Melody's Song

by

Kathleen E. Friesen

WestBow
PRESS
A DIVISION OF THOMAS NELSON

Copyright © 2012 Kathleen E. Friesen

All rights reserved. No part of this book may be used or reproduced by any means, graphic, electronic, or mechanical, including photocopying, recording, taping or by any information storage retrieval system without the written permission of the publisher except in the case of brief quotations embodied in critical articles and reviews.

WestBow Press books may be ordered through booksellers or by contacting:

WestBow Press
A Division of Thomas Nelson
1663 Liberty Drive
Bloomington, IN 47403
www.westbowpress.com
1-(866) 928-1240

Because of the dynamic nature of the Internet, any web addresses or links contained in this book may have changed since publication and may no longer be valid. The views expressed in this work are solely those of the author and do not necessarily reflect the views of the publisher, and the publisher hereby disclaims any responsibility for them.

Any people depicted in stock imagery provided by Thinkstock are models, and such images are being used for illustrative purposes only.

Certain stock imagery © Thinkstock.

Unless otherwise noted, all Scripture is taken from THE HOLY BIBLE, NEW INTERNATIONAL VERSION®, NIV® Copyright © 1973, 1978, 1984, 2011 by Biblica, Inc.™ Used by permission. All rights reserved worldwide.

Scripture taken from The Holy Bible, King James Version. Public Domain.

Scripture taken from The Message. Copyright © 1993, 1994, 1995, 1996, 2000, 2001, 2002. Used by permission of NavPress Publishing Group.

"You Are Here," lyrics by Jeanne Lynn Bellinger. Used by permission.

ISBN: 978-1-4497-6655-9 (e)
ISBN: 978-1-4497-6656-6 (sc)
ISBN: 978-1-4497-6657-3 (hc)

Library of Congress Control Number: 2012916433

Printed in the United States of America

WestBow Press rev. date: 9/13/2012

In memory of my beloved mother, Laura Boyer Smith, who taught me to love God and inspired me to share the stories of my heart.

*Because of the Lord's great love we are not consumed,
for his compassions never fail.
They are new every morning;
great is your faithfulness.
(Lamentations 3:22-23)*

*I have told you these things, so that in me you may have peace.
In this world you will have trouble.
But take heart! I have overcome the world.
(John 16:33)*

Acknowledgements

Many have walked beside me on this journey, and to you I offer my heartfelt thanks. First to my husband Ron, the love of my life, thank you for always supporting my efforts and forgiving my absentmindedness regarding meals and housework while this story was being birthed. You are my ever-loving hero.

To Gerry Meggait, Virginia Fairbrother, and Robin Flaten, my dear "pen pals," thank you for your unwavering love and encouragement. You are amazing!

To those who read and critiqued this story, Lisa Paul, Kathy Marie Smith, Annie Dyck, Eyvonne Johnson, Michelle Nortz, Vicki Mills, Sandra Neufeld, thank you! Your corrections and comments have improved this manuscript and gladdened my heart.

To Jonathan "Scooter" Clark (www.replant.ca) and Shaun Mitchell, I am tremendously grateful for your information and detailed, personal help in making the tree-planting scenes more accurate. Any errors remaining are mine alone.

To my sister Jeanne Bellinger, thank you from the bottom of my heart for allowing me to use your song "You Are Here" in this story and for preparing the musical score for "Melody's Song."

And to my readers, I appreciate each of you and would love to hear from you. Please feel free to contact me at kathleenefriesen@gmail.com.

1

Whap! The old screen door slammed and echoed through the nearly empty farmhouse, startling Melody Jamison as she wiped the bottom shelf of the cavernous refrigerator.

Her daughter Faith rushed into the kitchen, a white-gold banner of blond hair streaming behind her.

"Mom? There you are! Sorry we're late, but Jessica decided to nap an extra hour, and then she filled her diaper at the last minute, and … Mom, are you okay?"

Melody pushed herself upright and tossed her cleaning cloth into the sink, feeling much older than her forty-four years. She leaned back against the blue-tiled counter and rolled her aching shoulders.

"Yes, honey, I'm all right." She sighed, shoulders dropping. "I knew this move would be hard … leaving this old farm … saying goodbye … but it's even harder than I'd expected."

Her eyes welled up and she wiped them with the frayed hem of Tom's old denim shirt. "I just can't help feeling as if I've failed your father. You know how he loved this place. And after four generations of Jamisons …"

Faith circled slowly, looking like a sad ballerina as her chin quivered at the barrenness of what used to be their home. Then she crossed the room and wrapped her mother in a quick hug. "Yeah, I know."

Faith pulled back but didn't let go. "But Mom, you *are* doing the right thing. I still wish you were moving to a better part of the city, but at least you'll be in Saskatoon. I've been worried about you being out here all alone, working yourself into the ground. I couldn't bear to lose you, too. And Dad would never expect you to run the farm by yourself." She paused. "You do know that, right?"

She pressed her cheek to her mother's. "And we prayed about this, remember?"

She stepped back, peering into her mother's eyes. Melody looked away—too late. "You look exhausted. How long has it been since you've slept?"

That wasn't a question Melody wanted to answer. Nightmares had haunted her days and devoured her nights ever since Tom's death, but she wasn't about to share that with her daughter. Melody leaned into the hug and rested her head on Faith's slender shoulder.

"I'm so glad you and Jason are here. The movers left about fifteen minutes ago, but I was hoping you could take the houseplants in your van. My car is full of things from the freezer and fridge."

The screen door slammed once more, and Melody's eyes lit up. "Hello, Jason, and there's my darling! Come here, Jessie, Grandma needs a hug."

"Hey, Mom, I see we missed the movers. Sorry. Here, Jess fell asleep again on the way out, but now she's raring to go."

Melody eagerly took the baby in her arms, squeezing her so tightly Jessica whimpered. "I'm sorry, sweetheart. I guess Grandma's a little emotional today. But you sure are good for my soul. Mm-mm, you smell good!"

The baby giggled as Melody nuzzled her soft neck.

"Ouch! Oh, you do like Grandma's curls, don't you, little one?" Melody eased the plump little fingers out of her short brown waves, grimacing at the number of hairs still clenched in the small fist.

Faith came back into the room with a white African violet and a small jade plant. Jason followed, carrying a large philodendron in a patterned blue pot.

"Did you still have plants upstairs, Mom? I found these in the study, and we'll get the ones in the living and dining rooms. Are there any more?"

"Yes, there are a few in the bedrooms. I really appreciate your help. It's a long way to come, and it means a lot to me."

Her burly son-in-law grimaced. "Sorry we were so late. We'd meant to be here before the movers arrived, but you know babies. They sure can mess up a schedule."

"That's okay, Jason. I had everything ready, so it went fast. But I should get to the city so I can tell them where to put things. And you know how I feel about driving that highway. Do you mind?"

Faith shared a look with her husband before answering, "Of course, Mom. It won't take long to get these plants loaded. Here, give me the baby. Jason, you take those pots out to the van. I'll check upstairs, and we'll be on our way. I can direct the movers until you get there. And Mom? It will be okay."

A short time later, Melody wandered through the house for the last time. Life had been hard since Tom's accident, especially since there'd been no time to sit and grieve. Farm work wouldn't wait. *Is exhaustion triggering those nightmares? If so, maybe this fresh start …*

She looked out the dining room window toward the big old barn built by Tom's great-grandfather. The animals had been the first to go. A neighboring farmer had made her a generous offer for Tom's prized Jersey cows, and the chickens and various pets had made their ways to other farms in the last few months. Now the empty yard mocked her. She clasped her hands as though in prayer and brought them to her downturned lips. *I tried, but I failed. I'm so sorry, Tom.*

Even though she'd rented out the hay and grain fields, the four-acre yard and aging house were too much for one small woman. She'd done her best. For more than two years, she had struggled to keep the place operational, but five months ago she'd admitted defeat.

A crowd of neighbors from around Rosthern came to look for deals at the farm auction, but Melody had hidden indoors for the entire sale. Her old shyness had become a shield from nearly everyone since Tom had died. It was easier to stay home than face people and their pity—or their judgment.

Even the church she and Tom used to attend had become a place to avoid after overhearing some older members musing that "old George Jamison would roll over in his grave if he knew what that girl was doing to his homestead." She missed going to church, but she just couldn't face the whispers.

Melody sighed as she stepped into the living room. So much had changed since Tom's death. Hopefully this move would be a good one. *All I want is a pleasant, peaceful life. Is that too much to ask?*

Melody touched the wall where her family photos had hung. The dents in the carpeting outlined the sturdy furniture she and Tom had bought through the years.

Turning her back on those memories, she climbed the stairs. The first room had been Will's—walls hung with hockey posters and a perpetual mess on the floor. Snapshots of Will flitted through her mind: her bald, chubby baby, a bright-eyed little boy with blond curls she'd hated to cut, the shy pre-teen, and finally the tall, sullen stranger he had become just before he'd run away.

She whispered into the empty space, "Will, my son, what happened to you? Where *are* you?"

Pushing herself forward, she walked into Faith's old bedroom. Melody's eyes brightened at the memory of her tomboy daughter's eclectic decorating: embroidered patchwork pillows and piles of rocks. Pride lifted the corners of her mouth. *She's grown to be a lovely young woman. We'll get to spend more time together now, I hope. I've missed our mother-daughter times.*

Her steps slowed as she neared the bedroom she'd shared with her husband. Dreams forcing her to relive his accident made it feel as though the room was cursed. But when she'd still had Tom, this room had been their haven. She stopped outside the doorway and leaned against the wall. Would this move be what she needed? Or would her troubles follow her?

Melody turned back toward the stairs. She paused again at each doorway as memories tugged at her. *Stay,* they cried. *This is your home!*

But it wasn't any more. The sale was final, and it was time to leave. Melody straightened her shoulders, went back downstairs and out the back door. She turned the key in the deadbolt and shut the screen without a sound.

Will strained to lift his head. It felt as if it weighed at least fifty pounds. *What happened? Where am I? What time is it? Was I supposed to be somewhere?*

He stuck out his arm and peered at his watch. Too blurry. Pushing himself to a sitting position, he rubbed his eyes with the heel of his hand. He looked at the watch again. Five o'clock. *A.m. or p.m.?* He shook his head to clear it. *Unh. Bad move.*

Looking around, he saw that he was on a low-backed beige couch in a vaguely familiar apartment. But whose? And why did he feel like this, so stiff and groggy? Sure, he'd had a few drinks last night, but not enough to knock him out—or make him feel like a well-used punching bag. He looked down. His T-shirt was torn, and bruises were appearing on his hands and arms. *Aw, that was my favorite shirt.* He pulled up the torn hem and saw angry red marks on his abdomen. *No wonder I hurt!*

He was struggling to stand when a loud voice assaulted his aching head.

"Hey! Good afternoon to you, mister sunshine. I wondered when you would rejoin the land of the living."

Oh, yeah, this is Quentin's place. He's been letting me stay here while I find another place. But why …?

Quentin's voice rang with sarcasm. "Great party last night, eh? I *liked* that new club. Pretty girls, good service, and great music. Super night, in fact, until you mouthed off to those dudes outside."

Why did Quentin have to be so loud?

Will's host came over and stood in front of him. Hands clenching and unclenching, Quentin leaned in until the two were nearly nose to nose. Will blinked and tried to step back, but his legs hit the couch. Arms outstretched like a graceless tightrope walker, he barely managed to stay upright. Even with eyes still unfocused, he couldn't help but notice the ugly bruises on his buddy's face.

"I've tried to be a good friend to you, Will, but you're a mean drunk. And I can't afford to keep bailing you out of trouble. You're gonna have to find a new place to crash and someone else to lean on.

"Get your act together, man, before you get yourself—or someone else—killed!"

Hours later, Melody sank onto the big brown tweed couch in her new home and sighed at the chaos surrounding her. The movers and Jason had set up the furniture, and Faith had helped her get the kitchen functional, but boxes still covered nearly every visible surface.

Well, Tom, what do you think? Can this be home? Oh, how I wish you were here! Her face twisted. *But then I wouldn't have had to move, would I?*

Between Tom's life insurance and the sale of the farm, she had enough savings to live on, as long as she was careful. But she was used to being frugal. And she would get used to this new house. But could she ever get used to being alone? Melody shook off the depressing thoughts.

She pushed her exhausted frame off the couch and prepared for bed. She was thankful her son-in-law had taken the time to set up the oak sleigh bed before he and Faith took little Jessica home. *They're such good kids. And it will be wonderful to spend more time with that adorable baby.*

She slid between the sheets, the silky percale soothing her aching body. Just before closing her eyes, Melody admired the way the pale blue walls matched her favorite quilt and contrasted with the dark furniture. The surroundings were new, but the bed was comfortable and familiar. Melody hugged Tom's pillow and fell into a deep sleep.

But without warning the familiar dream began. She was standing at the kitchen sink, checking the time. *Where's Tom? He should have been in an hour ago, and he always phones when he's delayed. Of course, if that old baler acted up again, he'd forget about the time, just wanting to get it running and the field baled. He said he wanted to get the north quarter finished today.*

He's not answering his cell. Come on, Tom, answer it! Well, I guess I'd better make sure everything is all right. Otherwise I'll just keep worrying over nothing.

Okay, there's the tractor, but it's not moving. Now what's wrong with that baler? It looks so strange. What's that horrible red thing hanging from it? Looks like Tom's work boots. All that red ... is that blood? Is that TOM? No, God, no!

As always, the redness gathered itself into a haze that swirled and swam in front of Melody's face. She felt herself being pulled down into an abyss of blackness.

No, no, NO!

Her own moans woke her. She sat up in bed, her whole body trembling, dry eyes wide with horror. She rubbed her eyes, trying to erase the images burned into her memory. When would the nightmares end? Was she doomed to relive that horror night after night?

Shaking still, Melody got out of bed. *Where is it?* She rummaged through the boxes until she found the right one, pulled out Tom's plaid flannel robe, and wrapped herself in it. She padded softly to the living room, switching on lights as she went. Tom's brown leather rocker beckoned her, and she sat with her feet tucked under her, waiting for daylight.

As the first rays of sunshine hit the windows, Melody's eyes opened. *Good, I dozed off for a while after all.* She stretched her legs out, stood up, stumbled, and caught herself of the edge of the coffee table. Needle-like sensations shot up her legs as her feet regained circulation. *That'll teach me to scrunch up on the chair. Oh well, at least my feet got some sleep. Might as well make some coffee; it's going to be another long day.*

Across the street another woman woke up moaning. "Danny," she whispered, "will you please get me another pill?"

The man sprawled in the chair beside her snapped awake and automatically checked the pulse of the frail woman on the bed. It was faint but steady. The digital clock on the night table read five-thirty a.m.

"Hey, Mama." He leaned over and smoothed the wisps of white hair off her pale, lined face. "You must have slept a bit. That's good. I can't give you any more painkillers, though. I'm sorry; I wish I could. Valerie will be here soon and I'll tell her you need something stronger. Here, have a sip of water. I put a slice of lemon in it, just the way you like it." Her head moved against the pillow. "No? Okay, it's here if you want it."

Daniel Martens returned the glass to the nightstand and stood. *Another rough night. How many more would Mama—and he—have to endure? If God was as good as she always said, he would never allow such suffering. How could she keep believing?*

Yesterday afternoon while she'd rested on the couch, Rose Martens had asked Daniel to read Psalm 91 to her. He'd barely been able to choke out the words past his clenched teeth, but they'd seemed to soothe her. The pain-etched lines on her face had relaxed as he'd read:

> *"Because he loves me," says the Lord, "I will rescue him; I will protect him, for he acknowledges my name. He will call upon me, and I will answer him; I will be with him in trouble…"*

Empty promises! Bitterness nearly choked him, but he would do almost anything for his mother. And she knew it. *But did she know how hard this was for him?*

For a few minutes Daniel watched as his mother slipped back into the restless sleep of suffering. His rugged face softened as he leaned over and kissed her sunken, wrinkled cheek. Straightening again, he went to the kitchen to make coffee, his eyes squinting as he left the dim bedroom. It was going to take more than one pot of the stuff to get him through the day.

When the day nurse arrived at six o'clock, he took his coffee mug out onto the porch. The willow twig chair he'd built for his mother so many years ago welcomed his weary body as he sat. When the sun hit his face, he winced. He grabbed his extra-dark sunglasses out of his shirt pocket and covered his eyes with them. Another reminder of all he'd lost. He used to relish being out in the sunshine, but now he couldn't bear the brightness. *If it weren't for these glasses...* As though to emphasize the point, the back of his head started to throb, pulsing a dull ache in time to his heartbeat. He swore under his breath. The willow chair creaked as he shoved it back into the shadows of the porch.

Daniel looked over at the yellow house where the moving van had been parked most of yesterday afternoon. He hoped whoever had moved in would be nice and quiet, not like those people down there. He frowned as he glanced toward the gray house with black trim. His mother liked to have the windows open when a nice breeze was blowing, but when those people started yelling, the sound carried all too well. She didn't understand what was going on, but the noise agitated her. *Next time, I'm phoning the police.*

Looking back at the yellow house, Daniel noticed the living room curtains open. *Another early riser. Thought the hard work of moving would keep a body in bed a little longer. Not that it's any of my business.* But his eyes lingered on the little house.

As he watched, the front door opened and a petite woman stepped out. She sat down on her front step and raised her heart-shaped face to the rising sun. Her short, curly hair lifted in the breeze like a fluffy brown halo. Then she looked around as though she felt his eyes on her, like a doe about to bolt.

Timid little thing. What's her problem?

Daniel stood to go back inside. His sudden action was echoed by the woman across the street as she jumped to her feet. When she saw him, she half-smiled and her hand started to rise, then stopped. She turned, hurried into the house, and closed the door.

When Daniel checked on his mother, she was still dozing, but her breathing was ragged. He found the nurse at the kitchen table recording Rose's blood pressure and other details.

"Valerie, is there any way she can get more painkillers? She hasn't slept well the last couple nights." He rubbed the back of his neck. "I feel so helpless when she's in pain."

"I can't give her more pills, Daniel," the gray-haired nurse said. "She's already getting the maximum dose, but I can ask her doctor about an IV drip." She pursed her lips. "We'll do whatever we can to keep her comfortable. I'm sorry. I know this is hard."

Daniel just nodded and turned away. Good thing he had plenty of work these days. He would go crazy if he had to sit here the entire day watching his mother fade away. *Yeah, life is hard.*

2

Good grief! What is wrong with you? Melody scolded herself. *You're either afraid or too friendly, or both. That fellow is going to think I'm an absolute dolt! So much for making a good first impression on the neighbors.*

Embarrassment was good for one thing, Melody decided. It gave her incentive to stay indoors and empty some boxes. Hands on her hips, she gazed at the mess. How had she acquired so much stuff, anyway? She and Faith had accomplished quite a bit in the kitchen last night, but the rest of the house was littered with stacks of boxes.

The bathrooms should be an easy place to start. Melody located a box marked "Towels" and carried it into the main bathroom, humming as she worked.

By mid-afternoon, chaos had evolved into a semblance of comfort. Both the main bath and Melody's tiny en-suite were well organized, and the bedrooms looked much neater. The guest and sewing rooms still had boxes stacked in the closets, but until she could get some shelves installed, that's where they would stay.

The living room now looked ready for living, with only a few more boxes to unpack. Yesterday the movers had positioned the brown tweed couch opposite the picture window and Tom's leather chair, Mom Jamison's old piano against the inner wall, and the entertainment unit against the outer wall. Now the couch and chair were covered in colorful quilts and bright, fat pillows, Melody's own handiwork. End tables held tall brass lamps handed down from Tom's grandparents and mementos collected through the years. Pictures still leaned against the walls, waiting to be hung, but some smaller ones graced the coffee table and piano. It was starting to look comfortable. Melody sank onto the couch and put her feet up on the dark oak coffee table.

"Home, sweet home—I hope."

A few days later Melody shook her head at the boxes that still cluttered her living room. She'd wanted—desperately—to believe that this move would mean an end to her nightmares, but she couldn't seem to get through more than a night or two without the torment that consumed her strength and her faith. As a result she stumbled through her days in a sleep-deprived fog, accomplishing little and spending long nights on the couch huddled in Tom's old robe.

So much for leaving that nightmare back at the farm. Am I ever going to know peace again?

Melody picked up a framed snapshot of their family taken when the kids were preteens. Her finger touched the images of Faith and Will grinning over huge slices of watermelon. Both blond like their dad, Faith's straight hair was pulled back in a ponytail while Will's curls hung over his ears. He was already taller than his older sister. They were so cute! Behind them, her tall, handsome husband had his arm around her waist and, if she remembered correctly, was about to sneak a kiss.

Did I ever look that young? Where was that photo taken? Oh yes, at the church picnic in the park. Her childhood friend Tessa had been visiting and snapped it when they weren't looking. Tom had made a special effort to take a break from the farm and spend the day with his family. And what a wonderful day it had been! Melody kissed her fingertip and touched it to the faces of her loved ones. So long ago, they had been together and happy.

"Fur Elise" rang out, propelling her back to the present. *My cell phone! Where did I leave it? Oh, there it is.* Grabbing the phone off the piano, Melody hurried to flip it open before voicemail took over.

"Hello? Tessa! Really? I can't believe it's you! This is amazing! I was just thinking about you. It's true! Where are you? Are you in town?"

The responding voice was husky yet feminine and wonderfully familiar. "Hey, Mel, yes, it really is your long-lost friend, and yes, I am in town. I moved back two and a half months ago. I ran into your daughter at Midtown Mall a couple days ago, and she gave me your cell number."

Her voice lowered. "She said you'd sold the farm and were moving to the city. Are you moved yet? How are you? I'm so sorry about Tom."

She paused for a breath. "And I'm sorry I've neglected you for such a long time. You've been on my mind *so* much. When I saw Faith, I realized how much I needed to try and reconnect. May I come see you once you're settled? I really have missed you. Do you think you could make time for a visit from an old friend, maybe have a cup of coffee?"

As Tessa stopped to take another breath, Melody smiled into the phone. "Of course, Tessa, I would love to see you. You can come over anytime, as long as you don't mind a less-than-perfect house. It's only been a little more than a week since the move, so I still have some boxes here and there. When did you want to come?"

"Well, what are you doing for supper tonight? Want me to bring Chinese? I'll bet you haven't been eating very well. Do you still like egg rolls? How about sweet and sour pork? Should I bring wonton soup?"

Melody's smile widened. Her best friend from high school hadn't changed a bit! Fast talk and fast food. It would be good to get together again and maybe catch up on the years since they'd parted.

"Tonight would be great, and so would Chinese food—whatever you like, as long as you let me pay half. Did Faith tell you my new address? Good! It's the yellow house two doors down from the corner. I'll see you in a couple hours. And Tessa? Thanks. I can't wait to see you."

Three hours later the doorbell rang. Melody opened her door to the tantalizing smell of Chinese takeout, and standing on the second step looking uncharacteristically hesitant, a tall, slender redhead. The two women stared at each other for several heartbeats.

Tessa spoke first. "Mel, are you sure this is okay? I don't want to impose …"

"Of course it's okay, Tessa! Come in! Sorry for staring. It's just been such a long time. Come on, give me a hug. I can't believe you're here! You look great, and the food smells wonderful. Please, come in. Just watch out for that box. Here, let me help you with the food."

Melody led the way into the dining area and placed the containers on the table beside the dishes she'd already laid out. She turned to her friend and gave her another quick squeeze.

"Now, let me look at you. It's been an awfully long time, but you still look the same. What have you been doing for the last … ten or so years?"

Tessa pulled away from the hug. "Maybe we should eat before getting into catch-up mode."

"You're right, of course. Sit here, okay? We can visit while we eat. Would you mind asking the blessing?"

Tessa blushed pink. "Sure, Mel. I'm a little out of practice, but I'll do it."

It was almost as though the years and miles had never parted them when the two friends held hands across the table as Tessa prayed. "Dear Lord, thank you for bringing Mel and me back together. Thank you for never giving up on us, and thank you for this food. Amen"

Melody squeezed her friend's hand before releasing it. "Thanks, Tess. That was perfect."

By the time the last egg roll was shared, Melody was surprised to realize how much she had eaten. It was much more enjoyable sharing a meal than eating alone.

"Let's go in the living room. I'll make coffee—or do you want tea?"

"I don't need anything else, Mel. And I thought maybe I could help you unpack these boxes. Or, if you're tired, maybe we could just hang out for a while."

"Let's just visit for now, okay? The boxes can wait."

The two women sat side by side on the big brown couch as the setting sun threw shadows across the room. Melody cocked her head, puzzlement creasing her brow.

"Okay, old friend, what gives? You sounded like Tessa on the phone, but now … What's happened to you? Where's the gung-ho girl I grew up with?"

"If you don't mind, Mel, I'd really rather not get into that whole mess this evening. Okay? Let's just say I made some mistakes, learned some hard lessons, and now I'm glad to be back in Saskatoon. Mind if I unpack these books for you?"

As Melody opened her mouth to answer, Tessa continued, "Really, Mel. I'm not trying to hide anything. It's just that it's a long story, and I'd much rather hear about you and your family. What are your kids up to these days? "

Melody settled against the cushions. "Well, you saw Faith. She reminds me so much of her father; she has his energy and character. She makes me proud. She and Jason live on the east side of the city, and they've blessed me with the most beautiful baby girl. Did you see her?"

At Tessa's nod, Melody beamed. "She is such a darling! But I'd better not get started talking about Jessica. I do tend to go on and on about my littlest sweetheart! Anyway, Faith does medical transcription from home, and Jason works for Gorman Electric. They're not getting rich, but I think they're doing fine."

Melody leaned forward and hugged one of the bright, quilted pillows to her chest. She could feel pressure behind her eyes as she asked, "But Will … did you hear about him?"

"No," Tessa tilted her head. "What about my best little boyfriend?"

Melody sighed. "He dropped out of school halfway through grade twelve and took off to Vancouver. He'd gotten into some pretty serious trouble." Melody shook her bent head. "I know he was doing drugs—more than once he came home reeking of pot, but he'd always say it was others smoking. We just couldn't trust him anymore. So there was a big blowup between Tom and Will when we found out the police had nearly arrested him for beating up a classmate. Will was so angry, I was actually afraid of him."

She took a deep, shuddering breath. "Will said he was leaving, that he didn't need us or anyone. He was gone before we woke up the next morning."

Melody squeezed the pillow. "It broke our hearts. Tom was devastated. They'd always been close, but the last few months Will was like another person, and not a nice one. They argued almost nonstop, and when Will left, it nearly destroyed Tom and me. We didn't hear from him for three weeks, and then he just said we didn't need to worry and that he was looking for work."

Tessa grabbed a pillow for herself as Melody continued. "When Tom died, Will did come home for the funeral, but he hardly talked to anyone the two days he was here. He sat up in his room with his music blaring, just coming down to grab some food now and then. On the way to the airport, I told him what I thought of his rudeness. I could tell he was angry, but he didn't even respond."

She smiled wistfully at her friend. "Since then he's phoned every few weeks to let me know he's okay, but I'm afraid his idea of 'okay' and mine are miles apart. I know he's legally an adult now, and if he was making a life for himself, I wouldn't worry so much. But he's not. Every time he phones, he's in a different place and is often between jobs. I keep hoping and praying he'll come home, but so far …"

Tessa's eyes were wide with compassion. "Oh, Mel, I'm so sorry. You have had a hard time, haven't you?"

Melody threw the pillow back onto the couch and rubbed her arms.

"Tessa, I miss my son. But I wonder sometimes if the stress over

Will distracted Tom when he was working on that baler." She swallowed hard. "I guess I'll never know ..."

Tessa dropped the pillow she was holding and, without a word, wrapped her arms around her friend. Melody sniffled and returned the hug. After a few moments of silent comfort, Tessa picked up a photo from the coffee table.

"Hey," she said softly, "that's the picture I took of you guys—a long, long time ago."

"Yes, it is." Melody wiped her eyes. "That's why I was thinking about you when you phoned this afternoon. Amazing, isn't it? I think that may have been a God thing."

"Maybe so, Mel. That would be nice. I've got to admit, God and I haven't been on the best terms the last few years. I'm just starting to find my way back. Coming home is part of that." She stretched her long legs under the coffee table.

"Well, I'm glad you're here. I've really missed you, and I'm sorry we lost track of each other." Melody hesitated but then plunged in. "But what happened, Tessa? Did you move from Dallas? The last few times I wrote, the letters came back. It was as though you'd disappeared!"

"Well, Mel, I guess I did disappear, in a way."

Tessa reached into the box for the last book and lifted out Tom's well-used Bible. She sighed as she settled closer to her childhood friend.

"You want the condensed version? The whole story is too long and too depressing to get into tonight, okay? Please, try not to judge me too harshly. I know what I did was wrong, and I'm paying dearly for my sins."

"I'm in no position to judge you, Tess. Whatever you did has been forgiven already. You know that."

Tessa straightened and faced her friend. "Oh, Mel, I *don't* know that. I can't even forgive myself, so I don't see how God or anyone else could. Anyway, here's the scoop: I fell in love with a married man. He was a doctor at the hospital where I worked. Yeah, I knew it was wrong. I thought about calling it quits after I found out about his wife, but you know, I was sure he was The One for me.

"He left his wife and we moved to San Antonio to start a new life together. We did finally marry after a couple years, and I thought I was happy. I was such a fool!" Tessa shook her head and closed her eyes. "How could I expect someone who cheated on his first wife to be faithful to me?"

She looked up and whispered, "My divorce became final six months and three days ago."

Melody gasped. "Oh, Tessa, I had no idea. I'm so sorry. That must have been awful! But I'm glad you came back home. Home is a good place for healing."

Melody grabbed a tissue for herself and handed one to her friend. "Here you go. Aren't we a sight! Just when I think I'm all out of tears, they prove me wrong. If tears are good for cleansing the soul, mine must be pretty clean by now."

"Wish that was all it took, Mel."

Tessa wiped her eyes and glanced at her delicate gold wristwatch. "Melody, I'm sorry. I didn't mean to stay so long. You must be exhausted. And I've got an early shift tomorrow. Did I tell you I got on at City Hospital as a casual?"

"Good for you, Tess. How do you like it?"

"It's a job. Not what I'd prefer, but it will have to do for now. I'd love to get into a medical clinic or private home care, but there aren't many openings right now, and I'm at the bottom of the list."

She stood up, started for the door, and then turned back. "Before I go, I just want to say how much I admire you, Mel. You've been through so much, and yet you and your faith stay so strong. You're amazing!"

"No, Tessa, you're wrong!" Melody stiffened. "I'm not …"

"Still can't admit your own strengths, can you? Anyway, I've got to get going. I'll drop by in a few days, okay?"

"Sure, Tessa, but …"

"Love your new home, by the way. It suits you." Tessa opened the door and stepped through. "Bye for now, Mel, and thanks again!"

As the door closed behind her friend, Melody finally stood. She should have been more honest. Tessa had no idea.

I'm not strong, and neither is my faith. What would Tessa think if she knew I was barely holding on? Sometimes, God, I feel as if you've abandoned me.

Will pushed open the back door leading to the dark alley. He hoisted a garbage bag full of food scraps onto his shoulder. Stopping in front of a large dumpster, he pushed up the lid and flexed his muscles to shove the bag up and into the container.

"Wait! Please!" A feminine voice called out of the darkness.

Will spun around and lost his balance. The bag slipped from his hands, landed on the wet ground and split open. Half-eaten sandwiches, fries, egg dishes—everything the restaurant patrons had left behind was now splattered on the ground.

"Thanks a lot," Will muttered, staring at the mess.

"Sorry. I didn't mean to startle you." A slight young woman stepped into the glow of the light over the door. Even in that dim light Will could see the sores on her face and arms. She took a step closer.

"That looks good. Can I … ?" She gazed at the garbage on the ground and whimpered, "I'm so hungry."

Will shuddered as his stomach lurched. "Whatever. Go ahead, I guess. Take what you want, but hurry. I've got to clean this up and get back to work before that jerk fires me."

Will watched as the girl fell to her knees and, with shaking hands, began to shovel food scraps into her mouth. *That's disgusting. Why would anybody let themselves get that wasted?*

Flashes of memory sent Will reeling, groping for the nearest wall. He closed his eyes, but the sounds behind him merged with the scenes in his mind. *I would never have gotten that bad. Never.*

3

Wakened by the sun peeking in around the window blinds, Melody sat up and stretched. The last three nights had been pretty good—a few restless dreams, but no terrors. *Is the move finally making a difference?* Time would tell. And now it was a new day, the sun was shining, and she had a yard to inspect. She'd noticed a few straggly flowers wilting in the late-spring heat by the front walk on moving day, but now that she was starting to feel rested, it was time do a thorough evaluation of the yard.

The air felt refreshingly cool when Melody stepped outside the house, hands cupped around her favorite cobalt blue coffee mug. The prairie sun was well above the horizon, beaming down like a benediction in the stillness of the morning. Melody lifted her face to its blessing. *Thank you, God, for this new day and this new chapter in my life.*

As she wandered around the front yard, Melody grimaced at the lack of shrubbery and the general bareness of the small lot. It definitely needed something, but what? She'd never had the time to do more than maintenance on the farm yard, and the landscaping there was complete long before she and Tom took over, anyway.

The sad-looking front yard disappeared as memories played in Melody's mind like scenes from a silent movie. When she and Tom were newlyweds, they'd rented an apartment not far from the University of Saskatchewan. Tom planned to earn a degree in Agriculture and Land Management, but after their two children were born in quick succession, it became clear that studying full time meant no money and no time for family. So Tom found work as a mechanic, and after the kids were tucked into bed, he worked on his university courses. After seven years he was two courses away from graduating. That was twelve years ago. But in a heartbeat their world had turned upside down.

Melody sank to the front step as the scenes pressed on. One wintry night Tom's parents were driving home from Saskatoon on the two-lane highway toward Rosthern. Just past the little town of Hague they collided head-on with another vehicle, killing Tom's parents and the passenger in the other car and seriously injuring the driver. In an instant, life changed.

Melody stood, but the memories continued. Tom gave up his dreams and took over the family farm, moving his family from their cozy city life to the unrelenting work that was life on a farm.

Tom's parents had been wonderful people: warm, affectionate and hard-working. Melody had always felt welcome at their home, but taking their place while grieving their loss left her struggling to keep her head above a swirling pit of depression.

Melody shook her head to force the images away. *No wonder I'm haunted by nightmares, the way I keep dwelling on the past.* Taking a deep breath, she purposely stepped back from the house and studied the front porch. It wasn't a real porch, just preformed concrete steps leading to the front door. Melody squinted as she stared at the house, trying to picture what changes she could make to create a more welcoming entrance.

A real porch, that's what it needs, just like the one across the street. It could fill in between the bedrooms and the garage, and the overhang would keep the house cooler, too. A couple chairs or maybe a hanging swing … I wonder how much that would cost?

Inspired by her daydreams, Melody sat on the bottom step and surveyed the rest of the front yard. Other than some trampled petunias lining the narrow walkway, the yard was empty. The lawn looked fairly healthy but needed a good soaking. *Oh yeah, I'm going to need a lawn mower, too. I'd better start a list.*

A few minutes later, she was in the back yard with notebook in hand. A gnarled apple tree in the far corner was in desperate need of a thorough pruning, but it could be beautiful next spring. Melody tilted her head back and counted the green fruit on the leafy branches. Maybe a dozen tiny green apples. She jotted a note on her list. *Find loppers.*

Other than the tree and a small tool shed, the backyard's plainness echoed the front. It was like a bare canvas, just waiting for some loving attention from its new owner. Melody couldn't wait.

"Halloo! Are you the new neighbor? Come on over here so we can get acquainted!"

Melody swiveled toward the gravelly voice coming from the next yard. She couldn't see through the high board fence until she pressed her face against a gap between slats. And there she was, a stout older woman wearing faded jeans and a peacock-blue T-shirt sprinkled with sparkly white birds. Her gray hair was cut as short as a soldier's, contrasting with her bright red lipstick. Her gray-blue eyes held a friendly twinkle as she waved.

"Hello," Melody offered, "I'm Melody Jamison, and yes, I did just move in. I'm happy to meet you. And you are?"

"Bobbie Grant. Mighty pleased to meet you, Melody Jamison. Got time for a cup of coffee?"

"Actually, Bobbie, I do. Thank you! Shall I meet you at the front?"

As she followed her new neighbor into the beige stucco house, Melody blinked as her eyes adjusted to the dimmer light. Bright red walls, gold carpet and flowery overstuffed furniture—it was almost overwhelming. *Definitely from another era.* The kitchen was more subdued, with black and white tile floor and white cabinets. Melody sniffed. *Could it be?*

"So, you like saskatoon berry pie? Just made it this morning. Got six bushes in the back. Had to get up early to beat the birds to them." Bobbie dished up a generous slice and handed it to Melody. "Here, you look like you could use some fattenin' up. Coffee's fresh, and cream and sugar are there. Help yourself."

"Um, thanks, Bobbie. I do like saskatoon pie. I've never had it for breakfast before, but it smells absolutely wonderful!"

After one small bite, Melody decided pie for breakfast was a fine idea. The warm, flaky crust melted on her tongue, and the plump berries oozed purple sweetness.

"Oh my, this is fantastic! This is the best saskatoon pie I've ever had."

"Glad you like it. So … what's your story?" Bobbie plopped herself down in the chair opposite Melody's. "Divorced? Lesbian? Running away? Not many women your age around here. They're either old like me or young and surrounded by brats."

Melody gasped, nearly choking on her second bite. She grabbed her cup of coffee and gulped. Bad idea! It burned all the way down her throat. She coughed as tears sprang to her eyes.

"Sorry, Bobbie, you kind of caught me off guard there."

"Well, Kiddo, I'm not one to beat around the bush. Didn't mean to upset you, though. You okay?"

'Yes, I'm fine. This coffee is delicious too, by the way. I'd been hoping to meet my neighbors soon, so I appreciate this. Have you lived here long?"

"Okay, I'll take the hint. Yeah, me and Charlie bought this house nearly forty years ago and watched the neighborhood grow up around it."

"Do you know all the neighbors around here?" Melody took a careful sip of her coffee, this time enjoying its slightly bitter heat.

"Not all of them. Some houses can't seem to hang on to people. They move in, they move out. Just like that. I do know some, though."

Melody continued sipping her coffee and savoring each bite of pie as her neighbor leaned back and crossed her arms across her colorful T-shirt.

"Let's see … folks in the house other side of yours, they're a couple of yuppies. Always working or traveling, hardly ever home. Once in a while they'll throw a party. Then it's sorta loud, but nothing too bad."

She leaned forward again, resting her elbows on the table. "The guy down the street in the gray house, though, that's a bad one. Every couple weeks—payday, probably—there's yelling and all kinds of racket down there. I've phoned the cops a couple times myself. Nothing changes, though. I think the girl there is so scared she won't press charges. But I'll tell you," Bobbie's gravelly voice dropped to a stage whisper, "after those times, the girl wears long sleeves and sunglasses. No matter what the weather. Yup, it's bad down there."

Melody was speechless. Her eyes must have shown her shock, because her neighbor continued in a normal voice.

"That's the only bad ones. Guess every neighborhood has to have one bad egg, eh? But let's see … I used to get together a lot with Rose Martens before she got so sick with cancer. She lives in that purty blue house with the front porch across the street. Her son built that porch. Rose calls 'im Danny, but if you want on his good side, you'd better call him Daniel or Dan. Has a construction company in Alberta, but left his man in charge and came home a few months ago to help his ma. He lives with her now, hires nurses to take care of her while he works.

Keeps real busy, with keepin' track of the goins-on in Alberta and doin' small jobs here. Not sure how he manages it all. Good son, that one. Not real friendly, but steady. Can't be easy watching your mother die." Bobbie looked off into the distance, shaking her head.

"How awful!" Melody said. "But you and his mom—Rose?—are friends? What's she like?"

Bobbie's voice carried even more gravel as she answered. "Oh, she's a doll, that one. Husband was a preacher in Prince Albert for years. They moved here after he retired. How such a sourpuss could preach the 'good news,' I'll never know. Had a heart attack and died about six years ago. Anyway, Rosie was the sunshine to his clouds. Always cheerful. Always praying, too. Just out of the blue, she'd start talking to God like he was right there and they were best friends. At first it spooked me pretty bad, but after I got to know her better, it was like she included me in those holy gab sessions.

"When her old man died, I went over there a lot. I'd lost my Charlie just four months before that, so we helped each other through all those awful firsts. 'Cause we're friends, you know."

Melody reached across the table and covered her neighbor's broad hand with her own.

"Then when she got that cancer last fall, she went downhill fast. That's when her boy came home to help her out …."

Bobbie ran out of steam and sagged back against her chair, her hand still covered by Melody's. She looked at their hands as though unsure how they got there. When she looked up, there were tears in her eyes.

"Sorry, Kiddo. Got a little lost there, but Rosie's a true friend, and I'm already missing her. She does her best, of course, hobbles around the house a bit with her walker when she's up to it, but she's fading. Not that she'd complain. Told me she's good to go. But the drugs she needs now make her sleep more and more of the time. Last time I went over there, she tried to stay awake but kept fading out. Didn't even get to hear her pray."

"Oh, Bobbie, I'm so sorry." Melody's eyes mirrored the tearful ones across from her. "I do know what it's like to lose someone you love." She hesitated, wondered at her daring, but plunged in. "Um, would you mind if I prayed for Rose—and you?"

"Huh! Should've known Rosie's God would've sent someone to keep an eye on me. Sure, Kiddo, you go ahead and pray."

When Melody returned home, the red light on her answering

machine was blinking. She smiled as she listened to the message, and then picked up the phone and dialed.

"Good morning, Faith. Sorry I missed your call. What's up? Sounded as if you were out of breath when you phoned."

"Hi, Mom. Where were you? I was just checking to see if you wanted us to pick you up for church tomorrow. It starts at ten o'clock. Oh, and I *was* out of breath—from chasing your granddaughter. I can't believe how fast she can crawl. And to think I was anxious for her to start moving on her own!"

"Hmm ..." Melody said. "Wonder where she gets that need for speed? As for your questions, sure, I'd love to catch a ride with you. I wasn't looking forward to walking into a new church by myself. As for your other question, I was at my next-door neighbor's house. Bobbie invited me over when I was checking out the back yard, and we had a nice, long visit."

"Mom! You were visiting with a *man?*"

"No, silly, Bobbie is a woman." Melody lowered her voice. "We even prayed together.

"You mean she's a Christian?"

"I'm not sure, but she's certainly got a soft heart. I'll see you tomorrow morning!"

Late that night, Melody fell into a deep sleep. In her dream she walked hand in hand through a moonlit field with Tom, sharing sweet, soft kisses every few steps. Then her dream shifted. She could feel herself slipping sideways, losing her grip on Tom's hand, but she didn't fall. Instead, it felt as though she'd floated into another realm. She somehow knew she was lying in bed in her room, but she couldn't tell if she was awake or still dreaming. The air seemed heavy, and yet she felt as though she could float out of her body. Melody's eyes opened wide, and wonder filled her—Tom was coming into the room! Not really walking—more like gliding—and she couldn't see his face, but it didn't matter. She would recognize his tall form anywhere. Melody sat up in bed, astonishment making her voice tremble.

"Tom? Is it really you? Oh my love, I've missed you so much!"

The figure moved to the bed, sat down beside her without indenting the mattress, and touched her cheek. Melody froze. It *wasn't* Tom! Her cheek burned, and heat seared through her skin and down her throat.

What's happening? The room was suddenly frigid, the air thick with evil. As the dark figure leaned over her, a whiff of sulfur filled her nostrils and constricted her airway. She couldn't breathe! *Jesus, help me!*

Melody jerked awake, her whole body shaking. She reached for the lamp switch and sucked in a huge breath when the light came on. *It was just a dream. It was just a dream ... but what a horrible one!*

She slid out of bed onto shaky legs and turned on the overhead light. Darkness was dispelled, but still she shook. She reached for Tom's robe; her hand stopped midair. The nightmare was too real. She couldn't bear to wear anything of Tom's. It was as though evil hovered to touch her again.

After switching on nearly every light in the house, Melody opened her Bible and tried to read. She flipped through the pages, looking for something to hold onto. Nothing. Her thoughts scattered like sheep from a wolf, unable to latch onto any promises of peace. *Where are you, Lord? I need you!*

The air still felt stuffy, so Melody opened a couple windows. A cool breeze fluttered the kitchen curtains, caressing her face as she huddled at the table. *No!* She jumped up, ran to the window and slammed it shut. The guest room window was still open. *That will have to do.*

Curling up on the couch, Melody tugged the log cabin quilt off the back and wrapped herself in it. Leaning back against the matching pillow, she snuggled down, breathing deliberately. *It was just a dream. God is here. I can't feel him right now, but he must be here.*

She closed her eyes and was just starting to drift toward an uneasy sleep when a faint scream jolted her awake. *What was that?*

Melody sat up clutching the quilt around her with one hand, the other grabbing Tom's old Bible off the coffee table. She held it to her chest like a shield and strained to hear. Was that another scream? *Lord, have mercy!* She crept through her little home, trembling in fear. Then she heard another noise, this one a much harsher, louder voice. It seemed to be coming from the guest room!

God, what is going on? I am so afraid. Help me, please!

Walking into the dark room, Melody heard another coarse shout, but when she flicked on the light, no one was in the room. She sagged in relief. The noise was coming through the open window. She turned off the light so no one could see her, then pressed her cheek against the screen. Where were these dreadful sounds coming from?

Oh, it must be the 'bad ones' Bobbie told me about. God, it sounds so awful.

She shut the window, and the sounds faded. Melody leaned against the window frame as her shaking subsided. Then shame swept over her. *I can't just pretend it's not happening, can I? But what can I do?*

The quiet answer in her heart was clear in spite of the wail of sirens coming closer: "Go! Help my little one."

Melody gasped as a weight of fear and helplessness pressed her down to the floor. *Oh, no, Lord, you can't possibly mean that! I can't do that! I wouldn't know what to do. I ... I'm not even dressed—and it could be dangerous!*

Flashes of red and blue briefly illuminated the room as police and ambulance sped down the street, their sirens drowning out Melody's turmoil. When the wailing sirens stopped, she rose shakily and peered out the window again toward the not-quite-visible gray house. It looked like a scene from television. Guns drawn, two policemen advanced toward the house. More harsh shouts from the police as well as from inside, and then the officers disappeared into the house. Immediately the paramedics pulled a stretcher out of the ambulance, gathered their gear, and followed the police. The sudden silence seemed to echo in the night air.

A flash of light from across the street caught Melody's eye as her neighbor opened the front door and stepped out onto his porch. *What did Bobbie say his name was? That's right, Daniel.* He stood rigidly facing the action down the street until the ambulance sped away, lights and sirens slashing the night air once again, and the police came back to their car with a handcuffed captive. The neighbor turned to re-enter his house when the police car pulled over to the curb in front of his house. One officer got out, walked up to the porch, and exchanged a few words with Daniel. Melody couldn't hear what they were saying, but his stiff gestures made it obvious her neighbor was upset. He stepped back inside his house, back ramrod straight, as the officer returned to the car and drove away. The street was quiet and still once more.

What kind of neighborhood have I moved into, Lord? That was awful! Maybe Faith was right about this area. Have I made a mistake?

Melody backed away from the window, still clutching the Bible against her chest. *First that awful nightmare, and now this real-life horror.*

Arms and legs trembling, Melody curled up on the living room couch and opened Tom's Bible. There was no point in trying to sleep any more tonight. *Will I ever know peace again? Please, Lord, speak to* me! *I know I've ignored you for the last few years, but right now I need your comfort.*

An idea popped into her mind, and Melody flipped to the back of the Bible and searched the concordance for "comfort." There she found a notation for John 14. The flimsy pages seemed to stick to her shaking fingers, but finally she found it.

> *If ye love me, keep my commandments. And I will pray the Father, and he shall give you another Comforter, that he may abide with you forever. Even the Spirit of truth, whom the world cannot receive, because it seeth him not, neither knoweth him; but ye know him, for he dwelleth with you, and shall be in you. I will not leave you comfortless; I will come to you.*

Melody wasn't used to King James Version, so she stumbled a bit over the old-style language. Slowly she read the passage again. Yes, that was what she needed, the Comforter sent by Jesus himself to take care of her. Like the quilt wrapped around her shoulders, God's Comforter should make her feel better.

But even as her ragged breathing slowed and smoothed, something tugged at Melody's mind like words caught in the cobwebs of her brain. She read the verses once more, and once again stumbled over the language. Setting Tom's Bible down, Melody picked up her own New International Version Bible and found the same passage. The first verse jumped out at her:

> *If you love me, you will obey what I command.*

Barely breathing, she continued reading:

> *And I will ask the Father, and he will give you another Counselor to be with you forever—the Spirit of truth. The world cannot accept him, because it neither sees him nor knows him. But you know him, for he lives with you and will be in you. I will not leave you as orphans; I will come to you.*

"Okay," Melody mumbled, "this version calls him 'Counselor,' not 'Comforter.' I'll have to ask someone about that. But that first bit … what is it about that verse?"

As she tugged the soft quilt tighter around her, Melody heard an echo from the turbulent moments just passed: *Go! Help my little one.*

Her heart sank as she felt the familiar weight of failure. She had not obeyed the one she called Lord. Instead, fear had won. Again.

"Danny! Is everything all right?" Rose's clear voice stopped Daniel as he walked by the doorway to her room.

"Everything's okay now, Mama. Go back to sleep."

"But Danny, I heard sirens and saw flashing lights. What happened? Was someone hurt?" She struggled to sit up and bit back a moan.

"Mama, please, just relax." He moved to her bedside and stooped low to ease her frail form back onto the pillow.

Rose touched her son's cheek and spoke softly but firmly. "Tell me, Son. What happened? I want to know."

Sighing deeply, Daniel reached behind, pulled the chair closer and sank into it.

"It was that drunk from the gray house again. I called 911, and they sent the cops and ambulance. Looks like the girl got beaten up pretty badly. They took her to the hospital. At least the creep was arrested this time. Hopefully they'll be able to keep him in jail for a while."

He rubbed the back of his neck and closed his eyes. "I hate it that they woke you up. I hate this whole situation!"

Rose reached over and covered her son's free hand with her own and watched him as she prayed. "Heavenly Father, please help those poor children down the street. Send someone to that girl to show her your love. And touch that man; make him see his need for you."

Daniel jerked his hand back and stood up, anger deepening the lines on his face.

"Stop it, Mama! How dare you pray for those losers. And how dare you pray to a God who allows so much pain!"

Her voice was fading, but she continued, "And Father, please heal my boy. Take away his bitterness and pain …"

Daniel stormed out of the room, but not before he saw the flash of hurt in his mother's eyes—pain caused not by cancer, but by him.

4

"Thanks, Mr. Lee. You won't regret this!" Will towered over the older man, but right now he felt like a little boy being given an unexpected gift. "I can start right away if you'd like."

"Tomorrow will be fine," Mr. Lee said. "Here are the keys you will need. This one is for your room upstairs, and this one is for the shop. I will come at six tomorrow morning to train you. Be on time."

With that he turned and walked into his office at the back of the shop. Will resisted the urge to thank him again, shifted the weight of his backpack, and headed to his new home. Out the door, down the side alley and up the stairs he hurried. He was so excited it felt as if his feet barely touched the ground. Yesterday he'd been so desperate, he'd nearly phoned his mother for a ticket back to Saskatchewan. But today—today he had a job and a place to stay. He was set!

The room was furnished sparsely with a long couch, dinette table and two metal chairs. He spotted a coffee maker on the counter of the tiny kitchen. His mother's face swam before his eyes. *No! I'm not homesick—just hungry. I'll ask Mr. Lee for an advance after tomorrow's work so I can get some food. I sure was lucky to get this job. I'll make Mr. Lee glad he hired me.*

The peal of the doorbell woke Melody from her fitful sleep on the couch. She jumped up and peeked around the curtains. Jason and Faith's car was in her driveway, and her daughter was getting ready to press the doorbell once more. *What are they doing here? What day is it? Oh ...*

Melody grabbed the quilt off the couch and opened the door just enough to let Faith squeeze through.

"Mom! Why aren't you ready for church?" Faith's gaze took in Melody's disheveled hair, the shadows under her eyes, and the obvious distress on her face. "What happened, Mom? Are you sick?"

Faith started to press her palm against her mother's forehead, but Melody caught it in her own and kissed the open palm.

"I'm so embarrassed, sweetie. We had a bit of excitement down the street last night, and I didn't get much sleep. I'll tell you about it later. Can you give me a few minutes to get ready? I really want to go to church with you, and I'll hurry."

"Um, Jason has to be there early; he's in charge of the sound system. But I could drive him there and come back and get you. Would that work for you?" She paused as she turned to the door. "Are you sure you're all right?"

Melody patted her daughter's back. "That sounds perfect. I'll go hop in the shower. You have no idea how much this means to me. Thank you, sweetheart."

Melody hated to be late, especially to a new place. The curious glances as she followed Faith and baby Jessica into the sanctuary made her want to turn and run, but once they were seated, she felt herself relax a bit. Even though the congregation was in the middle of a song, people around them offered whispered greetings and smiles of welcome. Melody leaned back against the wooden pew and let the song wash over her. It was new to her, but the simple words and music bathed her with an unfamiliar peace and sense of expectation.

> *You are here, you are here*
> *And we're in awe of your presence.*
> *It's by your grace that we stand, Most Holy God.*
> *You are here, full of love,*
> *And you want us to know you.*
> *We're filled with wonder because you are here.*
> *You are here, you are here*

And I'm in awe of your presence.
It's by your grace that I stand, Most Holy God.
You are here, full of love,
And you want me to know you.
I'm filled with wonder because you are here.

Melody didn't feel the tears filling her eyes until Faith patted her hand and slipped her a tissue. "Here, Mom," she whispered, "that song gets to me, too."

As she dabbed at her eyes, Melody glanced around the sanctuary. It wasn't a large church, but it seemed to include every age group. She saw white-haired men and women singing and tiny tots jumping on the pews. No one seemed to mind the occasional ruckus or whispered reprimands. One gray-haired lady scooted over to help a young mother struggling with her three small children. It felt like a large, close-knit family—not at all like the rigid organization Melody had grown up in or the back-biting group back in Rosthern. *No wonder Faith and Jason enjoy it so much.*

The pianist was a lovely Asian lady with streaks of gray highlighting her glossy, shoulder-length dark hair. She sang as she played, often closing her eyes without missing a note. Melody was in awe. *She's not just playing by heart, she's playing from her heart!*

On the platform behind the song leader was a man she assumed must be the senior pastor. He wasn't a handsome man. In fact, he was quite homely, with a bulbous nose, bushy eyebrows, and receding hairline. But his face radiated joy as, eyes closed, he raised his hands as he sang. His sport coat and khaki pants looked well-worn and comfortable, not designed to impress. Melody was impressed by that.

The song leader introduced him as Pastor Dave as he stepped over to the podium. "This is the day that the Lord has made!" His rich bass voice resonated through the room.

"We will rejoice and be glad in it." The congregation responded with enthusiasm.

Immediately he began to pray. "Father God, thank you for this day, for being here with us and in us …"

As Pastor Dave talked to God, Melody was amazed at the intimacy of his prayer. It was as though he was talking to a beloved father. He prayed for the church all over the world, for governments and for "the lost and hurting."

Is that me? I certainly am hurting. Maybe I'm lost, too.

His prayer continued: "Lord God Almighty, give us courage to go out of our way to comfort those who grieve, to help the helpless and to love the unlovable."

Melody cringed as she remembered that quiet prompting the night before: *"Go, help my little one."* Guilt stabbed her, and she glanced around as though others could sense her failure. But no one seemed to notice.

The rest of the service was an emotional rollercoaster for Melody as she soared and dipped between hope and fear—hope that perhaps God really did care about her, and fear that she would always fail him. She felt relieved when the benediction was spoken.

Pastor Dave and his wife, Lydia, the pianist, greeted her warmly at the door, and Melody invited them to come for coffee later in the week. *Hopefully after I've recovered from last night.*

Melody sat curled up in Tom's chair working on a small quilting project when the doorbell rang. It was pressed again immediately, followed by loud rapping. Melody dropped her project, got up too quickly, and tottered to the door.

"Hello, Melody! Are you home? I need to talk to you!" Bobbie's gruff voice sounded stressed.

Before the door was fully open, Bobbie marched inside.

"Oh, good, you're here. I need help."

Melody bent over to massage her still-tingling legs. "Umm … come on in, Bobbie. Make yourself at home. Would you like some coffee or tea? I think I need some coffee."

"Oh, were you resting? Sorry. Doubt if anybody got much sleep the other night with all that ruckus goin' on. But that's what I need to talk to you about."

Bobbie perched on the edge of the couch. "Daniel called me over this morning to sit with Rose while he went to do a small job. Her nurse had an appointment, so he'd arranged to stay home, but one of his big-shot clients phoned with some cockamamie problem. And Rosie was still in a tizzy about the goin's-on down the street. So when he called, I went."

Melody smiled at her neighbor. "Of course you did. You're a good friend, Bobbie."

"Well, I try." Bobbie eased back onto the couch, strain emphasizing the lines on her forehead. "But after Val—that's her nurse—got back,

Rose asked me to do something for her. Before I knew what it was, I said I would. Now I don't know. This is way outta my comfort zone, you know."

"What is? What did Rose ask you to do?"

"Well, she got a real bee in her bonnet about that girl down the street. Daniel told her the kid ended up in the hospital, and now I've gone and promised Rose I'd go visit her. I hate hospitals! And I don't have a clue what I'd say."

Bobbie leaned forward, her gaze holding Melody's. "But you know Rosie's God. You would know what to say to that poor kid. If you went with me, you could do the talking, and I'd be keeping my promise to Rose. Okay? You'll do it, right?"

Melody's heart sank. Her faith was so shaky, how could she possibly be of any help to that girl?

Go! Help my little one!

The whisper echoed in her heart. Was this a second chance to obey? But what would she say? *God, this is too much for me! I don't know what to do. I don't …*

"Yo, Kiddo!" Bobbie's voice made her jump. "You daydreaming? I need an answer here."

Melody looked down at her hands as they clenched and unclenched. "I'm sorry, Bobbie. It's just that I'm not sure I can do what you're asking."

Bobbie's eyebrows lifted and her mouth turned downward. "Why not? Thought you and Rosie had the same God. She's always saying hers is all-powerful and stuff. What's yours?"

Melody gasped as Bobbie's words hit home. What was that the pastor quoted Sunday? "God doesn't always call the equipped, but he does equip the called."

She sighed in resignation. "Okay, Bobbie, I don't know what I'll do or say, but I will go with you. Do we have time for coffee first?"

As she sipped her coffee, Melody prayed silently. *Help me, God, help me.* "God, help me!"

"You prayin' or swearin'?" Bobbie interrupted her pleading.

"Praying. I didn't realize I'd said that out loud." Melody felt her face warm.

"Don't know why you're worried. You said your God is the same as Rosie's, and he's big enough to do anything, according to her."

Melody's blush deepened, and she looked down. "You're right, Bobbie. It's just that my faith isn't as strong as your friend's, and I'm scared. I don't know this girl ..." She looked up. "By the way, do you even know her name? How are we supposed to find her once we get to the hospital? And which hospital?"

"Don't worry, I did some snooping before I came over. Called a cop friend. The girl's name is Nila Black, and City was too crowded, so they took her to University. She doesn't have any family listed other than that creep she's shacked up with. No, they're not married. I don't get why she doesn't just leave him. Maybe you should ask."

Melody snorted at that. "I don't think so." She glanced at her watch. "I guess we should get going. I hope you don't mind if I keep praying all the way there."

"Of course not, Kiddo. 'If God is for us ...,' you know. Yeah, Rose taught me that. I'll drive, you pray."

Traffic was light on the drive to Royal University Hospital, but Melody didn't know whether to be thankful or more stressed. In spite of her prayers she was certain she would say the wrong thing or be unable to speak at all.

God, help me. God, help me. God, help me. It had become her mantra for the last half hour.

Next thing she knew they were stepping onto the steel and concrete elevated walkway leading from the parking lot to the hospital lobby.

The tunnel-like walkway seemed to swing like a rope bridge, slowing Melody's steps. Bobbie marched beside her, head forward, glaring at anyone that pushed past them.

"Come on, Kiddo, you're slower than molasses! Hey, you okay?"

Paralyzing fear snatched the strength from Melody's legs, and she wobbled beside her neighbor. "I think I need to sit down for a minute, Bobbie. Sorry."

They both sank onto the closest bench. Bobbie's face showed a mixture of concern and consternation as she looked at Melody's pale face.

"Hmph. For a woman of faith, you don't seem to have much. Maybe I was wrong about you."

"Please, Bobbie, just give me a minute. I don't know what's going on, but I feel as if something's sucking the strength right out of me." She pressed her fingers to her eyes. "I really think I need to pray again."

She closed her eyes and prayed silently, ignoring the curious glances of people streaming by. "Father God, I don't know why I'm here, except that you seem to be pushing me this direction. But Bobbie has more faith than I do. Please, please give me courage. I need your strength.

You know how fearful I am. Dear God, if this is what you want me to do, help me."

Like a quilt settling onto her soul, Melody felt the peace she desperately needed envelop her, just like the other night. The Comforter!

Thank you, Lord Jesus, for your Spirit. Melody took a deep breath. *Now I know for sure that you are with me.*

"Okay, Bobbie. I'm ready." Melody smiled and stood.

Bobbie stared at her for a moment, then stood and gave her a quick, hard hug. "That's my girl. Let's do this!"

Standing outside the door to the young girl's room, Melody hesitated once more. Bobbie pushed past her and opened the door. Then she stopped.

Melody walked around her statue-like body and entered the room. On the only occupied bed in the four-bed ward lay what appeared to be a broken doll. She was on the bony side of slender, and her face was a pale background for the dark bruises that stained her eyes, cheeks and mouth. Her long, dark hair was coming loose from its confining braids. She had stitches on one cheek, and her left arm was in a cast. Her eyes were so swollen Melody couldn't tell if she was awake or asleep. Above the neckline of the hospital gown more bruises colored the girl's collarbone.

Melody's stomach clenched. *How could anyone do this? God, help me help her.*

"Hello? Nila?" she called softly, not wanting to scare or waken the girl.

One bruised eye opened slightly.

"Who are you? What do you want?"

"We're your neighbors, Nila. I'm Melody; I moved into the yellow house down the street from you a few weeks ago. And this is Bobbie. She lives next door to me. We're concerned about you and want to know if there is anything we can do for you."

"Just take your concern and leave me alone. There's nothing anyone can do." Her eye closed again she turned her face away.

Melody felt tears fill her eyes at the hopelessness in that weak voice. "That's not true, Nila. We can help you."

She was surprised at the smoothness of her voice—not a waver to betray her nerves. "May I sit beside you? I promise I won't hurt you."

Nila's slight one-shouldered shrug gave permission, and Melody moved to the chair beside the bed. She glanced over at Bobbie, who was still standing just inside the doorway.

"Bobbie, why don't you come sit in this other chair? Then we can all visit for a few minutes."

Bobbie moved into the room and sat down without a sound, so Melody continued.

"Nila, I know you're in a lot of pain, so we won't stay long. But we do want to help you. Is there anything at all we could do for you? Perhaps bring you something to read? I notice you don't have a television in here. Would you like one? Or something special to eat?"

"Eyes hurt too much, and I can't eat much yet—mouth's too sore." The words came with their own pain, causing a spasm in the young, battered face.

"What if I read to you? Would you like that?" Melody stroked the slender fingers protruding from the stark, white cast.

"If you want. One of my foster moms used to read to me when I was a kid." Nila turned to look at Melody. "But why would you? I'm nothing to you."

Melody smiled through unshed tears. "Oh no, that's not true, Nila. You are very special. God loves you so much he pushed me to come to you even though I was afraid. He cares, and now that I've met you, I care too. I think I should read you my favorite psalm. It gives you a clear picture of just how much God cares for you."

Melody pulled her small Bible out of her purse and quickly found the page.

"Here it is, Psalm 139:

O Lord, you have searched me, and you know me.
You know when I sit and when I rise; you perceive my thoughts from afar.
You discern my going out and my lying down; you are familiar with all my ways.
Before a word is on my tongue you know it completely, O Lord.
You hem me in–behind and before; you have laid your hand upon me.
Such knowledge is too wonderful for me, too lofty for me to attain.
Where can I go from your Spirit?
Where can I flee from your presence?
If I go up to the heavens, you are there; if I make my bed in the depth, you are there.

If I rise on the wings of the dawn, if I settle on the far side of the sea,
Even there your hand will guide me, your right hand will hold me fast.
If I say, 'Surely the darkness will hide me and the light become night around me,'
Even the darkness will not be dark to you;
The night will shine like the day, for darkness is as light to you ..."

The girl's eyes were closed when Melody looked up, but she looked much more peaceful then when they'd arrived.

"Nila?"

No response.

Melody glanced over at the still-silent Bobbie. "Well, I hope she heard at least some of that. If nothing else, it seemed to calm her." She looked at her neighbor more closely. "Hey, Bobbie, are you okay?"

"Sure, Kiddo, don't mind me. That was a real good poem you read. I never heard anything like that before." Bobbie swiped at her eyes, swallowed hard, and stood. "Guess we should let her sleep, eh?"

As she turned toward the door, she grinned at Melody. "You did good. Rose would be proud."

Both women were silent as they left the hospital. But when they were almost home, Bobbie spoke up again as though no time had passed. "Speaking of Rose, we should go see her. She'll want to hear all about this. You up for that?"

"Umm ... I guess so, Bobbie. I've been hoping to meet her, but I don't want to impose. What if she's sleeping?"

"Don't be such a worry-wart. If she's asleep, we'll come back later. I know she'll like you."

Melody's timidity was back as she followed Bobbie up the front porch steps of the Martens house. She hung back as Bobbie pressed the doorbell. The door swung open, and a stern-looking woman glared at them from the doorway.

As Bobbie opened her mouth, the woman shook her head, frowning. "Quiet, please. She finally went to sleep just a few minutes ago."

The woman's expression softened as she stepped out onto the porch, pulling the door closed behind her. "Sorry, Bobbie. It's been a rough day." She looked past Bobbie to Melody. "Who's this?"

Melody smiled shyly. "Hi, I'm Melody. I live in the yellow house across the street."

"Yeah, Val, we wanted to report to Rosie about the girl from the gray house. She sent us to visit her at the hospital." Bobbie frowned. "What happened, Val? Is her pain worse?"

"I don't think so. At least, she wouldn't let me give her any more painkillers. Or any drugs, for that matter. She was moaning and muttering for more than an hour. It was as though she was fighting something. But when I tried to calm her, she shook me off and said she was 'waging war against the enemy.' I haven't a clue what she meant by that, but she finally calmed down a short time ago, and now she's asleep. So I hope you understand why I can't let you wake her."

"Sure, Val." Bobbie glanced back at Melody. "This one may have an idea what that was all about, but we'll let Rose sleep and come back later. Give her my love, okay?"

"Of course, Bobbie. Maybe try back this evening. It was nice to meet you, Melody. I hope you'll come again, too."

When Bobbie and Melody crossed the street to the blue house again several hours later, Daniel met them at the door. He was tall with deep-set blue eyes and dark, wavy hair streaked gray at the temples. Melody noticed that his nose was slightly crooked, and he had a scar between his eyebrows, but his face was somehow appealing in its ruggedness. He looked from one woman to the other without smiling.

"Hello, Bobbie. Valerie said you'd probably be back tonight. And you must be our new neighbor."

Daniel stuck out his hand toward Melody, so she smiled and took it. His hand was warm and rough, the hand of a working man. Suddenly a tingle shot from her hand to her shoulder. *What was that?* Melody felt her cheeks redden, and she pulled her hand back. *Did he feel that, too?*

"H–hello. I'm Melody, and yes, I do live across the street. Is your mother able to visit this evening?"

"Pleased to meet you, Melody." His frown belied his words. "Yes, Mother is sitting up right now and seems to be in good spirits. She'll enjoy visiting with you both. Bobbie, you know the way."

And with that, he turned and walked back inside.

At least he left the door open, Melody thought. *What a perplexing man.*

She followed Bobbie down a short hall and into a soft-hued bedroom. She stopped in the doorway as Bobbie greeted her old friend with a long, gentle hug.

"Hey, Rosie," said Bobbie. "It's awfully good to see you looking so chipper. I brought our new neighbor over to meet you. This here's

Melody, from the yellow house next to mine. She a good 'un, and she knows your God."

"Melody! What a delightful name!" Rose reached out a bony hand, and Melody took it in both of hers. "I'm pleased to finally meet you. Daniel told me a young lady had moved in across the street, and I so hoped I would get to know you. And you are a Christian! What a blessing—to me and to this whole neighborhood!"

"I've heard good things about you, Rose." She hesitated. "May I call you Rose?" Rose nodded with a smile, and Melody continued. "I don't know how I could be a blessing to you or this area, but you're awfully sweet to say that."

"You should have seen this girl today, Rosie," Bobbie interjected. "I got her to come with me to the hospital to see that kid from down the street, and even though she was chicken at first, she did good. Real good. Felt like God came right down into that hospital room for a few minutes. It was really sumthin'."

Melody blushed as Rose squeezed her hand and exclaimed, "I knew it! The enemy was mighty, but our God reigns!"

Rose leaned back against her pillow and closed her eyes. Melody wondered if they'd tired her, but then she heard that lovely soft voice praying.

"Lord God Almighty, thank you for bringing Melody to our part of this city. Thank you for giving her strength and courage. Thank you for carrying her when she could not go in her own power. You are good, oh God, and I praise you for your wonderful mercy, grace, and power."

She opened her eyes again, and beamed at Melody. "You *are* a blessing, my dear. God has chosen you to do mighty things for him. Trust him."

She turned to Bobbie. "And thank you, Bobbie, for being such a good friend. I know I asked a hard thing of you, but God knew what was needed. And you listened to his voice. Yes, you did!" She smiled at Bobbie's shocked expression. "I know he has plans for you, too, dear friend. Just keep listening for his voice. He loves to amaze us!"

Daniel's deep voice behind them made Melody jump. "And now, ladies, my mother needs to rest."

As he tidied the already-neat kitchen, Daniel scowled at his reflection in the window. His cheeks still felt hot after the quiet tongue-lashing his mother had given him. She had called him a rude child, as if he was eight years old. Told him she could judge when she needed rest. Didn't she understand he was just watching out for her? Valerie had told him what a rough day she'd had, so she didn't need visitors—even friends—wearing her out again.

"Especially," he muttered, "ones that get her all riled up about God."

Willing himself to calm down, Daniel took slow, deep breaths as he wiped the counter. His hands stilled as his thoughts turned to the new neighbor, Melody. Like a tune that wouldn't leave him, her curly brown hair, green eyes and shy smile teased his imagination.

"Yeah, she seems pretty nice," Daniel said to himself. *Pretty nice?* His conscience whispered, *Who are you trying to kid?*

Shoving his hands into his pockets, he shook his head to dispel her image. He had no business thinking about the new neighbor—or any other woman.

Daniel walked down the hall to his darkened bedroom and, without turning on the light, picked up a framed photo from his dresser. He sank onto the bed and traced with one finger the face he knew by heart.

"Angela," he whispered. "My angel ... I am so sorry ..."

5

"Pastor Dave, Lydia, welcome! Please come in." Melody opened the door wide to her guests and stepped back to let them in. "I'm so glad you could come today. Isn't this a beautiful morning?"

"Thank you, Melody. Yes, it is." The pastor's smile warmed her as he stepped past her.

"We're happy to be here, Melody," Lydia said as she reached out for a hug. "I've been looking forward to getting to know you better."

With coffee cups in hand, Melody and her guests settled into the living room. Lydia sat beside Melody on the couch, while Pastor Dave sat in Tom's recliner.

"You've made this a lovely home, Melody," Lydia said as she looked around the room. "Did you make these quilts and pillows? They are beautiful!"

"Thank you, Lydia. Yes, I did. I'm just starting to get back into it. It's good to have something to do when I can't sleep." *Oh dear, why did I say that?* Melody felt her cheeks warm.

"P-please tell me about yourselves." Melody stammered in her rush to change the subject. "Have you always lived in Saskatoon? How did you meet? I don't even know if you have children."

Dave's smile calmed her. "Well, Melody, I've always lived in Saskatchewan, spent my growing-up years in Nipawin, but Lydia is from the lower mainland in British Columbia."

His eyes twinkled as he grinned at his wife. "We met at a summer camp for inner-city kids near Vancouver when we were both counselors there. I was in my third year of Bible college, and she was fresh out of high school. I fell for her the first day we met."

"He sure did," Lydia agreed. Her almond-shaped brown eyes danced with laughter. "I was carrying my bags up to my cabin when we met on the trail. He stepped aside so quickly, he tripped over a stump and landed on his backside."

Dave chuckled. "It's not the recommended method of impressing a young lady, but it worked for me."

Lydia continued, "We married two years later, and now we have four children, all married, and seven wonderful grandchildren. When you come to our home, you'll see their photos everywhere."

Melody smiled at the implied invitation until Dave said, "We know a little about you, Melody, from visiting with your lovely daughter. She told us about your husband's tragic death and your struggle to keep the farm going until recently. She has also shared her—and your— concerns for your son. Could those perhaps be the reasons for the sleep problems you mentioned?"

Melody looked at her fists clenched in her lap and sighed. She really hadn't wanted to get into that this morning.

Lydia scooted closer and put her arm around Melody's shoulder. "Would you like to talk about it, dear? Why *do* you have trouble sleeping?"

Melody dared to look up. Both Dave and Lydia gazed back at her with such warm compassion, she felt her pride melt. "I haven't told anyone about it, but maybe I should."

Hesitantly at first, Melody shared her story of Tom's death and the nightmares that followed. Trembling as memories resurrected, she even told them of the most terrifying dreams where she'd felt herself slipping into another dimension.

"I had another one of those last night," Melody admitted. "First, it felt as if I'd slipped sideways without moving, and I heard my son crying out for help. He sounded so afraid! Then I heard another voice, sort of hollow and taunting, calling his name. And then I could see Will; he was near the end of a long tunnel. I tried to run to him, but I couldn't move. Then I saw a huge form—I don't know what it was—rise up behind him. It loomed over him and roared, and my son disappeared."

She leaned forward and covered her face with both hands. "I can still hear that horrible sound. I struggled so hard to reach my son, I finally woke myself, but I must have shaken for about an hour afterward. I couldn't even pray." She paused. "I don't know what's going on. Sometimes I think I'm going crazy. Do you think I might be?"

When she dared to glance up, Pastor Dave and Lydia were sharing a knowing look.

"No, Melody," Pastor Dave's rich voice soothed her. "Something *is* going on, but you're not crazy. Right now I'd like to pray for your son. Is that okay?"

When Melody murmured her assent, Dave looked toward heaven. "Father God, we lift young Will to you right now. You know his circumstances, and you know his heart. Shield him from the enemy. Turn his heart toward you and his family. Heal his hurts and make him whole for Jesus' sake. To you be all glory, honor and power, amen."

Melody's soaring spirit thumped back to earth when Dave tilted his head as he caught her gaze. "Now, Melody, what do you know about the kingdom of darkness?"

Melody shook her head. "Nothing, and it doesn't sound like something I want to know."

"Well, my dear, it sounds as if you're getting an education whether you want it or not." Dave's gentle smile softened his words. "I'm not an expert on the kingdoms of darkness and light, but they are real. And there is a real battle going on. I think God has, for whatever reason, given you the gift of actually seeing part of the battle."

"Gift? This doesn't feel like a gift." Melody frowned. "And I thought Jesus conquered Satan and everything evil when he died and was resurrected. That's what I was taught, anyway." She sighed. "But there's obviously a lot of evil still in this world. I just don't understand."

"You are right, Melody," Lydia said. "There is a lot of evil in this world. And you've been dealing with what feels like more than your fair share, haven't you?"

Melody nodded as Lydia patted her shoulder.

"When Jesus Christ died," Dave said, "he made it possible for us to be transferred from the kingdom of darkness, that kingdom of Satan and everything evil, into his kingdom of light and holiness. But until Jesus claims his kingship at the end of time, this world has been given to the kingdom of darkness. The battle continues because the devil does not want to lose any of his subjects to the Holy One. These battles are mostly unseen, but we do see the effects in all kinds of heartaches."

"But why am I having these horrible dreams? What good does

that do? I don't *want* to see or hear the kingdom of darkness!" Melody grabbed one of the cushions and hugged it to her chest.

Dave bowed his head and was silent for a full minute. His head tilted as though he was listening. When he finally looked up, his face was shining.

"Melody, I don't have an answer regarding those dreams. But it is apparent you've been made spiritually sensitive, and that—believe it or not—is a good thing. God must have something important for you to do or learn. You have his Holy Spirit within you, and he will protect you. You have to trust him. May I pray for you? There's a prayer Paul prays for the church at Colosse that I would like to pray for you. If you'd like to read it, it's from Colossians 1:9–14, and I'll paraphrase it."

"I would like that, Pastor. My Bible is in the bedroom; I'll be right back."

Once she had returned with her Bible and found the page, Melody followed along as the pastor prayed.

"For this reason, since the day we heard about Melody, we have not stopped praying for her and asking God to fill Melody with the knowledge of his will through all spiritual wisdom and understanding. And we pray this in order that Melody may live a life worthy of the Lord and may please him in every way: bearing fruit in every good work, growing in the knowledge of God, being strengthened with all power according to his glorious might so that Melody may have great endurance and patience, and joyfully giving thanks to the Father, who has qualified Melody to share in the inheritance of the saints in the kingdom of light. For he has rescued Melody and all his people from the dominion of darkness and brought her and all his people into the kingdom of the Son he loves, in whom we have redemption, the forgiveness of sins. In the name of our Lord and Savior Jesus Christ we pray this, amen."

The silence that filled the room as Pastor Dave ended his prayer felt glorified, as though they had been lifted into the presence of God Almighty. Melody was afraid to speak, unwilling to be jolted back to the "real" world.

But the atmosphere of reverence lingered as she said, "Thank you, Pastor Dave. That is amazing! I'm going to read those verses over and over again. Thank you for bringing me into God's presence."

The large man smiled gently. "You already were in God's presence, dear lady. In fact, his Spirit lives within you, so you are never without him. 'He will never leave you or forsake you.'"

"I've heard that before, but I guess I get caught up in fear, and that blinds me to God's love."

Melody turned to Lydia, but the pastor's wife still sat with head bowed and eyes closed. A heartbeat later, Lydia raised her head and looked at Melody. Her eyes shone as she reached for Melody's hand.

"Melody, I think I just received a word from the Lord for you. Your life is in God's hands, and he is making you a blessing to this neighborhood and to your family. You need to know that, no matter what happens, you are never alone."

Melody gasped. "That's almost exactly what my neighbor Rose Martens said! I still don't understand. How can I be a blessing to this neighborhood?"

Pastor Dave spoke up. "You cannot help but bless the area you live in when you follow the leading of the Holy Spirit, Melody. As you trust him and obey his guidance, his plan will become reality—not just for you, but also for those around you. I think that plan is already being revealed in your relationship with your neighbors."

At Melody's puzzled expression, Dave chuckled gently. "Don't worry, Melody, just trust. God will make it clear to you."

He glanced at his watch. "Oh my. I'm afraid we have to hurry away. I have a luncheon meeting downtown, and if we leave now, I can take Lydia home and still get there on time."

They all stood, and Lydia gave Melody another hug. "Thank you for having us, Melody. Getting to know you better has been a real blessing. I hope we can get together again soon."

"Thank you both for everything! I don't know whether to be relieved or terrified at what you've told me, but I really appreciate your wisdom and care."

Lydia patted Melody's arm. "We do care for you, my dear, but your heavenly father cares even more. Remember that."

Melody was slipping her lunch dishes into the sudsy water and nearly dropped a plate when her phone rang. Quickly wiping her hands on her jeans, she picked up the handset.

"Hello?"

"Did I catch you at a bad time?"

"Tessa! It's good to hear your voice. No, I was just washing dishes. You can interrupt that any time."

"Well, Mel, I was wondering if you could meet me for coffee this afternoon. My schedule at the hospital has been crazy, but I really need to talk to you. Would two o'clock work for you? Anyplace near the hospital is good for me; I have a short shift starting at four."

"Oh, Tessa, I'm sorry. I'm babysitting Jess here this afternoon while Faith gets her hair done. Her appointment is for two thirty. But could you come here? I know it's out of your way, but if you came early enough, we'd still get a chance to visit before you have to go to work."

There was a short pause, then, "Yes, I think that will be okay. I'd love to see that little darling of yours, anyway. I'll be there as soon as I can."

"Sounds good, my friend. I'll put the coffee on."

Less than an hour later, Melody welcomed her old friend with a big hug. "Ooh! I didn't realize it was raining. You're all wet!"

"It's really coming down out there. Gotta love these summer downpours!" Tessa grinned and hugged Melody again. "Now you're wet, too!"

"Thanks a lot. Come on, let's get you dried off and coffeed up. There are towels in the bathroom—down the hall to your right—and I'll pour our coffee. I'm so glad you could make it. Seems like forever since we've been able to chat."

A few minutes later, the two friends settled onto the couch, one at each end, feet up on the coffee table, coffee mugs cradled in their hands.

"Ahhh, this is the life!" Tessa sighed deeply. "I needed this."

"I'm glad you're here. By the way, that uniform is adorable. I love the teddy bears. Does that mean you're working on the pediatric ward?""

"Yes, I've been there for the last month. I enjoy working with the kids, but it's wearing me out." Tessa took a careful sip of her coffee and closed her eyes briefly. "Tired and lonely—not a good combination. I don't want to make another mistake, Mel."

"What do you mean? Have you met someone special?"

"Yeah. No. I don't know. There is a guy, but I don't even really know him. We just pass in the hall, chat a bit here and there. That sort of thing. Problem is, I'm so off-kilter from exhaustion, I think I'm reading something into his greetings that isn't there. Or shouldn't be."

She set her coffee on the table. "I'm so mixed up, Mel. I know you can't help me with this, but I just needed to unload on a friend. And you're the only one I've got. Sorry."

Melody put her hands on her hips and mock-scowled. "Wait just a minute, Tessa-girl, don't you dare apologize for unloading on me." She leaned back against the log cabin quilt draped on the couch. "We *are* friends, and have been for more years than I want to admit. So talk to me. Why are you so exhausted? You used to be an energizer bunny! And just who is this guy?"

"This energizer bunny got old, my friend. There's been a virus going through the staff, so I've been doing extra shifts. It's a lot more tiring than when I was young.

"As for the guy, he's an orderly at the hospital, and he has a beautiful Spanish accent. Everything he says sounds romantic." She gazed toward the window, a faraway look in her eyes. "His name is Orlando, and he's sweet, super good-looking, and rather shy. Like I said, I don't know him well, but I'm afraid I'm very attracted to him."

"But why are you afraid, and what do you find so attractive?"

Tessa winced. "I'm afraid because I'm probably reading more into this than I should—and because of my track record. As for the attraction factor, he is seriously hot, the real 'tall, dark and handsome' deal, and he's just about the sweetest guy I've ever met."

Her eyes sparkled as she twirled her empty coffee cup. "He not only takes pride in his work, he'll go out of his way to make a difference. I mean, last week I found him reading a story to several kids during his lunch break. They loved it! He put lots of expression into his voice, you know, making each character sound different. My heart just about melted. Three of those kids rarely get visitors; their families live too far away to come to the city very often. I didn't want to interrupt, so I waited in the doorway until he finished, and when I walked in at the end of the story, he blushed. When's the last time you saw a man blush? This guy is special." She sat back with a sigh. "Yep, I'm falling for him."

Melody swallowed the last of her coffee and looked into the mug as though seeking answers. "Hmmm…he does sound intriguing, Tessa. But in case you're right about reading too much into his responses to you—and especially because you are so vulnerable right now—I think you're wise be careful."

She shifted to face her friend. "Perhaps you can become friends without rushing into a romantic relationship? Even if this does develop into something else, friendship is a necessary foundation, you know." She paused for several heartbeats. "I hate to ask, but do you know if he's married?"

Tessa grimaced and shook her head. "That's the problem. I don't know, and that's one reason I'm wrestling with this. He doesn't wear a wedding ring, but dear Dr. Stephen didn't wear a ring. We were completely involved before I found out he was married." She sighed. "And we never really were friends. That whole relationship was wrong from the beginning. I messed up so badly." Another sigh. "And I never want to do that again."

"I'm sorry, Tess. I didn't mean to bring up bad memories. Can we pray together about this? My faith is pretty shaky, but I'm learning that the strength of my God is much more important than the strength of my faith."

Tessa's smile peeked through her melancholy. "I'd like that very much, Mel. I'm a long way from where I need to be faith-wise, but I do want trust God again. I guess praying is a good start."

Melody reached over and took Tessa's hand in hers. With eyes open she prayed, "Father God, Tessa needs your help and guidance. She needs you, dear God, to give her strength and wisdom. Please protect her, both from mistakes and from the enemy. Wrap your loving arms around her, I pray, in Jesus' name, amen."

Tessa spoke up, hesitantly at first. "Thank you, Jesus, from bringing me home to Mel and to you. Please do help me to do the right thing. And please help me to trust you completely. Amen."

Tessa looked up, eyes gleaming. "That felt good. Thanks, Mel."

At that moment the doorbell rang, startling them both.

"Oh, that must be Faith and Jessica," Melody said. She hurried to open the door. "Come in, come in! Oh dear, you're getting soaked."

Faith lugged the baby and bulging diaper bag inside and frowned at the water dripping from her coat. "Yeah, it's really coming down out there." She looked up. "Hey, Tessa, I wondered whose car was out front. It's good to see you again."

Faith passed the squirming baby to her mother and plopped the diaper bag onto the floor.

"Sorry I can't stay, but I've got to run. Jess will want a bottle in about half an hour, and then you can try to get to her nap. She didn't sleep after lunch, so she may get grumpy. There's diapers and anything else you might need in the bag. Give Mommy a kiss, sweetie. I've got to go. Thanks so much, Mom. I'll be back as soon as I can."

With that, Faith was out the door again.

"Whew! Nice to see you, too, Faith." Tessa grinned. "Why do I get the feeling someone was running a bit late?"

Tessa stood at the window watching Faith dash to her car as Melody struggled to remove Jessica's jacket. The baby was much more interested in grabbing her grandmother's curls than in cooperating.

"Tessa, could you give me a hand? I'm afraid I'm going to drop this wiggly little monkey."

"Of course! Here we go." Together they managed to free the baby's chubby arms from the raincoat, but not before she'd pulled out several Melody's hairs.

"Ouch! Good thing I'm crazy about you, little one." Melody squeezed the baby and smooched her chubby pink cheek. "Want to hold her while I put away our coffee mugs?"

Jessica took one look at Tessa's outstretched arms, scrunched up her face, and wailed.

"Uh-oh, I think she's making strange," Tessa said. "Maybe I'd better take care of the cups while she gets used to being here. I can't stay, anyway. Besides, I'm happy just seeing a healthy baby—especially such an adorable one." Tessa's smile faded. "That's the hardest part about working on Peds. It's heartbreaking to see those kids suffer, and there's often little I can do to help them."

"Oh, Tessa, I hope you get a better job soon. Miracles still happen, you know." Melody wrinkled her nose. "That sounded like a platitude. I'm sorry. But I do believe God cares."

"I hope you're right, Mel. Anyway, I'd better get going. You never know what traffic is going to be like. Thanks for listening—and praying."

She stopped halfway to the door. "By the way, Mel, have you thought about getting a porch added onto your house? I was looking at the one across the street. Something like that would look great and keep your company from getting soaked."

"Actually, I have. I've even thought about asking the man that built that one for a price, but …"

"Hey, are you blushing? I think you've been holding out on me, friend. What gives?"

"It's nothing. It's just that when we first met he was rather rude."

"You're kidding! Why? Maybe I should march over there and give him a piece of my mind."

"No, Tess, no! He has good reason to be grumpy. His mother has cancer, so he left his business in Alberta to care for her. He does construction jobs around town all day and looks after her at night. I can't imagine how he handles it. So if he's a bit prickly, it's understandable."

"Okay, but I still don't like it when someone mistreats my good friend." Tessa tilted her head. "And I think there's more to this story, but I've really got to rush. We'll talk later—I want to know everything."

She leaned over and gave Jessica a quick kiss on her soft cheek. "Bye, sweetie. Sorry I scared you. And Mel, we *will* talk."

After a twelve-hour shift of moving boxes and scrubbing floors Will was exhausted. He sprawled on the lumpy couch and wiggled his toes to the sounds coming through his earbuds. *Mr. Lee seems to have a good business here. They sure move a lot of goods every day. I can't believe how lucky I was to land this gig. It's pretty cool of Mr. Lee to let me keep my money in his safe, too, so I don't have to bother with banking.*

6

The next morning Melody awoke to sunbeams dancing on the walls, a meadowlark's trilling song, and sore muscles from playing with her granddaughter. She smiled even while wincing at the stiffness of her shoulders. *What a wonderful way to get a workout!*

But as she got dressed, those images of Jessica's bright eyes and happy smiles were replaced by thoughts of Nila's shadowed eyes and bruised face. By the time she was sipping her second cup of coffee, Melody knew she needed to visit her young neighbor again.

"Lord God," she prayed, "please give me courage and wisdom to speak the words Nila needs to hear. I think this is what you want me to do, but I can't do it alone. Help me, please."

After phoning the hospital to confirm that Nila was still there, Melody dialed Bobbie's number. Four rings later Melody began composing a message for Bobbie's answering machine. But just as it clicked on, Bobbie's gruff voice hollered, "HELLO! I'm here. Just a sec. Gotta shut this beepin' thing off."

"Good morning, Bobbie," Melody said. "I'm glad you're home. I have a favor to ask of you."

"Oh hi, Kiddo! What's up?"

"I need to go visit Nila at the hospital again, and I was hoping you'd come with me. Are you available?"

"Uh, visiting hours don't start until two, right? So, nope, can't make it. I gotta dentist appointment right after lunch. Gonna get a couple fillings. Sorry. But you should talk to Rose. She can't go with you, but I know she'd pray. And she's a real good pray-er."

"That's a good idea, Bobbie. Thanks. I will go see Rose. How about if I bring over some homemade soup for supper? You probably won't feel like chewing, and I can fill you in on my visit with Nila."

"Sounds good. Talk to you later, then." The line disconnected.

Melody glanced at her watch. It was just after nine o'clock. *What time does Daniel go to work? I don't want to risk running into him again.* But as she pictured her neighbor, her pulse quickened.

She looked out her living room window at the house across the street. Valerie's green Ford was parked in the driveway. *Daniel leaves shortly after the nurse arrives, so he must be gone by now. It should be safe.*

But before going out, Melody ran a comb through her curls and applied a touch of lipstick. *Just to look nice for Rose.*

After a final glance in the mirror, Melody straightened her shoulders and went over to the blue house. As she stepped onto the porch, she admired its welcoming feel. *I like this. A porch like this would suit my house, too. I wonder ...*

Shaking her head at her daydreams, Melody knocked lightly on the front door. After a few seconds, it opened to Valerie's questioning gaze.

"Yes? Oh, you're the neighbor from across the way, right?"

"Hello, Valerie. Yes, I'm Melody. I was hoping to talk to Rose this morning. Is she up to a visit?"

Valerie stepped back and opened the door wide. "She's feeling quite perky this morning, and I'm sure she'd enjoy a visit from you. Come on in; you know the way. I was just going to get a cup of tea. Would you like one?"

"Thank you, Valerie. That sounds lovely."

She entered the bedroom and was pleased to see Rose sitting upright, her wispy white hair fanned out like a halo framing her sweet face. Sunshine spilled through the open window, bringing birdsong and the heady smell of lilacs into the cozy room.

"Hello, Rose," she said softly. "How are you feeling today?"

"Why, hello, Melody. How lovely to see you, my dear. This is a good day, and I'm so happy you came to share part of it with me. Come, sit here." She gestured to a green upholstered chair beside the bed.

Melody obeyed, clasping her hands in her lap like a schoolgirl.

"So, dear child," the older lady said with a knowing smile, "how may I pray for you today?"

Melody's Song

Shortly after two, Melody hesitated once again outside Nila's hospital room. *Lord, thank you for protecting me from panic. Thank you for Rose's strong faith and encouragement, for speaking through her to me. Now speak through me, please, in Jesus' name.*

Pushing the heavy door open, Melody called, "Hello, Nila. I'm Melody, your neighbor. May I come in? Do you remember me? I was here a couple days ago with my friend Bobbie."

Nila was sitting up in bed, pushing some bland-looking mashed potatoes around her plate. The bruises on her face were even more colorful, and her encased left arm was propped on some pillows. Her eyes appeared to be healing nicely, and Melody could now see that she had beautiful brown eyes.

"Hi. I remember you. You read to me. It was nice." A slight smile touched the less-swollen side of her mouth as their eyes met.

"How are you feeling, Nila? Am I interrupting your lunch?"

The young woman leaned back against the pillows with a sigh. "I'm okay, I guess. I can't eat this stuff anyway; it tastes gross. And everything still hurts, but the docs say I can go home in the next day or two."

The battered young face crumpled and tears plopped onto the rejected mound of potatoes.

Melody grabbed a tissue from the bedside table and leaned over to gently wipe Nila's eyes.

"You've had a rough time, haven't you? Here, let me help. Let's just move the tray over here, okay?" She set the lunch tray on the bed nearest the door, then pulled a chair close to Nila's bed and sat down. "Do you want to talk about it?"

Nila turned away from Melody and gazed unseeing out the window. "It's no use. Nobody can help me."

"Sometimes it helps to talk things out, Nila. You don't have to carry your burdens alone, you know."

Nila's head swung around as she glared at Melody. "Of course I do! This is my problem—no one else's. Whatever you think you can do, it won't make any difference. Nick will still get drunk, he'll still hit me, and I'll have to stand there and take it. And in between, I'll pretend everything is fine. That's my life. I get what I deserve."

Melody struggled to hide her shock. *God,* she prayed silently, *give me your words. How do I respond to this?*

The bitterness in Nila's voice deepened. "So … nothing to say? That's what I thought. You might as well go. Leave me alone."

"No, Nila," Melody was surprised at the calmness in her voice. "I just needed a moment to ask God what he wants to say to you. Do you remember any of the things I read to you last time I was here? About how much God cares about you? It's true, you know."

"Of course I don't know. Look at me!" She gestured awkwardly at her injuries, eyes wide with despair. "Does this look like someone God cares about?"

"Oh sweetie, God does love you. I don't know why you're in such a terrible situation, but I do know you are loved. He sent me to help you, and while I don't know what I should do, I am willing to help you any way I can."

"You want to rescue me?" Nila snorted. "Are you gonna come over every time Nick starts drinking?" Her voice rose. "You gonna stand between him and me? Then there'd be two women getting a ride in an ambulance!"

Stunned, Melody felt her hands begin to shake. The room suddenly felt as cold as a prairie winter, and icicles of panic shot through her.

God, I know you're here. Help me, please! The temperature seemed to gradually moderate as Melody took several slow breaths and leaned back in her chair, hands clenching the armrests.

"Nila, I have to ask: why do you stay with him?"

The wall clock's ticking counted the passing seconds.

Finally Nila spoke into the void, her voice a whisper of hopelessness. "He loves me, and I belong to him. He is good to me most of the time. And if I didn't make him so mad, he wouldn't hit me. I just always do the wrong thing."

A surge of outrage replaced Melody's fear. "You *don't* deserve to be beaten."

She scooted closer to the bed and stroked Nila's hand. "Look at me, please, Nila. *No one* deserves to be treated like that!"

Just then there was a light knock on the door as it swung open. Nila's eyes widened as she pulled her sheet tight to her chest.

"Nick?"

A kind-faced woman stepped into the hospital room, and Nila sank back against the pillows. Her tension released in a deep sigh like a balloon deflating.

The woman stopped just inside the door, silently submitting to the young woman's wary inspection.

"Who are you?" Nila demanded. "What do you want?"

"Hello, Nila. My name is Anne, and I'm with Social Services. I'm here to talk to you about Haven House."

"Hey, blondie! Put a little hustle into it!" Will stiffened at the taunting call. *That Quan!* He was some relative of Mr. Lee's, so he acted as if he could boss Will around. *What a pain.*

Will was puffing as he unloaded yet another shipment of goods from overseas. He didn't have to open anything, just move the boxes into the storage room and stack them there. It was hard work and long hours, but he didn't mind the boring work, and the pay was decent. In another three or four months he'd have enough set aside to make things right and still be able to buy a cheap vehicle. *Freedom! That's what a car means. It would be great to have my own wheels.*

He placed the last carton from this load on top of the stack, stood back and wiped his brow. *Yep, I was lucky to get this, a place to stay and good pay. Everything is great!* He frowned. *Except for that Quan.*

While her chicken-orzo soup simmered on the stove, Melody dug through her recipe box for Mom Jamison's biscuit recipe. She used to know it by heart, but since Tom's death there'd been no one to enjoy her baking and no pleasure in the effort. As she pulled the worn, stained card out of the box, mental snapshots of family meals created a pang so intense it seemed audible.

Sighing, she pushed the memories away and concentrated on the task at hand.

"Even with a sore mouth Bobbie may be able to eat these, if I can remember how to make them the way Mom Jamison did."

As she measured ingredients and cut in the shortening, Melody reflected on her visit with Nila. The social worker Anne had managed to convince Nila to go to Haven House, a home for abused women.

"You don't have to stay if you don't like it," she'd promised. "But you will be safe there."

Melody had watched Nila's face as she listened to the social worker. The terror she'd shown at Anne's arrival changed to doubt, and as Anne explained the home's security, a faint glimmer of hope had brightened the bruised young face.

Melody felt a twinge of guilt even as she sighed with relief. She'd been on the verge of inviting Nila to stay with her even though she was uncomfortable with the idea. *Was that your way of saving me from a mistake, God? Or did I blow it again?*

Would she ever get this faith thing figured out? Melody blew out a breath of frustration. She slipped the pan of biscuits into the oven, set the timer, and gave the pot of soup another stir.

That evening Melody felt restless. She hadn't stayed long at Bobbie's. Her neighbor had mumbled her thanks for Melody's gift of supper, but her mouth was still too sore to talk. So Melody had crossed the street to visit Rose, but her nurse had said she was sleeping.

To calm her mind, Melody pulled out her latest quilt project, but the thread kept tangling. It was too warm to sit with a quilt on her lap anyway. Melody frowned in frustration and shoved the quilt back into her project basket.

"Nothing's going right. What is *wrong* with me?"

Whispers darted into her mind. *You're all alone. You are a weakling. You think you're doing good, but you'll fail. You always fail. And no one can help you.*

Melody slumped against the arm of the couch. Yes, she was alone. Ever since her children left home and her husband died, she'd been alone—and quite possibly an utter failure.

More accusations came, striking her heart like arrows: *You're not even a good mother. Where is your son? Do you know what he's doing? Is he hungry? Or maybe he's in danger …*

"No, I don't know. Oh Will, where are you? How can I help you when I don't even know where you are?"

He's lost, and so are you. Your faith has let you down. You might as well give up now …

The shrill ring of the phone startled Melody, interrupting the accusations.

"Hello?" Her voice trembled, dark whispers still swirling in her mind.

"Melody? Are you all right? It's Lydia."

"Oh…hi, Lydia. I'm okay. Just feeling a bit down. It's nice of you to phone. What can I do for you?"

"I was wondering if you'd like to come over. Dave is at a meeting, and I'd love to visit with you if you have time."

Melody hesitated. "I … I don't know, Lydia. I don't want to be a bother …"

"Of course you wouldn't be a bother." Lydia paused and her voice softened. "Melody, would you like me to come to your house instead?"

Melody took a deep breath. "Yes, I would appreciate that, Lydia. Thank you."

7

Daniel sat beside his mother's bed, quietly telling her details of his day. This hour after Valerie went home was a special time for them. Daniel could almost ignore the reality of his mother's illness as he described the quirks of the people who hired him for their small projects. Today he'd had to deal with an overly-friendly St. Bernard while building its owners a new deck. It had been frustrating at the time, but now he turned it into a humorous tale that made Rose smile.

Daniel felt himself relax, his trying day slipping away, lost in his mother's pleasure. He was tempted to ignore his cell phone when it buzzed against his hip, but he plucked it off his belt and recognized his site supervisor's number.

"Sorry, Mama, but I have to answer this."

Rose waved her fingers as Daniel rose and walked into the living room.

"Hey, Zach, what's up?"

"I've got a big problem, Boss. I'm really sorry, but I've got to get home as soon as possible. Farah just phoned, and her doc put her on bed rest for the rest of the pregnancy. With Tyler running around…Her mom already has a flight booked for the due date, and she can't change it. A friend is with Farah now, but she can only stay until tomorrow evening. Everything here is good at the moment, but we've got a new crew doing plumbing on the Rockridge site in a couple days and a framing inspection at Highview next Friday. Is there any way at all you can spell me off until Farah's mom gets here? It would be three weeks at the most. You know I wouldn't ask if it weren't an emergency."

Daniel stifled a groan. "Your family needs you, Zach. I get that." Daniel paced as he talked. "Let me get organized here; I'll need someone to stay nights with my mother … Listen, I'll phone you back in a couple hours. Go ahead and pack your things. We'll make it work—somehow."

Sighing deeply, Daniel sank onto the couch. The burden of his responsibilities pressed down on him as he struggled to corral his racing thoughts. His mother's needs came first, of course. He would have to tell her he was leaving, but he'd have to make sure he found someone he could trust to be with her. But who? And how?

Daniel walked down the hall and stopped in the doorway to her room. Rose was resting, eyes closed, but they opened and found his. Her eyebrows drew together as she studied her son's face.

"What's wrong, my boy? Who was that on the phone?"

Daniel crossed to her bed and sank onto the chair where he had relaxed just a few minutes earlier.

"It was Zach, Mama. He needs to go home and help his wife. She's expecting, remember? Well, something's wrong, and she's been put on bed rest. Her family is all in England and her mom can't get here for a couple weeks, so there's no one else to take care of her and little Tyler."

"Then of course Zach needs to be there." Rose tilted her head. "You're worried about me, aren't you?" She waggled a finger at him. "Well, don't be. God has already been working on this." She paused. "Talk to Melody."

Frustration and desperation battled for control of Daniel's thoughts.

"Is she a nurse?"

Rose smiled gently. "No, dear, but she has a friend who is, and she may be looking for a position like this." She gazed knowingly at her son. "It won't hurt to ask."

He frowned. *Are you sure about that, Mama? Every time I get near that Melody woman, I say or do the wrong thing. And I don't know why.*

∽ ∽ ∽

Melody was preparing coffee when the doorbell rang. "Come on in, Lydia!" she called.

She quickly wiped her hands on an embroidered towel and opened the door. "Oh!" She stared at her neighbor. Not Lydia, but Daniel stood a few inches away.

Suddenly breathless, Melody stammered, "I–I thought you were Lydia." She blushed. "I mean … I was expecting my friend. But you're here." *Good grief! That didn't come out right at all!*

Melody detected a hint of a smile growing at the corners of Daniel's mouth as she stepped back, took a deep breath, and tried again. "Hello, Daniel. Would you like to come in?"

The almost-smile was gone, and his usual scowl was back as Daniel stepped just inside the room, making her house feel strangely smaller.

"I need to talk to you. Do you have a few minutes?"

"Umm … sure," Melody responded. "I'm expecting company, but that's okay. What can I do for you?"

Daniel's scowl deepened. "It's not for me; it's for my mother."

He forced an uncomfortable smile. "I'm sorry. That didn't come out right. What I meant is that I do need help—for my mother."

Melody's heart clenched. "What's wrong? What can I do?"

"I need a nurse to cover nights while I'm in Alberta. My site supervisor has a family emergency, and I should only be away three weeks at the most, but I have to find someone dependable and available right away." He took a deep breath. "Mother said you have a friend who may fit the bill. Is that true?"

Melody's face lit up. "Tessa! Of course! I shared her work issues with your mother, and we prayed for her. Tessa would be perfect for your mother."

Daniel still stood just inside the door, so Melody gestured to the couch and chairs. "Please, won't you sit down? I'll phone Tessa right now. If she's not at work, I'll bet she'll come over right away." She glanced at Daniel. "I assume you'll want to talk to her as soon as possible."

"I don't like to leave Mother alone, but I will wait until you've phoned your friend. If she's not interested, I'll have to find someone else."

Melody dialed her friend's number and waited as it rang three times. *Please, God, let her be home.*

"Hello?" Tessa sounded out of breath.

"Hi, Tessa. It's Melody. Are you busy?"

"No, I've got a few days off, and I was just doing some aerobics. Gotta keep in shape, you know! Just a sec, I'll turn this video off." There was a pause and then, "That's better. What's up, Mel?"

Melody took a deep breath. "Tessa, could you come over right away? My neighbor from across the street is here and would like to talk to you about taking care of his mother. Starting tonight."

"Wow! Your mysterious neighbor is there? And he wants to talk to me? I'll be right there! Uh, give me a few minutes—I need to clean up. Bye!"

Melody's amused smile lingered as she turned to Daniel. "She'll be here in a few minutes. I know she'll be good with your mother."

"Just come over when she arrives." He put his hand on the doorknob. His eyes met hers, and his features softened. "Melody, thank you."

Oh my, he IS attractive when he's not scowling. Melody opened her mouth, but no words came.

Just then the doorbell rang. *Tessa, you're fast!* Melody thought as Daniel pulled the door open and stepped back.

"Lydia! Oh my …" Melody reached past Daniel to welcome her friend. "Please come in. I'm sorry, for a minute I forgot you were coming."

She introduced Lydia to Daniel as "my friend, the pastor's wife." Daniel nodded rather curtly, mumbled a "pleased to meet you," and walked out the door.

Her mind still reeling from her neighbor's quick-change moods, Melody sent a wobbly smile to Lydia.

"Let's go into the kitchen, okay? I'll explain everything there. Daniel lives across the street, and he has an emergency at work that's creating an emergency at home."

Lydia followed Melody into the cheery kitchen.

"Well," she said with a smile, "things seem to have changed since we talked on the phone. You look much perkier than you sounded."

Melody made a face as she poured coffee into two blue and white china cups. "Yes, I was having a pretty rough time. It felt as if my own thoughts were attacking me. Ever have that happen? But then my neighbor came over, and his problems superseded my own."

Melody shared what she knew about Daniel's situation, how he needed a caregiver for his mother —hopefully her friend Tessa—while he took care of business in Alberta.

"Well," Lydia said, "that sounds like an invitation for prayer. Shall we?"

"Oh, yes." Melody grasped Lydia's hand. "That's exactly what we need."

"Dear Father," Lydia prayed, "You know this situation inside and out. You know the needs of Daniel, his dear mother, his employee and family. Please work this out for your glory in the name of your son, amen."

Once more the doorbell rang.

"That must be Tessa!"

While Daniel interviewed Tessa in the living room, Melody led Lydia to Rose's room.

"Hello, Rose," Melody called softly. "How are you feeling this evening?"

"Come in, come in, dear! I am doing well." Rose responded with a smile that didn't quite hide the pain. "And who is this?" she asked, looking at Lydia. "Are you my new nurse?"

Melody answered, "Rose, this is my friend Lydia. She is my pastor's wife. Tessa is the nurse, and she's in the living room with your son right now. I'm sure she'll join us in a few minutes."

Lydia moved closer to the bed. "I'm so happy to meet you, Rose. Melody has told me how much you mean to her. I'm sorry to hear about this emergency with your son's employee and the crisis it's causing for all of you.

Rose patted the edge of her bed. "Come, dear, and sit with me. We are sisters in the ministry, you know. My husband was a pastor too."

Lydia sat carefully on the edge of the bed and turned to face Rose.

"I would love to visit with you and share stories, but right now I think I'd like to pray with you for your son and his company. Is that okay?"

Rose beamed. "You are a woman after my own heart. Yes, let's pray."

Several minutes later Daniel and Tessa stopped outside the bedroom door when they heard the women praying. Daniel stiffened as he heard his name, his face tightening. But as he listened to the prayers for his company, his employee's situation, and Daniel's own peace of mind, he relaxed.

Praying won't help, but it can't hurt—and it makes Mama feel better.

As soon as the prayer ended, Daniel cleared his throat and walked into the room.

"Mama, this is Tessa. She's going to take care of you while I'm away."

Rose held her hand out to Tessa. "Welcome, dear. I'm happy to meet you. And I know we'll get along just fine." Her smile enveloped Tessa.

"Hello, Rose. I'm happy to meet you, too, and I'm looking forward to getting to know you better. Now, if you don't mind, I'd like to check your vitals."

Melody took a slow, deliberate breath. Daniel's arrival into the room had made the cozy bedroom feel terribly small, stirring small sparks of discomfort. No one else seemed to be affected, though. *It's okay, just breathe,* she ordered herself.

She watched in awe as Tessa checked Rose's IV, respiration and pulse. She'd never seen her friend at work, and this Tessa was a revelation—self-assured and efficient as she took notes and talked quietly with her new patient.

Daniel cleared his throat. "You ladies seem settled, so I'll get packed. Tessa, I need to go over a few more details with you when you're done here. I'll meet you in the kitchen in, say, ten minutes?"

He gazed at his mother, worry and duty deepening the lines on his face. "Mama, once I get things settled on this end, I'll try to catch a couple hours' sleep. It's a long drive to Edmonton, and I need to be there before noon tomorrow. I'm sorry, but I have to go."

Rose leaned back against her pillow. "Of course, Son, go and do your job. I'll be fine. God is in control. He sent this lovely nurse and good friends to me, and I am at peace. Don't worry about me." She placed her hand over her heart as though making a pledge. "I'll be here when you return."

By the time Melody got home, it was nearly ten o'clock. *It all worked out perfectly,* she reflected. While Daniel phoned Valerie and her friend Lorraine, who agreed to work the day shift on weekends, Tessa arranged for a month's leave of absence from the hospital.

Lydia visited with Rose, sharing ministry stories that brought smiles and a few tears while Melody listened contentedly. *Peace in the midst of chaos. That's what you promised, isn't it, God?*

Exhausted after working fourteen hours, Will slept deeply until noises from the shop below woke him. He checked his watch. *Two o'clock! What's going on down there at this time of night?*

He leaned over the edge of the couch and concentrated on the sounds coming up through the floor. Quietly slipping off the couch onto his knees, Will pressed his ear to the floor. *That sounds like Mr. Lee, but who is he talking to?*

He listened more closely, plugging his other ear. *It's that little weasel, Quan. I saw him take cash from the till several times. Maybe Mr. Lee caught him. Wait a minute. What's he's saying?*

Quan's voice was loud and defensive. "No, Uncle, it wasn't me! I would never steal from you—certainly not heroin." A wheedling tone raised his voice. "I swear to you, it was that new guy Will Jamison. I saw him putting two packs inside his shirt yesterday."

All color left Will's face. *Heroin?*

Now Quan was whining. "I would have told you, Uncle, but you know how big he is. He scared me. He told me he needed more money, that you're not paying enough, and he said he would kill me if I told you."

Will was wide awake now. *WHAT?* He raised his fist to pound it against the floor—wishing it was Quan's face—but caution stopped him midair. *Gotta be quiet. Can't let them know I hear them.*

Mr. Lee was talking now. His voice was quiet but clear. "If you are lying to me, Quan, you will regret it. But you are my sister's son, so for now I will take your word. Young Jamison must pay for this betrayal. I will arrange it. You may go."

The voices ceased and Will crept to his backpack, adrenaline surging through his body. *I've got to get out of here!*

Daniel opened his truck's window a crack to let the brisk breeze tickle his face. The Yellowhead highway at that hour was quiet. Other than the occasional semi, it felt as if he had the road to himself.

He watched the kilometers disappear under his tires and let his thoughts drift to the business he'd been neglecting. He tried to formulate a working plan for the condo project Zach was leaving. There had been some problems with new crews not meeting his standards and resisting Zach's demands, so he would need to deal with that right away.

It's been too easy to offload everything onto Zach's shoulders. Something has to change. Maybe this trip will give me some answers.

But other thoughts kept intruding, teasing his thoughts away from the job at hand. *It was sure lucky that Melody's friend was able to book off the next three weeks so easily and that she'd been looking for a placement like this. Mama took to her right away too. Between Valerie, her friend Lorraine, and Tessa, Mama will have someone with her day and night. In spite of the time crunch everything worked out.* He felt his tension ease and he settled back against the leather seat. *Yes, things worked out just fine.*

Then he remembered his mother's words: "God has already been working on this." He stilled. Part of him, down deep, hidden in his heart wished he could believe that. He thought again of all the "happy coincidences." *Could it be true? Was Mama right?* Other memories surfaced. *No way. God doesn't care. Not about me, anyway.*

Daniel deliberately pushed aside his wayward thoughts and turned his attention once again to the long, boring highway and Zach's updates.

Pouring rain diluted the sweat streaking Will's face as he trudged toward Vancouver's downtown eastside. He knew he'd find a familiar alley there, someplace to hide until he figured out his next move.

He had run at least ten miles, and now putting one foot in front of the other required his full attention. His backpack seemed to weigh four times as much as when he'd fled the import shop.

"So much for being set, 'set up' is more like it," he muttered. "Drugs! How stupid can I get? Now I've got no home, no job, and some goons after me!"

A black Mercedes slowed as it came toward him, its headlights seeming to pin him. *You gotta be kidding! They found me already?*

Will glanced up at the well-lit sign above the doorway beside him. The Sanctuary. He'd heard about it from someone, something about good people and safety there. *It's my only hope.*

Ducking his head, he ran up the stairs and pounded on the door.

Will awoke to the smell of coffee brewing and bacon frying. "Mom?" he whispered. But when he opened his eyes, he saw several bunk beds, all empty. Not his mother's. *So where am I?*

Memories flooded in: overhearing Quan accuse him of stealing drugs from Mr. Lee, grabbing his few belongings, stuffing them into his backpack, and running until he couldn't run any more. Just when he'd thought he was finished, this place had saved him.

A heavy-set black man appeared in the doorway. A slow smile warmed his face as one eyebrow raised. "Mornin'. Breakfast is ready. Come on down if you're hungry."

Will untangled himself from the cozy blankets. "I'm starved!" He stood, pushed his golden curls out of his eyes, and followed the man out of the room.

"Name's Kane," the man said as they descended the stairs. "What's yours?"

"I'm Will. William Jamison." He sniffed enthusiastically. "Man, that smells good! I can't remember the last time I had a real breakfast."

"Heard you came in pretty late last night. Rough night?"

"You have no idea." Will paused, and a shudder ran through him. "My mom would say this place was a real God-send."

Kane looked at him sideways. They had entered the dining room, and the rumbling in Will's stomach nearly drowned out Kane's reply. "That's exactly what it is."

He gestured with a sweep of his arm toward covered dishes on the counter. "Looks like you're the last one down, so help yourself to whatever is left."

The first plate-full of bacon, scrambled eggs and toast disappeared quickly, and once Will was digging into his second helping, Kane settled across the long table from him.

"So, William Jamison, what's your story? You mentioned your mother. She live close by?" At Will's negative shake of the head, he continued. "Where you from? And what brought you to our doorstep in the middle of the night?"

Kane's calm, firm voice somehow reminded Will of his father, and sudden emotion threatened to choke him. He sputtered, gulped a mouthful of water, and swallowed hard.

"Uh, my family is in Saskatoon. We used to have a farm, but my dad died two and a half years ago. I'd left before then, anyway." He took another mouthful of eggs.

"Why?" Kane's question held no condemnation, and that gave Will the courage to answer honestly. He set down his fork and squared his shoulders.

"I made some mistakes. I'd been doing some drugs—I wasn't hooked or anything, but it messed me up. Couldn't get along with anyone, even my friends." He swallowed hard once more and looked away. "At a bush party I lost it and beat up a kid from school. Pretty bad, I guess. He'd been doing some stuff too, and we were both out of it. I don't really remember much, but I told the cops it was self-defense. They talked to my folks, said if I messed up again, they would have to charge me. Dad yelled at me and I blew up. Said I didn't need them and they would never see me again."

His breakfast seemed to congeal into a hard lump in his stomach as he looked into Kane's deep brown eyes. "I wish … I wish I could tell my dad that I'm sorry. I … I didn't mean what I said, especially about never seeing me again."

"That's a good start, son," Kane tilted the chair back and crossed his arms across his thick chest. "So what happened last night?"

Will told him how he'd felt so lucky to find work at Mr. Lee's import business, only to overhear Quan's false accusations that made him run for his life. His mouth twisted. "I should have known something fishy was going on, but desperation made me stupid, I guess."

"Hmm, that's quite the tale." Kane's chair came down with a thud. "I've heard rumors about Lee and his shop. I'll pass this information on to a buddy of mine on the force."

He pursed his lips and gazed into the distance while the clock kept time with Will's heartbeat.

"Meanwhile, seems like you need to get out of town. Any chance you're ready to go home? Sounds as if you've got a good thing going there. Lots better than most of our guests."

"No." Will shook his head. "I can't slink back home to hide behind my mother. Besides, I've got something I need to take care of first." A flicker of bravado crossed his face. "I know I can make it on my own. I just need a break."

"Well, I say you really need to think about going home. But if you won't, you still need to get away from this area. You won't be safe anywhere in the lower mainland with the likes of Lee after you."

He gave Will a thorough once-over, taking in his size, broad shoulders and callused hands, "I've got an idea. You ever been tree-planting?"

"Nope. Sounds like fun, though."

Kane snorted. "Don't kid yourself, boy. It's harder work than you've ever done. But it's honest work and good pay. And it's a long way from the city."

He rubbed his chin with one finger. "Old friend of mine who runs a crew phoned a couple days ago. He's coming down for a meeting tomorrow with some bigwigs, and we're meeting for coffee when he's done there. He doesn't usually hire rookies in the middle of a contract, but we may be able to arrange something for you—if you think you can cut it. Warner is a fair boss, plus you'd be a good distance from Lee and his gang. You'll have to buy your own gear, though. So what do you say? Think you're up for it?"

Will's mind raced. He knew how to work hard, growing up on a farm made sure of that. And he wasn't in a position to go out looking for another job. But how would he buy the equipment needed? All his savings were in the safe back at Lee's shop. *This may be my only chance to escape Mr. Lee. Whatever it takes, I have to do this.*

Kane pinned him with his gaze. "One more thing. Are you still into drugs? Because if you are, Warner won't touch you. He's had too much grief from kids who mess with that stuff."

"No, sir." Will straightened. "I've seen enough around here to swear off that junk forever."

Sunday morning dawned clear and bright. Melody woke early after a sound sleep, wrapped herself in her own robe and opened the living room curtains. Sure enough, Tessa's car was still in the driveway of the Martens house.

I wonder if she'll want to visit before heading home. Better get some coffee going.

While the coffee perked Melody prepared for the day. She was running a comb through her curls when the doorbell rang.

"Good morning, Tessa! I hoped you'd stop by this morning. How was your first night with Rose?"

"Morning, Mel. Do I smell coffee?"

The two friends filled their coffee mugs and sat at the oak dining table.

Tessa took a careful sip and sighed. "Just what I need. Thanks, my friend. As to your question, it was good. Rose slept most of the night, so I got some rest, too. It's going to take me a while to get back into night-shift mode." She took another sip of the strong brew and smiled. "But what a sweetheart she is. I can't thank you enough for suggesting me for this job. It's exactly what I was hoping for."

"It wasn't my doing, Tessa, it was God. Somehow he had it all worked out. I just sort of sat back and watched." She reached across the table. "He really does love you, you know."

Tessa tilted her head thoughtfully. "Yeah, I think he must, in spite of everything. Maybe one of these Sundays after I'm used to night shifts again, I'll come to church with you. I think it's time."

Melody was just finishing lunch when the phone rang.

"Hello?" She smiled at the responding voice. "Faith! What's up, sweetie? I missed you at church today."

"I tried to phone you Friday, Mom, to ask you to babysit this weekend—we were given a weekend at Temple Gardens in Moose Jaw by Jason's boss. And I tried again yesterday from there. You haven't been home much lately."

Melody heard the question in her daughter's voice. "You must have called while I was out buying groceries yesterday. You could have left a message, you know. And I was at my neighbor's house for several hours Friday. Remember me telling you about Rose Martens?"

Melody went on to briefly explain recent events resulting in Tessa's new position with her neighbor.

"That sounds great, Mom. But Tessa didn't give up her job at the hospital, did she?"

"Of course not; she just took a leave of absence. I'm sorry I missed an opportunity to babysit Jessica for the weekend, though. I assume Jason's mother took her? And why were you calling yesterday?"

"Yes, she did, but I wanted to give you a heads-up that Will might phone you. Did he yet? He phoned me on my cell saying he'd lost your new number."

Faith's voice held an undertone of disapproval, but Melody chose to ignore it. "No, he hasn't phoned. Did he give any indication what he wants? Did he say where he's living? How's he doing?"

"Mom, I know you worry about Will, but running away to British Columbia was his choice, and he doesn't seem to care much about his family any more. No, he didn't tell me anything except that he needs to talk to you. Probably wants more money, knowing my little brother." The censure was obvious now and impossible to ignore.

"Faith, I do worry about your brother because I love him. He's made some mistakes, but he's still my son. Anyway, did he leave you his number in case he loses mine again?"

"No, Mom, he said he really needed to talk to you. He sounded pretty stressed. Probably lost another job and needs Mommy's help. Same old story."

"Well, Faith, I'll wait for his call, then." She sighed. "I sure hope he's okay."

9

Lured to the kitchen window by the trill of a robin, Melody blinked in the bright sunshine and cringed at the barrenness of her yard. "That has to change—the sooner, the better."

She dug out the phone book and notebook and started jotting down numbers for landscape centers and companies advertising rototilling services. Then she found a recent mail-order catalogue for bulbs and seeds, refilled her coffee mug, and settled on the couch for some serious day-dreaming.

Halfway through a tantalizing variety of tomato seeds, dark whispers intruded into her thoughts. "Why hasn't Will called? He must be in trouble, and you don't even know how to contact him."

Melody tried to immerse herself in the garden catalogue again, but concern for her son engulfed her. Worry gnawed on her heart like a dog with a choice bone.

Whispers came once again: "Why did he have to leave? What did you do to make him go? Why can't he hang onto a job? Where is he staying? What's controlling him? You know you failed him, and now he's in trouble!"

As the accusations battered her soul, Melody paced the living room. "Phone me, Will," she pleaded to the air. "Please phone! I need to know you're okay."

Her pacing slowed. Condemning voices whirled around her,

pummeling her until she crumpled onto the couch. Finally another voice came, this one soothing and full of compassion.

"Come to me, my child. Give your burdens to me. I am willing and able to carry them."

"Oh, God," Melody whispered, "Please help me. Help and protect my boy. I don't know where he is or what he's doing, and I can't stand it. Help us both, please!"

"Do you think you love him more than I do?"

Melody sat up straight. She trusted God with her life. At least she tried to. Could she trust him with her son? And if not, why not? She didn't know the details of Will's life, but God did, and he could do something about it.

"Okay, Lord, my son is in your hands. Help me to trust you and not worry."

With a deep sigh of release, Melody hooked the phone onto her belt loop and walked out the back door.

As Melody stepped into her back yard, the familiar voice of her next-door neighbor greeted her.

"Hey there, Miss Melody! Ain't this a beautiful morning'?"

"Good morning, Bobbie," Melody responded with a smile. "You sound chipper this morning. Would you like to come over for some coffee? I've got news about Daniel and Rose."

"Whoa! Be right over! Make mine strong and hot—just like a good man!"

While the fresh pot brewed, Melody filled Bobbie in on the happenings of the previous evening.

"Rose said that God already knew what was going to happen and was working things out," Melody concluded. "It sure seemed like that was the case. So many little details just came together like a master-planned design. It was amazing."

"Well, that's sumthin'," Bobbie said. "I'd hope God would watch out for a person as special as Rose Martens. She's gotta be one of his favorites."

Melody got up and poured the coffee, handed a steaming mug to Bobbie and took her seat again.

"It wasn't just Rose that God was taking care of, though. He worked out the details for Daniel and his employee, and the perfect job for my friend Tessa. Maybe they're all his favorites."

She sipped her coffee. "I was just happy to watch it all happening. Oh, and did I mention that my pastor's wife was there, too? She'd come over to visit me when this all happened. Of course, Lydia and Rose hit if off right away. 'Sisters in the ministry,' they called it."

Melody sighed deeply, gazing into the depths of her coffee mug. "I wonder if Rose or Lydia ever had problems with worry and fear."

Bobbie leaned back and folded her arms against her ample chest. "Wanna talk about it? Sounds like you might need a shoulder, and mine are plenty wide."

"Oh no, I don't want to burden you, Bobbie. I'm just a little upset this morning about my son. I haven't heard from him since I moved here, and I found out he's planning to call me about something. Now I'm making myself crazy wondering what it's about and if he's okay. I'm *trying* to trust God to take care of him, since I sure can't, but it's hard."

"Hmpf! Kids!" Bobbie snorted. "Charlie and me were never blessed with the little darlin's, but I've seen my share of good ones and bad ones. Rosie's had her worries. Daniel's not an only child, ya know."

At Melody's questioning look, she continued. "Nope. He's got a sister a few years older than him."

"Where is she? What does she do?"

"And why isn't she here? That's what you really wanna know, right? Well, Hannah's clear around the globe, doin' God's work over in Africa. She'd be here if she could, but Rose said the politics there makes it pretty tricky." Bobbie smiled sadly. "She'll be here, though, one way or another, when Rosie's time comes. Guess you'll get to meet her then. She's a good un', just like her mom."

Melody's smile echoed her friend's. "I'm sure I'd love to meet Hannah, but not because of ..."

"Yeah, I know." Bobbie reached across the table and patted Melody's hand.

"Besides worries about Hannah's safety, Rose had a grouch of a husband, but she loved him anyways. And then there's Daniel ..."

"What about Daniel?" Melody leaned forward.

Just then the phone on Melody's belt loop rang out. "That might be my son!" Melody jumped up and unhooked the phone. "Hello? Will! How are you? *Where* are you? How are you doing?"

Bobbie got up and put her coffee mug in the sink. "I'll get home now, Kiddo," she whispered. "Thanks for the coffee and chat." She walked to the front door.

"Just a second, Will," Melody said into the phone, then called after Bobbie, "Thanks, Bobbie. I'll talk to you later."

She closed the door after Bobbie as she spoke into the phone. "Okay, what's up?"

"Hey, Mom, I had to get your new number from Faith. Sorry I haven't phoned."

Will's deep voice sounded so much like Tom's. Melody's heart twisted with love and grief, a bittersweet blend.

"I'm glad you finally did, Will. So how are you? Faith said you're out of work again. What happened?"

"Aw, her and her big mouth! Yeah, I quit my job." There was a slight hesitation. "You should be glad. It was in a nightclub, not a good scene. The boss promised big bucks, but it didn't pan out. He was a liar and a cheat."

Melody's heart sank. "Oh dear." This was worse than she'd thought. *God, are you listening?*

"Anyway," Will said, "I've got a better gig lined up. My friend knows this guy who needs help tree-planting in the mountains. I said I'd do it. I can make good dollars in just a few weeks, but I need to have my own equipment."

"I see," Melody said carefully. "Has your friend ever planted trees before? Do you know anything about planting trees? And how much equipment do you need?"

"Yeah, Kane did when he was a lot younger. He's a good guy and he knows this Warner pretty well." He paused. "It's exactly what I need right now, but I need good boots, a better sleeping bag, rain gear, planting bags, and some other stuff. Eight hundred dollars should cover it."

A pleading tone came into his voice. "Mom, I need your help here. I'm so done with Vancouver! And now I have this chance to make good money up in the hills, but I don't have the cash I need for equipment. Without the stuff, I can't do the job. And I haven't asked you for money for a long time. Please, Mom!"

What should I do, God? How can I not help my child? But is this the right way? Melody took a deep breath. "That's a lot of money, Will. I do have to be careful with my finances, you know."

"I'll pay you back, Mom. I promise. Don't you trust me? I'll even pay you interest, if that's what you want. But if I don't get the stuff in the next day or two, I'll miss out on this chance. I really need to do this, Mom. Please!"

Melody almost smiled at Will's little-boy whine. She could picture him begging for a dog when he was four years old. She'd always had a hard time resisting his pleading. In so many ways he was still her little boy. *It was easier when he was little. Then I usually knew what to do, and if I didn't, Tom did.*

She didn't hear an answer from God, so she took another deep breath—or was it a sigh?—and plunged in. "Okay, Will, I'll send you the money, but if you need it right away, I'll need to do a bank transfer. Do you have your account number handy?"

He relayed Kane's bank information almost breathlessly. "Thanks, Mom. I really appreciate this. By the way, since I'll be in the bush, I probably won't be able to phone until the contract is done. But don't worry, I'll be fine. Thanks again. Bye!"

With that, the line went dead. Melody stared at the silent phone in her hand and then slowly put it back on its charger. As she did, she thought she heard an evil laugh echoing in the stillness. Or was that just her imagination?

Melody quickly phoned her bank before she changed her mind. Doubts and whispers assaulted her again, following her like a swarm of mosquitos as she paced her living room.

"Leave me alone!" But the attack was relentless. After several minutes Melody was frantic.

She dashed out of her house slamming the door behind her, ran across the lawn and up Bobbie's steps. At her first knock, the door swung open.

"Howdy, neighbor!" Bobbie greeted her. "I was hoping we'd get to visit more after your phone call. Come on in and take a load off. How's your boy?"

They both sat on the flowery, overstuffed couch.

"Oh, Bobbie, I don't know." Melody rubbed her arms as though chilled. "He changed jobs again, but he needs special equipment for this one. I had to help him, even though I'm not at all sure it was a good idea."

"Of course you did, honey," Bobbie reassured her. "We take care of family, right?"

"Yes …" Melody hesitated. "But what if I helped him make a bad move? I just don't know." She slumped against the arm of the couch. "I'm trying to trust God with Will's life, but I'm not succeeding very well."

"Cut yourself some slack, Kiddo. Give God a chance to do his thing, eh?"

Melody looked at her friend with surprise. "Of course! You are so wise, Bobbie. Thank you."

She shrugged. "Naw, just repeatin' what I learned from Rose."

"Well, I appreciate your advice—and you. It was exactly what I needed to hear." Melody paused. "By the way, before I got so flustered by Will's phone call, I'd wanted to ask you for advice about gardening. Do you know of a good person to hire to rototill a small garden space? I'd love to grow some vegetables, even though it's a little late for planting. I thought I could do some lettuce, peas, and spinach. They're pretty fast. And maybe buy some started tomatoes. I've missed having home-grown tomatoes."

"They're the only ones that taste like anything," Bobbie agreed. "Sure, I know a guy. He does mine every spring. I can call him if you'd like." She winked and smiled. "Maybe you'll get the same price he charges me. He was good buddies with my Charlie, so he treats me right. Want me to phone right now? Do you know where you want your patch?"

"That would be great, Bobbie. Yes, I thought I'd like that back corner opposite the apple tree as a garden. Do you think that's a good spot?"

"Yep, that should work. Gets lotsa sunshine there. Just a sec, I'll get Roger's number."

She went to her kitchen and rummaged in a drawer. "Here it is," she said. "Any particular time you want him to come over?"

"Any time he can come would be great. I don't plan to go anywhere today, but if he's busy, he can set the time and I'll make sure I'm home. I can't wait to get started!"

A few minutes later, Bobbie hung up her phone and turned to Melody with a grin.

"How 'bout that? He'll come over right away. Said he was just about to store the tiller since planting season's just about done. He'll be here in about half an hour. Want me to introduce you?"

"Wow! Thanks so much, Bobbie. I'd just started dreaming about a garden, and now my dreams are about to become reality. Guess I'll have some shopping to do once the ground is ready. Maybe you could help me with that? I don't have any idea where the best deals are, and I'm betting you do."

"Glad to, neighbor. Let's go mark out that garden."

∽ ∽ ∽

Several hours later Melody groaned as she stood. Rubbing her lower back, she surveyed the changes to her front yard. *Why did I wait so long to do this? Roger was right, flowers make a huge difference!*

Bobbie's old friend had not only prepared the back yard garden, he'd convinced Melody to let him dig up along the front of the house and in the front corner beside her driveway. Melody had been wary of him at first, but after watching him joke around with Bobbie, she'd relaxed and enjoyed his dry sense of humor.

He was preparing to leave when Melody asked him how much she owed him. At first he refused any payment, but Melody insisted, pride firming her stance.

"Well, alrighty, missy," he'd grudgingly agreed. "You can give me a fiver if you're gonna be ornery about it."

"That's not enough! You've been here more than an hour."

Roger grinned through his curly grey beard. "Don't need the money, but I did need to check out this gal's new neighbor. I should pay you for bein' such a good friend to Charlie's girl."

In the end, Roger won. He left with a wave and five dollars, his tractor rattling as he drove down the street.

Her aching back eased for the moment, Melody picked up a large bag of fertilizer and spread it onto the new corner garden. "Who would have thought that composted manure was worth so much," she muttered. "We had a gold mine on the farm and didn't even know it!"

This was the last area she had to plant. The hollyhocks along the front of the house would soon grow taller than Melody, brightening the pale yellow walls with burgundy, pink and white blossoms. The petunias at their feet were a deep rose, some of them already blooming.

Melody dug three good-sized holes for her ornamental grasses. They anchored the corner garden, just as Bobbie promised. With the end of this gardening marathon in sight, Melody quickly planted more rosy petunias, white nicotiana, and some pale pink geraniums.

"Done! And I love it." Melody hardly noticed her aching back and knees as she gazed at the transformation.

"Wow! What happened here? It looks fantastic!"

Melody spun around to see Tessa walking across the street.

"Hey, Tessa, thanks." She glanced at her watch. Almost six o'clock. "I had no idea it was so late."

"That's not surprising, since you've obviously been *very* busy. I love this corner garden, especially the grasses and the way they flow with the breeze."

"Ooh, you're getting poetic on me!" Melody teased. "But thanks. I just wish I'd done this right away. Better late than never, right? Oh, and I've got a vegetable garden in the back, too. You'll have to come see it when you get off tomorrow morning."

"I'll do that, provided you have coffee ready."

"Give Rose my love, okay? Maybe I'll pop over this evening and see if she's up to a visit."

"Sounds good, Mel. I know she'd love to see you. See you later, then."

It was just after five when the truck Will was riding in turned off the highway and onto a logging road. His new boss slowed the vehicle while he set the radio transceiver to the frequency posted on the sign at the bottom of the steep, rough road.

Warner glanced over at Will. "Ever been on a logging road before?"

At Will's negative head shake, Warner grinned. "Hang on, then. This will be fun."

It had been a busy two days since Kane had set him up with this tree-planting job. Kane was the one who'd given him access to the home's computer and told him to read everything he could find about planting trees in the bush.

"Take your time and learn all that you can. You'll be coming in halfway through the year, so you're already behind. The more you know the better off you'll be. Besides, you need to stay out of sight until you leave—if you're hired."

He'd put his heavy hand on Will's shoulder. "If you stay inside here, you're safe. But if you step outside the door, we can't protect you. So, here's a pen and paper. Make a list of everything you need."

After Warner had hired him, it was Kane who had driven Will from store to store to buy all the equipment and articles he would need. But Will had noticed that his new friend kept checking his mirrors as he drove.

Now he and Warner were bumping and jolting up the mountain toward camp. Will had never tried bull riding before, mechanical or real, but he imagined it must feel a lot like this. The radio squawked every few seconds, but he couldn't make out the words.

"Umph!" he exclaimed as his shoulder bounced off the side of the cab. He looked to his right. Trees grew beside the road, but the steep drop-off made them look short. Far, far down he could see the road they'd been on a couple minutes earlier. An unfamiliar dizziness made him lean back.

"You got a problem with heights?" Warner asked.

"I didn't think so."

"Better not. You won't see much level ground in the next few weeks. You'll be part of Dusty's crew. He's a good foreman; he'll show you the ropes. Oh, and you'll get called rookie a lot. You are one, so just deal with it."

The radio squawked again.

Warner swore, hit the brakes and swerved sharply. The one-ton slid to a halt in a space barely wide enough for a small sedan. Will opened his mouth to protest, but shock silenced him as he stared at the loaded logging truck barreling around the bend toward them.

10

Tessa opened the door wide before Melody had a chance to knock. "Come on in, Mel. Look who's out of her bedroom. When I told Rose about your gardening effort, she insisted on coming out here so she could see the result."

And there was Rose, reclining on the couch with a big smile on her sweet face. "Melody, my friend, welcome! I'm so happy to see you. I am impressed with the change in your front yard. It looks lovely now, and it will be even more beautiful as the plants grow. Are you an avid gardener?"

Melody crossed the room and gave Rose a gentle hug before sitting across from her.

"It's wonderful to see you too. You must be having a good day. I'm glad. And I'm glad you like my little improvements. No, I never had the time or inclination to do any landscaping on the farm, so this is all new to me. Bobbie helped a lot." She chuckled. "Actually, she sort of took over, and I just followed her directions."

"Dear Bobbie, she does tend to take over when it comes to flowers. You can tell from her yard that she loves them, and she's always willing to share her enthusiasm." Rose paused. "She has a good heart, and God is gardening there."

They visited quietly for several minutes, until Rose admitted she was ready to return to her bed. Melody stood up to make her departure when the phone rang. Rose's eyes lit up as Tessa answered it.

"Hello, Daniel. Yes, she had a good day. In fact, she's on the couch visiting Melody right now."

As Tessa continued her to update her employer, Melody kissed Rose's soft cheek and said her goodbyes. "I always love visiting with you, Rose. I hope we can do this again soon."

"Goodbye and God's blessing on you, dear child."

Tessa was bringing the phone to her patient, so Melody let herself out and went home.

By the time they reached camp, the sun was playing hide-and seek with the mountain tops. As the truck slowed, Will gazed around the site.

It's a lot bigger and more complex than I expected. He shivered. It had been hot on the highway, but it was much cooler here.

Warner noticed. "You did bring a warm jacket, right? You'll need it. Soon as the sun goes down, it'll get cool—sometimes downright cold. Especially if it's raining."

"Yeah, Kane made sure I got everything on the list. I think I'm set."

Warner didn't smile. "We'll see about that."

That night Melody decided she was too tired for her new habit of Bible reading before bed. The relentless assault on her emotions all morning and the afternoon of planting had exhausted her to the point of numbness.

She fell asleep almost immediately in spite of aching muscles. But dreams of flowers and overflowing garden centers soon morphed into the old nightmare. As she watched it unfold like a familiar horror film, Melody fought to wake up. Tossing and moaning, she struggled against the nightmare dragging her to its heart-breaking conclusion. Once again, she was pacing the farmhouse, wondering why her husband was so late. Once again she tried his cell phone over and over. Once again, she walked with leaden feet to the hayfield. And there was the baler, just like every other time.

Don't look! Don't look! Melody groaned aloud as she resisted the scene. She was unable to fight it, though, and the dream continued. Once again, mangled in the machine, was … *NO! Not Will!*

Her loud cry finally woke her, but the horrific scene replayed in her mind. Will was trapped. Will was dead. Not just Tom, now Will too. As she struggled to wake completely, Melody heard the echo of a mocking, evil laugh.

Desperate for light, Melody reached for the bedside lamp and switched it on. *That's better.* But the haunting laugh still lingered.

Melody sat up and reached for her Bible. "Please, God, speak to me. I need you!"

Flipping through the pages, the underlined verses of Lamentations 3 caught her eye. She had discovered these verses shortly after Tom died. They'd brought her comfort at a time when comfort could not be found. Settling against the headboard, Melody's frantic gasping slowed as she read:

> *I remember my affliction and my wandering, the bitterness and the gall.*
> *I well remember them, and my soul is downcast within me.*
> *Yet this I call to mind and therefore I have hope:*
> *Because of the Lord's great love we are not consumed, for his compassions never fail. They are new every morning; great is your faithfulness.*
> *I say to myself, "The Lord is my portion; therefore I will wait for him."*
> *The Lord is good to those whose hope is in him, to the one who seeks him;*
> *It is good to wait quietly for the salvation of the Lord.*

Melody let the words sink into her soul. Slipping out of bed, she knelt with her face against the covers.

"Dear God, these words say you do care, that even when everything goes wrong, you are there. Help me, please, to trust you with my son. Wherever he is, whatever he's doing, please take care of him. Protect him from the enemy, dear God. In the name of your son I pray, amen"

The words comforted Melody's heart, but the bed's tangled covers and tear-stained pillow repulsed her. Wrapping Tom's old robe around her, Melody stripped the bed.

"Maybe clean sheets will bring dream-free sleep. Then again, I might as well wash these now. I won't be sleeping anymore tonight."

∽ ∽ ∽

Will felt as though he'd barely fallen asleep when his tent was invaded by a booming voice.

"Top o' the mornin' to you, young rookie! It's 5:45—time to rise, shine, and plant some trees!"

"Wh–what?" Will groaned. He forced his eyes open, looked toward the doorway of the tent, and stifled a gasp.

A large head filled the doorway to his small tent. It was framed by an enormous amount of bushy red hair, and the craggy face was dominated by a wide grin surrounded by an equally bushy beard. The eyes were deepset and dark brown, almost black.

"Morning," was the best Will could muster. "Who are you?"

"Elias T. Carter, at your service. But call me Eli." One eye winked. "Get yourself out here. 'Early bird catches the worm,' or in this case, the early riser gets lots of breakfast and the best lunch makings. We make our own lunches, you know."

The head disappeared, so Will wriggled out of his sleeping bag and dressed. The sun was just peeking over the mountain tops when he stepped out of the tent. He stretched, leaning to the right and left with his arms high overhead. He shivered. He could see his breath!

The big redhead was standing about four feet away. Will peered up at him through sleep-hazed eyes. *He's huge! I'm six foot two, so he's got to be at least six eight. And those muscles! Looks like a pro wrestler or maybe a football player. Seems to be friendly enough, though. Good thing.*

"So how was your first night?"

"Okay," Will said. His sleep had been interrupted several times by dreams of logging trucks chasing him.

"Well, I hope you're rested up. It's going to be a long, hard day for you. By the way, what's your name?"

"Will. Will Jamison."

"Pleased to meet you, Will. Got your jacket? Let's go get some grub!"

∽ ∽ ∽

Sunlight streaming through the kitchen window stirred Melody. Opening one eye, she was surprised to realize she'd slept soundly on the couch. She sat up and stretched.

"Thank you, God," she said out loud. "I didn't think I'd dare close my eyes again, but that sleep felt good!"

She glanced at the wall clock—nearly six o'clock. *Oops! Tessa will be here soon; I'd better get moving.*

The tantalizing smell of coffee filled the house when the doorbell rang a short time later.

"Mornin' Mel. Umm-mm, that smells good—just what the doctor ordered!"

"Good morning, Tessa." Melody greeted her friend with a quick hug. "How was your night?"

"Fine, but I'll tell you about it later. First I need coffee and then I want to see this vegetable garden you bragged about."

As they filled their china mugs, Melody grinned at her friend. "I didn't exactly brag. I am excited about it, though, especially the promise of fresh-from-the-garden tastes."

She led the way into the back yard and gestured toward the little garden patch at the back of the yard. The sprinkler was creating sparkly rainbows as it watered the newly-planted seeds.

"See, it's pretty small, and it will be quite a while until that promise is fulfilled, but it's a start."

"It is, indeed." Tessa gazed in silence at the mostly-bare earth with a few small tomato and pepper plants.

"I'm proud of you, Mel," she finally said. "You really are making a new home here by yourself. You've come a long way from the shy little girl that hated to try anything new."

Melody's smile was more of a grimace. "Well, Tess, in this case it's not as though I had a choice. But I do think this move was planned by God. He's been working in me a lot since I came here."

"Me, too," Tessa responded. "Let's go back inside, and I'll tell you about it."

Melody topped up their mugs before they sat across from each other at the table. "Okay, Tess, I'm all ears."

Tessa grinned. "No, you're not. You've got a few other parts here and there. But I will tell you about my relationship with Rose. Just in the last few days of working with her, I've come to think of her as my own special angel. She is so loving! When her son phones, and he does every evening, she lights up like it's Christmas."

Images of Will intruded into Melody's thought, but she pushed them away. *Not now. I can't compare my son to Daniel. He's much older; of course he's more mature and caring toward his mother.*

"Hey, where'd you go?" Tessa was looking at her quizzically. "Did my mention of Mr. Neighbor get you dreaming or something?"

Melody blushed. "Of course not! Tell me about Rose."

"Sure, Mel, sure." She grinned, then sobered. "Well, Rose sleeps pretty well much of the night, usually, but now and then pain or something else keeps her awake. Last night was pretty rough, maybe because she'd been up during the day."

"It was great to see her up," Melody interjected. "But I hope I wasn't to blame for aggravating her pain."

"No, it wasn't anything you did. She insisted on getting up. She wanted to see your yard, but she also wanted a change of scenery. It just wore her out, that's all. But last night she was restless and couldn't sleep. When that happens, she likes me to read the Bible to her. I think I've read more scripture since I started working with Rose than I had in the last ten years."

"God works in mysterious ways," Melody quoted with a grin. "I knew it was his idea, you getting this job."

"I think you must be right, Mel. Anyway, last night Rose asked me to read from a book I didn't even know existed. Ever heard of Lamentations?"

A little tingle started at the back of Melody's neck. "Um-hmm," she murmured.

"Well, I hadn't. But I found out that's where my favorite hymn comes from." She began singing: "Great is Thy faithfulness, O God my Father ..."

"That's amazing!"

Tessa stopped singing and gave her friend a puzzled look. "What? That I know a hymn? That I can sing? What?"

"No, silly, I remember you sang that hymn as a solo when we were kids. I'll never forget how proud I was of you! You've always had a beautiful voice." She hesitated. "It ... it's just that God led me to those verses last night, too. They were exactly what I needed after a bad dream."

"Wow! Talk about mysterious ways! Want to tell me about the dream?"

"Not really, Tess. I'm trying not to think about it. But I'm so glad you shared this with me. God is certainly doing something. I'm just not sure what yet."

"Well, old friend, maybe we can talk more about this another time." Tessa looked into her coffee mug. "Empty! Guess that's my cue to get home and try to bring some order into the chaos that's my apartment."

She put her mug on the kitchen counter and blew a kiss to her friend still seated at the table. "Thanks again for the coffee and for the visit. I know my way out. Same time tomorrow?"

Melody looked up. "Sure, Tessa. See you tomorrow."

Melody was moving the oscillating sprinkler to the front yard when she heard her phone ringing. She dropped the sprinkler onto the lawn and ran into the house.

"Hello?" she answered breathlessly.

"Hi, Mom. What did I get you from? You sound winded."

"Oh, hi, Faith. I was just moving the sprinkler; today's my day to water. How's everything at your house?"

"We're all fine. But Jason just found out he's going to be working out of town for a couple days, so I was hoping we could get together tomorrow, maybe go shopping or something."

"That sounds like fun, honey. Where's Jason going?"

"He's got a job to do in Leroy. It's not a big job, so he should be home by Friday night. But I know I'm going to be lonely even with Jess to keep me busy." A wistful note came into her voice. "Besides, we haven't had a mother-daughter date for a while."

"I would love that, Faith. When and where do you want to go? Should I pick you up? Since I bought that baby seat, my car is all ready for my littlest sweetheart."

"Great! Jess is usually ready for the day around ten. That gives us a couple hours before lunch and naptime. Would you mind if we went to Midtown Mall? The elevator there makes it easier to get around with a stroller, and Sears has some sales on baby stuff right now."

"Sounds like a plan, Faith. I haven't been to Midtown in ages. We can shop to our hearts' content and then come here for lunch. Would that work for you? That way Jess can crawl around or sleep; she'll have a lot more freedom than in a restaurant."

"Perfect. I can hardly wait! Thanks, Mom."

11

By ten o'clock the next morning, Melody was at Faith's door. "Good morning, dear daughter. And there's my little angel. Come to Grandma, Jessie."

Jessie squealed with delight when Melody plucked her out of her swing. She gurgled a happy sound as her fist closed around Melody's curls and pulled.

"Ouch! You little monkey, why do you like my curls so much? Maybe you just need some of your own." She nuzzled the downy fuzz covering the baby's head.

"I think we're ready to go, Mom. Let me check Jessie's diaper one more time. Sometimes I think she does it on purpose, filling her pants just when we're ready to walk out the door."

A few minutes later, they were on their way. Jessica gurgled and cooed from the back seat, kicking her chubby legs so that the bells on her sandals jingled merrily.

"She's such a happy baby, Faith. You're obviously a very good mother."

"Well, I had a good teacher," Faith retorted. "By the way, did Willful phone?"

Melody pursed her lips at the nickname Faith had bestowed on her brother when they children. Unfortunately it fit—back then and even more so now.

"Yes, he phoned," she admitted. "We didn't talk long, though."

Faith gave a ladylike snort. "Huh! He wanted money again, right?" At her mother's wry nod, she exclaimed, "I knew it! What was his deal this time?"

"To be honest, Faith, I don't know if I should have given in. But he was offered a job planting trees and needed money for his equipment. It sounds as if he could make quite a bit of money this summer, and it would get him out of the city."

"So how much did he get from you?"

"Faith, I didn't give more than I can afford. And I think that's between your brother and me." She reached over and patted her daughter's knee. "Don't worry, honey, this situation—and Will—are in God's hands. And I'm trying to leave them there instead of worrying. Can we change the subject?"

"Okay, Mom. I'm sorry I got on your case. But I worry about my little brother. He seems determined to choose the hardest way possible."

"Yes, you're right about that. He's good at pushing me into trusting God, though."

She smiled into the rear-view mirror at her grandbaby. "Okay, sweetie, here we are!"

Melody slowed her vehicle and turned into the parking structure. "What do you think our chances are of finding a spot near the elevator?"

An hour later, Jessica tired of charming passers-by and started fussing, gaining volume by the minute. She strained against the straps on her stroller, making it difficult to steer. Faith stopped in the middle of the walkway and crouched down beside the stroller.

"All right, all right, I get the message. Looks like my princess wants her bottle." She glanced up. "Are you ready for a break, Mom?"

"Absolutely," Melody responded. "I'd forgotten how big this mall is; I'm totally ready for coffee."

While Melody bought the drinks, Faith released Jessie from the stroller, settled her onto her lap, and popped a bottle into the wailing mouth.

"That's better, isn't it?" Faith soothed her little one. "Oh, thanks, Mom. That smells wonderful. I was just about ready to wail, too."

By noon they were all more than willing to head home. Jessie was fussing again, needing lunch and a nap. The trunk of the small car was filled with bags of baby clothes, the stroller, and some stuffed toys Melody couldn't resist.

As she pulled into her driveway, Melody turned to Faith. "That was a lot of fun, daughter dear, but I'm beat—and starved. Are you ready to eat?"

"Sure am. Let me get this baby fed and put down for her nap, then we can relax. Let's just leave this stuff in the car, okay? No point in moving it twice."

Melody had prepared chicken salad with grapes and almonds, fresh vegetables, and bakery-bought croissants that morning. So while Faith fed Jessica, she set everything on the table and started a fresh pot of coffee.

After lunch Faith stacked the dirty dishes in the sink and turned on the faucet.

"Leave the dishes, Faith." Melody said. "That will give me something to do later. Let's go sit in the living room. Do you want more coffee?"

"No thanks, Mom, I'm trying to cut down. You go ahead, though. I know it's your favorite addiction."

"Watch it, missy!" Melody warned with a smile.

Faith sat in Tom's recliner and raised the footrest. She sighed as she leaned back. "This chair is so comfy, but it makes me miss Dad even more. How do you handle it, Mom? Being surrounded by so many reminders?"

Melody put her feet up on the coffee table and sipped her coffee. "Well, honey, I'd have to say it's easier here than it was on the farm. *Everything* there was a reminder of what I lost when your father died. It became unbearable." She shuddered and shifted to face her daughter more directly. "But the things I brought with me, like that chair, bring more comfort than pain. At least most of the time."

She paused, sighed. "I will always miss him, but I have no choice. I have to go on."

"I think I understand. If I hadn't had Jason to lean on, I don't know what I would have done when Dad died. I know you and Dad thought we were too young to get married, but looking back, I really think the timing was a God thing. He knew." She smiled wistfully at her mother. "And I admire the way you've picked up the pieces and are starting a new life for yourself. And speaking of that, Mom, there's something I want to talk to you about."

Something in Faith's tone had Melody on alert. "What is it?"

"Don't worry, it's nothing bad." Faith reassured her. "It's just that Jason and I have been talking, and we want you to know that if you want to start dating, it's okay with us. In fact, we think you should."

"Wait just a minute!" Melody nearly dropped her favorite mug. "You're telling me to *date?*"

"It's been more than two years since Dad died. You're still young…"

"Thank you very much," Melody muttered.

"Let me finish. You are young, and we hate it that you're alone. You have a lot of living left, and you should be able to share it with someone special."

Melody sat up straight and glared at her daughter. "I *do* share my life with special people: you and your family, Tessa, and several new friends. I don't need anyone else."

Faith looked only slightly chastened as she murmured, "Okay, mother dear, whatever you say. Consider the subject dropped."

After taking her daughter and barely-awake granddaughter back to their house, Melody was still fuming. *I don't need "someone special." I'll always miss my Tom, but I'm finally doing fine with my life just the way it is.*

But no matter how hard she tried to displace it, the face of her handsome neighbor lingered in her mind.

༶ ༶ ༶

The following morning Melody had coffee perking and muffins in the oven by the time she heard Valerie's car pull into the driveway across the street.

"Perfect. Everything should be ready when Tessa comes over."

Sure enough, she was just taking the blueberry muffins out of the oven when the doorbell rang. "Come on in, Tessa." Melody called. "It's unlocked."

Tessa swung open the door, stepped inside, and stopped with her hand on her heart. "Oh, Mel, you read my mind. Coffee *and* muffins! Those smell absolutely heavenly."

"I hope you like them." Melody upended the muffin tin onto the cooling rack, and plucked four onto a waiting plate. "It just felt like a muffin-type morning. Let's eat."

Tessa was buttering her second muffin when Melody cleared her throat.

"So … what's it like working for my neighbor?"

"Rose? She's great! Such a sweetheart!" Tessa smirked. "But you already knew that, didn't you? I'll bet it's her son you're wondering about. Am I right?"

Melody tried not to blush, but she could feel her cheeks warm. "Well, yes. I was just wondering if he's as grumpy with you as he's been every time I've encountered him."

"No," Tessa said. "We don't actually talk that much; he just wants to know how his mother's night went. He's always been polite. Once I give my report, I give the phone to Rose so they can visit. I can tell from her voice that there's a very strong bond between them."

A look of longing came into Tessa's eyes. "It must be nice to be loved that much."

"Aw, Tessa, you're loved!" Melody protested. Her head tilted. "But you're talking about a different kind of love, aren't you?"

At her friend's slow nod, Melody asked, "So what happened with that guy at work? Orlando? I thought maybe …"

"Yeah, me too." Tessa slumped in her chair. "But I'm glad I took your advice and just kept being friendly without pursuing anything more. I almost did …"

"So what happened?"

"Well, about two weeks ago I decided to take my lunch outside. And when I stepped out onto the patio, there he was, sitting with his back to me. I decided this was the perfect time to get to know him better, so I headed his way. Just as I was about to call out to him, I realized he was talking on his cell phone. He was speaking Spanish, and I heard him say, 'I love you, Carmelita.' I learned some Spanish while in Texas, you know." Tessa's mouth twisted. "The way he said her name, it was like a tender caress. I stopped in my tracks. I should have turned and walked away, but I couldn't move. He said a few more sentences in Spanish that I couldn't follow, and then he ended with 'I'll see you when I get home.'"

Tessa's eyes were pools of misery. "I did it again, Mel. I fell for a married man. What is *wrong* with me?"

Melody's eyes were damp, too. Her friend didn't need any more heartbreak, especially over men. "Tessa, there's nothing wrong with you. You are a wonderful person!"

Tessa shrugged. "Well, now you know why I was so pumped to get this job taking care of Rose. I had to get away from the hospital, even for a while. After that little revelation I tried to steer clear of Orlando, but even in a big place like that it's hard to avoid someone completely." She sighed. "The few times we passed in the hall, I tried to be friendly in a professional sort of way, but I was so angry with myself, I'm afraid I was almost rude.

"At least I hadn't let him know how attracted I was toward him. I am thankful for that small mercy." She grimaced. "I know I won't be able to avoid him when I go back to the hospital, but maybe this time away will give me some emotional distance."

After Tessa left, Melody headed for her little vegetable plot. As she pulled the green shoots already popping up between the neat rows, Melody grumbled at God.

"Why did Tessa have to get her heart broken again? She thought this guy Orlando was so wonderful, and now she finds out he's married. Why didn't you protect her heart? Why didn't you prevent this from happening? I just don't get it."

Pulling weeks somehow soothed her. It was as though she was a warrior, protecting her seeds and seedlings from the dangerous weeds that would harm them. One clump of crabgrass at the edge of the plot was especially stubborn. Several inches tall, Melody had to stand up and pull it with all her strength.

"Oomph!" She landed on her backside with a thud. She rolled onto her knees and stood up again, still holding the offending weed. "Well, at least I got it!" She looked at the clump of grass in her right fist. The roots stuck out of the bottom like a small shrub. "No wonder that put up such a fight!"

But looking more closely, she saw that the roots were broken at the ends. "Rats! That means I'd better dig up the rest of this monster."

Heading into the house for her basket of garden tools, Melody heard the "Beep, beep" of her answering machine. She pushed the "play" button and heard silence, then finally Nila's timid voice.

"H–hello, Melody. You said I could call you. I need to talk to you. Please call me back."

Oh, Nila, I forgot about you. I haven't even prayed for you since I saw you last. God, forgive me!

It took a few minutes to get through the protective red tape at Haven House, but finally Nila's voice came through the phone again.

"Hello?"

"Hi, Nila. It's good to hear your voice. How are you doing? Is your arm healing okay?"

"Melody," the timid voice said, "thank you for phoning me back. I didn't know who else to phone."

"What's wrong, honey? What can I do for you?"

"I want to go home, Melody." Urgency raised her voice. "I *need* to go home! I don't even know if the doors got locked. You know, anyone could just walk in and take stuff. And a friend told me Nick's getting out of jail. If things aren't just right, he'll be awfully mad."

Melody's heart twisted at the fear in Nila's voice. "I hadn't heard anything about him getting out so soon. Are you sure? But if he is, that's even more reason for you to stay where you are. You're safe there, Nila. And it's only been a week. You need more time to heal, don't you?"

Nila's voice dropped to a whisper. "I just want to go home."

Melody took a deep breath. *Give me the right words, Lord. Please tell me what to say.* "Are they treating you well there?"

A mumble came through. "Um-hmm."

"Well, can you give it at least one more week? Your cast comes off in another four weeks, right? If you can stay there until then, your arm will have a much better chance of healing properly. But at least give it another week, okay?"

After another deep breath, Melody heard herself say, "Nila, I'll keep an eye on your house for you if that will help. In fact, I'll walk down there today and make sure everything is okay. If Nick is home, I'll let you know." *After I run home and hide!*

"You'd do that? Really?" Nila's voice held a whisper of wonder. "Oh." There was a long pause. Finally, "Okay. I guess I could stay here a little longer. Good-bye."

Melody hung up the phone, reached behind her for a chair, and sank into it. *Well, God, now what have you gotten me into?*

"Hey, Bobbie, would you like to go for a walk with me?" Melody stood on her neighbor's front steps, anxiety crinkling her brow.

"What's up, Kiddo? Why the sudden urge to get some exercise?" Bobbie stepped back and motioned with her hand. "Come on in; take a load off and tell me about it."

A few minutes later, after filling Bobbie in on her phone conversation with Nila and the promise she'd made, Melody and Bobbie headed down the street. The gray house was near the end of the long block, and the closer the two women got, the less Melody wanted to actually go up to it. It felt like only a few seconds until they were standing at the end of the narrow walkway leading to the house.

"Looks like nobody's been takin' care of this place for some time,"

Bobbie muttered. "Could use a fresh coat of paint. And look at that lawn! Mostly weeds gettin' way outta hand."

"I wonder if I should bring my mower down? Maybe run a sprinkler for a couple hours? Nila was awfully worried about things not being just right when Nick got home."

"Put those ideas right outta your head," Bobbie ordered. "Why do anything for that monster? You saw what he did to that little girl. He doesn't deserve any kindness!" Her face softened with concern. "You'd just be puttin' yourself in danger, too."

"Okay, okay, you win." Melody held up her hands in surrender. She straightened her shoulders and started up the walk. "I promised Nila I'd make sure the doors are locked. Let's get this over with."

"Yeah, let's. I'll check the back door while you do the front." A grim smile twisted Bobbie's lips. "Race you!"

Darts of panic shot through Melody, increasing their intensity with each step closer to the black front door that looked like a black hole waiting to devour her. Her feet seemed to sink deep into the ground, forcing her to strain as though pulling stubborn roots with each step. By the time she reached the front door, she was panting from fear and exertion. Up one step. She paused, gasping. Another step. Why was the air so thick? Top step. *Why am I doing this? I'm so afraid!*

The darts became voices. "You should be afraid. You're walking into danger, and you are powerless. Why did you drag Bobbie into this? Do you want her to get hurt, too? This is too big for you! Give up!"

Trembling, she reached for the doorknob as though it was electrified, and with a deep, shaky breath, took hold and turned it.

12

"Hey! Rookie!" Will spun around, lost his balance and nearly fell on the seedling he'd just planted.

The checker strode toward him, smirking and shaking his head. "You've got to pick up the pace, man," he said. "Right after you redo that last row." He gestured toward the sad-looking little trees. "Do those look straight to you? Nobody gets paid for work like that!" With that, he moved on.

Probably to yell at some other poor dude. Will looked back at the row he'd just completed and groaned. Miniature Towers of Pisa, that's what they looked like. He wiped the sweat out of his eyes with the hem of his shirt, readjusted his planting bags, and headed back down the row. His back ached, his calves burned, and his boots were caked with heavy clay mud. Carrying his shovel in one hand, Will swatted futilely with the other at the swarms of bugs following him down the steep slope.

"Now I know why other guys quit," he muttered. "Hard doesn't begin to describe this." He had made less than seventy-five dollars yesterday, and after camp costs of twenty-five dollars, he'd wondered if he'd made a mistake. *But I'm far away from Mr. Lee and his goons, and Warner said the work would get easier. I wonder when?*

He stopped at the bottom of his section, set down his shovel for a moment and took a long swig of water from his water jug. Then he began pinching the base of the rejected seedlings to straighten them.

"Hey, rookie!" This time the nickname came from a female voice, so Will raised his head, searching for the source. "Over here!"

About fifty yards away a cute girl was smiling and waving at him. A red flowered bandana covered pony-tailed dark hair, and a skimpy tank top and very short shorts completed her outfit. Will straightened his back and waved back. "Hello!"

"Wanna buy me a drink in town tomorrow?"

In town tomorrow? Oh yeah, this is day five of the shift, so tomorrow's a day off. He grinned and yelled, "Sounds good to me!"

Still smiling, he bent to his work.

After supper that night Will headed toward the showers. He could hardly stand his own smell after two days of planting. He didn't want to offend that hot girl when they met down in Vanderhoof. *Hmmm ... I don't even know her name. Better find out somehow. I'll bet Eli knows.*

Eli seemed to know pretty much everything about camp life. And he'd been friendly when no one else in the camp paid him any attention. Until now ... He decided to find Eli and get that girl's name before showering.

But as he passed by the mess tent, Warner hollered at him from the doorway. "Jamison! I need to talk to you. Get in here."

"Now what?" Will grumbled. "This is supposed to be my free time."

As he entered the large tent, Warner waved him to an empty table. "Have a seat."

Will sat, but his thoughts raced. *Am I being fired? Already? That's hardly fair.*

Warner settled on the opposite side of the table and waited until Will's eyes met his. "As you know, tomorrow is the crew's day off. Almost everyone plans to head into town, but you've only been working two days, not enough to earn a day off."

Will opened his mouth to protest, rebellion heating his face, but his boss continued.

"You seem to be having trouble meeting quota so far. Everyone has to pull their weight and finish their piece at a good pace. I've heard complaints that people have to wait for you at the end of the day. Plus you missed the safety lecture. Eli Carter has volunteered to give you some concentrated training. He's good at this job. If you're smart, you'll take full advantage of this opportunity. When the two of you are done, you can rest up for the next shift." He stood. "It could mean the difference between a successful summer for you, or a very short one."

Will didn't move, trying to absorb the news. His whole body ached, he was exhausted, and he'd been counting on this break. Sure, it was good of the big redhead to say he'd stay here and help him, but … *what about the girl?*

Melody dialed the number for Haven House. After six rings, a breathless voice answered. "Hello. Haven House, Sofia speaking."

"Oh hi, Sofia, it's Melody Jamison. I talked to Nila Black earlier. Is she available?"

"I'm sorry, but she's busy right now. May I take a message?"

"Please tell her that her house is locked and everything looks okay." *And I hope I never have to go there again.*

Will was still sitting in a daze of anger and disappointment when he heard, "There you are!" It was the girl, and he hadn't even found out her name yet.

"Yeah, here I am," he responded, mouth turned downward.

"Well, are you ready to head out? We're leaving in just a couple minutes. Where's your stuff?"

Will stood and looked down at the girl, eyes pleading for understanding.

"I can't go. Sorry. Apparently I need some more training if I'm going to make it here."

The girl's eyes blazed, and her mouth twisted. "Yeah, right!" she retorted. "What, I'm not good enough for you? Look, if you're not interested, at least be man enough to say it."

She turned and stomped toward the doorway. "Don't worry, I'll find someone else to keep me company tonight."

Will stormed toward his tent, boot steps keeping time with his thoughts. *Forget the shower. Doesn't matter now, anyway. It's just another workday for me tomorrow, while everybody else gets to goof off. It's not fair!*

The sun was high in the sky as they hiked away from camp with their shovels and practice trees. Eli led the way through the bush as he whistled a tune. It sounded vaguely familiar, but Will couldn't place it. He started to ask what the song was when Eli stopped.

"Everyone else got this training on day one." He looked intently at Will and continued, "So why'd you come up when you did? Warner wasn't looking to hire when he went down to the city."

Will stopped three steps behind Eli and shrugged his shoulders. "It's kind of a long story."

Eli shrugged. "I'm a good listener. But on second thought, let's leave that until after I enlighten you on the fine art of planting trees. This spot should work."

A couple hours later the two headed back to camp. On the way, Will worked up the nerve to ask Eli about the enchantress he'd had to turn down.

"Flowered headscarf, about up to here," Will raised his hand to shoulder level, "and really cute. Really short shorts too."

"She calls herself Vixen," Eli said with a shake of his bushy head. "Hate to burst your bubble, but she's hit on every guy around here. Not the kind of girl you want to hang out with."

Will snorted. *Oh, no? Sounds like my type exactly!*

∞ ∞ ∞

Melody was kneeling in her garden when she heard her neighbor's voice behind her.

"Mornin', neighbor! Looks like your garden is doin' real good. You're gonna have to thin those carrots, though."

"Good morning, Bobbie!" Melody pushed herself upright and brushed the dirt from the knees. She looked down at the row of carrot tops, fluffy green wands pushing against one another.

"You're right. Looks as though I planted them much too thickly. How soon should I thin them?"

Bobbie shrugged. "Any ol' time. Well, the sooner the better, actually. They need room to grow straight."

Melody smiled her thanks. "I'm so blessed to have you for a neighbor, Bobbie." She gestured toward the house. "Want some coffee?"

Bobbie chortled. "Do one-legged ducks swim in a circle? I need to ask you a favor, anyway."

Filled mugs in hand, Melody and Bobbie sat at the table.

"So what's the favor you need, Bobbie? What can I do for you?"

Bobbie took a gulp of the dark liquid. "Well, Miss Melody, I'm going away for a week, and I was wonderin' if you'd watch my place for me."

"Of course I would," Melody said. "What would you want me to do?"

Bobbie leaned back. "Sprinklers are automatic, so there's no worry there, but the raspberries are just gettin' ripe. If you'd pick and use 'em, I'd be relieved. That and pickin' up the mail and paper. Maybe check inside the house once or twice. That's about all."

"I'd be happy to do that, and I love raspberries." Melody tilted her head. "So when and where are you going?"

"Leavin' early Sunday, flying to Edmonton. Got an old friend who's turning seventy-five, so her hubby's puttin' on a surprise party. He said I should plan on a whole week, though, since Ella's kinda bummed about that big number." She chuckled. "Guess she really is my *old* friend now!"

After lunch Eli went to wash his clothes in a couple buckets while Will sprawled on his bedroll.

That wasn't so bad. Eli's a pretty good teacher. Wish I'd known those tricks two days ago. I'd have done a lot better, made more money.

His eyes started to close, but his next thought snapped them open.

Strange, he didn't seem surprised or anything when I told him about having to get away from Mr. Lee and the way Kane arranged things with Warner. It was almost as if he knew and was testing me. I wonder why.

His eyes slowly closed, and within seconds he was drifting asleep while Eli's haunting tune played in his mind. In his relaxed state, the words came unbidden from somewhere deep in his memory: *"Great is Thy faithfulness ..."*

Sunday morning Melody put together a simple casserole, stuck it in the oven, set the timer to start in an hour, and glanced at the clock again.

Tessa said she'd be here by now. Hope she didn't chicken out on me. She was pulling dishes out of the cupboard when a flash of red outside caught her eye. *There she is.*

A few minutes later, the sporty Honda pulled into the church lot.

"Looks like Faith and Jason beat us here," Melody said, unbuckling her seatbelt. "Come on, if we hurry, we should all be able to sit together."

"I–I don't know about this," Tessa said. "Now that we're here, I'm getting nervous again. Are you sure I look okay?"

Melody gave her friend a slow, thorough once-over. Shoulder-length coppery hair held back with silver clips, matching earrings and necklace, and a simple but stunning royal blue wrap dress ... *She looks like a model!* Melody thought just a bit enviously.

"Good grief, Tess, you look gorgeous. Quit worrying. I told you there is no dress code here, and even though you're making me look frumpy, I'm quite happy to be seen with you."

"It's just been a long time since I've been to church, any church." Tessa shook her head and let out her breath slowly. "But we're here now, so let's do this."

∞ ∞ ∞

Two hours later, Tessa and Melody sat at opposite ends of the big brown couch and propped their feet up on the coffee table.

"That was a great lunch, Mel. I'll have to get the recipe from you for that casserole." She patted her trim midriff and smiled. "And that raspberry sundae was just too yummy! Think I'll have to jog ten miles tomorrow."

"Seriously? You're jogging now?"

Tessa grinned sheepishly. "Well, I'm trying to. There's a fitness club next to my apartment block, so I joined up to use their treadmills. So far I'm just walking with short spurts of jogging." She sighed. "If I ever *do* meet Mr. Right, I don't want to be all saggy and out of shape."

Melody squinted at her friend. "Hmm ... can't quite picture you saggy. It's fun to try, though."

"Not to change the subject or anything, but wasn't that a great sermon? Did you tell your pastor about my past? Is that why he preached on God's forgiveness?"

"Of course not, Tessa. I would never do that." Melody clasped her hands together. "And yes, it was a wonderful sermon. You're not the only one who needs to hear about God's forgiveness and grace, you know. I rather thought he was talking to me."

"You! What are you talking about?"

So Melody shared how unwilling she'd been to keep her promise to Nila and her panic once at the house.

"I felt so silly when the knob didn't turn and it was obvious her boyfriend wasn't home. But I'd forgotten to trust God, as usual. Pastor Dave quoted that verse that says perfect love overcomes fear. For me, too often fear overcomes love."

Silence filled the room until Tessa asked, "Mel, would you mind if I played your piano? "

"Of course you can, Tess, but I really don't think of it as my piano. It's always been Mom Jamison's. Both Faith and Will took lessons on it, but I've never played. I just kept it for memory's sake." She smiled. "You're the musical one, not me."

So Tessa pulled out the padded bench, sat down and began playing. Melody knew the first one, since it was her cell's ringtone. After that she just leaned back, closed her eyes and enjoyed the music flowing from Tessa's fingers.

Several minutes later, Tessa put her hands in her lap. "Oh that was fun. It's been ages since I've had a chance to play. Thanks, Mel."

"Thank you, my friend. Any time you feel the need to let some music out, that piano's here for you."

Daniel paced his hotel room. It was seven o'clock. When he'd gotten in from the jobsite, there was a message at the front desk from Zach saying he'd phone back at seven.

Now what? Sure hope his wife is okay. What if there were more serious complications than they'd thought? What if he can't return to work in two weeks as planned? That new nurse has to go back to her hospital job then. What if…"

The phone buzzed. He nearly dropped it in his haste to answer it. Tension throbbed at the base of his neck "Yes? Zach. How are things?"

He listened for several seconds, a smile spreading across his face. "That's great news, Zach! Congratulations!" He paused, listening. "Yes, I understand. Glad to hear she and the baby came through it okay. Sounds as if Farah's going to need your help for a while. I should be able to run things here for another week or so. Farah's mother will arrive next week, right? Sounds good."

He twirled around, eyes searching. "Wait a minute, Zach, let me get a pen and paper. My mother's going to want the baby's specs."

Tessa was reading to Rose from 1 Corinthians 13, the love chapter. Rose settled back against her pillows, the deep lines on her face easing as she soaked up the words.

Love is patient; love is kind. It does not envy, it does not boast, it is not proud. It is not rude, it is not self-seeking, it is not easily angered, it keeps no record of wrongs. Love does not delight in evil but rejoices with the truth. It always protects, always trusts, always hopes, always perseveres. Love never fails.

Tessa stopped and looked toward the ceiling, gulping back a lump in her throat. Would she ever know love like that? Would she ever be able to *give* love like that?

Rose looked at her, questions in her eyes. Tessa dropped her gaze to the Bible again just as the phone rang.

"That must be Daniel," Rose said with a smile.

Tessa answered the phone, wondered at the cheer in Daniel's voice, and delivered the phone to Rose's outstretched hand.

"Hello, my dear," Rose sang into the phone. "How's everything in Alberta tonight?"

Tessa turned to leave the room, but Rose motioned her toward the chair beside the bed.

"Oh, that's wonderful news, Danny! I'm so happy for Zach and Farah, and for little Tyler, too. A baby girl—what a blessing! So are you coming home soon?"

Rose listened for a minute or two, her face sobering. "I see. Well, I'm glad they're all doing well. I will be praying for the whole family."

She turned to Tessa and made a writing motion with her free hand. While Tessa found pen and paper in the nightstand drawer, Rose spoke into the phone again. "Do you know the baby's name? How do you spell that? S-a-m-i-r-a. Oh, that's lovely." She smiled. "More information, please. Six pounds, five ounces and eighteen inches long. That's a good, healthy size. Thank you for that happy news, Danny. Give my love and blessings to Zach and family. Now, how are *you* doing?"

13

The following Thursday Nila phoned again. Melody cringed when she heard the timid voice. *Now what?*

"Hello? Melody? Umm … this is Nila."

"Hi, Nila. How are you doing?"

"It's been a week. I stayed another week like you asked. Now I want to go home. They can't keep me here, and my arm is good. I can use it now, even with the cast on." A pleading tone came into her voice. "You said you'd help me, Melody. Would you please come get me?"

Melody's thoughts raced. *I haven't been by her house in the last week. What if that monster is back? How can she want to go back to him? What am I supposed to do?*

"Umm, Melody? Are you there?"

Melody closed her eyes and sighed. "Yes, Nila, I'm here. Listen, is Anne there? I'd like to talk to her if I could."

"Yeah, she's here. I just talked to her. She said I can leave any time I want."

"I would like to talk to her for a minute, Nila. Please."

After a few moments, a pleasant voice spoke. "Anne here. How can I help you, Melody?"

"Tell me what to do, Anne. Nila says she wants to go home, but I don't think that's wise. Her boyfriend may or may not be there, and if he is, what's to prevent him from hurting her again?"

"Well, Melody, we don't keep anyone here against their will. Nila told me you convinced her to stay another week, and that's fine. She has healed physically in the time she's been here. Emotionally, not so much. But if you made promises to her, you need to keep them.

"It's true that she may be going right back into danger, but that's her choice." Her voice lowered. "Unfortunately, we see that a lot. What you can do is continue to be her friend. Be there for her as much as possible. Can you do that?"

"Not on my own," Melody admitted. "But I'll try. Please tell Nila I'll be there by two o'clock."

It was a warm, sunny day, not hot enough to justify turning on the air conditioning, but too warm to keep the windows up. Melody was just going to ask Nila if she minded the breeze when Nila laughed quietly.

"That wind feels so good on my face. Nick always rolls down the windows on nice days like this." She turned to Melody, face alight. "I just can't wait to get home!"

Melody turned off the main boulevard two blocks away from their street.

"Well, we're nearly there."

There were so many other things she wanted to say: "Don't go! You'll just get hurt again, eventually if not right away. Let me help you."

But Anne had warned her to stay supportive and not criticize Nila's decisions or her boyfriend. So she clamped her mouth shut and kept driving.

As they neared the gray house, Nila sat up straight, trembling. "Look, there's Nick's truck. He's home!"

Sure enough, there was a big, black half-ton truck with lots of chrome and vivid flames painted on the sides. Melody instinctively slowed. Just beyond the truck was a young man pushing a lawn mower. He was average in size, shirtless, and a backwards baseball cap covered most of his short, sandy brown hair. *He's not nearly as big or mean-looking as I'd imagined.*

Nila covered her mouth with her fingers. "Nick," she whispered. "I didn't really think he'd be here yet." She looked at Melody, uncertainty widening her eyes. "Do you think he's gonna be mad that I wasn't here?"

"I don't know, Nila, but I guess we're about to find out." She pulled into the driveway, stopping just behind the truck.

The young man stopped, wiped his brow with his hand, and stared. He saw Nila and strode toward the car. He smiled, showing deep dimples on both sides of his mouth.

"There you are, baby girl! Where you been? I've been here since eight this morning."

He opened Nila's door, grabbed her arm before Melody could utter a word, and pulled her out of the car and into his embrace.

"I missed you, darlin," he said into her ear. Then he pressed his lips on hers until Melody felt embarrassed.

Abruptly, Nick released Nila and swatted her backside. "Get into the house. I'll be right in."

Nila was flushed and seemed jittery, but she waved goodbye to Melody and obediently headed inside.

As soon as she was out of sight, Nick walked around the car and leaned in Melody's window. His dimples were gone, replaced by a leering snarl.

"I don't know who you are or why my old lady was with you, but I don't wanna see you around here again. Got it?"

Melody's pulse started to race. Those familiar panicky darts raced up and down her spine. *God! Help!*

She took a slow, deep breath. "My name is Melody. I live down the street, and I'm Nila's friend."

Nick's eyes glittered and his teeth bared as he sneered. "Oh, no, you ain't. Nila don't need no one but me. Keep your interfering little nose outta my business, or I'll break it for you. Now get out of here!"

He slapped the roof of the car and stepped back without breaking eye contact.

Melody looked at him for a moment, unable to respond. Then with shaky hands, she put the car into reverse and backed out of the driveway.

Someone banged two pots together somewhere, but they sounded as if they were right beside his ears. Will groaned and moved his head carefully.

"Ooh, that hurts. But at least it's still attached." He winced at his own joke.

Fumbling for his work clothes, Will rolled out of bed. His watch told him he'd have to hurry if he wanted breakfast, let alone have time to make a lunch. He grabbed his equipment and headed for the mess tent.

By ten o'clock that morning, Will was sweating profusely. He glanced over at Vixen's parcel. She didn't look too good this morning, either. But night before last … He reached for his water jug and took a long swig.

Bending to his work once more, he let his mind wander over the last two days. Eli had tried to convince him to stay behind again on the night off, but he'd made up his mind. Nothing was going to keep him in camp this time around.

Down in Vanderhoof their first stop was the laundromat. The promise of clean-smelling clothes to the tired, grubby crew was like nectar to bees. Next stop, check into whatever motel or hotel was handy and cheap. The ones with pubs attached were snapped up quickly.

Will ended up sharing a room with some guys he knew only by name. Then he headed for the nearest pub. Luckily for him Vixen was already there, and she looked as if she was willing to give him another chance.

Yeah, it was a good time, worth feeling wasted yesterday and today. He plucked another spruce seedling out of his planting bag, pushed aside debris with his boot, plunged his shovel into the exposed dirt, and stuck the tree in the opening. He tamped the ground around the small tree to keep it straight, the way Eli had shown him.

Wonder how Eli's feeling today? Saw him at the laundromat, but then he disappeared. Must have gone to a different pub.

By the end of the day, Will felt as exhausted as he had his very first day. He looked around the mess tent, almost too tired to bring the roast-laden fork to his mouth. Pretty much everyone who'd partied down in town looked as rough as he felt. But Eli and some guys who'd stayed in camp looked like they'd just flown in from Hawaii or something.

So what? Bet they didn't have as much fun as I did.

∞ ∞ ∞

By the time Sunday came around again Melody felt as though she'd been shredded. Every time the phone rang, she expected to hear Nila's voice begging for help. Every night was filled with tormenting dreams about Nila or Will.

This morning Tessa was picking her up, so she tried to cover the shadows under her eyes and dug out her rarely-used blush powder. She looked at her reflection in the mirror and grimaced.

Well, if no one looks too closely, I look okay.

"Hey, Mom, are you having trouble sleeping again? What's up?" Faith confronted her mother as they hugged in the church entrance.

Lot of good that makeup did. Melody stepped out of the hug and reached for baby Jessica.

"I'm fine. Here, let me hold Jessie. Come here, fussy girl. Why so sad?"

"I think she's teething again, Mom. If she gets too cranky, we'll take her home after church instead of coming over for lunch. Is that okay?"

"Sure, honey. I understand. When you're not feeling well, only your own bed will do. Tessa and I will just have to eat more, right Tess?"

Tessa groaned. "I don't think so. If you keep feeding me so well, I'm going to balloon!"

She groaned again a couple hours later. "I shouldn't have eaten that extra biscuit. But they were *so* good."

She put their dishes in the dishwasher, helped herself to coffee and poured some for Melody.

Once they were settled in the living room, she raised her eyebrows at her friend. "Okay, Mel, what gives? The shadows under your eyes make it obvious you're having sleep problems again, plus you've been yawning all morning. Don't think I didn't notice."

Melody tried to stifle another yawn. "You're right. I am short on sleep." She took a sip of coffee and put the cup on the coffee table. "I'm so worried. I haven't heard a thing from Will since I sent him the money for his new job, and I've been having terrible dreams about him. Between that and worrying about Nila, I haven't had a good night's rest in quite a while."

"Why are you so worried about Nila? Isn't she still at Haven House?"

"Oh, I forgot to tell you. She convinced me to take her home, and that boyfriend of hers was there."

"Yikes!" Tessa's eyes widened. "So what was he like?"

Melody shuddered. "Well, he wasn't built like Shrek, which was how I'd pictured him. He was pretty average in size, actually,"

Then she described his actions, how he'd manhandled Nila and then threatened her.

"He changed so quickly," Melody shook her head, "it was scary. I don't think he's stable. And Nila is like a lamb to the slaughter. Every day I expect to hear that she's been beaten again—or worse. And I delivered her to him, so I feel responsible."

"No wonder you're not sleeping! What a nightmare."

Tessa sat in silence for several moments, her brow creased in thought. "Didn't you tell me it was Rose and Bobbie who first got you involved? Have you told either of them about this?"

"No," Melody said, "I don't want to burden them. It's not their fault."

"Of course it isn't, but I'd bet Rose would have some wisdom for you—and some prayers. She's the most praying, caring person I've ever met."

Melody brightened. "You're right, Tess. I should talk to Rose. My prayers don't seem to go past the ceiling a lot of the time, but hers seem to have a direct line to God."

∽ ∽ ∽

Several hours later Melody entered Rose's room.

"Hello, my dear," Rose greeted her. "Come, sit here." She patted the edge of her bed. "Tessa told me you were coming. How can I help you?"

Melody obediently sat beside her friend and mentor and turned to face her. "I do have a problem, Rose, but I'm concerned about burdening you with it."

Rose took Melody's hand in hers and squeezed lightly.

"Don't worry about burdening me, Melody. I've learned to give my burdens to God. He can handle them much better than I can. So if I can be a stepping stone on the way to heaven ... well, that blesses me. Now tell me, what's troubling you?"

Hesitantly at first, Melody shared her fears. She described Nick's quick change in appearance and mood, his threats, and Nila's meek submission.

"I'm so afraid for her," she said. "And I feel as though I am responsible for her. I just don't know what to do."

Rose squeezed Melody's hand once more and lifted her face upward. "Father in heaven, you have blessed your daughter Melody with a caring heart. You love young Nila, and now you have given Melody a love for her, too. You love them both with all your heart. But you love young

Nick, too, and gave your son to atone for his sins. Now give Melody wisdom, peace, and strength to do everything you ask her to do, in the name of Jesus, I pray."

She looked at Melody with love-filled eyes. "You have been given a great burden, but it is for the glory of God. Read Joshua chapter one; I think it will speak to you."

"O–okay," Melody stammered. "I'll read it tonight." She frowned. "But Rose, that boyfriend of Nila's is so horrible. How can you pray for him like that?"

Rose smiled wanly. "I can pray for him with love because God loves him." She tilted her head and sighed. "You know, Melody, quite often people who hurt others carry great wounds themselves."

As soon as she got home Melody picked up her Bible and found the book of Joshua. As she read, goosebumps tickled her arms. She read the entire first chapter, and then she read it again.

Joshua was about to lead God's chosen people into the land he had promised them, but there would be fierce battles ahead. Melody tried to imagine herself in Joshua's place.

Was Joshua afraid? Is that why he needed so much encouragement? I would be! Ah, and I am. I love this promise: "As I was with Moses, so I will be with you; I will never leave you nor forsake you." And this: "Be strong and courageous … be strong and very courageous … be strong and courageous. Do not be terrified; do not be discouraged, for the Lord your God will be with you wherever you go … Only be strong and courageous!"

Melody closed the Bible and let those words soak into her soul. Four times God had commanded Joshua to "be strong and courageous," because God would always be with him.

"Those commands and promises are for me, too, aren't they, God? Help me to trust you, to be strong and courageous."

"What a miserable day," Will grumbled out loud. No one could hear him over the howling wind and pouring rain. "Good thing we're outta here tomorrow."

The crew had to finish this block today, so everyone was hurrying to get their piece planted. Will wiped his face, readjusted his raincoat, and bent to his work again. He'd gotten a pretty good rhythm going: scrape, dig, insert seedling, tamp. His piece was nearly done, and he was nearly done in.

"Hey, Will, how's it going?" Eli came up from behind him. "Want a hand? I had an easy piece."

Will looked up in surprise.

"I just mean to help; you can still claim the trees," Eli said, squinting through the rain.

Did he just read my mind? "Sure." Will shrugged. "I'm doing okay, but if you want, go ahead. I've just got two more rows to go."

"Yeah, I see that. But most of the crew are done. And I'm as anxious to get dried off and warmed up as everyone else."

With that, Eli climbed over to the last row and began working. Will watched him for a minute.

"What's up with that guy?" he muttered. "Why does he keep helping me?" His eyes narrowed. "Seems a little too good to be true."

ೞ ೞ ೞ

"Hello?" *Please don't let it be Nila,* she begged silently.

"Hey, neighbor, I'm home!"

"Bobbie! Welcome back." Melody breathed a sigh of relief. "How was your visit with your friend?"

"Super! Lots of folks showed up for Ella's party—it was a blast! The rest of the week Ella and me just goofed off, doin' whatever we felt like every day. Best holiday I had in ages."

"That's wonderful, Bobbie. Do you want me to bring your key over tonight, or is tomorrow morning better for you? I've got some news to share with you."

"Mornin' will be fine. We'll have coffee and catch up then." A chuckle burst through the phone. "Make that catch–up, not ketchup!"

14

It was late the following afternoon by the time the crew arrived at their new campsite. They'd had a long drive with stops for more equipment and supplies, and now they were about four hours north of Golden, British Columbia, high in the Rockies.

Everyone had to pitch in to set things up, sometimes forming a chain to pass supplies to their new location. Will had tried to position himself beside Vixen, but she'd turned her back on him and maneuvered herself between A.J. and Gordo, who laughed and jostled her as they passed the boxes. Will scowled as he watched the three until he nearly dropped a case of eggs.

Eli stepped in beside Will and spoke quietly. "Don't let her get to you. That's just the way she operates. Anything for a good time, and if someone gets hurt in the process, so much the better."

By ten o'clock, the camp was set up, and the warmth of the day had disappeared along with the sun. Clouds had appeared in the west, building all evening, and now the sky was dark gray.

Will's tent was next to Eli's, so they trudged up the trail together. All Will could think about was crawling into bed and sleeping as long as possible.

Eli interrupted his thoughts. "Looks like we could get snow."

Will stopped. "You gotta be kidding. It's the middle of June!"

Eli shook his head. "And we're high in the mountains." He pointed just over the treetops. "See that cloud? I'm pretty sure we're going to wake up to a white world. Good thing our trees are already here."

Will stifled a groan. *Yeah, right.*

By mid-afternoon Monday, Melody was tired of flinching each time the phone rang. "This is ridiculous! I guess I just need to find out how Nila is doing. Maybe I'll wander down the street, and as long as Nick is gone, I'll pop in and see her."

As soon as Melody walked past Bobbie's, she could see that the driveway at the gray house was empty—no ominous black truck. She breathed a sigh of relief and continued down the street.

Her breathing quickened as she neared the house, but she shook off the panic with a prayer. *Lord, calm me and guide me, please.*

She walked resolutely up the steps to the door, raised her hand to press the doorbell, and *whoosh!* It felt as if a blast of winter wind cut through her. Fear froze her.

"Help me, Jesus!" she begged out loud.

Like a wave of comfort, warmth flowed through Melody from her head to her feet, thawing the fear. "Thank you," she breathed.

As soon as the doorbell chimed, the black metal door opened. There stood Nila, a big smile brightening her pale face.

"Hello, Melody!" She stepped back and opened the door wide. "Can you come in? I was just thinking about you."

"Thank you, Nila. I've been thinking about you, too." Melody entered the house and stopped in surprise. "Wow! What gorgeous flowers."

A large bouquet of roses, lilies and baby's breath graced the dining table.

Nila flushed pink. "Aren't they pretty? Nick got them for me. Said he'd really missed me."

Melody tried to hide her surprise. "That's nice. I'm glad he ..." She didn't know how to end that thought.

Nila rushed to fill the awkward pause. "I'm doing good. Really good. Nick is being super nice, and I'm really happy. You don't have to worry, Melody. Things are great now. He's never going to hurt me again. He promised!"

Melody bit back her disbelief. From what Anne at Haven House had told her, this was typical. The abuser would shower his victim with gifts and promises until he erupted once again in violence.

How can I warn her, God? Didn't she hear this at Haven House? But if she didn't believe them, why would she believe me? What should I do?

"Umm, can I get you something to drink?" Nila asked uncertainly.

"That sounds good," Melody said. "Do you have coffee? Or water would be fine."

"I can make some coffee. I'll be right back." Nila turned and went into the kitchen.

Melody sat on the plaid couch and looked around. It was nicer than she'd expected, very clean with cheap but decent furniture except for the large-screen television on the wall and an extensive gaming system in the unit below.

The dining set was against the far wall next to the kitchen. Other than the bouquet of flowers, there were no feminine touches anywhere.

It looks like a well-kept bachelor pad—not a good sign.

The sounds and smell of coffee brewing stirred Melody from her inspection. "Nila, can I help with anything?" she called.

"N–no thanks. I can handle it. You stay there."

Unsure what to do, Melody stood and walked over to the entertainment unit. She picked up a game case and was shocked at the violence depicted on the cover. *But why am I surprised? I should have expected this.*

Nila walked in carrying a plastic tray with two large mugs of steaming coffee. She saw the game case in Melody's hand and nearly dropped the tray.

"Melody! Don't touch that!"

She spun around. Nila was trembling, and the coffee was in danger of slipping off the tray. Melody quickly replaced the game case and took the tray from Nila.

"I'm sorry, Nila. I didn't mean to cause trouble. Here, let's put this on the table and we can take our mugs from there. Come, let's sit down."

As though she was the hostess, Melody led the way back to the couch. They sat at opposite ends, neither saying anything for several moments.

Finally Melody broke the silence. "I noticed you're using your arm very well in spite of the cast. How is it doing?"

"It's fine. If I do too much, it hurts, but I don't mind. I'm just happy to be home, back with my boyfriend."

She placed her coffee cup on the floor and clasped her hands together as though in prayer. "He really is a good person, you know."

Melody glanced at her watch. "Speaking of Nick, what time does he get home?"

Nila's face paled. "Oh! What time is it? He gets home around four thirty."

"It's four twenty now." *I've got to leave!*

She stood and drained her coffee cup, trying not to choke on the panic in her throat. "Thanks for the visit and coffee, Nila. We'll have to do this again, maybe at my house next time." She started toward the kitchen. "Shall I just put this in the sink?"

Nila jumped up. "No! I mean, I'll take it." She was trembling again. "Just let me take care of things. You'd better go."

৯৵ ৯৵ ৯৵

Eli's forecast was right. Tuesday morning Will was awakened by laughter and a *whump* on the side of his tent.

"Hey! What's going on?"

He stuck his head out the door of his tent just as a snowball struck just beside him.

"Oomph!" He grunted and wiped the snow off his face. "All right, who did that?"

Snowflakes still clung to his eyelashes, making it difficult to see. But the laugh that followed confirmed his suspicion—Eli stood about ten feet away, molding another fluffy projectile. About a six inches of snow covered the ground, the trees, everything!

Eli laughed again at the shock on Will's face as he stepped out of his tent and gazed at the whiteness. "Isn't this great? It's like being inside a giant Christmas card—in June! It's beautiful, and it gives us a morning off."

That clicked. "You mean we can go to town?"

Eli lobbed the snowball at Will's chest so that it exploded up into his face again. "Think again, rookie. This snow will melt soon, probably by lunchtime. There's no time to go to town and back."

"Oh." Will's face fell. "So, what do we do now?"

"Well, we still get to eat," Eli said. "Get yourself dressed, and let's go get some grub."

After breakfast Warner called everyone together for a safety review. Two hours later Will was tired of sitting. He looked around as Warner wrapped up his demonstration. Several others were fidgeting, and A.J. and Gordo seemed to be planning something. He noticed them glance his way a few times as they whispered together.

Finally, the crew was released for the rest of the morning. If enough snow melted, they'd be planting after lunch.

While Eli stayed behind to talk to the boss, Will walked outside the tent and right into a barrage of hard-packed snowballs. Snow and ice were in his face, down his neck, and all over his front.

"What the ... !" He wiped the snow out of his eyes. "That hurt!"

"What's the matter, rookie? Can't take a little snow?" A.J. and Gordo were laughing as they packed more snow projectiles. "Here, let us help you adjust!" And they let loose again, this time aiming only for his head.

Will covered his face with his forearms and pushed forward through the onslaught. He lunged toward his attackers when they turned and ran. Will swore loudly. "Run, you cowards!"

Soaked and angry, Will headed for his tent. *Better get these things into the dry tent. Sure hope I still have some dry stuff. Those stupid ....*

Eli spotted Will heading into the dry tent with his wet garments. "Hey, Will, what happened? You fall into a snow bank?"

His grin disappeared as Will told him about A.J. and Gordo bombarding him with icy snowballs. "Sounds as if they went a little overboard. Snowballs are fun, but icy ones can do damage." He inspected Will's face. "Looks like they got you good."

Will touched the scrape on his cheekbone. "Yeah, that was a hard one. What's their problem, anyway? I've never done anything to them."

"Territory would be my guess," Eli answered. "Vixen is pitting them against you with her flirting."

"Naw, I think they're just jerks." He walked into the dry tent with Eli behind him.

"Here, let me help you hang up those things," Eli said. "Then I'd like to take advantage of this free time in a drier fashion. You up for a game of cards?"

"Sounds good. What kind of card game?"

Eli stroked his bushy beard. "Ever play two-handed kaiser?"

Will grinned. "You bet!" Then his face fell as scenes of the kaiser games between him and his dad flashed through his mind. "I used to play it a lot."

It was Will's turn to deal. He shuffled a couple times, but then he stopped, cards in hand, and studied Eli.

"So what's up with you? Why are you so straight-edge? You don't lose your temper, you don't even complain, and I've never heard you swear. Are you a saint or something?"

Eli gave a laugh that was almost a growl. "I wish! No, Will, I'm not a saint."

"Then what are you? You sort of remind me of my folks, but even better."

"Well, young Will," he said kindly, "I get that straight edge you mentioned from knowing the Truth and obeying him."

"What?" Will frowned in thought. His lips twisted as he realized, "You mean religion. I know all about God; I went to Sunday school and church, but it didn't work for me." He slammed the cards onto the table. "God was nowhere around when I needed him."

Eli's eyes burned, their dark glow pinning Will to his chair. "No, my friend, you've got it wrong. It's not religion, and God was with you. He was there, but you refused him access. He has been protecting you all your life in spite of your resistance to him."

He smiled, but it didn't reach his eyes. "You think you know God, but you only know a few concepts about him. You don't really know him at all."

∞ ∞ ∞

"Hi, Mom, what are you doing this Saturday?"

Melody smiled into the phone. "Well, Faith, this Saturday I'm getting older, but not so old I forgot my birthday. Is that by any chance why you're phoning?"

"Aw, you spoiled my surprise. Yes, that's why I'm calling. Tessa, Lydia and I are going to take you out for a special lunch. How does that sound?"

"That sounds absolutely lovely, my dear. Where are we going?"

"Nope. I'm not telling you. At least that can be a surprise! I'll pick you up just before noon, okay?"

"That sounds wonderful, Faith. I can't wait!" She paused. "I was rather dreading facing another birthday on my own. You are an angel."

15

Will glanced sideways at Eli as the two jostled together in the back of the van. He'd been surprised when Eli said he was coming down into town with the gang. After the talk they'd had, Will had expected Eli to avoid him. Instead, he'd offered to share accommodations.

Will looked at him more closely. Eli's head was bent low, and it looked like his eyes were closed. *Is he dozing or deep in thought ... or maybe praying? Strange guy. Decent, but strange.*

After their laundry was done, Will showered, put on his best clothes, and headed toward the door.

"I'm going to find some action," he said to Eli. "Want to come?"

"I think I'd better." Eli ignored Will's shocked grunt as he rose and grabbed his jacket. "Mind if I hang with you tonight?"

Will swallowed his disappointment. He'd been hoping to hook up with Vixen again, but Eli seemed kind of down, and Will prided himself on never turning his back on a friend. He forced a smile. "Sure, buddy. Let's go."

The small pub was packed by the time they got there, mostly by the planting crew. Will peered through the dimness, but he couldn't spot Vixen. *I thought everyone was meeting here. Where is she? Rats, I don't see A.J. either.*

"How about this table?" Eli led the way deeper into the room. "I'm famished. Want to order some wings?"

"Yeah, okay." Will's enthusiasm for the evening had vanished, but a growl from his stomach aroused a different appetite. He ordered a plate of wings and a beer, while Eli drank a cola with his.

Yeah, he's straight-edge, all right.

A short time later Will noticed Eli's expression suddenly darken. He swiveled his head toward the door. A.J. had just arrived, alone and looking upset.

A.J. walked straight to the bar and ordered a drink. His hands shook as he picked up the glass and drained it in one gulp. He ordered another one and drained it, too. His whole body shuddered. Several other crew members looked over at him, but no one went to him. Will could see some of them whispering together, shrugging their shoulders.

Eli got up from the table. "Something's wrong. Stay here."

Automatic defiance pushed Will to his feet, but something forced him back down. He sat, confused.

He watched Eli put his hand on A.J.'s shoulder. The smaller man jumped as though struck, and Eli leaned in close to say something. A.J. gestured wildly, eyes frantic. Will couldn't make out what he was saying, but it obviously wasn't good. Eli put his arm around A.J.'s shoulder and half-led, half-carried him to their table.

"We've got a problem." He addressed Will while depositing the shaking man into the chair beside Will. "Vixen's in trouble. I need to go."

Will half-rose from his seat. "I'll come with you!"

"No," Eli ordered. "You need to stay here. See if you can keep this one from any more stupidity until I return."

Anger flooded Will. He glared at the distraught man beside him. "What did you do to her?"

"I–I–I didn't ..." A.J. stammered. "Sh–she ..." He collapsed in sobs with his head in his trembling hands.

Will stared at him in disgust and ordered two more drinks.

A few crew members drifted over and tried to question A.J., but he was incoherent. They looked at Will. "What's going on? What's his problem?"

"Other than being drunk and stupid?" Will's anger spilled over. "I don't know, but it has something to do with Vixen. This"—he couldn't think of a word strong enough— "got her into some kind of trouble. Eli's gone to check it out."

Fear brought a lump to his throat, but he swallowed hard and forced it down. His co-workers shrugged and returned to their drinks.

It felt as if weeks had passed by the time Eli returned. A.J. was still sprawled on the table, more drunk now than hysterical. Eli barely glanced at him. He sat heavily across from Will. His eyes were reddened, and his wide shoulders bowed.

He spoke quietly. "It's not good, Will. I couldn't help her." His sigh came out like a groan. "She got hold of some bad Ecstasy. By the time this one," he glanced again at A.J., "caught on that she was in trouble and phoned 911, it was too late."

Will couldn't breathe. He gasped, "How … bad …?"

"She's in the hospital, but the cops I spoke to don't expect her to make it."

Will had never seen such sorrow up close; Eli wore it like a leaden cloak. His entire being seemed darker, weighed down. Will couldn't handle it. He turned his head and stared unseeing at the wall.

Images of Vixen played through his mind: her dancing eyes and inviting smile, her amazing body, and the way she made him feel like he was the only man around, even though he knew she was a flirt. An image of their evening together seared his heart. With his arms wrapped around her, he'd wished he could hold her forever, never let her go. And now she was … gone?

He gulped back a shot of loss.

Just then a ripple of whispering spread through the room. Will turned and froze. A uniformed policeman was striding toward their table. Eli saw him and stood.

"Officer," he greeted him solemnly.

The policeman nodded once without smiling. "I have bad news, Mr. Carter. I already contacted your boss, and he asked that I let you know."

Will felt a buzzing in his ears. *Don't say it. Don't say it! I can't handle it.*

Eli spoke the words as though each one lacerated his throat. "She's dead, isn't she?"

"I'm sorry."

Tessa opened the door at Melody's first light rap. She spoke quietly. "She's waiting for you. Thanks for coming, Mel. I'm glad I didn't wake you when I phoned. I don't know what's up, but she's been asking for you. I've got some things to take care of before Valerie arrives, so go on in."

"Melody, my dear, thank you for coming." Rose reached out a thin hand in greeting. "You have been on my mind all day." She smiled feebly. "Well, actually all night and this morning." She motioned to the chair beside her bed. "Come, sit."

She must have had a rough night, Melody thought as she sat next to Rose. *She looks frailer than ever. I'll have to ask Tessa ...*

"How was your sleep, Melody?" Rose always said her name with a musical inflection.

"Umm ... it was okay." It had been awful, but she didn't want to burden her dying friend with her nightmarish dreams.

Rose looked doubtful, but her voice was compassionate. "I don't mean to pry. I just wondered because you and your son were on my heart all night."

Melody's eyes widened. "Oh!" *How ...?* She took a deep breath. "You're right, Rose, I did have a rough night. I dreamed about Will several times." She shuddered at the memory. "They were the kind of dreams that seem to continue even after you wake."

"I wondered. I have been praying and will continue." Rose took Melody's hand in hers and squeezed. "Worries for our sons can plague the mind and heart, can't they?"

Melody sighed. "They sure can. I'm trying to give my concerns about Will to God, but I must not be doing it right. I still have nightmares."

"You are doing well, Melody. Just keep praying, giving everything to our Father. Perhaps our hearts are burdened because the enemy is attacking more fiercely as he loses ground."

"That makes sense." Melody tilted her head and smiled. "How did you get to be so wise, Rose?"

"I'm not sure that I'm 'so wise.' But I believe that some wisdom comes directly from the Father's heart, and some comes through suffering."

Melody heard a new weariness in her friend's voice. Fear rippled through her, making her voice tremble. "Is the pain worse? Should I call Tessa? "

"No, no, Melody, don't bother my nurse. I'm not talking about this physical pain." She closed her eyes. "Before we do anything else, let's pray."

Rose prayed first, her soft voice carrying Melody to the throne of

God as she pleaded for intervention on behalf of Will. Melody followed, asking for strength, wisdom, and courage for herself, peace for Rose, and salvation for Will.

"Yes, Lord," Rose prayed again. "Save both our sons. Tear down the walls they have built between them and you. Show them your truth, in Jesus' name."

Melody raised her bowed head and squeezed Rose's hand gently. "May I ask you a question?"

"About my son?" Rose smiled gently at Melody's hesitant nod. "Of course, child. He isn't always easy to understand, but he is a good man. What would you like to know?"

Now that she had opened this door, Melody wasn't sure how to proceed. "Well, in your prayer you mentioned walls." She took a deep breath and plunged in. "Was Daniel hurt somehow? Is that why he is so …?"

"Prickly?" Rose finished for her. "Oh yes, he was hurt—physically, emotionally, and spiritually."

A soft knock announced Tessa's entrance. "Sorry to interrupt, but Valerie is here, and I'm going home. I just wanted to say goodbye."

"Goodbye, dear one," Rose said. "I'll see you this evening."

Melody waved her fingers. "I'll call you later, okay?"

Tessa nodded and left, leaving the door open.

"Perhaps we will have to continue this talk later," Rose said. "Valerie will be coming in to help me with my bath." She gave Melody's hand one more weak squeeze and let go. "Meanwhile, Daniel could use your prayers, too."

Melody felt her face warm. Just thinking about Daniel made her flustered. How could she pray for him?

Daniel stormed into the construction trailer that served as his site office. He flung his hard hat onto a chair and grabbed a pile of papers from his desk.

"Where's that phone number?" He growled to the empty room. "That inspector was supposed to get here yesterday!"

His carefully-arranged schedule kept getting sabotaged by delays, and each delay was costing him. This entire project was turning into a headache. As though to prove the point, pain began throbbing at the base of his skull. Daniel rubbed his neck with one hand while continuing to search through the papers on his desk. He finally found the business card, dialed the number, and got an assurance of action from the inspector. He hung up the phone and tilted his chair back, still massaging his neck.

"Good thing Zach is coming back in a few days. I'm more than ready to hand this back to him and get home. Logan Construction sure picked the perfect time to try to buy me out. It's tempting, very tempting."

He closed his eyes and felt a wave of tiredness and remembered disquiet. It had been a rough night. He couldn't recall exactly what he'd dreamt, but it seemed to be the same thing over and over, and it left him feeling out of sorts. Something about some kind of danger stalking someone close to him.

Shake it off, man, he told himself. *It was just a dream.*

The group gathered in the mess tent at camp that afternoon was a somber one. They had returned early; no one wanted to stay in town any longer. Their boss had just returned and announced a meeting before supper.

Will looked around at the weary faces. He doubted if anyone had gotten much sleep last night. He knew he hadn't.

Now Warner stood in front of them and waited for the whispering to stop. He cleared his throat a few times and finally spoke. "You have heard the news, I'm sure. Vixen died last night of a drug overdose." He seemed to be struggling to find the right words. "You all know the company policy on drugs: we have zero tolerance for anything other than prescribed meds and things like aspirin. This is why. If you need to talk, I'm available. That's all."

Will looked over at Eli. He was sitting on the far side of the tent, alone. He hadn't spoken a word to Will since the previous night. When they'd finally returned to their motel room, Will had tried to talk to him, but Eli had put a heavy hand on his shoulder and mumbled, "I'm sorry, man. I just can't talk now."

All through the night Eli had moaned and muttered as he tossed on his bed. Will wasn't sleeping anyway, so he'd sat up and switched on the small television, keeping the volume low. What was on he couldn't say, but it had kept him from thinking too much.

Even on the trip back to camp Eli was silent. The van was

crowded as usual, but Eli seemed to be alone even while his seatmates jostled him.

A dark suspicion had been growing in Will's mind as he considered his friend. Eli had made it sound as if he didn't think much of Vixen, warning Will away from her. *Could it be that he just wanted her for himself? Why else would he be so broken up now?*

Jealousy pricked him, stirring up anger. *Hypocrite! Here I thought he was being a good friend, but he was just being territorial. So now he can't talk to me. Fine! That can go both ways.*

Eli looked over at him just then, his eyes red-rimmed and dull. Will got up, turned his back, and strode out of the tent.

Will headed out of camp, not caring where he was going or that he was missing supper. Last week's snow was long gone, but the ground was still soft and mucky. His boots were soon caked in heavy mud, but Will ignored the growing weight as grief, anger, and betrayal pushed him further and further from camp. After several hours of long strides, his steps slowed as his churning emotions burst through clenched teeth.

"He talked about the truth as though that was the ultimate answer. What a fraud! I thought he was my friend, but friends don't lie. Good people don't lie."

"What's that make you?" something whispered. "Think about all your lies, how they hurt your parents, your friends, yourself. How good are you?"

His parents? Memories of his childhood flashed through his mind. Happy times, carefree years. Then the pictures slowed; his last year at home became billboards of rebellion, deceit, and withdrawal.

"How do you think your mom and dad felt when you left? You wanted to prove that you were a man, that you could take care of yourself. How are you doing so far?"

"Stop it!" Will cried out. But the mental billboards continued. Jobs lost because he stole from the boss or just didn't show up. Friends lost because he'd used and abused their friendship. Nights and days lost because he'd gotten drunk. And now Vixen lost because he couldn't protect her.

A sob tore from his throat. He stumbled over a fallen branch, fell and landed hard on his hands and knees. Shock kept him still for a moment, and then he dropped his head to the ground between his muddy hands.

"I give up," he moaned against the wet ground. "It's no use.

Everything I've done, I've messed up. I'm no good for anything or anyone."

He stayed there, numb with misery, for several minutes. Finally, the damp cold seeped through his bones into his consciousness. He pushed himself to his feet and looked around. Nothing was familiar. Dusk had deepened the shadows in the forest, and the chill of the approaching night cut through Will's jacket.

Will wiped the mud from his face with his jacket sleeve and shivered. *Take it easy*, he told himself. *Just turn 180 degrees and walk straight. That'll take you back to camp.*

The safety training Eli had given him pricked his conscience. "If you get lost, STAY PUT!"

He considered it, but pride resurged. "No way, I'm not staying here. I can find my own way back."

He carefully positioned himself in the opposite direction and started walking. Darkness was his enemy, though, and so was the cold. With each step he shivered harder as the dark forest seemed to close in around him.

After what must have been hours Will stopped. He could hardly see his hand in front of his face, let alone where his feet were. He had fallen over forest debris several times, and each fall sapped more of his strength. He wrapped his arms around his torso, trying to still his uncontrollable shaking. His shoulders slumped as he faced the truth: he was lost, totally lost.

Fighting rising panic, Will stumbled around in the dark until he bumped into a large boulder. It took a few attempts but he finally managed to climb up onto it. He pulled his knees to his chest and wrapped his arms around them. Shivers racked his body as he fought the tears welling up in his eyes. He put his face down on his knees.

Blackness pressed down on him, and forest noises became amplified. *Was that a bear?* He clamped down on that thought, but then the tears forced their way out. Once started, Will was powerless to stop them.

Wetness rapidly chilling on his face, he finally cried out, "God, if you're there, help me!"

∽ ∽ ∽

From a deep sleep, Melody bolted upright in bed as her son's name tore from her throat. "Will!"

16

Melody slid out of bed onto her knees, pressed her face against the mattress, and prayed. "Lord, have mercy on my son. Please, Lord God, whatever is happening to him, help him, protect him. Save him! Lift him up if he has fallen; bring him back to the light if he's in darkness. You told me you love him. Now my heart tells me he's in trouble. You can help him. Reach out and save him, oh God."

She prayed until she ran out of words and could only hope God could hear her heart.

∽ ∽ ∽

Deep in a misty blackness, Will sensed a warmth settle on him. He felt himself being lifted. The part of him that could still think wondered, *Is this death?* He thought he heard a grunt as he was hoisted over a shoulder. *A bear?* But he couldn't seem to care.

"Will. Will Jamison!"

The voice was like a rumble of thunder far away. Will moaned and tried to cover his ears, but he couldn't move his arms. They were too heavy. It didn't matter.

"Come on, buddy, wake up!" The voice was right in his ear now, pulling him out of the deep, black nothingness.

Leave me alone, he wanted to say. *I'm dead. Let me be.*

Something patted his face. "You're alive and safe, Will. Wake up now!"

That got through. Will opened his eyes and saw nothing but Eli's worried face. "Wh–what ...?" Will blinked and tried to focus. Were those tears in Eli's eyes?

"Thank you, Master!" Eli's face tilted upward, and in the darkness of the tent, his face seemed to glow.

The flap on the door rustled, and another voice came from behind Eli. "He's awake! Good." A hand appeared on Eli's shoulder. "Well done, Eli. I guess your stubbornness paid off."

The voice was familiar. Will struggled to put a name to it. Finally it clicked: Warner, his boss. *He sounds upset. What did I do? Am I going to be fired?*

Warner stepped around Eli and looked down at Will. "You gave us a real scare, young man, disappearing like that. I had to call off the search when it got too dark for safety, but your friend here," he looked at Eli, "refused to quit. Insisted he could find you." Warner paused. "I'm glad he was right."

He turned to go. "We'll talk later this afternoon, after you've both had some rest. I don't expect either of you to work today." Then he was gone.

Will struggled to sit up, but he couldn't move. He looked down at himself and saw the pile of blankets wrapped around him.

"Wh-what happened?" Will finally got the words out.

Eli crouched down beside him. "You were lost, but now you're found. God was merciful." His eyes bore into Will's. "Someone was praying for you, my friend."

He stood up slowly, as though in pain. "We will talk later. Right now you and I both need to rest." Eli turned and walked out.

Alone in his tent, Will tried to remember. He was warm now, but he recalled shivering so hard he'd thought he would shake apart. He remembered darkness. Loneliness. Fear and despair. *But why?*

His tired mind refused to remember anything more as warmth and exhaustion pulled him back down into blackness, this time of healing sleep.

The doorbell woke Melody. She opened one eye and looked at the clock on the bedside table. *Six-thirty? Too early.* She pulled the covers over her head. Another loud chime pierced the covers. Melody sat up and threw the blankets back.

How did I get back into bed? Last thing I remember was being on my knees, praying. How odd! Must have crawled back into bed in my sleep.

She rushed to the door and opened it while tying her bathrobe.

"Tessa, I should have known it was you. Come on in."

Her friend stood there with eyes wide and one hand over her mouth. "Oh, Mel, I'm sorry. Obviously I woke you. I just needed to talk to you, but it can wait."

Melody rubbed her still-sleepy eyes and smiled. "It's okay, Tess, it was time to get up anyway. Please, come in."

Now that she could see more clearly, Melody noticed dark circles under Tessa's eyes. There were also lines beside her mouth that she'd never seen before.

"Coffee," she pronounced. "We need coffee. Sit down and rest while I get it going."

Tessa sank onto the couch, leaned her head back and closed her eyes. "Coffee sounds perfect, Mel. Thanks."

Melody quickly dressed while the coffee was brewing. As it was sputtering its finish, she popped a few muffins into the microwave and set up a tray.

"Here we go, my friend," she said as she carried the tray into the living room. "I made some lemon-blueberry muffins yesterday. Hope you like them."

Tessa opened her eyes and sniffed. "Yum, they smell wonderful!"

Two muffins had disappeared and their coffee mugs were half empty before either spoke again.

Melody brushed some crumbs off her lap. "Okay, Tess, what happened? Did Rose have another rough night?"

"Yes, she did." Tessa sighed and rolled her shoulders. "I almost phoned Daniel at one point, she was moaning so much. He'd asked me to phone him before contacting her doctor, and I thought I might need to."

Melody's eyes widened. "So what happened?"

"About one o'clock she woke up and called for me. I was right there, of course, and tried to calm her. I asked her what she wanted me to do for her, and she said, 'Pray!'"

She turned to Melody. "But when I started praying for her—you know, for less pain—she just squeezed my hand and said 'Will ... Melody.' So we prayed together for both of you."

She drew a shaky breath. "It was amazing, Mel. It was as though Rose carried me right up to God's throne. And after that, she slept more peacefully. But I kept praying for you, Will, Rose, and for myself too. I couldn't stop. It was strange, scary, and wonderful all at the same time. And now I feel totally wrung out."

Melody stared into her coffee cup. "That's surprising and yet not, Tess. I had to pray last night for Will, too. Something woke me up in the middle of the night, and I just had to get on my knees and pray." She turned to Tessa. "What do you suppose is going on?"

"I don't know, Mel. This is way out of my league." Tessa rested her head on the back of the couch again. "All I know right now is that I'm too exhausted to drive home. Could I crash here for a few hours?"

Melody lightly swatted Tessa's shoulder. "Of course you can! You can be the first one to use my new guest room. I'll just get a fresh pillowcase for you."

She stood up and tilted her head. With a half-smile she said, "And welcome to the reluctant warriors' club, my friend."

It was the excessive warmth that stirred Will from his deep sleep. *Too warm. Gotta move.*

He wrestled to free himself from the blankets confining his now-sweating body. He finally got one arm free and shoved the pile of covers onto the floor of the tent. Now fully awake, Will pushed himself upright.

"Unh. That hurts." He looked down at himself. Rips in his clothes, scrapes and cuts on his skin, and stiffness in his joints ... *What happened? Did I get into a fight again? I don't think ...*

He sank back down onto his bed as memories came flooding back: vague impressions of being carried, darkness and terrible, bitter cold, anger pushing him to run, but from what?

It hit him in the gut with a force that took his breath away. *Vixen is dead. Just like Dad. Why? Why did you let it happen? Where were you, God?*

The door to his tent opened, and Eli stepped inside. "How are you feeling, Will? I figured you'd be waking up by now. Here, I brought you some sandwiches and coffee."

The tantalizing smell had already penetrated Will's despair. His stomach rumbled. He pushed his hair out of his eyes and reached for the tray Eli carried.

"Uh, thanks, man. I'm starved." He took a swig of coffee and bit into the first sandwich. He was halfway through the second thickly-stuffed sandwich before he realized that Eli was still standing.

"Want to sit?" he asked around a mouthful. He motioned to his backpack. "Best seat in the house."

Eli sat. His steady gaze was starting to bother Will as he gulped the last of the coffee. He wiped his mouth on his sleeve and set the tray on the floor.

"What's on your mind, Eli?" More memories washed over him. Eli's deep sorrow over Vixen, and Will's suspicions. His mouth tightened. "Got something we need to talk about?"

Eli's gaze didn't waver. "Yes, we do need to talk. I am very concerned for you, young Will."

Pride flared. "What are you talking about?" he demanded.

"Why did you run?" Eli's face showed only concern. "What were you running from?"

"What do you think?" Will's mouth turned down. "A girl I cared about died, and then the guy I thought was my friend carries on like she was *his* girl!"

"You thought I'd lied to you, betrayed you?" Eli shook his bushy head.

Anger drove Will to his feet. "Yes! You warned me off Vixen, and then you act like she was the most important thing in your life! What am I supposed to think?"

Eli looked up at Will, his eyes full of pain. "I understand why you would conclude that. But Will, my grief over Vixen is not what you assumed. I had no desire for her."

Will opened his mouth, but Eli put up a finger. "Let me finish. I warned you away from her because she would have led you into trouble. She was on the downward path and would not be turned from it. No, Will, I do not sorrow because of lust or desire. I sorrow because Vixen is lost." He lowered his eyes and then his head. "She had no one to intercede for her, no one to show her the Savior."

Will sat stunned, his thoughts swirling and clunking like ice in a blender. "What do you mean? How do you know? Why does that matter? Who *are* you?"

Eli looked at him again, a ghost of a smile on his lips. "You will understand better someday." The smile disappeared. "But now the most important question is: why do you believe God failed?"

"God?" Will sputtered, half rising. "Yeah, he failed, all right. He's supposed to care—that's what I was taught—but where *was* he?"

He sank down, deflated. "Where was God when Vixen took that Ecstasy? Where was God when my dad got caught in the baler? Where was he when I got in trouble?"

Eli didn't hesitate. "He was there, William. He was there all the time."

"Then why didn't he stop it? Why didn't he keep Vixen, my dad, and me from getting hurt?" He shook his head angrily. "I don't believe you."

Eli suddenly looked much older. "Vixen refused to listen to anyone who would help her. As for your father, there are some things you won't be able to comprehend this side of the divide. Young Will, his death was not a punishment."

Will gasped. *How did he know ...?*

Eli continued, "It was part of the Master's plan. It was heartbreaking for many—not just you, Will—but God was there. Your father's death was not without purpose. God was watching over you too, keeping you from serious harm. But do you suppose that God's job is to prevent any pain from touching his people?"

Will shrugged. "Well, he's supposed to be all-powerful, right?" At Eli's somber nod, he continued, "So why not? Why do good people get hurt, get sick, die? WHY?"

Eli looked upward for a moment. His lips moved, but Will couldn't make out what he was saying. "No answer, eh? That's what I thought." Anger was replaced by an enervating disappointment.

The radiance on Eli's face sparked a shiver of awe in Will. "You are asking powerful questions, William, and I will answer with another question. What did God do to make it possible for people like you, like your dad, even like Vixen to come to him?"

Will knew the answer to that one. Sunday school and his parents had made sure of that. "He sent Jesus to die."

"Yes, he did." Eli's glowing eyes bore into Will's. "And do you think that might have hurt?"

Will's puzzlement crinkled his face. "Well, yeah. It had to hurt."

"It did. It was more excruciatingly painful than you will ever comprehend. But it was the only way to redeem humanity. Jesus loved you enough to literally go through hell for you." He paused. "William, the way to redemption often involves great pain."

Will's thoughts felt jumbled. He turned away from his friend, unable to bear the radiance on Eli's face.

"I–I need to rest," he said. "I can't think anymore."

Eli stood, looking like just another tree planter. "Okay, young Will, rest up. Suppertime is in a couple hours. You'll want to come down for that."

The tent felt darker once Eli had gone. Emotions and questions swirled in Will's mind. *Could it be true? Does God really care? And just who is Eli Carter, and how does he know so much?*

Saturday morning Melody opened her front curtains to enjoy the beautiful morning, but her eye was caught by the sight of a blanket of portulaca weed crowding the flowers beneath the picture window.

"Aargh!" she muttered. "Guess I know what I have to do this morning."

A short time later, she was on her knees pulling the invasive plants. She knew that any speck left behind would start a new plant. *Just like fear, right, Lord? It digs itself in and takes over if we don't deal with it.*

"Mornin', neighbor!" Bobbie waved from her front step, still in her plush purple bathrobe. "Hard at work already? Come on over when you're done there. I need to talk to you."

Something in her voice made Melody hurry. Before long the narrow flower patch was clean. "Much better." she said aloud. "Now if it would only *stay* weed-free."

Bobbie was dressed in her usual garb of colorful t-shirt and denim jeans when Melody arrived. A pan of cinnamon buns was cooling on the counter, the delicious smell mingling with the rich aroma of fresh coffee.

"Bobbie, you spoil me!" she protested with a smile.

Bobbie just grinned and handed her a large mug of coffee and a still-hot cinnamon bun. "Bet you tackled those weeds before you even ate. Right?"

"You're right." Melody nodded sheepishly. "I just couldn't stand seeing them invading my flowers like that."

She took a bite of bun. "Ooh, these are SO good! Can I get your recipe?"

"Sure thing. Just an old'un I got from my mama years ago. Charlie always liked 'em, so I used to make 'em a lot. Not so much anymore."

"Well, I'm glad you made them today." Melody closed her eyes in pleasure as she took another bite.

Bobbie waited until Melody swallowed. "Got something to tell you, but first I got something for you."

Melody looked up, surprised. "Really? What?"

Bobbie opened a cupboard door, took out an envelope, and handed it to Melody.

"Here." Her smile was almost shy. "A little birdy named Faith told me it's your birthday today. Happy birthday, Kiddo!"

Melody's laughed in delight. "Why, thank you, Bobbie! You know, I totally forgot that it's my birthday today. When I saw those weeds, that's all I could think about."

"Open it," Bobbie ordered. "It ain't much, but I hope you like it."

Melody opened the flowery, sentimental card, and a gift certificate fell unnoticed onto her lap. She smiled as she read the card, tears welling in her eyes. "Oh, that's so sweet! Thank you!"

She looked down to hide the tears and saw a gift certificate for the best garden center in town. She picked it up, eyes wide. "Oh, my! This is too generous, Bobbie."

"Nope." Bobbie shook her head. "Got nothin' better to spend my money on these days. And you've done me a heap'a good." Her eyes were looking a little misty, too. Then she shrugged. "I'd be glad to help you pick out somethun' for your yard, if you want."

Melody's smile shone through tears. "Oh, Bobbie, I'm so thankful for you. You are one of a kind—and I mean that in the best possible way."

She jumped up and gave her friend a quick hug. Stepping back, she asked, "Are you coming to my 'surprise' party this afternoon?"

"Sorry, Kiddo, can't make it. Wish I could, but I gotta go see Rosie." Bobbie paused. "That's only one reason I called you over." Her sudden seriousness alerted Melody.

"O … kay, so what's the other reason?"

"Ran into the kid from the gray house at the grocers yesterday. Nila."

Melody's smile disappeared. "Is she okay? Did she say anything to you?"

"Don't know how okay she is—looked scared, as usual. Nearly jumped outta her skin when I touched her arm." Bobbie shook her head, lines deepening around her mouth. "No bruises showing, anyway. She didn't know me at first, but I told her I saw her at the hospital that time with you. Then she got all excited and said she needs to see you but lost your number. Said she's not allowed to come over. So I gave her the numbers for your cell and your house." Bobbie looked unsure. "That okay?"

"Of course. But I wonder what she wants. Maybe I should go see her, as long as that boyfriend of hers isn't anywhere around." Melody shuddered. "Did I tell you what he said to me when I took Nila home?"

Bobbie shook her head. "Nope. What?"

Melody recounted her brief but terrifying experience with Nick. Just telling the story sent prickles of fear racing up and down her spine.

"There's something unnerving about him. He looks as if he's not much older than my kids, so I've tried to think of him as someone's child. But that day, the look he gave me was pure evil."

∽ ∽ ∽

Daniel paced the office trailer as he dialed Zach's number. "Come on, Zach, pick up!" His patience had worn thin. Reports from home told him his mother's health was declining, and Daniel was anxious to get back. Two weeks had become three-plus, and he'd lose the night nurse in a few more days.

"I hired Zach to run the crews. He's had his time off; now he needs to get back here. Family is important, but not just for him."

Valerie's latest report ran in an endless loop in the back of his mind: "She's failing, Daniel. You need to come home as soon as you can."

Finally, a British-sounding female voice answered. "Hello?"

"Zach, please. This is Daniel Martens."

"Oh, yes sir, Mr. Martens. I'll get him for you."

After a pause, Zach came on the line sounding uncomfortable. "Daniel, I was going to call you today. It's been more than a little crazy here."

Daniel frowned. That didn't sound promising. "It's been more than three weeks, Zach, and I need to get back home. I told you I'd cover for you for two or three weeks. I can't wait much longer."

"I know, I know. It's just that Farah's mom arrived with a nasty cold, so she hasn't been able to help much, especially with the baby. Farah's still weak from her C-section, and …"

"What are you saying? Are you ready to work or not? I need to know one way or the other. If you can't make it, I have to find someone who can." Frustration seeped through Daniel's voice as he struggled to calm himself. "You're a good man, Zach, but if you don't want this job, I'll find someone who does. I'm going home in two days. Will you be here?"

A few minutes later he set the phone down with a care that belied his annoyance. Sinking onto the well-used office chair, he rubbed the back of his neck.

"Zach said he'd manage to be here tomorrow. That gives me one day to go over everything with him before I leave. It'll be hectic, but I should be able to go home Monday."

He made several more phone calls to various crews to confirm their schedules. After the delays of the last week, he needed to tighten things up. He studied his recent notations on the flow chart pinned to the office wall. If everyone showed up as promised, the project could be completed on time. "Okay, that's all I can do about that."

His mother's promise echoed in his mind. "Hang on, Mama, I'm coming."

From the time she'd admitted she had terminal cancer, he'd known the day for final goodbyes would come. "But not yet. I can't handle it yet." News of his father's death had brought more relief than sorrow, but his mother …

He shook off that train of thought and glanced at his watch. It was nine p.m. He phoned his mother's home.

"Daniel here. I need to speak with my mother, please." He listened for a moment. "Oh, all right. No, don't wake her. Just tell her I'll be home in two days."

17

Melody paced her living room. She'd walked partway down the street after leaving Bobbie's, just far enough to make sure Nick's truck was not in the driveway of the gray house.

I should have kept going, gone to see Nila right away. Why am I such a chicken? Why is it so hard to do the right thing? But what am I supposed to do? How much am I supposed to risk?

A raspy voice whispered in her ear. "It's your birthday! You shouldn't have to do such a hard thing on your special day."

That's a tempting thought. Maybe I don't have to ... She stopped short. *Where did that thought come from? Just how immature am I? God, help me. Give me strength to do the right thing.*

Before she could reconsider, she walked out of her house and down the street.

Nila opened the door as though she'd been watching out the window.

"Hi, Melody!" She smiled shyly. "I'm happy to see you. Come in, please."

"Thank you, Nila," Melody responded as she followed Nila inside. The room looked the same except for different flowers filling the vase on the small table.

"Lilies!" Melody said. "They're lovely."

Nila nodded, then looked away. "Yes, they are, aren't they? Nick gave them to me."

She turned back to Melody and clasped her hands together. "I'm really glad you came over. I need to ask you something." She faltered. A faint flush rose in her cheeks as she gestured to the couch. "I'm sorry. I forgot my manners. Sit, please."

Melody sat. Nila perched on the opposite end of the couch and pulled her knees up to her chest. She glanced at Melody and looked away.

She is SO timid. But she wants something. I hope I can help. "What can I do for you, Nila?" Melody spoke as though to a skittish colt.

Nila hugged her knees, still not looking at Melody. "I-I've been thinking about some of the things you said to me. You know, about God loving me and stuff."

Melody's heart thrilled. "He really does, Nila."

The young shoulders began to quiver as she continued. "I don't know, not really. But I want to." She finally turned and looked at Melody, eyes bright with unshed tears. "Are you sure it's true?"

Melody scooted over and put a hand on her arm. Nila flinched. *Poor kid. Lord God, give me the right words to reach her, for Jesus' sake.*

"Yes, Nila, I'm sure. God's word tells us how much he loves us, no matter what we've done or what we've been through. And in my life, he has proven it over and over."

An idea brightened Melody's face. "Would you like to come to my house some time? I could show you lots of places in God's word that tell about his love."

Nila looked away again, and her shoulders slumped. "I–I can't. Nick likes me to be home. And he calls to check up on me, make sure I'm okay and stuff."

Melody bit back her outrage and took a deep breath. *She is so bound, Lord!*

"Well, then would you like a Bible of your own? I could bring you one of mine. I have several. Or perhaps you'd like a new one?"

"Oh … no," Nila sighed and regarded Melody somberly. "I don't need a new one. But would you really give me one of yours?"

"Absolutely!"

Nila took a deep breath. A hint of a smile peeked through. "I'd like that. A lot. I'd take good care of it, I promise."

"Then I'll go get one right now." She glanced at her watch. *Yes, I have time to do that before Faith picks me up for my birthday lunch. Oh-oh…*

Realization dawned, and Melody shivered. "It's Saturday, Nila. Where is Nick? He doesn't work weekends, does he?"

Nila shook her head. "No, he's not at work. He went fishing with some guys from work. He won't get home until late tonight." She rubbed her cast.

Melody could just imagine the condition he would be in when he arrived home. *Lord God, protect her, please!*

She mentally tried and discarded several questions before asking, "Nila, will you be okay? Do you want me to be here when Nick gets home? Is there any chance you'd be willing to go back to Haven House?"

Nila shook her head, rearing back. "No! You shouldn't be here. And I'll be fine. Really." Her hands went up as though to ward off a blow. "As long as I do what he says, Nick is really nice to me."

Between phone calls and consultations, Daniel's mind sped homeward. How was his mother, really? Was Valerie overreacting? He considered and dismissed that hope. No, Valerie was too professional for that. "If she says Mama is failing, I need to be there."

He cursed himself for letting so many of his responsibilities here slide. Because of the backlog, he hadn't been able to take a day off since he'd arrived.

His site supervisor did a good job, but there were aspects that only he could manage. For the last three weeks, his construction company had consumed him. The long hours and never-ending stress used to be all he cared about; his business had been his life.

But in the last few months his priorities had changed. Between barely sleeping most nights listening for his mother's voice and his construction work in Saskatoon, he hadn't had the energy or desire to run this business properly.

Two weeks ago another contractor had called offering to buy him out. He'd asked for a few weeks to think about it.

"It's tempting," he admitted, "especially at that price. But do I really want to give it up? Or will I need this again after Mama's gone?"

Melody was quite certain her flaming face was heating the entire restaurant as her friends and the staff sang loudly and not quite in tune, "Happy birthday to you, happy birthday to you ..."

When the serenade finally ended, Melody laughed along with Faith, Lydia, and Tessa. "Thank you all, I think!"

"Okay," Faith announced. "Time to open gifts. Here's mine."

Seconds later there were three fancy gift bags in front of Melody. She opened Faith's first. On top was a whimsical plaque decorated with hearts and flowers and the words "Grandma is another word for Love." Underneath a stack of fat quarters in Melody's favorite colors was a CD of classical music.

"Oh, Faith, this plaque is beautiful. Thank you! I know just where I'm going to hang it. And I'm already planning my next quilt project, so these fabrics are perfect. I'll enjoy listening to this music while I work on it." She reached over and squeezed her daughter's hand. "I love you," she whispered.

"Mine next," Tessa said.

Melody obediently opened the purple-striped bag. The card inside made her laugh. "Yes, Tessa, I will always be older than you, but you're not that far behind!"

Removing the tissue covering, Melody pulled out three books. "Romance novels? Tessa!"

"Yes, ma'am," Tessa replied with a wink. "I thought it was about time you allowed a little romance back in your life, even if it's just fictional. And they're Christian novels." She pointed to the book in Melody's hand. "I have that one; it's really good. And I'll borrow the rest of the set once you're done, if you let me."

"Well, thank you. I haven't read a book since ... I can't remember when. I'll start this one soon, and I'll picture you as the heroine." She grinned at her friend.

"Here, Melody," Lydia touched the tall bag in front of her. She tilted her head and smiled. "This made me think of you."

Curious, Melody pulled the gift out of the bag and carefully lifted the tissue.

"O–oh," she gasped.

The framed picture showed a child sleeping in his bed, toy sword and shield on the floor beside him. Standing at the boy's head was a large angel, his huge sword and heavy shield shining bright. The angel's massive wings curved protectively, and his attention was fixed on the sleeping child.

"Lydia, this is perfect."

Tears welled up as she gazed at the picture. Blindly, she rummaged in her purse for a tissue. When she looked up, she noticed that her tears seemed to be contagious—all three of her friends were wiping their eyes too.

"Thank you, Lydia. This means a lot to me, as you must know." She smiled at each one in turn. "Thank you all. I think this has been the best birthday ever. I am so blessed to have you in my life."

Tessa leaned forward. "But wait, there's more!" She stage-whispered. "I have some news for my dear, romance-starved friend."

"What are you talking about, Tess?"

Tessa paused as though awaiting a drumroll before announcing with a sly grin, "Daniel is coming home in two days!"

Will was struggling. His whole body ached as though it was his first exhausting day all over again. He glanced around. Almost everyone else was finished their piece, and he still had two long rows to plant. It hadn't helped that he'd caught himself looking around for Vixen more than once. Each time reality struck with an enervating depression. He just couldn't seem to find his rhythm.

"Not gonna make much today," he muttered. "And the crew's not going to be happy with me making them wait again. Or maybe they'll just leave me here to walk back to camp."

"Unh!" He stumbled and nearly fell as someone swatted him on the shoulder. "What ...?"

"Hey, rookie, looks like you could use some help." Eli grinned at him through his bushy beard. "Mind if I join you?"

He looked at Eli. It if weren't for the dirt clinging to him and the sweat staining his shirt, he'd look as if he hadn't planted a thing yet. But his planting bag was filthy and empty, evidence of a long day's work.

Again? He wants to help me finish again? How—and why—does he do it?

Will wiped the sweat from his eyes. "Sure. Be my guest."

They split up the seedlings still in Will's bag, and Eli took off for the far end of Will's assigned piece. "Meet you in the middle."

A short time later the two men trudged up the hill to the waiting van. The sun was still high in the sky, but the hollow ache in Will's stomach told him it was definitely suppertime.

Just before they reached the group resting in the shade of the vehicle, Will reached out and clapped Eli on the back. "Thanks, man. You saved my skin. Again."

Eli chuckled, a deep, rumbling sound that came out like a growl. He spoke so softy that Will wasn't sure if he'd heard right. "Just doing my job."

It was nearly eight o'clock by the time Faith brought Melody home. Melody carried her gift-bagged treasures into the house and set them on the coffee table. She sat on the couch and reopened the embellished bags, carefully examining each gift. "Chosen for me by my precious friends. I am a wealthy woman, aren't I, Lord?"

She leaned back and closed her eyes, enjoying the warmth that radiated from deep inside her heart. "Forty-five's not so bad, if today is any indication."

After the party, she'd spent the rest of the day with Jason, Faith and baby Jessica. Jason had prepared one of his special dinners in her honor, another delightful surprise.

"My heart is overflowing, Lord. My precious family—I'm thrilled to live so much closer to them." She stilled. A pinprick of disappointment deflated a corner of her joy. "Except for my son. Where is he? What is he doing right now?"

Melody squared her shoulders. "Leave him in God's hands," she ordered herself. "Only God can tear down those walls he's built around his heart."

An echo fluttered at the edge of Melody's memory. "Walls. What is it about walls?"

The picture focused: Rose asking her to pray for Daniel. She'd said he had walls, too.

"Rose was going to tell me something about her son, but we got interrupted. I wonder if she's up to a visit this evening?"

Valerie opened the door at Melody's first soft knock. "Hello, Melody."

"Good evening, Valerie. I was wondering if Rose might be feeling well enough for company."

The nurse stepped back and motioned for Melody to enter. "She's on the phone with her son right now, but if you'll to wait a few minutes, I'm sure she would enjoy seeing you."

Valerie's stern expression softened to an almost-smile. "She told me it's your birthday today. Happy birthday."

"Thank you, Valerie." She looked around the tidy living room. "Should I wait here?"

"Yes. I'll let Rose know you're here as soon as she's done talking to Daniel."

Just the mention of his name sent shivers up Melody's spine. *Why does he make me so nervous?*

A few minutes later Melody stopped in the doorway to Rose's room. It had only been two days since she'd been here, but the change in Rose was unmistakable. She looked thinner and frailer in that short time. Her eyes, though still bright, were now more yellow than white. Melody smiled brightly to cover her shock.

"Hello, Rose. How are you feeling this evening?"

"Come in, come in, dear child," Rose's voice was weaker too. "I was hoping I'd get to wish you birthday blessings today."

Melody pulled the chair as close as she could to the side of the bed and sat forward on it. "Thank you, Rose. It really has been a special day."

She told her about the luncheon party and the time spent at Faith's. She shared some of Jessica's cute antics and was rewarded by a wistful smile on Rose's face.

"I would love to meet your granddaughter. Perhaps the next time she's at your house, you could bring her over. I wasn't blessed by grandchildren of my own, you know."

"I didn't know that. I would love to bring Jessica to meet you. She is a handful, I must admit, but we could pop in for a minute or two. Maybe next week?"

"Whenever it's convenient, Melody." Rose closed her eyes.

Is she tiring already? Perhaps I should go. Melody scooted her chair back just enough so she could stand.

Rose's eyes opened. "Must you go so soon?"

"I thought you needed to rest," Melody said, easing back into the chair. "Are you sure you don't want me to leave?"

That brought another wistful smile. "Quite sure, my dear." She gestured at her frail body encased in blankets. "This old vessel is wearing out, but I'm not ready to go yet. There are many things I hope to tell you."

"Oh?" Melody took the bony hand in hers. "Whatever you want to tell me, I want to hear. But I don't want to tire you. Please promise me you'll rest when you need to, and I'll stay as long as you want."

Rose smiled at her. "You are a sweetheart, dear Melody. It's a deal." She squeezed Melody's hand lightly.

"My son … I need to tell you about my son." She closed her eyes again, but only for a moment. "He was such a handsome boy, with his dark, wavy hair, beautiful eyes, and sweet smile. He was always independent, wanting to do everything on his own, but he was a considerate child, too."

Melody struggled to reconcile this picture of young Daniel with the scowling neighbor who flustered her.

Rose continued. "He rarely squabbled with his sister, and from what I've seen in other families, that was a rare gift. Although I remember that since Hannah was four years older than Daniel, she sometimes tried to make him her 'dolly' when they were both young." Rose smiled at her memories. "That did not please my boy."

She was quiet for a moment, apparently lost in the past. Rose sighed, a mournful release, and looked at Melody with a pensive expression.

"Daniel and his father had some rough times. Daniel's independent nature did not please my husband." Rose looked away, seeing only her memories.

"My husband was a hard man," she admitted. "He did not see anyone's viewpoint but his own." Another deep sigh. "Ezekiel was a good man. He preached about grace, but I don't believe he comprehended its meaning. When Daniel decided as a teen to attend a different church, Ezekiel ordered him to recant his decision or leave our home. My son left."

Rose faced Melody again, distress shadowing her pain-etched features. "That, my dear, was a terrible, dark day."

"Oh Rose," Melody could only murmur, "I'm *so* sorry!"

Rose rallied herself, dabbing at her eyes with a tissue. "But the thing I need to tell you, Melody, is that before he left, Daniel came to me. He told me that if I ever needed him, he would be there for me."

An odd mix of pride and sorrow radiated through the lines on her face. "He made a vow, Melody, and my boy always keeps his promises."

Understanding dawned. "That's why he came home to care for you, isn't it? That's why he left his business in Alberta."

"Yes, dear," Rose nodded. Melody had to lean in to hear her now. "I didn't ask for such a sacrifice when I told him about this illness. I only intended to make him aware, so he would be prepared when my time came. But he remembered his vow, and he came home to care for me."

She seemed to sink into the soft mattress as she released another sigh. This one sounded more like a moan. "I think I must rest now, dear child. Would you please ask Valerie to come in?"

"Yes, of course." Melody stood, emotions swirling. "Thank you, Rose, for sharing this with me. I had no idea …"

Rose reached toward Melody, her voice a mere whisper. "Will you come again? Perhaps tomorrow? There is more to tell."

18

Will sat down at the back of the mess tent. As he chewed his first bite of bacon, he studied the rest of his crew. They sat in couples or groups, laughing and talking loudly. Will frowned and bit off another chunk of meat.

The bench depressed as Eli sat beside him. "Morning, Will," was all he said.

They ate, neither talking until frustration burst from Will. "Don't they care?" He gestured with a slice of bacon at the rowdy bunch near the front of the room. "How can they act like nothing happened? Like Vixen didn't exist … or didn't matter!"

Eli's eyes followed Will's gesture. He continued to chew methodically for a few moments. Finally he swallowed and put down his fork.

"Perhaps they don't care as much as we do, Will, or perhaps they simply can't face this reminder of their mortality. For some, life is more about running from death than it is about really living."

Will stared. *Eli, my friend, you are one strange guy. Where do you get this stuff?*

"You know, tomorrow may be my last shift with Rose, since Daniel's coming home then. I'm hoping he'll want me to stay on for another night or two, but I'm already booked to start back at the hospital this Friday. Do you still want to ride together on Sundays if I'm not working?"

No response from the passenger seat. Silence dragged for a minute.

Tessa took her eyes off the road long enough to peer at her friend. "Hey, Mel, where are you?" She chuckled. "It's a good thing you're not the one driving this morning!"

Melody patted her own face as though to wake herself. "Sorry, Tess. I am a little distracted this morning. Sure hope Pastor Dave's sermon is a rousing one."

"He does preach from the heart, doesn't he? I really appreciate his messages. But what's up? Why so distracted?"

"Oh, I was over at Rose's yesterday. She decided she needs to explain Daniel to me for some reason. That's worrisome." She grimaced. "But what's really bothering me is her decline. She seems so much weaker this week than last."

Tessa pulled into the church lot and parked. She turned to face Melody and spoke softly. "You knew this was going to happen, didn't you? She has never hidden the fact that she is dying." She sighed. "I hate it, too. In the short time I've known Rose, she has become like a beloved mother to me."

"Me, too," Melody said. "She's ready to go, but I'm not ready to give her up."

The two friends sat without speaking for a moment. Then Tessa took her keys out of the ignition and said, "It's hard, very hard. But we're not without hope, are we? Let's go see what God has for us today."

୧୨ ୧୨ ୧୨

A few hours later, Melody was welcomed into Rose's house by Lorraine. "She was napping, but she's awake now. Go on in. She's expecting you."

Melody greeted her frail neighbor with a smile. "Hello, Rose. Are you up to a visit?"

"Oh, yes, my dear. Please, come and sit." The voice was faint but steady. "Today I must tell you about Daniel's wife."

Shock pushed Melody down onto the chair. *Wife? I didn't even know he was married!* Shame swept over her as she realized she'd been attracted to a married man. *Guess Tessa's not the only one with that weakness.*

Rose was looking at her with questions in her eyes. Melody flushed. "Please, do tell me your story. I–I didn't realize he was married." She looked out the window, unable to meet Rose's gaze.

Rose cleared her throat. "Yes, dear Melody, Daniel *was* married. He met Angela when he decided to become a journeyman carpenter. Her father owns Bridge City Construction, and Daniel apprenticed under him. Anyway, Daniel and Angela became good friends, friendship eventually became love, and after he'd established his own company, they married. Daniel adored her, called her his angel."

Rose's eyes held a faraway look. "I called her my sunshine girl. She was tall like our friend Tessa and just as willowy. With her long, golden hair and cheerful disposition, she was a ray of sunshine."

For some reason, Melody felt dowdy. She absently pulled at a short, brown curl.

"Even before they married," Rose continued, "Angela tried to help Daniel reconcile with his father. It was the only source of friction between the two of them. Angela had a great relationship with her own father, and she wanted the same thing for Daniel."

Rose took a long breath and closed her eyes. She lay motionless for several heartbeats.

Is she still breathing? Oh, God, don't take her yet, Melody pleaded silently.

She leaned forward and spoke softly, "Rose? Are you okay? Should I go get Lorraine?"

Eyes still closed, Rose responded as though from a distance. "I am still here, Melody. I just need to rest for a moment. Don't go."

Melody listened to the beating of her own heart as she waited. Finally Rose reopened her eyes. It seemed to take her a moment to focus.

"Where was I? Oh yes ... Angela. I will see her soon."

Uh–oh. Melody steeled herself. She slid a tissue out of her pocket.

"Daniel refused to have anything to do with his father. We still lived in Prince Albert then, and he and Angela would come visit me only when Ezekiel was away. This hurt Angela terribly, but she could not give up. Then one day an arrow of pure love pierced my boy's wall of animosity."

Rose paused, pale with pain and memories. "Angela was expecting. They were both thrilled, and in his joy Daniel agreed to share the news with us—both of us."

Melody released the breath she hadn't realized she'd been holding. "Oh, I'm so glad!"

Rose moved her head against the pillow. "It didn't go well." She frowned in puzzlement. "I don't know what got into Ezekiel," she said with a quivering sigh. "I intend to ask him when I see him."

Melody kept silent, dreading the story's conclusion.

"Harsh words were said by both men. Daniel stormed out, pulling Angela with him. On their way out the door, my son turned and told his father he would never see their baby, his grandchild."

A sob escaped Rose's trembling lips. "Daniel was so angry, he shouldn't have been driving, especially when the roads were so icy with blowing snow. They were near Hague when their car hit black ice. Daniel overcorrected, and they hit a car coming north head-on."

Rose's eyes were open, but she was obviously seeing the carnage of the past. Her face was taut, and tears flowed freely.

"Angela was killed instantly, as were the couple in the other car. Daniel was in the hospital for two weeks with head injuries and several broken bones."

Melody wiped her own tears, but they kept falling. She couldn't speak.

Rose's hand reached for Melody's, and Melody grabbed it as though it was a life preserver.

"Melody." Rose looked into Melody's eyes, tears to tears. "This is the reason I shared this with you: I am asking of you a great favor."

"Anything!" Melody promised.

"I told you Daniel keeps his vows. Well," another sigh, "while he was still in the hospital, he told me he'd vowed never to love again, not another woman and certainly not God. He believes our Lord turned his back on him, just as his father had."

She squeezed Melody's hand faintly. "My dear, I am asking you to pray for my son. Pray that God will pierce his heart again with love. I have been praying that for these last twelve years, but my time is nearly up. Will you carry that burden for me?"

Melody sat stunned, speechless, and unable to move as a tsunami of awareness hit. *Twelve years? Near Hague? Blowing snow and black ice?*

Wave after wave of shock rolled over her until she thought she'd drown in it.

But this sweet, dying woman was waiting for an answer. Melody shut her eyes tight against the terrible memories flooding every fiber of her body. She shook her head to clear it and removed her hand from Rose's.

"Yes, dear Rose," she choked out the words through teeth clenched against pain, "I will pray for your son."

She stood on shaking legs, leaned down, and kissed Rose's sunken cheek. "I'm sorry. I have to go now."

God! How could you do this to me?

Melody ran blindly out of Rose's house, across the street and into her own. She groped her way to the bedroom, leaning against the walls for support. She reached for her bed and collapsed onto it.

Sobs tore her throat as an avalanche of grief and anger beat down on her. Old wounds ripped open; the freshness of each loss making her cry out. Her in-laws, her husband, her son—grief upon grief flowed from Melody's heart.

"Why, God, why? Why did Tom's parents have to die? If they hadn't, Tom wouldn't have had to take over the farm so soon, Will could have been saved, my family would be *whole!*"

She cried until her body had no more tears. Her fists still clenched the pillow as sobs became shudders, then deep, gasping sighs.

"Are you there, God? Can you feel my pain?" She whispered against the pillow.

She didn't hear an answer, but slowly, almost imperceptibly, the chill in her exhausted body was replaced by gentle warmth.

Melody lay there, numb, until Rose's plea echoed in her heart: "Pray for my son." Daniel: the catalyst that turned her life upside down and inside out.

"How can I pray for him? Why should I? After all he's responsible for? I can't bear to even think about him!"

You promised Rose. This is her dying wish. Do you love her?

"Of course I love her!" In frustration Melody rolled over and raised her clenched fists. "But she didn't know what Daniel's accident cost me! She wouldn't ask that if she knew."

Do you love me?

She stilled, her shoulders slumped, and her hands dropped back onto the covers. "Yes, Lord, I do."

Her tumbling thoughts slowed, sorted themselves. "And you love Daniel, don't you," she whispered. "He lost more than I did that terrible night. He lost his faith as well as his loved ones."

Tears came again, quiet ones now, flowing from somewhere deep inside. "Dear God, please do help Daniel. Break down the walls of pain that keep him from you. Heal his heart. He is suffering, so much misery, Lord. Remove the blinders from his eyes so he can see and know your goodness and great love. And ... and help me to forgive him."

୶ଡ଼ ୶ଡ଼ ୶ଡ଼

Melody stirred. *Wh–what?* Someone was pounding on her front door. She tried to focus on the clock beside her bed. Her puffy, salt-crusted eyelids didn't want to open. She rubbed her eyes and tried again. *Six-thirty? Who ... .oh, Tessa?*

She untangled the sheets and climbed out of bed, stumbling over her clothes on the floor. Her head pounded in time with the knocking on the door.

"Coming," she called, but it came out as a croak. She tried again. "Coming!"

Tessa's fist was poised to knock again as Melody opened the door. "Oh good, you're up." Tessa's crooked grin didn't quite hide the concern on her face. "May I come in?"

Melody wiped some curls off her face and straightened her pajama pants. "Sure, Tess, come on in." She looked down at her rumpled pajamas. "Guess I should get my robe. You know where the coffee makings are, right?"

A few minutes later, worry haunted Tessa's face as the friends faced each other over the table, coffee mugs in hand.

Melody couldn't think of any small talk. Her brain and emotions felt bruised, crippled.

"Okay, Mel, what's going on?" Tessa finally burst. "What happened at Rose's yesterday? Lorraine told me you ran out of there as though monsters were chasing you."

One side of Melody's mouth lifted, more of a grimace than smile. "Yeah, that's about right." She paused, took a deep breath. "I–I don't think I can talk about it yet, Tess."

Tessa shook her head. "This is not good. Whatever it is, you can tell me. It can't hurt—I hope—and it may help."

She reached across the table for Melody's hand. "This is your old friend talking, Mel. We can handle just about anything together, right?"

Melody pulled her hands back and clasped them in her lap. She spoke slowly, softly. "I'm sorry, Tess. I know I'm upsetting you, but I really do need some time. I promise I'll tell you in the next day or two, but please give me today at least to sort things out in my mind. "

"Can you give me a hint?" Tessa pleaded. "Because you're right. I'm really worried about you, especially now. Is there anything I can do to help?"

Melody's sorrow-filled eyes met Tessa's. "Just pray for me, Tess."

She closed her eyes, trying to shut out tormenting images. "I can tell you this much: I'm being challenged—by love—to forgive." She propped her elbows on the table and lowered her face into her hands. Through her fingers she murmured, "And I don't know if I can."

Tessa carefully set her coffee cup down, got up and walked around the table to enfold her friend in an embrace.

"I'll pray," she whispered into Melody's ear, "that you'll come through this even stronger than before and that forgiveness will fill your soul. I'll leave you now." She stood and turned toward the door. "But remember, Mel, God must have a purpose, even for this."

19

Daniel set the cruise control on his truck for 125 kilometers per hour and pulled an open bag of sunflower seeds closer. Munching them was an old habit, and it helped him stay alert while driving. He'd gotten away much later than planned, and now it would be around midnight by the time he got home.

"Zach had better snap out of that 'new daddy' fog, and quickly. How many times did I have to tell him to focus? If he doesn't make sure everyone sticks to the schedule, we'll have late penalties to deal with. And if that happens, he'll have me to deal with."

He hadn't slept well, as usual, and he'd hoped he could be rested before this trip and the sleepless nights sure to come.

He zipped past several vehicles on the divided highway until the distinctive light rack of an RCMP car materialized on the horizon. He muttered a word his mother would not approve and touched the brakes. As soon as the police car disappeared from sight, he reset the cruise.

By the time he passed Vegreville, his construction company and its stresses had been replaced by apprehension about his mother. "How bad is it? How much longer does she have? Valerie said her eyes are yellowing, a sign the cancer is into her liver. That's why she told me to hurry. Hurry … hurry."

Lights suddenly flashed from a vehicle coming toward him. Daniel blinked and checked his speedometer. Without realizing it, he'd pressed down on the accelerator, and now he was doing 140. "That would rate a whopper of a ticket," he reprimanded himself. "Watch it, man!"

He hit the brakes just as another police car appeared. Daniel watched the car closely, but it continued heading west. "That was close. Glad that other guy warned me."

He popped a few more sunflower seeds into his mouth. As he crunched, he made a mental list.

"I need to contact Hannah. Sure hope she can get here in time. She'll want to see Mama before …" Daniel nearly choked on a seed but managed to swallow it. "I'll have to talk to a preacher, too. I wonder if Mama has that all arranged. Probably. She's been talking about being ready to go for a long time already."

Sudden tears blurred his vision. He wiped them quickly and focused on the road. "Think about something else."

He switched on the radio and found a station playing golden oldies. That worked well until Whitney Houston's lustrous voice tore open his heart with her song, "I Will Always Love You." That had been his and Angela's special song back when they were dating, and now its melancholy message reminded him of all he'd lost.

Angela.

But when he tried to conjure her image, her long blond hair and blue eyes seemed to morph into short brown curls and green eyes.

"What? Oh no, you don't …"

A few hours later Daniel zipped past the lights of Langham. "Almost home."

He considered that. "It's strange that after living in Alberta for so many years and building my company there, Saskatoon is still home." He mentally reviewed the proposal he'd received from his would-be buyer. "Maybe it's time to come home for good."

He hadn't spent much of his earnings over the years. Other than paying off his mother's mortgage when Ezekiel died and helping with his sister's support, he'd invested everything above his cost of living.

He had several jobs waiting for him in Saskatoon, work he'd had to delay while he filled in for his site supervisor. A flicker of irritation disturbed his musings.

"Zach really pushed the limits of my tolerance this time. If he hadn't come back, I would have had to replace him. But then what? I'd still be stuck there. Well, it worked out. Lucky for him. For both of us."

Before long Daniel could see the bright lights at the Credit Union

Centre marking the edge of the city. A quick stab of homesickness surprised him. "Nearly there."

Minutes later Daniel pulled into the driveway, shut off the truck and sat, unable to move. Now that he was home, he dreaded seeing the changes that Valerie had described. He couldn't face the preparations that needed to be made. "I don't think I can do this."

The door to the house opened, and Tessa peeked out. She recognized his truck and waved. "Welcome home!" she called.

Daniel opened his door and stepped out on stiff legs. "Thank you, Tessa. Is my mother still awake?"

Tessa came down the walkway to meet him. "She slept for a little while, but she's awake now. She's anxious to see you. You may be shocked at her appearance, Daniel, but she's still in good spirits."

Apprehension slowed him. "How bad is it?" he asked through tight lips.

Tessa stopped just outside the door. "She probably won't last much longer, I'm afraid. She has weakened a great deal in the last few days. I'm sorry, Daniel."

Yeah, I'm sorry, too.

He followed Tessa into the house, his stiff legs feeling as though they ended in concrete boots.

In case she was napping, Daniel walked as quietly as possible to his mother's room. He paused at her open door. Her eyes were closed, but other signs of decline were obvious. She was much thinner than when he'd left, her skin looked jaundiced, and her hands trembled on the covers as she slept.

He crossed to the bedside chair and eased into it. Rose's yellowed eyes opened and fixed on him immediately. "Daniel. You're home! It's good to see you, Son."

"Hey, Mama, how are you feeling?" Daniel spoke softly, as though even a loud voice might shatter this fragile woman.

She beamed. "Wonderful, now that you're here." She reached for him. "Come here, Son, and give me a hug. I won't break."

Are you sure, Mama?

He leaned over and enclosed the frail body in his strong arms. "It's good to be home," he whispered.

Her body felt as fragile as she looked. Daniel struggled to smile again as he eased back into the chair.

"You look tired, Mama," he said. "I should let you sleep."

"But you just got home," Rose protested, "and we have much to talk about."

He shook his head. "I'm not going anywhere. We can talk in the morning."

Rose looked as though she was going to argue, but then she reached out and traced the lines on his forehead. "You're tired too, aren't you? I forgot what a long drive it is from Edmonton." She patted his cheek. "All right, dear, we'll talk in the morning. But do you know what I'd like?"

"No, Mama. Tell me."

"I'd like you to hold my hand until I fall asleep. Would you do that for me?"

The tears he'd been fighting filled his eyes. "Of course, Mama. Of course I will."

Melody had heard Daniel's truck. She'd somehow known it was him even before she peeked through the curtains. As a result she'd hardly slept, and this morning no amount of coffee could raise her spirits.

So he's home. Rose must be thrilled. I'm happy for her. But I'm not happy for me. This is too hard, God. How am I supposed to deal with all this confusion and anger?

"Give it to me, child." The voice was inaudible but clear. "I will carry your burdens."

But how? How do I do that? Just wrap up all this hurt and grief in a bag of anger and push it upwards?

"Oh dear, I'm sorry, Lord," she prayed aloud. "That was terribly sarcastic. But you know how horrible I've felt ever since Rose told me about the accident. Help me, please."

"Open your troubled heart to me, dear one. Open yourself to love. Do you love Rose?"

"You know I do."

"Yes, I know. Do you trust me?"

"Y–yes."

"Then keep your promise—not your distance—and allow me to work out my purpose in this. I will never leave you."

"O–okay, God. I will try."

It was mid-afternoon before Melody found the courage to phone her best friend. After three rings, Melody's nerve was failing, but Tessa answered on the fourth ring.

"Hey, Tess, did I wake you?"

"No, Mel, I was just vacuuming. Didn't hear the phone at first."

"Good." She hesitated, then took a deep breath. "Tess, I'm ready to talk. I'm sorry it has taken so long, but you'll understand when I tell you. Are you working at Rose's tonight?"

"Yeah, it's my last night, though. Daniel's exhausted and was afraid he wouldn't waken if Rose needed something, so he asked me to work through tonight."

"Oh." A pang of sympathy twisted Melody's bruised heart. "It must be so awful ... Anyway, if you'd like to come for an early supper, we could talk."

"That sounds good, Mel. How much time do we need? Should I come over right away?"

Melody sighed. "That might be a good idea. I have no idea how long this will take."

"Give me half an hour, okay?" Her voice softened. "Hey, Mel, thank you for trusting me."

20

High in the Rockies north of Golden, a van full of dirty, sweaty tree planters headed back to camp. This was the last day before their day off, and since town was four hours away, they'd finished early.

Excitement trumped fatigue as arrangements were made for the evening and following day. Loud voices hammered on Will's nerves, and he felt his irritation building.

"Do they have to be so loud?" he complained to his seatmate. "I can't hear myself think!" He looked at Eli. His friend looked relaxed and at peace. "How do you do that—stay so cool?"

A ghost of a smile crossed Eli's face. "I *am* cool, my friend."

Will punched him playfully on his bulging bicep. "Ri–i–ght."

"Are you going in to town tonight?" Eli asked, a line creasing his brow.

Will shook his head. "Naw. Don't feel like it. You know, bad memories. Partying doesn't feel right. It's just too soon. How about you?"

"I plan to stay in camp. It's much more peaceful there, and I could use the rest."

"Yeah, I figured I'd hang out, maybe catch up on sleep. I feel like it's been my first week all over again."

They sat in silence the rest of the way, the noise of their boisterous crewmates swirling around them.

A short time later as they trudged side by side up the hill toward their respective tents, Will slowed his steps. Eli turned, inquiry in his eyes.

"Um ... Eli ..." Will faltered. "Later, when the rowdies are gone, do you think we could talk?"

"No problem, Will. Any particular subject you want to talk about?"

"Well ..." He hesitated again and looked down. "I ... um ... I've been thinking a lot about what you said about redemption. You know, about its cost and stuff."

A light came on in Eli's eyes. "And?"

Will met his eyes, blinked and looked down again. "I-I think I'd like to know more about that." He glanced up with a casual shrug. "If that works for you."

Eli's grin illumined his whole face. "Absolutely!"

Daniel rested his elbows on the kitchen table and rubbed his temples with his fingers. He had spent most of the day visiting with his mother and making phone calls, and the stress of trying to hold his emotions in check had produced a massive headache.

Rose had been anxious to hear about his work in Alberta, so he'd made his time there sound like a pleasurable and productive holiday.

"Didn't know I could be such a good actor," he muttered. "But she seemed to enjoy my stories."

Rose hadn't said much. She'd seemed content to listen to him, smiling even as she fell asleep every few minutes. Valerie told him this was natural and to "go with the flow." She'd said that eventually Rose would slip into a coma, but she couldn't predict when that would happen.

Daniel groaned, resting his head in his hands. "Too soon, God. I'm not ready. Please let me have a little more time with her."

His body tensed. *Was that a prayer?* He blew out a deflating breath. *Hopelessness does strange things to a man.*

He picked up the phone again. This time the call reached his sister in Niamey, Niger.

"Hello, Hannah, it's Daniel. How soon can you get here?"

Melody had just finished setting the table when Tessa arrived. She welcomed her friend with a firm hug and a hesitant smile.

"I'm sorry I practically shoved you out of the house yesterday, Tess. I'm glad you're here now. Want some coffee?"

"Of course!" Tessa walked into the kitchen and helped herself to the fragrant brew. "Have you sorted things out? You were pretty out of it."

Melody took a slow, deep breath. "Well, I'm not sure if I'll ever feel 'sorted out' again, but God and I have been having some heart-to-hearts. That has helped."

They took their usual spots on the brown couch, leaning against the arms and facing each other.

Melody concentrated on her cup of coffee, not sure how to start or how much to share. *I don't know how much of Daniel's story was for my ears only. Help me, God, to do this right.*

Tessa made a show of looking at her watch. "So?"

"Patience, my friend," Melody retorted softly. "I'm just trying to figure out how to say this." She shifted on the couch. "You see, Rose decided she needed to talk to me about Daniel."

At Tessa's grin, she held up her hands. "No, not like that. For some reason, and I don't understand why, she felt I needed to know his background. It seemed really important to her."

She set her cup on the low table and pulled her knees to her chest. "His relationship with his father was pretty awful, but I won't go into that. But Tess, did you know he'd been married?"

"Well, sure. Didn't you ever look at the photo on Rose's dresser? The one where Daniel's got his arms around a beautiful blonde? Rose told me a bit about their story, how she died."

Melody felt her cheeks burn. *Why didn't I notice that? I wouldn't have been so shocked when Rose told me about her.* She put her hands on her hot cheeks. "I guess I never looked around the room; I was always focused on Rose. So that was a shock to me. But Tess, the thing that really threw me was when Rose asked me to pray for Daniel."

"Why? What's the big surprise in that? Rose is always praying."

Melody hugged her knees again but couldn't stop the trembling sensation as it worked its way up from her toes to her shoulders. She swallowed hard, shook her head, and closed her eyes for a moment.

"Mel? What is it?" Concern filled Tessa's voice, but it seemed to come from a distance.

Scenes of the horrible crash flashed through her mind without mercy, as they had since Rose's revelation. Melody shook her head more forcefully, trying to dispel the images. *Tess is waiting. Get hold of yourself!* Then, *help me, God.*

She breathed deeply and plunged in, her distraught gaze fastened on her friend. "Tess, did Rose tell you much about Daniel's accident?"

At Tessa's negative gesture, Melody continued. "Rose told me that he hit black ice near Hague, causing a head-on collision with a northbound car. Does that sound familiar?"

Tessa gasped. "You don't mean …"

Once again Melody felt as though she couldn't get enough air. She gulped a breath and let it shudder back out. "Yes. When Rose asked me to carry her burden of prayer, she mentioned she'd been praying for his faith since the accident twelve years ago." She choked out, "Twelve years, Tess!"

Tessa exhaled forcefully. "But what if it's a coincidence, Mel? Are you sure?"

Melody bowed her head into her hands, letting them muffle her words. "Yes, I'm sure. I found the news reports online." She raised her head, her eyes frantic. "Daniel killed Tom's parents."

Several moments of silence passed before Tessa spoke. It was only a whisper, though, as the facts clicked into place. "What are you going to do?"

"I–I don't know. That's why I couldn't talk about it yesterday. I feel steamrolled. All the wounds I thought were healing have been smashed wide open again, with Daniel's losses adding to the misery."

She reached her hands out in supplication. "It's so much more than I can handle. What would you do?"

Tessa wiped tears from her face and mirrored Melody's posture, hugging her own knees. "I sure don't know, Mel. That's a tough question." She was silent for a moment. "Do you think it would help to talk to Pastor Dave and Lydia about this?"

A sliver of sunshine broke through Melody's despair. "That's a really good idea, Tess. Why didn't I think of that?"

"Maybe because you've been so overwhelmed with emotions, you haven't been able to think clearly."

Melody smiled wanly. "You're right, my friend. Thank you. I'm going to phone them and make an appointment. Then we should eat before you have to go to work."

"Good plan."

Tessa stood, started for the kitchen and stopped halfway there.

"This is my last night with Rose, and Daniel will be there. I don't know if I can face him tonight."

Melody rose and gave her friend a one-armed hug as she passed her. As she picked up the phone, she paused, sighing. "I made your favorite chicken salad for supper, but I don't know if I can eat. I think we're both going to need an extra helping of prayer, though."

21

"Daniel." His mother's voice carried a note of something—longing, weariness, pain?

"I'm here, Mama." Daniel set his newspaper on the floor and leaned toward his mother. "What can I do for you?"

"Melody," she whispered. "Talk to Melody."

Daniel stiffened. "Why?" He tried to keep his voice soft, but he could hear his frustration.

Rose's right hand fluttered toward him. "I'm sorry, son." She paused, gathered her strength. "I think … I may have … upset her."

And now she's upset you! I'll talk to her, all right.

He forced himself to sound calm. "Why do you think that, Mama?"

Rose closed her eyes, but not in time to prevent a tear from slipping out. "I told her … accident, Angela … pray."

"Mama! What did you do that for?" His voice rose in spite of his efforts, and Valerie rushed into the room.

"Is everything okay in here?" she inquired, one eyebrow lifted. She quickly crossed to Rose's bed and checked her pulse and respiration.

"I think you'd better let your mother rest." She looked pointedly at the doorway. "I'll finish my report in here. You may go."

Daniel sagged. He hadn't meant to get angry, and he certainly hadn't intended to upset his mother. He walked into his bedroom, shut the door, and leaned against it.

Why would Mama tell our neighbor my life history? What does that have to do with her?

Melody's face materialized in Daniel's mind. He swiped at his eyes as though that would erase the image. *She's just a woman, nothing to me.*

He felt for his bed and sank onto it. *So why does she make me feel so incomplete?*

It was late afternoon in the BC Rockies as Eli led Will through the forest to a babbling stream, clear and bone-chillingly cold.

Eli knelt beside the stream and scooped up a drink in his cupped hand. "Ah, refreshing!" He grinned. "Come on, Will, have a drink!"

Will shrugged, knelt and stuck his hand in the water. "Hey! That's so cold it burns!" He threw several drops of water at his friend. "Thanks a lot. Now my hand is frozen."

He steeled himself against the cold, and just to prove he could do it, scooped and gulped down several handfuls of the frigid water.

Eli laughed as he settled himself on a nearby fallen log. Patting the spot beside him, he invited, "Here, have a seat. This is a good place."

Will sat, shivering slightly. Eli seemed to be listening to something, his head back and face alight, so Will listened, too. He heard birds chattering somewhere in the trees; he heard the brook. He heard the wind brushing past branches and boulders. But he didn't hear anything that made his face light up. *What's with this guy?*

He cleared his throat rather loudly. Eli turned. "You have some questions, Will," he stated.

"Yeah, I do." He hesitated. "I just don't know how to ask them."

"You are wondering about redemption, right? You do understand the basic concept, though."

"Sure," Will countered. "What I don't get is the 'why.' And I don't know what it has to do with me."

Eli's eyes glowed like embers. "Are you sure about that? You don't think you have any need for redemption?"

Will leaned back and nearly fell off the log. Face flushing, he repositioned. "Well, I admit I mess up sometimes, but there's a big gap between that and Jesus dying. Isn't there?"

One side of Eli's mouth lifted. "You mess up? Don't you think that's a bit of an understatement?"

Will tossed a pebble into the water and scrunched up his face. "Maybe. I just don't get it, though. I mean, I heard most of this stuff at church, but it doesn't make sense. If Jesus is God, how could he die? And why would he let those losers nail him to the cross?" He thought of the picture in his childhood Bible that portrayed the crucifixion of Jesus. Will shook his head. "You're right, that had to have been horrible. I can't even imagine…"

Eli leaned back, clasping one knee with his large hands. "Have you heard this, Will? 'Greater love has no man than this, than to lay down his life for a friend.' That's what Jesus did. Even though the world hated him, he still loved you enough to die for you. 'The payment for sin is death.' No one took Jesus Christ's life. He gave it willingly." He looked at Will. "He gave it for you, William. That's redemption: his life for your sin, your messing up."

Will couldn't stand the brilliance of Eli's gaze. He turned his head; his thoughts and emotions twisted around and around like a maze with no solution. "I–I think I'll go rest now. Maybe I'll figure it out later."

He could feel Eli's eyes on him as he stood and walked back toward camp. *Yeah, I'm running again,* he admitted to himself, *but I just can't deal with this now. Later … I'll think about it later.*

༄ ༄ ༄

Valerie had given Tessa her updates and left, and now Tessa was preparing Rose's supper, a liquid meal replacement.

Daniel watched her measure four ounces and pour it into one of Rose's prettiest glasses, adding a bright pink straw. *How's that little bit going to keep her alive?* He felt his spirit droop even further. *Of course, it won't. Nothing will now.*

Tessa turned with a strained smile.

Is she feeling it, too? She should be glad she won't be here for the end.

"Daniel, would you like to feed your mother? She likes to hold the straw, but if she's too weak …" She held out the half-full glass.

"I think I can manage that." Daniel knew he sounded surly, but he couldn't seem to help it. He accepted the glass and sighed. Snarling at the nurse wasn't going to help. "I'm sorry for that snide remark, Tessa."

"I understand. This is a difficult time, and you have a lot on your mind." Tessa forced a smile. "So don't worry about snapping at me, Daniel. I can handle it."

"Thanks," Daniel mumbled. He turned and started down the hall. Just before entering his mother's room, he paused. *Tessa is good friends with Melody. Maybe she'll tell me if Mother is right, and if so, why she is so upset about something that has nothing to do with her.*

"Thanks for coming so quickly," Melody greeted Dave and Lydia. "I really appreciate your taking the time to talk with me."

"That's what we're here for," Pastor Dave said while Lydia gave Melody a warm hug. "I'm just glad we had a free evening for a change!"

Lydia shared a quick grin with her husband. "Yes, that was a happy *coincidence*, wasn't it?"

Melody stepped back. "Are you saying God may have arranged your schedule to fit my needs?"

Lydia's smile felt like a benediction. "And why wouldn't he? He loves you very much, Melody."

"Oh." Melody felt flustered, undeserving. "Well, I'm glad you're here, anyway." She turned toward the kitchen. "Would you like coffee?"

Pastor Dave shook his head. "No thanks. Coffee after supper keeps this old guy awake at night."

"Me, too, I'm afraid." Lydia shrugged. "But you go ahead if you'd like, Melody. We don't need anything."

"Then let's sit in here, shall we?" Melody sat in her usual spot on the couch; Dave and Lydia sat beside her, questions in their eyes.

"I'm not sure where to start," Melody said. "I just know I need help sorting things out."

"Start wherever you want, Melody." Lydia patted her knee. "Take your time. We're in no hurry."

Melody took a deep breath and exhaled forcefully. "It's about Rose Martens. I know you've gotten to know her in the last few weeks. She *doesn't* have plenty of time."

She paused, fighting the sudden pressure of unshed tears. Dave and Lydia said nothing, but when Melody glanced at them, compassion shone from their faces. She gnawed on the inside of her lower lip as she tried to find the right words.

"She told me some things about her son that must have been a real burden to her." She gulped air and swallowed hard. "She asked me to pray for him."

Her pastor frowned in puzzlement. "And why is that a problem? Are you unable to pray for him?"

"I'm sorry, I'm not making sense." She pressed her fingers against her eyes. "What Rose told me was that Daniel's wife and unborn child were killed in a head-on collision twelve years ago." She stopped, unable to face the horrific images once again flashing in her mind.

"And …?" Lydia encouraged.

Melody turned to her, anguish releasing the tears. "My husband's parents were in the other car. They were killed that night, too."

"Oh, Melody." Lydia's arms pulled Melody close. "And your life was changed forever," she finished for her.

Melody pulled back and wiped her face on the backs of her hands. "I just can't stop the 'what-ifs' raging through my mind. What if Mom and Dad Jamison hadn't been killed? What if we'd stayed in Saskatoon until the kids were through high school? What if Will hadn't gotten into trouble? Would Tom still be alive? Would I have been spared all this heartache?" She leaned back and appealed to the ceiling. "Why? Why did all this have to happen?"

Dave scooted forward until his eyes met hers. "Melody, I believe that our Lord would rather have his children yell and scream at him than ignore him. He wants to bear even your deepest sorrows. He longs to hear your heart's cries. So I must ask: have you yelled at God yet?"

What a strange question! Melody tilted her head. "Umm, yes, I guess I did."

"Did he respond?"

Melody lowered her head, remembering. "Yes, he did. It felt as if he asked me if I loved him, and if I loved Rose." She looked at her pastor. "I think I know where you're going with this."

"And where is that, Melody?" Dave's voice was gentle.

"To trust him even though I cannot understand. Right?"

Now he smiled. "Gold star for you, dear lady! One more question: have you prayed for Daniel yet?"

Melody pursed her lips. "Yes. I have to keep my promise to Rose."

Lydia wiped a tear from Melody's face. "May I say something, Melody?"

"Of course!"

"You know the verse Romans 8:28, don't you?"

Dave and Lydia quoted together, "And we know that in all things God works for the good of those who love him, who have been called according to his purpose."

Lydia squeezed Melody's hand. "I hope and pray that you will cling to that truth, Melody. We may never understand the hows and whys, but we can know without a shadow of a doubt that he is working in every circumstance. As you keep your promise to pray for Daniel, you may be surprised at what our Lord does in both your hearts. Now may I pray for you?"

"Yes. Please do."

"Tessa, may I have a word with you?"

It was nearly ten, and Rose was asleep, pain-numbing drugs dripping into her veins. Tessa made a notation on the chart and set it down.

"Of course, shall we go into the living room?"

She sat on the edge of the easy chair while Daniel sank onto the couch. Tessa clasped her hands together and looked at Daniel, a question in her gaze.

Daniel cleared his throat twice. He'd thought this would be easier, but now he wasn't sure what to say.

"Uh, Tessa," he said, "you're close to our neighbor Melody, aren't you?"

Tessa looked wary. "Yes, I am. Why do you ask?"

Daniel rubbed the back of his neck and frowned. "Well, my mother seems to think Melody is upset with her for some reason, and it's causing her a great deal of distress. She asked me to find out what the problem is." *And fix it,* he finished silently.

"Just what are you asking of me?" Tessa's scowl matched his own.

Daniel reared back. *Whoa! She obviously knows something, and it's not good.* "I hoped you could tell me if Melody *is* angry with Mother, and if so, why."

He watched various emotions play across Tessa's face. She seemed to reach a decision as she pinched the bridge of her nose between her thumb and middle finger.

"Okay." She sighed. "I can tell you this much—Melody is *not* upset with your mother."

"Then why did she run out of here the other day? And why hasn't she been back?"

Tessa looked out the picture window toward the yellow house across the street. When she turned back to Daniel, her expression was stony.

"Melody would never avoid your mother. It's hurting her to stay away, especially now." She took a deep breath and exhaled through pursed lips. "You're the one she's avoiding, Daniel."

Daniel stood abruptly. "What did I do? I haven't even been around until last night!" The back of his neck throbbed, and he rubbed it reflexively.

Tessa glanced around the room as though seeking an escape. She opened her mouth and closed it again. Her shoulders drooped, and she shifted back in the chair.

"I really think you should have talked to Melody about this," she said. She gazed out the window again. "But I guess I can spare her that particular hardship—she's hurting too much already."

What? He sat again, confusion numbing his brain. "Please go on," he said through stiff lips.

"Fine." Tessa met his eyes again, and hers seemed to be ablaze. "Rose told her about your accident, Daniel. It was the details—the place and time—that are tormenting Melody."

Daniel knew his face showed his inner turmoil. Grief, anger, and confusion battled for prominence. He closed his eyes as images of that terrible night assaulted him. He groaned. "Why would that impact *her* so much?"

Tessa waited until his eyes reopened, then she glared at him. "What was the last name of the couple in the other car?"

Huh? Bewilderment evicted the painful memories. *The other car? I never even saw them.* "I–I don't know," he admitted.

Tessa sighed, her face softening. "It was Jamison, Daniel. They were Melody's husband's parents."

Daniel felt his heart rip open, a new wound over so many old ones. "Oh" was all he could say. Guilt joined his grief, a caustic mixture. He felt as if his heart would burst into flame from the searing pain.

"So what am I supposed to do now? What should I tell Mother?"

Tessa shook her head, tears in her eyes. "I don't know, Daniel. But I will tell you this: Melody is praying for you."

Oh, God.

22

Will lay on his bed, one arm across his forehead, staring at the ceiling. The weariness in his body seemed to press him into the bedding, but his mind refused to settle down.

"Redemption. Eli said it's all about love and redemption. He made it sound as though Jesus would have died just for me. I wish I could believe that. Then maybe I'd be more like Eli. He really seems to have it together. Not like me. Maybe I'm really not good enough. I get mad too often; lying comes so easy; I mess up over and over. Not exactly love material."

"You're right about that." A raspy whisper seemed to float in the night air. "You'll never be good enough, and you might as well accept that."

"Who's there?" Will sat up, instantly alert. No one answered. He lay down again, pulse racing. Was it true?

"Am I hopeless? Or is Eli right? Did Jesus really die for me?" He covered his eyes with one hand. "God, if what Eli said is true, help me understand."

Melody woke Wednesday morning to bright sunshine squeezing ribbons of light through her window blinds. She sat up and stretched, lifting her hands high above her head. After the stress of the last few days she'd expected to toss and turn all night, but she'd slept well. She rubbed the sleep from her eyes and smiled.

"Thank you, Lord, for this new day." She paused and took a deep breath. "And thank you for that wonderful, restful sleep."

She continued praying as she prepared for the day. She prayed for her family and her friends. She prayed for Nila and even for Nick. She prayed for Rose and for Daniel.

As she prayed, her heart felt cleaner, lighter. *Much better,* she mused. Aloud she quoted, "You are good, oh Lord, and what you do is good. Help me to keep remembering that, in Jesus' name."

After a quick cup of coffee, Melody headed out to her little garden, basket in hand. Kneeling in the soft dirt, she plucked fragrant green beans from their bushy plants.

"These are going to taste so good!" The large basket filled quickly. "Fresh vegetables from my own garden—I love this."

As she continued picking a thought came to her. *Give some to Daniel.* Her hands stilled as she wondered at that. "Was that you, God, or just my imagination tricking me?"

Her basket was nearly full, so she finished the row she was on and headed into the house.

"Well, I guess it couldn't hurt to share these with my neighbor. I wish Rose could have some." Pressure ached behind her eyes. "Rose. I need to see her. She must be wondering why I didn't come over yesterday."

She found her colander tucked under some bowls and placed it in the sink. As she was dumping the beans into the colander, the cell phone on her hip buzzed. She nearly dropped the basket but caught it against the edge of the sink.

Melody fumbled for her phone and opened it as it buzzed the third time. "Hello?"

"Uh, hi, Melody." Nila's voice was quiet, as usual, but there was something different about it.

"Good morning, Nila," Melody spoke as though to a small child. "How are you?"

"I–I'm good. Real good." There was a pause. I … umm … Melody …" Another pause.

Melody waited.

"M–Melody," Nila finally said, "I've been reading the book you give me. You know, the Bible." Another pause. "I really like it."

"I'm so glad!" Melody smiled into the phone.

"Well, I–I need to ask you about some stuff. Could you come here?"

Maybe she could come to my house instead. Then I wouldn't risk running into Nick. But before she could open her mouth, something stopped her.

"Don't ask that of her. Go to her." The voice was silent but clear.

"Of course, Nila, I would love to help you any way I can. When do you want me to come over?"

"Uh … I'll be here all day. So any time is good."

Melody did a quick review of her plans for the day. She needed to go visit Rose, and she'd wanted to do that in the morning. Tessa said Rose was usually fairly alert mid-mornings. And she didn't want to rush Nila—or be at her house when Nick got home.

"Okay, Nila, I'll come over right after lunch, if that's good for you."

Nila's voice sounded almost carefree. "Thank you, Melody! I'll see you then."

The warmth in his tent finally roused Will. He stretched leisurely and glanced at his watch: eight-thirty! "Wow! I really slept in. Hope there's still some breakfast and lunch makings left. Better get down there."

When he arrived at the mess tent, a few other crew members who'd stayed behind were making lunches or just sitting and talking. Will found some pancake batter, a package with a few slices of bacon, and a carton of eggs. He'd just starting cooking when he heard Eli's friendly voice getting closer with each word.

"Morning, rookie! Thought I might have to throw some water on you to wake you up."

Will refused to look up until he nearly fell forward from the clap on his back.

"Hey, watch it!" he flared.

Eli stepped back, chuckling. "Sounds like somebody hasn't had his coffee yet."

Will scraped his breakfast onto a waiting plate. "Sorry." He turned and walked past Eli without meeting his eyes.

He downed half his plate-full before he raised his head. Eli still stood by the grill, head tilted as he peered at his friend. Will turned his attention to his food again, but out of the corner of his eye he saw Eli lower his eyes and walk out of the tent.

A stab of guilt pierced Will, sparking more anger. "Why does he have to be so chummy? Can't he see I need some space?"

His appetite gone, Will pushed the half-full plate to one side. He didn't enjoy feeling guilty, and Eli had a way of making him feel ashamed. "All that talk about redemption—I'm okay just the way I am. I don't need that."

The look on Eli's face haunted him, though. He tried to block it, but he knew he'd hurt his friend. "Okay, I'll tell him I need more space and time to think about everything he said. That should fix it."

But when he went looking for Eli, he wasn't anywhere in camp.

"Maybe he's gone for a hike. Actually, that sounds like a good idea. Maybe a walk will clear my head."

He went back to the mess tent, put together a snack, and filled his water bottle. Shoving them into his backpack, he headed up the winding logging road.

As he walked, he let his mind wander. He thought about the farm and all the good times he'd enjoyed there, even the chores he'd grumbled about. But that brought memories of fights with his dad. His dad, now dead. Will discarded that mental file and tried to picture the car he would buy when this job was done. But for some reason, his dream sports car became the dented beater his parents had given him when he'd gotten his license and their proud smiles when they'd handed him the keys. Too bad he'd totaled it after a bush party that same year. At least they'd believed him when he said he'd swerved to miss a deer.

"Stop it! "

But the memories kept coming, each one heaping on more feelings of shame. He stumbled on a loose rock and nearly fell.

"Unh," he groaned. "Man, I can't even walk today. What is wrong with me?"

You're a mess, his conscience answered. *You're not making it on your own, no matter what you claim.*

"No," he retorted. "I'm not dealing with that—not today."

He increased his pace and hummed loudly, trying to drown out the roaring in his head. Reclaiming the middle of the road, he pushed on. The roaring refused to be drowned out, though, and it even seemed to shake the ground.

Will rounded a sharp bend and froze. That roaring was coming from the logging truck racing toward him! A long blast from the air horn immobilized him in shock until something shoved him out of the way just as the loaded truck thundered by.

Crouched against the bank, battered by the truck's slipstream, he gasped. "That was close—too close!"

"Good morning, Bobbie!." Melody greeted her neighbor as they walked down their steps toward the street. "Are you going to visit Rose?"

"Yup. Mornin' to you, too." Bobbie carried a towel-wrapped pot away from her body. "Thought Rosie might be able to sip some of this here chicken soup."

"What a good idea. That's a lovely thing to do, Bobbie."

Bobbie shook her head. "Naw. It ain't much, but I want to do *something*. She's goin' downhill fast, and even though she's ready to go, I'm not nearly ready to say goodbye just yet."

Melody moved closer and patted Bobbie's broad back. "I know. I feel the same way."

Bobbie pointed with her chin towards Daniel's truck. "Glad to see her Danny-boy got home. Sure hope his sister makes it on time."

Melody didn't want to talk about Daniel. "You told me, but I can't remember. Where is Hannah working?"

"Way over in Africa," Bobbie said. "She teaches at a boarding school. Summertime like this, she and her hubby travel around to clinics. He's a doc and she shows moms how to take care of their kids with the little they got. Rosie's awfully proud of her Hannah."

"I hope I get to meet her," Melody said. "She sounds like she takes after her mother."

"Yup, pretty much."

They had reached the porch of Rose's house, so Bobbie rapped lightly on the door. Melody felt a quiver in her stomach like a thousand tiny butterflies as her heart began to race.

Valerie opened the door, and Melody breathed deeply again.

"Is Rose up to a visit this morning?" she asked.

The nurse moved back and motioned for them to enter. "I think she'd be happy to see you both." Her mouth smiled, but her eyes remained solemn. "You have to understand that she's sleeping much of the time now."

"Yeah, we know." Bobbie held out the steaming, covered pot. "Brought some chicken soup, thought Rosie might be able to drink a little. And I doubt her boy is eating like he should."

Valerie's smile warmed. "Thank you, Bobbie. I know they will both appreciate this." She took the towel-wrapped pot. "I'll just put this in the kitchen for now. You two can go on in. If Rose is sleeping, you can still talk. She seems to appreciate knowing someone is in the room."

Bobbie led the way down the hall with Melody following a few steps behind.

"Hey, Daniel," Bobbie stage-whispered to the man sitting beside Rose's bed. "Good to see you again. Glad you made it home."

Melody stopped in the doorway. *Oh no, those butterflies are migrating to my throat!*

Daniel looked up, the beginning of a smile on his face. Then his eyes met Melody's frantic ones, and a scowl replaced the smile as he looked away.

"Good morning," he muttered. "I'll go get another chair."

He headed toward Melody, but she quickly moved out of the doorway, bumping her elbow on the wall in her haste.

"Go on in," Daniel called over his shoulder. "Mother will be glad to see you both."

Melody obeyed but stood against the far wall, rubbing her elbow, while Bobbie settled in the chair Daniel just vacated.

Only a moment later Daniel returned, carrying a kitchen chair. "Here." He barely glanced at Melody as he set it in front of her. "I've got some errands to take care of." And he left.

Rose was sleeping, so Bobbie and Melody visited quietly across her still form. Melody told her neighbor about her conversations with Nila.

"She phoned me this morning," Melody said. "She's been reading the Bible I gave her and wants to ask me some questions." She paused, remembering the lilt in Nila's voice. "She sounded happier than I've ever heard her."

Rose's eyelids fluttered, catching their attention. "Rosie," Bobbie's voice was gentle. "It's Bobbie and Melody here, honey."

Rose opened her eyes and looked at Bobbie and then Melody. The deep lines on her face smoothed as her mouth lifted. "Dear ones," she said. Melody had to lean forward to hear her soft voice. "Bless you." Her eyes closed again.

Valerie walked into the room and felt for Rose's pulse. She checked the IV bag and line, nodded at the two visitors, and turned to go.

"Wait, Val." Bobbie held up her hand. Valerie turned, and Bobbie whispered, "Do you know, is Rosie's girl gonna make it?"

The nurse shrugged her shoulders. "I hope she gets here in time. Daniel said she's flying out Friday to arrive Saturday. He said the flight takes twenty-six hours and crosses nine time zones."

"Oh," Melody said. "That is a long trip. She's going to be awfully jet-lagged, isn't she?"

Valerie just nodded once and left the room.

Melody's mind was racing, and its restlessness compelled her to pace the small room. She ignored Bobbie's questioning look until the small picture on Rose's dresser caught her eye. She picked up the silver-framed photo and felt a strange twist somewhere near her heart.

"This is Angela with Daniel, isn't it?"

"Yup."

Melody examined this memento of long-ago love. Angela was beautiful, there was no denying that. Her long, golden hair was braided and wrapped around her head like a crown. She had bright blue eyes with dark lashes that seemed to need no makeup for enhancement. Her radiant smile reached out to share her joy.

Melody felt her spirits sag, but she forced herself to take in Daniel's appearance, too. She hardly recognized him, he looked so happy. No scowl, no frown lines, and of course no streaks of gray in his dark hair. A spasm of empathy shuddered through her.

"Good-lookin' couple, weren't they?" Bobbie said quietly.

Melody replaced the photo, her eyes still on the happy faces. "Yes, they were. No wonder Daniel seems so driven and miserable. He lost so much. And now …" She turned toward Rose.

Bobbie's face mirrored her sorrow. "Yeah." She swiped at her eyes with a wadded-up tissue.

"Bobbie, I have an idea," Melody said. "Do you think Daniel and Hannah would mind if I made some meals for them?"

Bobbie's face lit up. "Great idea, Kiddo! I could do that, too. Nothing fancy, mind you, but I can whip up a mean batcha spaghetti sauce."

"We could take turns, if you'd like. Do you think we should ask Daniel first?"

"Why? A body's gotta eat, and I don't imagine Daniel or his sister are gonna feel like cooking."

Melody's stomach rumbled, and she glanced at her watch. "Oh dear, it's noon already! I promised Nila I'd come over right after lunch. I'd better get going."

"I think I'll stay here a bit longer." Bobbie's gaze rested on the sleeping Rose. "While I can."

"Okay, Bobbie." Melody turned to go. "I was planning to make meat loaf, scalloped potatoes and fresh green beans for supper. That's an easy meal to share. You can tell Valerie I'll bring some over around five-thirty."

"Sounds good. I'll cover tomorrow." She looked up at Melody. "Hope your visit with kid from the gray house goes okay."

Melody paused in the doorway. "Thanks. You know, I really don't like going there. It feels as though I'm walking into a snake's pit, but as long as I remember God is with me, I guess I can do it." She sighed, eyes downcast. "I wish I could have heard Rose pray for me, though."

෴ ෴ ෴

Will leaned on his shovel and wiped the sweat from his face. Gnats and flies buzzed around him; no amount of spray deterred them on hot days like this.

"Think of their buzzing as music," Eli had advised that first week. "That way they won't drive you crazy."

Good advice, if you can do it. He swatted at one part of the swarm, put his head down and resumed planting. He hadn't slept well, and now he was struggling to find his rhythm. He looked back down the row of freshly-planted seedlings.

Rats! I messed up on ... five, maybe six. I'll have to go back and fix them.

He glanced around. The crew members he could see were working well ahead of his pace. He would be the last one to finish—again.

Maybe Eli...No! I don't want or need his help.

He hadn't run into Eli yesterday on his hike, but after that truck nearly ran over him, he'd only ventured another mile or two before turning back. He'd had a close call, but he was still here. He could take care of himself.

I don't need anybody, he told himself. He hummed a tuneless melody to drown out the incessant buzzing as he marched back down the row to fix his crooked seedlings.

23

Nila opened the door before Melody could knock. "Thank you for coming," she said. "I made coffee. Come on in, and I'll get it."

"That sounds good. Thanks." Melody crossed the room to the couch and sat at the end nearest the door. She could hear Nila in the kitchen, so she looked around the small living room. No flowers this time. *I hope that doesn't mean he's back to "normal."*

Nila came back into the room carrying two coffee cups. "You like yours black, right? Here you go."

"Thank you, Nila." Melody accepted the offered cup and stiffened. Nila's cast-free forearms bore yellowing bruises, four in a row and one beneath. *Not again!*

Nila followed Melody's gaze and flushed. "I–It's nothing. I bumped into … some stuff the other day."

"Oh, honey," Melody breathed. *Should I pursue this, Lord? Help me.*

But Nila pulled her sleeves down as she sat at the opposite end of the couch. She set down her coffee cup and pulled out of her pocket the copy of The Message New Testament that Melody had given her.

"I've been reading this," she said softly, "and I love it. One of my foster homes had a Holy Bible, but it was really confusing—too many strange words. But this one talks right to me."

She looked at Melody with shining eyes. "I really like Jesus! He's so smart. I don't understand lots of the things he says, but you just know he's really smart. He's strong, too, and isn't afraid of anybody." She looked down at her lap. "And he's kind. He's always kind. I like that a lot."

"Yes, you're right, Jesus is all those things." Melody's heart pulsed with sympathy and joy.

"But," Nila continued, eyes still downcast, "I don't like what's coming next."

"What do you mean?"

Nila scooted closer to Melody and opened her Bible to a bookmark made from a torn piece of paper. "Look. Right here. You can tell something bad is going to happen."

It marked the middle of Matthew 27, and Nila pointed to the scene in the Garden of Gethsemane.

"Look at the way he's talking to his father." She looked at Melody, eyes haunted. "He's going to die, isn't he?" Her mouth turned down, and she set the book in her lap and rubbed her arms. "I don't want him to die."

Melody couldn't help herself. She scooted even closer and put one arm around Nila's slender shoulders, trying to ignore the slight flinch.

"Keep reading, honey."

"Why? It's going to be bad."

Melody took a deep breath. *Help me, Jesus!* "Yes, Nila, you're right. Jesus did die. But he did it for a very good reason, and he didn't stay dead."

Nila pulled out of Melody's embrace and stared at her. "What do you mean? What was the reason? And how ...?"

"It was planned from the beginning of time, honey. Jesus came from heaven to live and die, even though he never did anything wrong, to pay the price for everything we have ever done wrong." She paused. "Does that make sense to you?"

Nila twisted her lips. "Umm ... I guess so. But why?"

Melody reached for the Bible. "May I?" At Nila's nod, she took it and found John 3:16. Pointing to the verse, she held the book in front of Nila. "Read this."

Nila looked down at the words, her brow knotted. As she continued reading aloud to the end of the section, her face smoothed out until a smile broke through.

This is how much God loved the world: He gave his Son, his one and only Son. And this is why: so that no one need be destroyed; by believing in him, anyone can have a whole and lasting life. God didn't go to all the trouble of sending his Son merely to point an accusing finger, telling the world how bad it was. He came to help, to put the world right again. Anyone who trusts in him is acquitted; anyone who refuses to trust him has long since been under the death sentence without knowing it. And why? Because of that person's failure to believe in the one-of-a-kind Son of God when introduced to him.

"Oh!" Nila sighed. "That's beautiful!" She beamed at Melody. "Jesus is God's Son, isn't he?"

Melody nodded. "Yes, you're right."

Then Nila's smile disappeared. "I want to read to the end of this part." She flipped back to Matthew. "But I don't think I can do it when I'm by myself." She lifted her face to meet Melody's eyes, and she begged, "Would you stay here with me while I read it? I just hate it when people get hurt."

Melody glanced at her watch. It was only one-thirty—lots of time before Nick would return. *I hate that, too,* she agreed silently. *Protect us both, Lord God.*

Settling back against the arm of the couch, Melody reassured her hostess, "I'll stay as long as you want."

Nila managed a wobbly smile. "Thank you," she said and lowered her eyes to the book in her lap.

Melody prayed silently as she watched Nila read. The young woman clutched the Bible, her knuckles turning white as her face began to crumple.

"Oh, no," she whimpered, tears leaking from her eyes. She continued reading, and her tears became a steady stream. "No, Jesus, don't let them do that!"

Hear her heart, dear God, Melody prayed. *Help her understand.*

Nila was sobbing now. She dropped the book to her lap and covered her face with her hands.

I wonder if she remembers I'm here. Do I dare put my arm around her?

"I'm sorry, Jesus. I'm so sorry!" Nila sobbed into her hands, rocking back and forth.

Dear Jesus, Melody marveled, *have I ever grieved over your suffering the way Nila is right now?*

She could feel wetness on her own cheeks as she gently touched Nila's shoulder and whispered, "Keep reading, Nila. You'll like the ending, I promise."

Nila raised drenched eyes to hers. "How can that be? They're *killing* him!"

Now Melody scooted over and stroked Nila's back tenderly. "That was part of the plan, remember? Jesus paid for our sins with his own blood. But Nila," she picked up the Bible and placed it in Nila's hand again, "that's *not* the end. Keep going."

Nila's breath shuddered out as she lowered her eyes to the open page. Melody watched, seeing the crucifixion, burial, and resurrection through Nila's body language. *It has never been this real to me, Lord Jesus. All the times I heard or read about your death, I never experienced it the way Nila is right now.*

After a few minutes, Nila raised her face again, but now her eyes sparkled and her whole face radiated wonder.

"You were right, Melody! Jesus came back to life!" She sagged back against the couch, some of the sparkle gone. "But he went through an awful lot for me."

Daniel heard Valerie go to the front door and greet someone warmly, but he couldn't hear who it was. He was holding the glass so his mother could sip her meager meal through a straw, watching closely to ensure she didn't choke. Rose must have heard Valerie, too, because she pushed the straw out of her mouth with her tongue and raised her eyebrows at him.

"Who?" she asked faintly but clearly.

"I don't know. Valerie is dealing with whoever it is. Here, Mama, you need to drink some more." He held the straw close to her mouth, but she avoided it.

"Go ... see," she insisted.

Daniel sighed and set the glass on the bedside table. "Okay, I'll check it out."

As soon as he stepped into the hallway, an enticing assortment of flavors tickled his nostrils, creating an immediate rumbling response from his stomach.

Could it be ...?

Valerie was actually smiling when he got to the kitchen. She gestured to a large box on the counter. "Your neighbor brought supper," she said. "Smells good, doesn't it?"

Daniel was salivating now. The sturdy BC Apples box seemed to carry several dishes, but a towel covered them. He reached for the towel, asking, "Bobbie?"

"Nope. Melody." Daniel could swear the normally-stern nurse was on the verge of chuckling.

He pulled his hand back and straightened. His brow furrowed. "Why? Why did she bring food?"

Valerie's eyes were definitely twinkling. "Melody and Bobbie discussed this when they were here earlier. They're going to take turns bringing supper over for you and for your sister when she arrives."

She stepped close to the box and pulled the towel off with a flourish. "Pretty nice neighbor, eh?"

Daniel couldn't resist. His stomach rumbled noisily as he lifted the lid off the closest casserole. Three small meat loaves were nestled side by side in the shallow dish. *Oh man, my favorite!* He licked his lips as he lifted the second lid. Creamy scalloped potatoes steamed their fragrance up to his face. More quickly now he checked the remaining dishes: fresh green beans, a fruit salad, and finally, a still-warm apple pie.

All my favorites! When's the last time anyone made me my favorite meal? Christmas before last? How did Melody know? And why …?

His stomach growled demandingly. *When did I last eat? I can't remember. Maybe breakfast?*

Guilt interrupted. *Mother! She's still waiting for the rest of her drink.* He looked again at the tempting array waiting for him. *Hmm, I wonder if Mama could swallow some potatoes if they're mashed thoroughly?*

He hurried back to Rose's room, a small bowl of steaming potatoes in his hand.

"Hey, Mama, look what Melody brought over."

Rose looked more alert, as though the wonderful smells had revived her will to live. "It smells delicious, Danny. What is it?"

He rattled off the array of dishes, enjoying the smile that softened the lines on his mother's face.

"Your favorites," she murmured.

"Yes. Did you tell her?" he said.

She shook her head no, and he held out the small bowl. "Anyway, I mashed up some of the scalloped potatoes. Would you like to try some?"

"Yes, please!" She looked up at him. "And you'll be sure to thank Melody, won't you?"

Daniel extended the spoon with a tiny amount of potatoes without answering. "Here you go, Mama. Be careful."

She accepted the offering and leaned back against the pillows, eyes closed, and swallowed—and gagged.

Daniel dropped the bowl onto his lap, grabbed a water bottle from the nightstand, and held the straw to her lips. She took a sip, swallowed again, and smiled.

"Thank you, dear," she whispered. "I guess ... I'll have to stick ... to liquid meals." She touched one finger to her lips. "But I'll recall ... that tasty bite ... the rest of my life."

Daniel felt a surge of anger rising like bile in his throat. *I hate this! Enough already!* He sagged in defeat. *She keeps saying she's ready to go. But why does it have to hurt so much?*

He retrieved the nearly-empty glass of meal replacement and offered it to his mother. "Here, Mama, try to finish this. I'm sorry about the potatoes."

"I enjoyed them, Danny. You're a good son." She accepted the straw, sipped a tiny amount and leaned back against her pillows, eyes closed.

"Go and eat, Son," she said quietly. "I'll rest now. But we'll talk ... later."

24

Melody looked down at her nearly-untouched plate. She'd eaten a few bites, but she couldn't say if they tasted good or not. "My heart is so full there's no room in my stomach, I guess. I hope Daniel enjoyed his meal."

She glanced in the direction of the blue house and waited for the familiar boiling emotions at the thought of Rose's son. Instead, she felt a bubbling of joy welling up until she lifted her hands and face upward.

"Thank you, Lord Jesus, for the miracles you worked today, for letting me watch the beauty of Nila's new faith in you, and for giving me peace in serving Daniel. You are awesome, dear God, and I praise you with my whole heart, the heart you are making whole."

Melody felt something stir inside her, pushing her away from the table and in search of a writing tablet. She hadn't written any poetry since her kids were small and she'd made up silly rhymes to entertain them.

"But now I need to write. I don't know why, but I need to get these feelings on paper."

She quickly located a new pad of paper and returned to the table, shoving her plate to one side.

"God, if this is from you, help me, please." She took a deep breath and began writing:

The enemy had bound me

With chains of doubt and fear,
Until your word spoke to my heart,
Its message true and clear.
I longed to feel the freedom
That only you can give.
I needed, Lord, to know you,
I need your strength to live.

Melody sat back and reread the words. "Yes, that's it. That's what you've been working in me, isn't it, God."

Restless now, she paced around the table until more words settled into lines.

You touched my eyes, they opened.
I saw the pain outside.
The battle raged around me.
I saw kingdoms collide.
But when I fell in terror,
You set me on my feet.
You're teaching me to listen
To follow where you lead.

"Thank you, Jesus," she breathed at last. She got up from the table and went into the living room to sprawl on the couch, feeling completely spent.

Daniel set his fork down and looked down at his empty plate. "That was really good. I didn't think I could eat, let alone an entire plate-full, but it tasted as good as it smelled—even better."

Leaning back, he patted his satisfied stomach. "Melody is a great cook, but I don't understand why she'd do this for me. Maybe Mama asked her to. Anyway, I guess I'll have to thank her. "

He recalled his mother's words as she'd sent him to eat, and a trickle of disquiet dampened his contentment. *I wonder what she wants to talk to me about.*

Rose appeared to be sleeping when Daniel sat in the bedside chair, but after a moment she looked straight at him. She smiled gently.

"How was your supper?"

He answered her with a smile of his own. "Really good. And yes, I'll thank Melody." He reached for her trembling hand and enfolded it between his strong fingers.

"You wanted to talk to me about something, Mama?"

Rose struggled to sit more upright, and Daniel adjusted her pillows to support her.

"Yes, Danny, and thank you." Her voice sounded surprisingly strong. "You're not going to like this, but hear me out."

He stiffened, rebellion ready to flare, but he damped it down. "Go ahead, Mama. I'm listening."

"I know this is hard for you, my son." Rose spoke softly but clearly. "But I am quite ready to leave this tired old body for my new one in paradise."

She reached over and traced the frown lines on his forehead. "Listen, my dear. I feel the wall you have built around your heart. I know you blame God for your misery, almost as much as you blame yourself."

Her hand fell back onto the bed, and her voice wavered. "God loves you, Danny. He always has and always will. But I think you have a distorted picture of God because of your father."

Daniel had to concede. "Perhaps," he grumbled. "But Mama, you're tired. This doesn't matter. You need to rest." He flexed to stand.

"Sit!" Rose's voice rang clearly once more. "This *does* matter—a great deal. This is my request of you, Daniel Martens: you need to let God's love melt those walls around your heart." She looked him until his eyes reluctantly met hers. "Will you do that for me?"

Frustration battled with devotion, and Daniel knew his face showed his turbulent emotions. "I guess I can try. But how do I do that, Mama?" he asked through tight lips.

"You can start by reading his word." Rose motioned to her Bible beside her. "Would you read to me now, Son?"

"All right, Mama." Daniel breathed deliberately in an effort to calm himself as he picked up the book. "Any particular place?"

"Ephesians chapter 3. My prayer for you is there."

Curious, Daniel found the place and began to read aloud with a growing sense of wonder. *Oh, Mama.* He could almost hear her voice echoing his own. When he finished the chapter, he looked up. His mother lay still.

Terribly still.

Melody relaxed in a warm, sunlit garden beside a clear stream. Her young children played beside her on the soft, green lawn …

The doorbell pealed, scattering the sweet scene. Melody sat up, rubbed her eyes, and tottered to the door.

"Hey, Tessa, come on in." Melody opened the door wide. "I didn't hear your car. I guess I dozed off."

She looked more closely at her friend standing immobile on the step. Tessa's face was drawn and her eyes dry but red-rimmed.

"What's the matter?" Fully awake now, Melody grabbed Tessa's arm and pulled her inside. "What happened?"

Tessa allowed herself to be led to the comfy couch, and she sank onto it with a small groan. "It's Rose," she finally said.

"Is she …?" Melody couldn't say it.

Tessa shook her bowed head. "No, Mel, she's still with us, sort of. Daniel phoned me, and I called her doctor who confirmed what I thought. She's slipping into a coma, Mel." Tessa looked at her friend, her eyes no longer dry. "He said her time is short—a day or two at the most."

Melody frowned as she calculated. "What's today, Wednesday? Daniel's sister isn't arriving until Saturday. Oh, God," she whispered, "let Hannah get here in time to say goodbye."

"Amen," Tessa agreed. She shifted on the couch to face Melody. "I phoned Pastor Dave, and he's on his way. Is there anyone else who needs to know right now?"

"Bobbie!" Melody said. "She'll definitely want to know."

Just then a blur of movement outside caught her attention. She stood to see what was happening.

"Oh, there goes Bobbie now. Daniel must have phoned her." Melody nibbled her lower lip. "Poor Bobbie. She and Rose have been close friends for several years. This is going to be awfully hard on her."

She sank onto the couch again. "And poor Daniel. My heart aches for him."

Tessa's eyes widened. "Really? Then God's been working on you, hasn't he?"

Melody smiled wanly. "He sure has. Daniel still makes me feel … I don't know … strange and bothered, but my bitterness toward him seems to be disappearing."

She shook her head at Tessa's amused expression. "I know what you're thinking, but it's not like that," she protested. "You know how upset I was when I found out he was responsible for Mom and Dad Jamison's deaths … well, as responsible as a person can be for a terrible accident."

"I'm not likely to forget that any time soon," Tessa responded. "You really had me worried."

"So God has been working in me, because when I made supper for Daniel tonight—Bobbie and I are taking turns with that—it was as if my service set me free from those terrible emotions."

Now Tessa smiled. "That's great, Mel. Love does cover a multitude of sins. And I mean that in the best possible way."

She leaned toward the coffee table and picked up Melody's tablet. "What's this?"

"Oh, it's just a poem that came to me."

"I didn't know you wrote poetry," Tessa said. She read it silently and then aloud. "This is really good, Mel. In fact, when I read it, I think it must be a song."

Melody felt her face warm. "I'm not a poet, and I'm sure that's not worthy of becoming a song."

Tessa put the paper on her lap. "Well, do you mind if I play with it a bit? I'd love to put it to music if I can."

Melody smiled faintly. "Okay, Tessa-the-musician. Give it a try. Knock yourself out."

She looked toward the blue house visible from the picture window. "But right now would you pray with me, Tess? I promised Rose I'd keep praying for Daniel, and he's probably never needed it as much as he does now."

The two friends prayed for Daniel, for Rose, and for a miracle. "Somehow, Lord God, let Hannah arrive before you take Rose home. Work out all the details, in Jesus' name."

After several minutes of prayer, the two friends sat silently, their heads still bowed. The sound of car doors opening and closing alerted them, and both jumped up and looked out the window.

"Oh, good, there's Pastor Dave and Lydia," Melody said.

She watched as the door of Rose's house opened. Daniel stood stiffly and then stepped back to let them enter. He stood in the open doorway for a moment, his head hung low and his shoulders stooped. Then the door closed again.

Tessa sighed. "He looks broken."

"He looks like he needs a hug." Melody clapped her hand over her mouth, but it was too late. She glanced at Tessa.

Tessa's grin was weak, but her eyes danced. "I think I know just the person for that."

Will could hardly contain his excitement. Ever since he'd found out their final block necessitated helicopter transport, he'd been anxious for this morning. Now the crew stood huddled in the cool air, waiting to board. The helicopter seated five besides the pilot, and Will was determined to be in the first group. He felt like jumping up and down, waving his arms in the air and yelling, "Pick me! Pick me!" With effort he stuck his hands in his jacket pockets and stood nearly still. He couldn't help doing a restrained little dance, though, hopping from one foot to the other.

"So," the pilot drawled, "we got any rookies in this bunch? Any 'copter newbies?"

Will's hand shot up. He looked around; no one else had responded.

"Alrighty then." The pilot nodded to Will. "Guess you're riding shotgun."

"Woohoo!" He couldn't hold it in, but when his crewmates looked his way, some snickering, he sobered a bit. But his grin remained and widened as he stowed his gear and climbed into the seat beside the pilot.

The flight from Vancouver to Saskatoon for his father's funeral had been his first airplane trip, and he'd loved the rush of takeoff. The rest of the flight was a blur of misery, but he'd enjoyed the sensation of flying.

Will shook off the memories and looked around. The windshield's curve made it feel as if he was barely inside at all. *Just that glass between me and the sky.* A little tickle started in the pit of his stomach. On the jumbo jet, he'd been entrenched among rows and rows of seats with only a small window beside his seatmate. This was totally different. *Awesome!*

The other four crew members were soon buckled in, and the pilot started flipping switches. As the rotor began whirling, the butterflies in Will's stomach multiplied until he thought they'd fly up his throat. *Sure hope I don't get sick. That would NOT be cool.*

He was grateful for the sound-cancelling headphones as the metal and glass beast began to roar. He twisted to look at his crewmates. Three had their eyes closed as though this was just another ride, and the other watched out her side window. No one was paying any attention to him or sharing his excitement.

Liftoff was smooth, but those butterflies in his innards moved frantically as they rose into the deep blue sky. The nose of the helicopter tilted downward as it lifted, and Will's hands gripped the side of his seat until his knuckles turned white.

"So, whaddaya think?" The pilot's voice came through Will's headphones.

Gulping back the fluttering in his throat, he grinned. "This is great!"

"Just relax and let this ol' bird carry you." The pilot looked pointedly at Will's white knuckles.

Will felt his face warm, and he flexed his fingers as he moved his hands to his lap.

A few minutes later, the pilot's voice came through the headphones again. "We're almost there, but first I want to show you all something."

Will sat up straighter, and sounds from behind him told him the others were alert, too. His hands automatically gripped the seat edge once more as the pilot maneuvered the helicopter into a slow swing. Will felt as though he swung on the end of a pendulum as they flew over an open area bordered by a sharp drop-off.

"Look down there," the pilot ordered. He pointed the nose of the helicopter at what appeared to be the edge of the world. Will's butterflies soared, lifting his breakfast perilously close to his mouth. He clamped down on his lips.

"You'll be planting that burned-out area," the pilot continued. "So stay several feet away from that cliff. In case you weren't listening to your boss's warning, I'll tell you again: don't work too close to the edge. Look down, and you'll see why."

Will looked down—he had no choice, unless he shut his eyes. First he took in the devastation left behind by the forest fire and marveled at the sharp demarcation between barrenness and lush forest. Then his eyes were drawn to the drop-off. He tasted bile.

25

Dark clouds were piling up over the city as Melody pulled a pan of ham and cheese muffins out of the oven.

"My family always devoured these. I hope Daniel likes them." She placed eight of the dozen into a cloth-lined basket and folded the cloth over the top. "Looks awfully windy out there. I'd better get these delivered before the storm hits."

Moments later Daniel opened his door to her light knock.

"Good morning, Daniel." She forced a bright smile. "I made some muffins for you. My kids always liked them, and they freeze well, and I thought maybe …"

I'm babbling, and he looks exhausted. What must he think?

"Come in, Melody." Daniel's voice was nearly monotone. "Thank you for your kindness."

Melody stepped inside and looked up at her neighbor. The shadows around his eyes and deep lines beside his mouth spoke of grief and exhaustion, a state Melody knew all too well. She had a sudden urge to reach up and smooth away those lines. Her face flamed. *Get a grip, woman!*

"Shall I take these to the kitchen?" She didn't wait for an answer, but walked in and set the basket on the kitchen counter.

Valerie came into the kitchen and nodded a greeting to Melody. "I thought I smelled some baking," she said. Her face, too, was drawn into lines of sorrow.

"Hello, Valerie. How is Rose this morning?"

"Not good. She wakes up now and them for a minute, but those minutes are becoming further and further apart." Her eyes welled up, and she hurried away.

Melody turned and nearly bumped into Daniel. "Oh, excuse me!" She quickly backstepped as her eyes met his. A frisson of emotion rippled through her. *Shared grief, that's all,* she told herself.

"Your mother is loved by so many," she murmured.

"Yes, she is." Daniel closed his eyes for a moment and then met her gaze again. "Would you like to sit with her for a while? I know she and you are very close."

Melody smiled through sudden tears. "She is precious to me. I–I don't know what I'm going to do without her."

"Yeah, me too." Daniel turned away, his shoulders drooping even more.

Melody clasped her hands together to keep them from reaching for him. "I'm so sorry, Daniel."

With his back still toward her, he mumbled, "Excuse me, please," and walked out of the room.

Feeling flustered, Melody looked around blankly for a minute. Then she took a deep breath and went down the hall to Rose's bedroom.

Her dear friend lay completely motionless except for the ever-so-slight rising and falling of her chest.

"Rose?" she called softly. "It's me, Melody."

Rose's eyelids fluttered but did not open. Melody eased herself into the chair closest to Rose's bed. Her Bible was on the nightstand, and Melody picked it up. The well-used book opened to Psalm 139.

"Lovely," Melody said. "This must be one of your favorites. It's my favorite, too." She looked at the still form on the bed. "May I read to you, Rose?"

She read quietly, more for herself than Rose, but she hoped her friend could hear the words. She read to the end of the psalm and glanced up. Daniel was sitting in the chair on the other side of the bed.

"Oh! I didn't hear you come in." Her voice was louder than she'd intended, and she put her fingers to her lips. "Sorry."

Daniel didn't smile. "I didn't mean to startle you. But please continue reading. My mother appreciates that." He gestured with his chin toward the Bible.

Melody obediently turned a few pages, but before reading more, she glanced up and asked, "Did you get any sleep last night?"

"A little." Daniel must have seen the doubt in her eyes, because he continued. "Bobbie was here with Mother all night, and she made me lie down for a while."

Melody's smile didn't reach her eyes. "Bobbie's good at caring for people. I'm glad she was here."

"She'll be back tonight and every night until... Said it's the least she can do for her friend." Daniel studied his mother's still form before meeting Melody's eyes. "I need to be with my mother, and she'd like you to read to her. Are you okay with that?"

"Y–yes, of course," Melody stammered. She flipped through several pages, found another passage and began reading. Keeping her head down, she continued to read until her voice gave out. She rasped out the last few verses of Psalm 111 and finally looked up. Daniel's head was back, his mouth slightly open, and he was snoring softly.

Poor man. Guess that "little" sleep wasn't enough.

Melody took advantage of this opportunity to study her neighbor. His dark hair was liberally sprinkled with gray at the temples. *Quite distinguished.* She let her eyes roam slowly over his face. *Rose has a very handsome son,* she admitted. She couldn't help noticing how much younger he looked while asleep. Something deep inside her ached, a bittersweet longing.

Melody carefully set Rose's Bible back on the nightstand and tiptoed out of the room.

She found Valerie in the kitchen, but the nurse was on the phone, so Melody stepped into the living room until she heard Valerie hang up.

"Valerie, I need to go home for a while, but I'll come back in a few hours." She turned to go but hesitated. "By the way, Daniel is asleep in Rose's room."

Valerie shook her head gently. "Poor boy, this is wearing him out." She sighed and stared out the window. "It's hard on all of us." She blinked away an unseen tear as she turned back to Melody. "By the way, I called your pastor."

Questions widened Melody's eyes.

Valerie held up one hand and shook her head. "No, it's not for Rose. I just thought I should talk to him. A person can't work with Rose Martens for long without realizing there's something to this God business." She looked sheepish but hopeful.

Melody's heart felt light for the first time that day. "That's wonderful, Valerie, and Pastor Dave is the right man to help you figure things out." She paused. "So when would you like me to return?"

"Any time. I'm sure Daniel appreciates your company."
Was that a wink? Oh dear.

Daniel woke with a start, nearly falling off the chair. The doorbell sounded again, and he heard steps and then Valerie's voice welcoming someone.

He sat up straight and cringed at the kink in his neck. Disoriented, he blinked hard to clear his vision and gazed around him. *Mama's room. Wait, wasn't Melody here? What happened?*

He plucked several scattered pieces from his drowsy mind and realized he'd fallen asleep while Melody read. *How embarrassing—and rude.*

He felt the heat coming up his neck to redden his face and was glad no one else was in the room. *Except for Mama.* He rested his elbows on his knees and propped his chin on his hands. *Is she still here? Or is she gone?*

He felt wetness on his hands. *God, please let heaven be real.*

Valerie bustled into the room and checked Rose's vitals. As though she'd read his mind, she said, "She's still with us," and walked out again.

Daniel heard footsteps coming down the hall. He started to rise and realized his legs had gone numb from sprawling in the hard chair. The nerves protested with jolts of electricity.

"Ouch!" He sat down again.

Bobbie walked through the doorway and spoke as quietly as her rough voice would allow. "Hey, Danny. I brought ya some supper, spaghetti and meatballs and the fixin's. Hope you like it. How's your mama? I'm stayin' with Rosie all night, so you go on and eat." She plopped herself down on the other chair, and motioned with her head, "Go on. Give me some time with your mama."

He pushed himself upward again and this time his legs held with just a few painful prickles.

Half an hour later Daniel pushed his chair away from the table and began clearing away the leftovers. Bobbie's spaghetti supper was tasty, but he just didn't have much of an appetite tonight.

Maybe I ate too many of those muffins Melody brought this morning. His hands stilled. *I don't get it. I haven't treated either of them well enough to deserve this kind of generosity. Especially Melody. How can she even look at me after what I did?*

Deep in thought, he walked quietly back to his mother's room to thank Bobbie for the meal, but a rusty monologue stopped him halfway down the hall.

"And I almost forgot, Rosie. Your gal Val an' that Pastor Dave are havin' a talk tonight about your God—yours, Melody's, Tessa's and mine, too. Yeah, Rosie, your lessons got through." She cleared her throat noisily. "Ya know, seems there's gonna be a humdinger of a reunion up there in heaven one of these days!"

Daniel walked quietly to the living room and sank into the nearest chair. He hunched over as his heart twisted. *A reunion?*

The chorus of an old hymn resurrected in his mind. "When we all get to heaven, what a day of rejoicing that will be. When we all see Jesus, we'll sing and shout the victory!"

His head dropped to his hands. *But where will I be?*

Melody had just stepped out her door into the night when headlights flashed and Tessa's Honda pulled into her driveway. As her friend extracted herself from the low-slung car, Melody met her with a hug.

"Hey, Mel," Tessa greeted her, "are you heading to Rose's?"

"Yes, I am. But that can wait if you need something."

"I came to be with her, too. This is my last free evening for a while, and I want to spend it with Rose." Her mouth twisted. "While I can." She sighed. "Anyway, I thought I'd park here so I wouldn't block Daniel's driveway. Is that okay?"

"Of course." Melody squeezed Tessa's hand. "We'll go together."

"Hello, Daniel." Melody's heart twisted at the hopelessness in her neighbor's eyes. "Is there any change?"

Daniel shrugged and moved aside to let them enter. "No, not really. Bobbie's already here, but I'll bring more chairs. Go on in."

When they entered Rose's room, Bobbie was clasping one pale, inert hand with both her broad ones. Bobbie looked up and smiled, but it didn't reach her red-rimmed eyes.

"Hi, Bobbie, I hope we're not interrupting," Melody said softly.

"Naw, come on in, kiddos. Me and Rosie have had our little talk.

Now I'm just tryin' to help her hang on. I know she wants to see her daughter."

Daniel carried in two kitchen chairs, set them down, and left without a word.

"Thank you, Daniel," Melody said to his back.

She and Tessa pulled their chairs close to the bed. "I don't know how Hannah will get here in time, but Tessa and I prayed about that earlier today, and I'm sure God is working on it."

"There's a lot of that goin' around," Bobbie stated. She grinned crookedly. "Maybe we should put up a sign on our street: God at work."

Tessa's face brightened marginally. "Great idea, Bobbie."

Rose's eyelids fluttered, catching their attention. All three watched closely, willing her to wake up, but there was no more movement other than the barely-perceptible rising and falling of her chest.

Melody smiled through tears as she cleared her throat. "Hey, Rose, I have some wonderful news for you." She looked at Bobbie and Tessa. "And for you, too."

She told them what had happened at the gray house the day before, how she'd experienced the reality of Christ's suffering through Nila's eyes. "She loves him," Melody said. "And she met him because of you, Rose, and you too, Bobbie."

Rose's eyelids fluttered once more. *Please wake up,* Melody begged silently.

Bobbie's gruff voice interjected, "Wasn't me. That was Rosie's God at work, and he used you, Kiddo."

Tessa had been sitting quietly, but now she began to sing, her rich voice filling the room. "Great is Thy faithfulness, O God my Father …"

When the song was done, Melody wiped her eyes and looked up. Daniel stood in the doorway, shoulders shaking.

"Mama's favorite," he choked out.

Melody glanced at Rose, and when she looked toward the doorway again, Daniel was gone. She held out her hands to her friends. "Let's pray."

Melody prayed for Daniel and Hannah that God would comfort them and bring them peace. Tessa followed, thanking God for the privilege of working with Rose. Then, to Melody's delighted surprise, Bobbie broke in.

"Thanks, God, for Rosie here. She's a good 'un, and she always told me the truth. I know she's ready to see you, but I'm gonna miss her somethin' terrible. So I hope you'll keep workin' on me so I can see Rosie again someday."

Melody and Tessa murmured together, "Thank you, Jesus, thank you."

For more than an hour they prayed, visited, and prayed some more. Shortly after midnight Tessa pulled out her stethoscope to check Rose's heartbeat. She listened for a minute and wrote the results on the chart at the foot of the bed.

"Weak, but fairly steady," she said. "Her breathing is slowing, though."

Dear Jesus, Melody prayed silently, *get Hannah here in time. Please!*

Bobbie's head was bowed, whether in sleep or prayer Melody couldn't tell, but all three women snapped alert at the buzz of the doorbell.

"Who could that be?" Tessa said, echoing their thoughts.

Daniel pushed himself off the couch, unlocked the front door, opened it and stared. Standing on the porch was a woman with long, graying hair coming loose from a low ponytail, a suitcase by her side, and an exhausted expression on her face.

For the first time in days, Daniel beamed. "Hannah! You made it!"

His arms opened wide, and he pulled his sister into a fierce embrace. "It's great to see you, Sis," he said into her neck.

Hannah wrapped her arms around his waist and squeezed. "It's good to see you, too, Danny." She pulled back and gazed up at him. "Is Mama still with us?"

Daniel nodded once, sorrow drawing lines on his face once more. "Yes, but she's failing. The doctor said it could be any time …"

He paused, confusion deepening the furrows on his forehead. "But you weren't due here until Saturday. What happened?"

She reached behind her for the suitcase and shut the front door. "It took a series of miracles, Danny, but God made it happen. I'll tell you later. First, I need to see Mama."

A moment later they entered Rose's room and met three expectant faces. Bobbie, Melody and Tessa vacated their chairs and moved together against the window wall as Daniel introduced his sister.

"Hannah, you remember Bobbie from across the street." Hannah smiled a greeting, and Daniel continued, gesturing with his hand. "This is Melody; she lives next to Bobbie, and this is Tessa, Melody's friend who nursed Mama while I was away."

"Hello," Hannah responded to their welcoming smiles and moved quickly to her mother. She stroked a few wispy white hairs away from Rose's face and whispered, "Hey, Mama, it's Hannah. I'm here, and I'm *so* thankful you are too."

As Daniel and the three friends watched, Hannah's face crumpled, and she sank into the chair closest to the bed. Tears streamed down her face as she brought Rose's hand to her mouth and kissed it gently. "Oh, Mama, I should have been here for you."

Daniel stepped behind his sister and massaged her shoulders with his strong hands. "It's okay, Hannah. Mama knew you were where you belong. She told me many times how proud she is of you and the work you do in Niger."

Hannah twisted around to see his face. "Really?"

"Yes, really."

All eyes were drawn to Rose's face as her eyelids fluttered—and opened. She looked straight at Hannah, and her mouth lifted in a smile.

"Hannah ... daughter."

Her voice was a faint whisper, and everyone moved as close as possible to the bed, Daniel and Hannah on one side and the three friends on the other.

Rose turned her head slowly to look at each one, her smile like a benediction. "Dear ones," she whispered, "I love you ... so much." She closed her eyes briefly but opened them again, fixing her gaze on her son. "Danny ... remember ... your promise."

Her eyes closed again. Five people barely breathed as they sensed time melt into eternity.

And after what seemed like mere moments, Rose lifted her head, her face alight. "Music! Can you hear the music?"

She sagged back against the pillow and lay motionless. A sweet, ethereal fragrance filled the small room as Rose released one long, last breath.

26

Six days later Melody struggled to concentrate on the recipe in front of her. Hannah was flying back to Africa the following morning, just two days after her mother's funeral. Daniel's sister was so like Rose that Melody had felt an immediate affinity with her, and in those grief-filled, difficult days preparing for the funeral, their friendship had blossomed.

Melody and Bobbie had continued to bring food over, and Melody had helped as much as possible with planning Rose's memorial service. Even though Rose had dictated her wishes several weeks prior, there were several details to finalize.

The day of the funeral the small church had been filled to capacity with people wanting to honor Rose. Afterward Hannah had pulled Melody close and begged her to stand beside her and Daniel through the interment. So Melody had stayed by Hannah's side, slipping her tissues when Hannah's ran out.

"Lord, I'm going to miss Hannah. Saying goodbye to her is almost like losing Rose all over again. I'm surprised she and Daniel agreed to come over this evening since it's their last one together for a long time. But I'm glad they're coming."

Since Valerie had told her the meat loaf dinner was Daniel's favorite, she'd decided to make it again. She knew each recipe by heart, but today the grief enveloping her was clouding her memory. She read the ingredient list again for Grandma Jamison's meat loaf and gathered several spice jars out of the cupboard.

"I miss Rose so much already, God, and Daniel and Hannah must be devastated."

She grabbed a tissue and wiped her eyes.

"I know Rose is free from pain now, and that's a reason for joy, but we're still hurting. Please, somehow, bring peace to our hearts."

For the last several days, Will had felt a stab of guilt every time he saw Eli, and he was tired of it. He was tired of his self-imposed loneliness too.

It's time to 'man up,' he ordered himself. *Quit acting like such a jerk.*

He unfastened his planting bag and propped it against a stump. It was time to take a lunch break, two hours after his stomach started complaining. Hunger pushed him toward the clearing with the tarped shelter. He was anxious to eat, but first he had something to do.

Will grabbed his bag lunch and went looking for Eli. He rounded the corner of the shelter and was almost bowled over by the big man coming the opposite way. He stopped too quickly and lost his balance.

"Whoa, young rookie." Eli chuckled as he reached out and steadied Will. "What's the rush?"

Now that they were face to face, Will wasn't sure what to say. "Um, no hurry. I was just looking for you."

Eli raised one bushy eyebrow and said nothing.

"I–I mean, I need to talk to you," Will stammered.

"Okay." The big man crossed his arms and stood statue-like.

"Um … can we go somewhere …?" Will looked behind him and gestured toward a couple crewmates openly listening as they refilled their water jugs.

Eli shrugged, turned and headed into the forest. Will followed. Once they were out of sight of the rest of the crew, Eli sat on a stump and gestured for Will to follow suit.

"So, Will Jamison, you want to talk to me, after eight days of doing your best to ignore my existence?"

Shame colored Will's face. "I–I'm sorry, Eli. That was rude and wrong, and I really am sorry."

"And now?"

Will took a deep breath and plunged in. "Even though I've tried not to, I keep thinking about the things you said about God and, you know, redemption. It's been bugging me worse than these gnats." He swatted at a swarm without pausing. "I can't seem to wrap my head around it, but that's no reason to avoid you. That was stupid." He stopped for a breath. "Can we be friends again?"

A smile slowly lit Eli's face, like the glow of the halogen yard light at the farm. "I never stopped being your friend, Will."

He stuck out his hand, and Will shook it solemnly. "Thank you."

Eli opened his lunch bag. "Now let's eat and get back to work."

Just before five o'clock, the dark clouds that had threatened all day decided to pour down sheets of rain. Melody was watching for her guests and opened the door before they got up her steps.

"Come in!" she greeted them. Hannah was followed by an enormous bouquet of flowers with Daniel's head and legs behind it. He thrust it at Melody, saying "Here, this is for you," and stepped back outside to shake off his raincoat.

"Thank you," Melody murmured, looking around for a place to set the huge display.

"I thought you might enjoy that one," Hannah said. "Even though we'd requested no flowers, some people sent them anyway. Bobbie took several home with her, and some faded quickly, but this one still looks lovely." She hesitated. "Do you mind?"

"Of course not, Hannah, it's gorgeous. I'll think of your mother and you every time I look at it."

Melody moved aside some books and pictures on the coffee table and centered the bouquet in the middle. She stepped back and admired the lilies, roses, mums, and several plants she couldn't identify.

"Beautiful," she smiled. "Thank you both."

Daniel's discomfort showed plainly on his face as he re-entered the living room, but he nodded solemnly at Melody. "You're welcome."

Now Melody felt awkward. "Valerie told me you liked the first dinner I brought over, Daniel, so I made it again. I hope you both like it."

She turned and headed for the kitchen. "Everything is ready, so if you'll have a seat at the table, I'll get the food."

Was that my imagination, or did Daniel almost smile?

The atmosphere eased during supper as they talked about special moments during Rose's funeral.

"Your pastor gave a wonderful talk, Melody," said Hannah. "Even though he didn't know Mother long, he obviously cared for her. And Bobbie—wasn't her eulogy great? I'm so proud of her!"

Melody smiled at the memory. "She had me laughing and crying at the same time. I had no idea she would be so comfortable speaking to a crowd like that. She is a real treasure."

Daniel swallowed the last bite of apple pie, put his fork down and leaned back. "That was excellent, Melody," he said. "You do know the way to a man's heart." His face turned a dull red. "I mean ..." he faltered.

Hannah laughed in delight. "After all that wonderful food, how in the world did you find room in your mouth for your foot, brother dear?"

Daniel's discomfort propelled Melody out of her chair. "Would either of you like coffee or tea?" she offered, looking at Hannah.

"Do you have decaf?" asked Hannah. "I need to try to sleep tonight."

"Sure. How about you, Daniel?" She barely glanced at his still-red face.

"Decaf sounds good to me," he mumbled. "Thanks." He was gazing at his empty plate as though it might become a hole he could disappear into.

While the coffee brewed, Melody and Hannah cleared the table. By the time the dishes were dealt with, coffee was ready.

"Let's sit in the living room," Melody suggested.

Mugs in hand, the two women settled onto the couch while Daniel sat in Tom's leather recliner.

Melody glanced at him and stilled, waiting for the expected pang. It didn't come.

"Are you okay, Melody?" Hannah asked.

Melody eased back against the cushions. "Yes, I'm fine." She shifted to face Daniel's sister. "I'm going to miss you, you know. The last week was terribly hard, but getting to know you was a rainbow in the storm."

Hannah smiled, her eyes misty. "I'm going to miss you, too. You've become like a sister to me the last few days. I don't know what we would have done without you and Bobbie." She tilted her head and looked at her brother. "Right, Danny?"

Daniel massaged the back of his neck. "Yes. You've been very kind, Melody." His unease was reflected in Melody's face.

Hannah glanced from one to the other, got up and gazed at the driving rain pounding the picture window.

"Melody, have you ever thought of putting a porch on your house?"

She looked up in surprise. "Actually, I have. Well, I've thought about hiring someone to build it. Carpentry is not my forte. I've often admired your mother's porch."

Hannah looked pointedly at her brother. "Well, I happen to know an excellent carpenter who might have some time on his hands soon."

Daniel frowned at his sister, but Hannah ignored him and continued, "He's considering selling his company in Alberta and moving back here for good."

"Oh," Melody said—and wondered at the sudden warm glow deep inside.

"Hannah," Daniel warned, "I haven't made a final decision yet about the sale. But," he turned to face Melody, "if you'd like me to build a porch on your house, I'd be glad to do that. Or if you'd rather hire someone else, I could give you some names."

"I prefer you," Melody blurted and felt her face burn. "I mean … the porch you built for your mother is perfect, and I'd love to have one like that."

Where IS that hole in the floor when you need it?

Daniel walked out of the John G. Diefenbaker Airport and winced. Yesterday's storm clouds had blown away, and the morning's brilliant sunshine stung his eyes. Snapping on his dark glasses, Daniel climbed into his truck and drove homeward.

He'd waited until his sister's plane had taken off, soaring into the bright blue sky, leaving him with a dull ache of loneliness. He didn't want to go back to his mother's empty house, but that was the only home he had now. He'd rented out his Edmonton condo when he'd first come home to help Rose.

"I can't face the emptiness. Not yet."

He pulled into the drive-through for a popular coffee shop, ordered his dark brew, and drove into the adjoining lot. He shifted into park and sipped his steaming coffee. The taste took him back to the previous evening at Melody's house. Daniel pictured her heart-shaped face and pansy-like green eyes, and his heartbeat increased noticeably. Irritably he shoved the take-out cup into the cup-holder.

"Okay, I'm attracted to her, very attracted. But I don't have a chance. She's suffered too much because of me, and I'm damaged goods. How she can be so kind to me, I'll never understand. But it's no good thinking about her. It would never work."

Daniel ground the starter on his already-running truck, muttered at himself, and pulled back onto the busy road.

As soon as he walked into the house, silence met him. No nurse, no visitors, no sister, no mother. A wall of loneliness hit him, and the force of it rocked him back on his heels. But he squared his shoulders, strode to his office, and sat at his desk.

"Work, that's what I need. It saved me after the accident, and it will get me through this. It has to."

27

Melody wandered through her house doing chores mechanically. She wiped a fine layer of dust off the piano and coffee table and watered the fading bouquet meant for Rose. Her heart and mind both felt anesthetized, except when she looked at the flower arrangement or out the window toward the blue house across the street. Then a rush of sorrow blanketed her until she could barely move. Old habits resurfaced, and she drew the curtains closed. But it didn't help; it was as though the drapes didn't exist.

"I can't hide from this, can I? God, I miss Rose so much. What am I supposed to do now?"

Go, help my little one.

"Nila!" Melody flinched at the realization that she'd forgotten her young neighbor so new to faith in Jesus. Before fear could stop her, she rushed out the door.

The driveway of the gray house was empty, but the drapes were closed, giving the house a forlorn look. Melody hesitated. *What if she's sleeping?* That thought was followed by another: *or hurt?*

Melody knocked on the door, waited, and knocked again with more force. No answer. A prickle of unease crept up Melody's back, and she pounded her fist on the door.

"Nila, are you in there? It's Melody. Let me in, please!"

She heard slow steps moving toward the door, and it finally opened a crack. Nila peered through the opening.

"Hi, Melody." Her voice was halting. "Th–this really isn't a good time. I'm sorry."

She started to shut the door, but Melody pushed it open, shocked at her own boldness.

"Nila, I need to see you. What is wrong?" She stopped. "Oh, honey."

The now-open doorway revealed a dark purple handprint-shaped bruise on Nila's face and makeshift bandages on both her hands.

"I–I didn't want you to see me like this." She looked down at the floor.

Melody gently took Nila's arm and led her to the couch. "What happened, Nila? You know you can talk to me."

"You're gonna be mad at me."

"I doubt that." Melody forced herself to breathe deeply. "Please tell me. I promise I won't be upset with you."

Nila gazed at her injured hands and touched one bandaged finger to her bruised face. Finally she looked at Melody.

"I–I'm sorry, Melody, but I lost the book you gave me."

Melody frowned in disbelief but kept her voice calm. "What do you mean?"

Nila looked at her hands again. "N–Nick … um … I told him about Jesus, about him dying to save me." She lifted her face, confusion puckering her brow. "Nick got awful mad, and he wasn't even drinking. He made me get the book, and …" She gulped and turned away.

"It's okay, Nila, tell me." Melody struggled to control her surging temper. "What happened next?"

After several shuddering sighs, Nila scooted out of Melody's reach and continued. "He yelled at me, said that no one could save me but him. Then he grabbed my Bible, lit it on fire, and threw it into the sink."

She held out her hands. "I grabbed it, but the fire burned my hands. Then Nick slapped me and knocked me down." Tears dripped onto her bandaged hands. "I dropped the Bible, Melody, and Nick stomped on it until it was in pieces. I couldn't save it."

Melody looked down at her own hands. Horror and anger held them clasped so tightly her knuckles were white. *Calm down,* she told herself. *Anger isn't going to help right now.* She glanced up again. *Look at her, she's shaking.*

"I'm not mad at you, Nila," she said. "I am worried about you, though. This is not a safe place for you, is it?"

The young woman shook her head. "You don't understand. Nick loves me. He loves me so much he can't stand it if I talk about anyone else. This was *my* fault!"

Oh God…

"How can I help you? What do you want me to do? Can I take you to a doctor to get your hands treated?"

Nila shook her head. "No. It's okay, I'll be fine." Her smile twisted. "But I miss my Bible. I really miss reading about Jesus."

"I can get you another one, if you'd like," Melody said.

Nila's face lit with hope. "Would you? Oh, I'd like that. I'll put it in a special hiding place every day before Nick comes home. It will be safe there."

But how safe will you be?

That afternoon Melody walked into her pastor's home and into Lydia's hug.

"Welcome, Melody," Lydia released her and smiled gently. "I'm so glad you called. Please make yourself at home. This is your first time here, isn't it?"

"Yes, it is, and thank you for letting me come on such short notice." She looked around her with appreciation. "This is a beautiful home, Lydia."

"Thank you, dear. Would you like a little tour before we visit?"

The older two-story had been tastefully renovated, making it functionally modern while keeping its charm. Melody admired the contrast of dark beams on the high, white ceiling and the gleaming oak floors.

"Beautiful," she murmured.

Their final room was the kitchen at the back of the house. "This is my favorite room," Lydia said. "We took down a wall here," she pointed to the edge of the granite-topped island, "and combined the kitchen with the formal dining room." She winked at Melody. "We're just not formal-type people, you know."

"You mean you and your husband did all this work yourselves?" Melody was in awe.

Lydia smiled proudly. "Well, Dave did the work. I just drew up the designs."

"You both did a fantastic job. It somehow reminds me of our old farmhouse. Not that it was elegant like this, but it's the warmth, the feel of permanence ... I love it."

"Thank you, Melody." Lydia filled two ironstone mugs with rich, aromatic coffee. "A little bird told me you enjoy the occasional cup of coffee."

Melody just grinned as she accepted the cup and took a sip. "Mm–mm, this is yummy! Is that a hint of mocha?"

"You're good. Yes, it's one of my favorites. Now, would you prefer to sit in here or go into the living room?"

"Hmm, let's stay in here. These stools look comfy, and I love looking out at your back yard. You've obviously done a lot of work there, too."

"Yes, that's my 'baby.' But we'll talk about that another time. You said you needed to talk to me about something."

Melody sighed as she pictured her young neighbor's bruised face. She told Lydia about Nila and her situation. "I just don't know how to help her. I mean, she won't leave him even though he hurts her. She's totally under his control."

Lydia patted Melody's hand. "It sounds to me like you *are* helping. You're being her friend, and she needs that more than anything. And while it seems as though she's being controlled by her boyfriend, the fact that she asked for another Bible tells me there's a spark of independence there."

Melody brightened. "You're right. Her love for Jesus gave her enough spunk to stand up to Nick when he burned her Bible." Her sparkle dimmed. "But what if that courage gets her hurt even worse next time?"

"Let's pray. And, if you don't mind, I'd like to share this with Dave when he gets home."

"Yes, of course—to both."

The two women raised Nila up to their heavenly Father, asking for protection for her and her new faith. Lydia also asked for wisdom in how they should respond.

"Thank you so much, Lydia," Melody said as she wiped her eyes. "My heart feels lighter now." She tilted her head and asked softly, "Do you mind if I make you my 'Rose'? She was my prayer warrior, and I think I miss that most of all."

Lydia slid off her stool and put one arm around Melody, squeezing gently. "That would be a privilege, my dear. I can never take the place of Rose Martens, but I can certainly pray with you and for you. By the way, Dave and I are continuing to pray for your son. Have you heard from him lately?"

"No," Melody shook her head. "He told me not to expect to hear from him until his tree-planting work was done, but that should happen soon, I think."

"Well, we will keep on giving him to the Lord." She gave Melody a quick squeeze. "Try not to worry. I just know God is working in Will's heart."

She released Melody after one more hug. "Wait here a minute, and I'll go get another copy of The Message for Nila."

She chuckled and shook her head at Melody's expression. "We always have extras around here. My husband buys them by the case. 'Never know when someone might need one,' he says."

Daniel closed his laptop, walked to the room he'd been avoiding, and pulled open the closet doors. He stood there, eyes closed, as his mother's favorite fragrance filled the room.

"I could almost believe she's still here." He shut the doors. "But she's gone."

The last several days had been filled with questions. Questions from his mother's lawyer, questions from Zach, and questions from his own mind about his future. Pressure built inside him until he felt as though even a casual bump might cause an explosion. "I can't handle any more. I've got to get out of here."

Daniel pulled a suitcase out of his closet, opened it and quickly packed it. He started to zip it shut, but instead he picked up the framed photo from his dresser.

"Angela," he whispered. The expected stab of pain was more like the pull of an old scar, making him pause. But he wrapped the photo in tissue paper and placed it inside the suitcase.

He made a few phone calls, loaded his truck, and walked across the street. Taking a deep breath, he pushed the doorbell.

The door opened, and Daniel was met by a questioning expression.

"Hello, Bobbie. May I come in for just a minute? I have a favor to ask of you."

Will felt a prickle at the back of his neck, as though he was being watched. He straightened and looked around, but everyone in sight was busy with their own work. He shrugged and bent to the task once again.

That uneasy feeling kept nagging at him, though, and he became careless in his haste to finish the row closest to the dark forest.

"Rats!" he muttered when he checked behind him. "I've messed up this whole row." He groaned at the thought of fixing all those seedlings. "I'll finish up this row and make sure it's right before I fix those down there."

Just as he placed another seedling, a loud rumble from his stomach made him pause and check his watch.

"No wonder I'm hungry." He quickly positioned the tiny tree, took off his planting bag, grabbed his water jug and lunch, and trudged up the hill to refill his water.

He ate as he climbed and was relieved to realize that the disturbing prickle had disappeared. He swatted at the swarm of gnats hovering around him and increased his pace.

"Must have been my imagination."

֍ ֍ ֍

Melody walked back toward her house, deep in thought after delivering Nila's new copy of The Message.

Nila had accepted the gift and held it to her chest. "Thank you. I can't believe you're giving me another one."

But she'd stiffened when Melody had tried to hug her.

Pulling away, she'd protested, "You can't stay, Melody. I have to get this mess cleaned up before Nick gets home."

Glancing around, Melody had seen only a few items out of place. *This is a mess? Maybe to a control freak.* So she'd simply reminded Nila to call her if she had any questions or needed anything. "Anything at all," she'd said. Then she left.

"I want so much to snatch her out of the danger she's in, Lord. Please help me to know what to do."

"Hey, Melody!" Bobbie was standing on her front step as though she'd been watching for her. "Got a minute?"

Melody changed direction. "Sure, Bobbie. What can I do for you?"

"Come on in. I tried a new cookie recipe, and I need a guinea pig."

Melody grinned as she climbed Bobbie's steps. "Hmm, sampling your baking? Sounds like the perfect job for me."

A few minutes later, Melody wiped a stray crumb from her mouth. "What do you call those? They're delicious!"

"Chocolate Temptations," Bobbie answered. "They *are* good, aren't they?" She picked up another cookie.

"Did you make these for Daniel?" Melody asked. She picked up her cup of coffee and sipped the hot brew.

Bobbie bit off a chunk of still-warm cookie, chewed thoroughly and swallowed before answering. "Nope. That's what I want to talk to you about. He's gone."

Melody gasped, inhaled coffee, and coughed. When she caught her breath, she frowned at her neighbor. "Gone? When? And where?"

Bobbie chuckled dryly. "Mighty concerned about his whereabouts, ain'tcha?"

"Well, I just …" She faltered. Heat warmed her face as she carefully took another sip.

"I shouldn't give you such a hard time, I guess." Bobbie leaned forward and propped her elbows on the table. "So here's the scoop: Danny came over yesterday and asked me to look after his place for a week or two. Said he has to take care of business in Alberta."

Melody raised her eyebrows, and Bobbie shook her head. "Naw, he didn't give any details. Just that he'd be gone for a while."

"Okay," Melody said slowly, "so what does that have to do with me?"

Bobbie immediately sobered. "Well, he did ask me to do another favor, and that's where you come in."

She took a deep breath, and her shoulders drooped. "Danny asked me to clean out Rosie's clothes and things while he's gone. Said he just can't do that, and I should take anything I'd like for a reminder."

Sorrowful eyes met Melody's. "I can't face that alone, Kiddo. Will you help?"

28

The next morning Melody and Bobbie crossed the street to the blue house in silence. Their steps seemed to echo on the front porch, and when they entered the house, silence so thick it seemed impenetrable accosted them.

"Feels strange, don't it?" Bobbie whispered. "No wonder Danny took off."

Melody looked around. The living room appeared unchanged, but even Bobbie's whisper seemed to echo.

"You're right," she whispered back. "But why are we whispering?"

Bobbie cleared her throat and spoke normally. "Guess that's kinda silly. But it's sorta like walkin' through a graveyard. Know what I mean? Anyway, let's get at it. Danny said to take anything we want from Rosie's closet an' dresser and chuck the rest."

"Maybe we should tackle the dresser first," Melody suggested. "I doubt that there's much there we'll save."

But when the top drawer was pulled open, Melody gasped softly. Two deep stacks of embroidered, lace-edged handkerchiefs lay neatly folded in the drawer.

Melody touched one reverently. "I would love to take these, if you don't want them."

Bobbie looked surprised. "Go ahead. Don't think anyone uses hankies anymore. I sure don't."

Melody stacked the treasures on the bed while Bobbie cleared out stacks of underwear, also neatly folded.

"Just feels wrong," Bobbie muttered as she dumped Rose's things into a large garbage bag held open by Melody. Contents of the second and third drawers followed, but when Bobbie opened the bottom drawer, she grunted and sat heavily on the floor.

"What is it?" Melody asked. When Bobbie didn't respond, she dropped the garbage bag and knelt beside her. "What's wrong?"

Bobbie just pointed to the open drawer. It was full of spiral-bound notebooks, plain except for the flowing script written across each one: *Rose Martens, Journal,* and the dates.

"Oh," Melody breathed, "these are real treasures. We have to keep these for Daniel and Hannah." She picked up one and held it close, as though the private musings of its writer could soothe her hurting heart.

Bobbie sat on the floor with tears running down her lined cheeks as she traced the elegant handwriting with one blunt finger. "Hope there's still some tissue around here," she blurted.

Melody quickly replaced the notebook and grabbed a box from Rose's bedside table. "Here you go, Bobbie." Then she used one for her own face.

While Bobbie vigorously blew her nose, Melody stacked the notebooks on the bed. "You know, I've got a plastic container at home that would hold these. Maybe we should take a coffee break now, and then bring it back with us."

"Sounds like a plan, Kiddo," Bobbie said gruffly. She blew her nose again. "I could use a break."

A short time later Melody carefully stacked Rose's journals into a lidded container while Bobbie emptied the bedside table. Hannah had taken her mother's precious Bible, so all that remained were a few odds and ends.

"You ready?" she asked, tying the bag shut.

Melody nodded mutely. As though choreographed, they each grasped one of the decorative knobs on the closet doors and pulled simultaneously. Rose's fragrance wafted out, and they stood silently for a moment, accepting it as a blessing.

Bobbie was the first to speak. "It's just clothes. Don't know why I'm gettin' all choked up again."

Melody reached out and touched a pale blue cotton dress bordered with white daisies. She gulped back a sob as she realized she'd never seen Rose wearing anything but bedclothes.

"What was she like, Bobbie, before she got sick?" Melody was whispering again.

Bobbie smiled wanly. "She was a doll, just like she was right up to the end. Only spunky. She had lots of spunk, lots of energy."

Melody began dividing the dresses and blouses into two piles while Bobbie sat on the bed and reminisced.

"She loved to have folks over. She'd feed 'em and love 'em until they were plumb full. Me an' Charlie were over there a lot, even though it was more comfy when Ezekiel was outta town. Charlie didn't think much of him." She sighed. "But if there was a missionary ever in town, well, she just had to have them stay at her house. She just soaked up their stories and prayed for them forever after. Then again, she did that with everybody. Love 'em and pray for 'em. That's … that was my Rosie."

She sat lost in her memories for a full minute. Then she wiped her hand over her eyes and noticed the piles Melody had formed. "You keepin' some of those?"

"Is that okay? Did you want some?"

"Naw, they wouldn't fit me. You, either." Bobbie's puzzlement was obvious.

Melody smiled gently. "I think I could make one or two small quilts from these." She touched one of the piles. "They're mostly cotton, so it should work, but I might have to add some other material. Working with Rose's clothes would be therapeutic for me, and I hope the results will be something Hannah—and maybe Daniel—would appreciate."

Bobbie's smile reached her eyes for the first time that day. "That's a great idea. Go for it!"

That evening, with Faith's gift of piano and cello music lilting through the stereo's speakers, Melody spread out her treasures on the kitchen table. She smiled through tears as she touched each one tenderly. She picked up her scissors.

"Dear, sweet Rose, I miss you so. Lord Jesus, can she see me? Does she approve of what I'm about to do?"

"Good morning, sweetheart. I hope you don't mind my popping in like this, but I missed you at church yesterday. Jason said you weren't feeling well."

Melody examined her daughter's flushed face and shadowed eyes. Immediately she placed a palm on Faith's forehead.

"You don't feel feverish, but you look pretty miserable. What's going on?"

Faith pulled her bathrobe tighter around her and shrugged. "I think it's a flu bug, Mom. Don't get too close, or you might catch it." She shuffled toward the kitchen. "I'll put coffee on for you. Jessie's playing in her room."

"I've already had coffee, Faith, so don't bother with it unless you want some. I'll just go get that little darling."

"Thanks, Mom. Oh, she may need a diaper change."

"No problem. I've done that a time or two." She gazed at her daughter for a moment. "I have an idea. How about I play with your daughter for a while, and you can relax in a nice, hot bath. Then maybe you'll want to lie down for a while."

"Mom, you're the best!" Faith leaned forward and gave her mother a quick hug. She pulled back just as quickly. "Oops! I hope you don't catch this bug."

By lunchtime Melody had tidied the living areas and entertained Jessica to her heart's content.

A refreshed Faith came into the living room where grandmother and granddaughter were snuggled on the couch. Melody was reading Dr. Seuss to baby Jessica, who responded with giggles and grins.

Melody looked up when Faith cleared her throat. "Are you feeling better? You look perkier."

"Yeah, thanks, Mom. That quiet time was just what I needed." She came and sat beside the two. "Has Jess talked to you?"

Melody raised her eyebrows. "She's talking?"

Faith grinned. "Well, just a few words." She held out her arms to the baby. "Come here, Jessie. Come to Mama."

"Ma–ma–ma–ma," Jessica gurgled and leaned toward her mother.

Faith grinned proudly as she took her daughter and set her on her lap. "And where's Daddy?"

"Da–da–da–da."

"Now, Jessie, where's Grandma?" She pointed to Melody.

Jessica peered wide-eyed at Melody and giggled. "Na–na!"

Melody's heart soared. "You sweetheart. I am totally impressed." She tickled Jessica, making her chortle. "I like the name 'Nana.' Works for me!"

Faith beamed but suddenly sobered. "Speaking of family, have you heard from my little brother lately? He's been on my mind an awful lot lately, and last night I had a terrible dream about him. He was being attacked by something—I don't know what—and I couldn't do anything to help him. It was horrible!"

She hugged her baby close. "I'm afraid for him, Mom."

A few days later Melody welcomed her friend with a warm hug.

"I've missed you, Tessa. How have you been? I haven't seen you since the funeral."

Tessa returned the hug and patted Melody's back as she let go. "It's good to be here, Mel. I'm still adjusting to shift work again while mourning Rose."

She continued as they filled their coffee mugs. "I'm working on the orthopedic ward this month, and every time I see a white-haired lady …" She shook her lowered head.

"That must be terribly difficult," Melody said. "But wait, before we sit down, I want to you to see something."

Melody led the way to her sewing room. Piles of fabric shapes covered Melody's cutting table, but the hankies were still untouched. Melody unfolded a piece of off-white material and spread it out on top of the fabric piles.

"I'm making this for Bobbie," she said. "She and I cleaned out Rose's dresser and closet, and I decided to made some lap quilts out of some dresses. This one is called 'Rose of Sharon.'"

"Oh," Tessa breathed, "it's beautiful." She traced one flower shape with her finger.

The intricate flower design was only half completed, so Melody apologized. "You'll have to imagine the finished project. I'm using four dresses for this one, and these," she pointed to more flowery prints," will be a quilt for Hannah." She picked up the stack of dainty handkerchiefs. "I thought you and Valerie might each appreciate a pillow made from these hankies once the quilts are done. What do you think?"

"I think you're much too good to me, my friend. I would treasure it forever, and I'm sure Val would too." She smiled gently, but then a twinkle sparked in her eyes. "But what about Daniel?" Tessa teased. "Does he get a quilt, too?"

Melody felt tell-tale warmth rising in her face and turned away from her friend. "Actually, yes. These plain and plaid fabrics will be enough for a lap quilt. I may add some others, though. Daniel doesn't seem like a lap-quilt kind of guy."

Tessa laughed out loud. "You've got that right. Maybe when you two are old and snuggling on the couch ..." She laughed again at the outraged expression on Melody's face.

"All right, I'll quit teasing now."

Once they were sitting in their favorite spots at either end of the big brown couch, Melody decided it was time for some payback.

"So, my romance-loving friend, how is *your* love life?"

To Melody's satisfaction, Tessa blushed. "My love life is non-existent, and I don't see any positive change on the horizon." Tessa closed her eyes and pressed her lips together.

Melody grimaced. "Sorry, Tess, I was just trying to get back at you for teasing me. But I didn't mean to poke you in a sore spot."

Tessa sighed. "It's okay, Mel. I've just been feeling sorry for myself lately. I got an email a couple weeks ago that my ex-husband has already remarried. Makes me wonder if I'll ever be able to trust my own judgment when it comes to men."

"What about—what was his name—Orlando? Are you sure he's married?"

Tessa nodded her head. "I think he must be. I didn't see him the first week I was back at the hospital, but the other day we met in the cafeteria. His face lit up like moonlight on snow, and he came over and told me he'd missed me."

She held up her hands in supplication. "What was I supposed to do? I told him I'd missed him, too, because I had. We visited that entire half-hour and every lunch break since then. But as soon as shift is over, he's out of there. He must have someone special waiting for him at home." She pursed her lips. "Someone named Carmelita."

Melody felt a pang of fear for her friend. "Sounds like you're becoming quite close."

Tessa drew a deep breath, looked up at the ceiling and sighed. "Yes, we are." Her troubled eyes met Melody's. "I think I'm falling in love with him, Mel."

∽ ∽ ∽

Will and Eli grabbed their equipment and climbed out of the helicopter. Will folded his bug-spray soaked bandana and tied it around his head, matching Eli's actions.

"Thanks again for that new spray," Will said. "It seemed to make a difference yesterday, and less swatting and more planting is a good thing. I might just make my goal after all."

"What goal is that?"

Will shrugged and picked up his planting bags. "Just a dollar figure I'm trying to hit. No particular reason." He felt a flush of shame and turned away from his friend. *It's none of his business, anyway.*

The two fell into line behind the rest of the crew as they hiked further up the mountain to the final planting block.

"I don't know why Dusty had to give me the piece closest to the drop-off," Will complained. "It gives me the creeps, and it's going to take at least two days to finish."

"Well, two days is all we've got. We're supposed to wrap up tomorrow. Just remember the first rule of safety."

"Yeah, I know: 'Be aware of your surroundings at all times.' But that's harder than I'd thought. Once I get my planting rhythm going, I just go without thinking about anything else." He shrugged. "Works for me, anyway."

Eli looked at him with a strange expression on his face. "Just be careful, okay?"

29

Daniel stormed into the construction trailer and slammed the door so forcefully the wall clock crashed to the floor. He bent to pick up the pieces and groaned.

"What is wrong with me? I nearly snapped Zach's head off out there for no reason. He was right to call me on it. I can't afford to lose him."

He dumped what was left of the clock into the garbage, sat in his swivel chair and propped his feet on the desk. He looked around the trailer. Photos showed his accomplishments of the last several years. Framed newspaper clippings bragged about his award-winning company.

"Nothing, it means nothing any more. Is this numbness because of grief?"

He got up and paced the small room. "I don't think so. This was my refuge after the accident, and I was certainly grieving then. I miss Mama, but she made it clear she was eager to go. And this," he searched for the word, "dissatisfaction started before then, anyway. "

He stood still. "I'm going to be fifty in a couple years, and I want something more in my life than work."

Melody's image moved from the edges of his thoughts into the center. He pictured her shy smile and endearing awkwardness each time they'd met. Her love for his mother warmed his heart as he remembered the snippets of conversation and prayers he'd overheard.

He recalled her generous giving of herself and her talents as she made meal after meal for Hannah and him. Hannah had immediately adored Melody too.

"Too?" he asked himself. "Do I adore her?" His face felt as warm as his heart, but he considered the question. "Until I packed Angela's photo, I hadn't looked at it in weeks. She'll always be my first love, but twelve years is a long time to mourn. Is my heart finally ready to move on? Is that why I'm so restless, why I can't get Melody Jamison out of my mind?"

He sat again and picked up the phone. He found a business card under several papers and punched in the number.

"Logan, Daniel Martens here. If you're serious about buying me out, I'm ready to talk."

Melody sat bleary-eyed at her kitchen table nursing her third cup of coffee. It had been a rough night, and she could still hear echoes of the whispers that had tormented her sleep.

"Faith is sick. Maybe it's serious, and she won't tell you. You lost your son. You'll never see him again. You lost your husband. You'll never know love again. You can't protect Nila; she'll soon be gone. Rose is gone. Daniel is gone. Everyone you care about—gone!"

"Leave me alone," she moaned. "Jesus, help me!"

The phone rang, and it was Faith calling.

"Hello, honey, how are you feeling this morning?"

"No better, but I have a doctor's appointment this afternoon. But you sound as though you caught it. Are you okay?"

Melody sighed deeply. "I'm not sick, Faith. I just had a rough night."

"Me, too, Mom. That's why I called. Have you heard anything at all from Will?

"I did it!" Will swung his shovel over his head in celebration. He could faintly hear some of the crew, but he was alone near the bottom of the steep slope. The clearing where the helicopter would soon land and where other crew members were gathering was out of sight. Several boulders, a few barely surviving trees, and the irregular slope separated Will from the others.

"Dusty did me a favor this time," he said aloud. "Nobody distracted me, and this is my best tally yet." He brushed off the now-familiar prickle at the back of his neck.

Will gazed back over the seedlings he'd planted in the last two days. The ones he could see stood straight, but boulders and trees hid some from sight.

"I'd better check, just to make sure. I don't want to get docked now."

He trudged up and down the rows, fixing a few, until all that remained was the row in the bottom corner close to untouched forest.

That annoying prickle spread until it felt as if millions of bugs were attacking him. Will slapped at a lone gnat.

"What's going on?"

He stepped over a fallen log and saw the last seedling near a huge rock. "Rats! Looks like I must have stepped on that one. Good thing I checked."

He bent down, adjusted the tiny tree, and stood slowly, rubbing his back. "It's been a long day, but I'm done."

"Whoof!"

Will froze. On the other side of the boulder stood a huge bear, swaying slightly, lips curled back in a snarl.

Time slowed to a crawl as Will's mind raced. *What was that saying? Stop, drop and roll? No, stupid, that's for fire. What was it? Oh yeah, don't run.*

He dropped his shovel, turned, and ran. He only got two steps before razor-sharp claws sliced his back, knocking him to the ground.

Will curled into a fetal position, arms protecting his neck. Someone screamed. It sounded like his own voice. Teeth dug into his left arm, and the screaming intensified.

This is it. I'm done. Mom, I'm sorry. God, I'm sorry!

"Will!" Eli's voice came through a fog of pain.

The bear let go and stood, and Will scrambled to crawl away. "Unh!" The bear swatted him flat, raking his shoulder. Will curled up again and hoped the end would come quickly.

Whumpf! A force struck the bear, knocking it backward. "Will, stay down!" Eli's voice was muffled but firm. Will turned his head just enough to see.

Eli seemed to be dancing with the huge bear, pushing it by brute force away from Will. But as Will watched in horror, the bear bared its teeth and bent to bite Eli's neck. The two fell to the ground, still entwined, and they rolled down the steep slope.

"NO!" Will struggled to his knees but could do nothing as Eli and the bear rolled to the edge of the drop-off. They fought there for a moment, seemingly unaware of the danger. Then, as Will watched, they disappeared over the cliff.

"Eli!" Will cried out as he tried to stand. He got halfway up when dizziness struck. He wobbled, saw only black spots, and passed out.

Will buckled his seat belt and winced at the fiery pain. As he waited for the plane to take off, he mentally thanked Warner again for the kindness he'd shown. When Will had regained consciousness, he was flat on his stomach in the hospital in Golden, and his boss was by his side looking as though he hadn't slept in days.

He'd rolled partway onto his right side, and his moans had roused Warner.

"How're you doing, Will? Anything I can get for you?"

"Eli?" he'd asked, but Warner shook his head.

"I'm sorry, but he's gone." Warner had looked out the window at nothing and reported in a monotone: "Apparently your friend landed underneath the bear in a deep crevice about two-thirds of the way down. I don't know when or how his body will be recovered, as it's pretty much inaccessible."

Will had buried his face in his pillow until his tears soaked it.

When Will had insisted on checking himself out of the hospital two days later against the doctor's wishes, Warner had driven him to the Calgary airport and made sure he'd made his flight.

"Best job, best boss I ever had," Will murmured, "but worst ending ever."

The jet's engines roared, and Will anticipated the rush of takeoff. But the force was excruciating as it pushed Will's torn back against the seat. He cried out in agony and hoped no one heard him. He shoved his fist into his mouth to keep his moans from becoming screams. His back burned as though the bear's claws raked them afresh while the plane rose in the sky.

When the airplane leveled off, Will leaned forward, and the refrain that began with Eli's action resumed: "Eli died to save me. I'm alive because he rescued me from that bear. The good guy died, and I'm still here."

And then he'd hear Eli's voice: "Greater love has no one than this, that he lay down his life for his friend."

Over and over it played until Will leaned forward and buried his head in his hands.

"Okay, I get it, God. I understand now. Eli did what Jesus did. He died for me. He was right, redemption really hurts. Worse than I'd ever thought." His shoulders shook, but he ignored the fierce pain.

"I'm sorry, Jesus!"

30

Melody had just come in the back door from weeding her garden when she heard a light knock at the front door. She quickly wiped her dirt-covered hands, but before she could answer the door, the knob turned, and the door opened.

"Hey, Faith …"

"Mom! You left your door unlocked again! You're not on the farm anymore, you know."

Melody stopped halfway across the room. "Well, hello to you too."

Faith blushed. "Sorry, Mom. You know I worry about you. That's not why I popped in, though. We just came from the doctor."

Worry creased Melody's brow. "What is it, Faith? Come, sit down and talk to me."

"No, Jason needs to get back to work, and he and Jess are in the car. I just had to tell you right away."

"What?" Melody reached for her daughter and pulled her close. "Talk to me, sweetheart."

"Well, Mom," Faith whispered into her mother's ear, "you don't need to worry about catching what I've got."

Thoughts of all kinds of terrible diseases raced through Melody's mind until she pulled back and saw the sparkle in Faith's eyes.

"You mean …?"

"Yep. I'm pregnant, Mom!"

Melody squeezed her again and laughed with relief. "I guess you're right about me not catching that, my dear. Oh, I'm so relieved—and thrilled! Are you sure you can't stay for a little while?"

"No." Faith shook her head. "Jason took time off work to go to the doctor's with me, and he has to get back." She headed out the door again. "We'll see you on Sunday, though, as long as I can keep some breakfast down."

Melody followed her daughter to the car and leaned in the driver's window to kiss Jason's cheek. "Congratulations, Jason. I'm so happy for all of us! Hi, Jessica. How's Nana's sweetheart?"

"Na–na," Jessica cooed.

"Thanks, Mom, but we've to go." Jason put the car in gear. "See you later."

A few minutes later, Melody heard a vehicle pull into her driveway. *Did Faith forget something here?*

She looked around the living room but couldn't spot anything that didn't belong. She peeked out the window and saw a taxi pulled close to the walkway.

"Who could that be?" she muttered. "I wonder if someone got the wrong address."

She walked out onto her front step to confront the stranger. But as a tall man awkwardly emerged from the taxi, Melody's hand moved to her suddenly-pounding heart.

The golden curls were long enough to tie back, and she'd never seen him with a beard before, but this … this was her son!

"Will!" she cried, running down the steps on shaky legs. "You're home!"

The tall, stooped young man flung up a hand to stop her from grabbing him. "Hi, Mom. Don't hug me, please."

Melody skidded to a stop and stared at this beloved stranger. She noticed an odd bulkiness on his left shoulder and arm. His shadowed face was etched with pain-lines and exhaustion, and he looked as though he had aged a dozen years.

The cabbie had removed one bag from the trunk and was waiting to be paid.

"My purse is in the house," Melody offered, but Will was already digging into his pocket with his good hand.

"Here." He handed two crisp bills to the cabbie. "Thanks for everything."

As the taxi pulled back onto the street, Will picked up his bag and followed Melody to the house.

"Nice little house, Mom," he said. "Ever think of putting a porch on here?"

"Thanks, Son, and yes, I have." She moved back to give him room to enter. Since he was in obvious distress, she held herself back from touching him even though her heart yearned to hold him close, close enough to obliterate all the pain of the last two and a half years.

Will stopped just inside the door, swaying slightly as he gazed around the room.

"Aw, you kept the old couch and Dad's chair." He seemed to be staying upright by sheer stubbornness.

"Sit down, Son. All the furniture is from the farm; I didn't replace anything. So make yourself at home." Her smile was wistful. "Only the location has been changed."

A spasm marred his face as he gingerly lowered himself to the couch and sat as far forward as possible.

God, what happened to my boy?

"Are you hungry?" Mother-mode kicked in, numbing her anxiety for the moment.

Will shook his head and winced at the slight motion. "No, but thanks." He started to lean back and moaned when his back brushed the couch fabric.

"Will, what happened? You're obviously hurting, and," she moved around the side of the couch, "you're bleeding!"

She reached out a hand to touch him but pulled it back. "Please talk to me," she said. "What happened to you?"

"It's a really long story, Mom. Can it wait? I think I need to lie down for a while." His face had paled, and he looked as though he was about to pass out.

Melody swallowed hard. *He's here. He's hurt, but he's here. Give him what he needs, and the rest can wait.* "Would you prefer your old bed or the couch?"

One side of Will's mouth lifted slightly as he murmured, "My own bed? I've dreamt about that." He looked at his mother with not-quite-focused eyes. "I might need some help getting there. Could you…?"

Melody nodded and reached for him.

"Just my right arm, Mom," he directed. "If I could lean on you, you can show me the way."

With her son's right arm draped around her shoulder, Melody helped him down the hall to the guest room. She had him sit on the padded chair from Faith's old room while she took off his shoes and pulled back the bed covers.

"Mom?" His voice was as weak as he looked. "What time is it?"

She stopped fluffing the pillow she held and glanced at her watch. "Just after four. Why, honey?"

"Pills ... in my bag. Would you ... get them?"

A few minutes later, Will was sprawled diagonally across his old bed, lying on his uninjured arm. Melody stood in the doorway for several minutes, until his deep breathing told her he slept.

She walked into the kitchen, poured a cup of coffee, stared at it for a minute, and dumped it down the sink. Leaning against the counter, she raised her face, distress filling her eyes.

"What is going on, God? I gave him to you to keep safe. I trusted you! Yes, he's home at last, but he's wounded! Is this how you take care of him?"

Her head dropped, and she let her tears fall into the sink.

Early the next morning, Melody phoned Tessa. "I hope I didn't wake you, Tess, but I need your help. Will is here, but he's sick. Can you come over? Right away?"

"Wait a minute, Mel, slow down! Did you say Will is home? And he's sick? What happened?"

Melody took a deep breath and tried to calm her frantic mind. "He arrived yesterday and hasn't said much yet. He's got huge bandages on his back, and even though I gave him his pain pills last night, he's been moaning and groaning for hours. He won't wake up, and I'm sure he's running a fever. I don't know what to do, Tess!"

"Okay, okay, I'll be right over. While you wait, phone your doctor and see if you can get him in today. And if he's feverish, try holding a cool cloth on his head." Tessa sighed into the phone. "Hang on Mel, he'll be okay."

Tessa stopped in the doorway of Will's room, hand over her down-turned mouth. "My poor little boyfriend," she whispered.

"Not so little," Melody muttered, rolling her stiff shoulders. "But what do you think?"

Tessa crossed the room, felt Will's forehead and grimaced. "You're right; he's burning up. I wonder if he'll wake if I have a look at his back."

She leaned down and raised the hem of the loose shirt. Gently, carefully she lifted the bottom edge of the thick padding covering much of Will's back. She froze.

"Mel," she groaned, "do you have any idea what happened? His back is a *mess*. We need to get him to a doctor—as soon as possible."

"He hasn't told me anything yet. And I phoned like you told me, Tess. But my doctor is booked for more than two weeks, and when I explained the situation to his nurse, she suggested taking Will to Emergency at City Hospital."

Her legs gave out, and she sat heavily on Faith's old chair. "Do you really think that's necessary?"

"Yes," Tessa answered bluntly. "Do you have coverage for an ambulance?"

∽ ∽ ∽

Tessa led Melody to the sun-filled atrium cafeteria in the hospital. The young intern in Emergency had been so overwhelmed by Will's injuries, an older doctor had been called from his rounds.

"Here, Mel, have a seat." Tessa pulled out the chair for her dazed friend. Melody sat.

"Dr. Harris is one of the best," Tessa patted Melody's shoulder. "He'll have Will re-stitched in no time. I think we should have some coffee while we wait, though. Don't you agree?"

Melody rubbed her eyes with one hand and tried to focus. "Coffee? That sounds good."

It seemed like only a second later when Tessa placed a steaming cup of coffee in front of her. She picked it up and sipped. "Um–mm, that's good."

After several sips, Melody felt part of the fog lift. She turned to her friend. "Tessa, did that doctor really say those looked like claw marks? Bear claws?"

Tessa nodded. "I'm afraid so, Mel. Looks like your boy had a wrestling match with a bear." She looked off into the distance. "I wonder what happened to the bear?"

She went rigid, and then as Melody watched curiously, Tessa's face warmed to a rich shade of pink.

"Mel," Tessa whispered urgently out of the corner of her mouth, "don't look, but Orlando is sitting by the window behind you. And he's with someone. Someone with long, dark, gorgeous hair. Oh, my goodness, he just spotted me and waved!"

Melody quickly turned. Her eyes widened, and she turned back to Tessa. "That is one tall, dark, and handsome man, my friend." She turned for another look. "And he is signaling you to come over there." She leaned forward. "What are you going to do?"

"Nothing," Tessa whimpered. "He's *with* someone."

Melody checked behind her and smiled for the first time that day. "And that someone, along with your friend, is coming this way. She's beautiful, isn't she?"

"Yes, she is," Tessa said grumpily. "She looks awfully young."

A minute later, the handsome man stood beside their table. "Good morning, Tessa. What a pleasant surprise to see you. I thought this was your day off?" He made it a question with one dark eyebrow raised.

"And who is this lovely lady?" His smile charmed Melody.

"Um, hello, Orlando. This is my friend Melody. It is my day off, but we had to bring Melody's son in to Emergency."

"Hello," Melody said. "I'm pleased to meet you."

Now the dark eyes held concern. "I hope it is not serious?" He reached his arm around his companion and drew her close.

Tessa looked around as though seeking an escape. "He has some deep cuts and punctures that needed attention. We don't know the whole story yet, but maybe we should go check on him."

"I will not keep you. However, I had hoped to introduce you to mi amor, Carmelita." Orlando released the young lady and gestured gallantly toward her.

Tessa blanched and said nothing, so Melody smiled kindly at the girl. "Hello, Carmelita. What a beautiful name!"

Carmelita curtsied. "Thank you."

Then she looked at Tessa through lowered lashes, pretty head tilted. "Are you the Tessa my papa keeps talking about?"

31

Melody excused herself to check on Will in the emergency ward. She was still smiling when she ducked through the curtain hanging at the entrance to her son's cubicle.

Her smile disappeared. Will was lying on his stomach, left arm propped on an extension on the table, and Dr. Harris was re-stitching the final slice on Will's shoulder. Melody closed her eyes as the room began to spin. The nurse assisting Dr. Harris looked up, saw Melody wobble, grabbed a chair, and pushed her down onto it.

"Put your head between your knees," she ordered quietly.

Melody obeyed, taking deep, slow breaths. *God, what did you do to my boy?*

Dr. Harris cleared his throat. "Are you all right, Mrs. Jamison?"

She nodded and lifted her head, focusing only on the doctor's face. "I think so."

He continued, "We're just about done here. We'll get new dressings put on your son's wounds, and then you can take him home. His back has been anesthetized, so he won't feel much pain for the next hour or so. I'm giving him a stronger antibiotic, as this bite has become infected. If his fever continues past tomorrow, bring him back in and we'll put him on IV antibiotics. For now, he needs to rest and give it time to heal. He's young and strong, and he should recover completely." The doctor looked over his glasses at her. "But it will take time. Any questions?"

He tied off the last stitch and nodded to the nurse, who gently applied clean bandages over the horrific gashes until Will's injuries were once again bulky and white.

Melody's voice had deserted her. Mutely she watched Will struggle into his shirt with the help of the nurse. When at last he looked her way, his face pale and drawn, she stood and leaned on the back of the chair.

"I'm sorry you saw that, Mom." His voice was shaky.

"I–I'm sorry you were hurt so badly." She'd finally found her voice. "I hope you're ready to tell me what happened."

He hung his head. "When we get home, okay?"

Tessa's mood was so bubbly as she drove back to Melody's, she didn't seem to notice the lack of reciprocation from Melody or Will.

"Isn't Carmelita a doll? No wonder Orlando is so protective; she's only fourteen but seems much older. They'd just stopped by to visit a friend when they saw us. Amazing timing, eh? Oh, did I tell you the three of us are going out tomorrow night?"

"Only four times now, Aunt Tess," Will responded dryly. But he managed a weak grin when she glanced at him in the rearview mirror. "It's okay. I'm happy for you, since you're way too old for me."

Tessa made a face at him and began to hum a tune, quiet at first and then upbeat and bouncy.

"I like that, Tess," Melody said, "What is it?"

Tessa smiled mysteriously. "Oh, just something I've been working on. It's not quite ready for unveiling, but it's going to be pretty special. I hope."

Will hunched forward as he sat on the couch, resting his bandaged left arm on the couch's arm at an awkward-looking angle.

"You look so uncomfortable," Melody said. "Your dad's recliner is pretty soft; would you like to try sitting there?"

Will shook his head. "No, I can't. I have to keep this arm up so it doesn't throb too much. And leaning back against anything hurts. The doc said to keep the bandaged areas away from any friction. Guess that's what made so many stitches pop on the way here." He grimaced. "I'll sure be glad when I can sleep on my back again and sit like a normal person."

Melody sat beside him, close enough to touch him but not so close she'd bump him. She leaned forward to match his posture and said, "Okay, Son, I think it's time you told me what happened."

"Yeah, I guess it is." Will shrugged his shoulders and immediately groaned. "Not so smart."

He turned to face his mother. "That pretty much sums up my life the last few years: not so smart. I thought I was. I thought I was smarter and tougher than anyone, but all I did was mess up."

He told her about his "prime" job with Mr. Lee and how he'd ended up at The Sanctuary.

"I lied to you, Mom, and I'm sorry. I thought you'd worry less if you thought I'd quit a bad job at a nightclub than if I admitted I'd been working for a drug boss." He hung his head. "But I mostly didn't want to admit I'd been so stupid."

"Oh, Will," Melody murmured. She stroked his good arm. "You've been through so much."

"But things worked out, Mom," he continued. "Kane, the guy at The Sanctuary, was the one who hooked me up with Warner and the tree-planting job."

He straightened carefully and turned to face his mother. "If that hadn't happened, I wouldn't have had the best job ever, and I wouldn't have met Eli."

Will's expression crumpled, and tears filled his eyes. "Eli was the best friend I ever had. He talked to me a lot about redemption. You know, how someone pays someone else's penalty for messing up."

Warmth began radiating from Melody's heart. *God, did I misjudge you? Were you watching over my son after all?*

"Go on, honey," she encouraged, squeezing his arm gently.

"I didn't want to hear it at first, but he just kept being my friend, even when I was a jerk." Will lowered his head. "I've never met anyone like him."

Melody remained quiet, steeling herself for what was to come.

"Anyway, it was the last day of the contract, and I was nearly done, just fixing a few seedlings that weren't straight."

He told her about the bear attack, how he'd been sure he was going to die. Then he told her about Eli rushing in to save him, and how Eli and the bear had fallen over the edge of the cliff.

Will's head dropped and tears dripped onto his lap. Melody's emotions soared and dipped as she waited. Her hand reached out on its own volition to wipe away Will's tears, but her son shook it off as he raised his head and faced her.

"Eli died to save me, Mom. Just like Jesus. I understand that now." He wiped his tears on his shirt sleeve. "I understand a lot of things better now. But maybe ... if only I hadn't been so stubborn ... "

Melody wanted desperately to wrap her arms around him, but she restricted herself to patting his leg. "I wish I'd been able to meet your friend," she whispered.

"Me, too. You would have liked him." Will swallowed hard. "But Mom, there's something else I need to tell you."

"I'm listening. You can tell me anything."

He took a deep breath. "I–I lied to you a lot, even before I left. When I got into that fight that the cops told you about, it was because I was drunk and high." He shook his head. "Yeah, I did some drugs. I was so dumb!"

Melody patted his leg again. "We weren't completely unaware, you know. Your dad and I made mistakes too, and I'm awfully sorry for the ways we let you down."

Will looked at her in disbelief. "You never let me down. You guys were always there for me! I was just stupid."

"You were young, Will, and while you did make some bad choices, it sounds like you've learned from them."

"But that's not all," he protested. "I stole from you, too. Before I left, I found five grand in your jewelry box. I took it. The last few months I've been trying to save up to pay you back, and I will when I get my last paycheck. But I *stole* from you! I'm really sorry, Mom."

Several emotions swirled around in Melody's heart. Love, relief, thankfulness, regret and joy turned into tears that ran down her face.

"Will, that money was for you!"

At his shocked expression she explained, "Your dad and I planned to surprise you with a car for graduation. A friend of his had a nice eight-year-old Chevy for sale, but he wanted to sell it for cash right away. We were going to store it until you graduated. So you see, you didn't really steal from us. You just took what was going to be yours anyway."

Will sat immobile as he processed this news. After several moments, he lifted his wet face toward the ceiling and groaned, "I can't believe how dumb I was. All this time of trying to prove I didn't need anyone else, and all I did was blow it. Over and over again."

He dropped his head once more. "How can you forgive me?"

Melody beamed through a veil of tears. "It's easy, Son, because I love you. And now I'm rejoicing because you were lost, and now you're found."

Will's head jerked up. "That's exactly what Eli said."

Two days later Melody invited Faith, Jason, and Jessica to a welcome-home dinner for Will.

"He's in a lot of pain," she'd warned, "so don't hug him yet. But he's anxious to see you all. He especially missed you, Faith."

When they arrived that evening, Faith held back while Jason shook Will's hand and said, "Great to see you again, Will. It's been a long time."

"It's good to be home," Will responded. "Good to see you, too."

He smiled and gently touched Jessica's chubby arm as she clung to her dad. "You must be Jessica. I've heard a lot about you."

They all laughed when she gazed up at her uncle with wide blue eyes and pronounced, "Pret–ty!"

She then held out her arms to him expectantly, but Will shook his head and stepped back. "Not yet, little one, but soon, I hope."

Now Faith stepped forward, reached up to cup Will's face in her hands, and said, "Welcome home, little brother. I was mad at you for leaving, but I'm awfully glad to have you back." She swallowed hard. "God heard our prayers."

She moved one hand to make room for a kiss on his wet cheek. "I love you, Willful."

Daniel tossed his briefcase onto the hotel room bed and picked up the phone. He'd been phoning Bobbie every few days for updates on his house while hoping for word on Bobbie's next-door neighbor. But for some reason, Melody's activities were absent from Bobbie's reports.

She wasn't absent from his thoughts, though. All through the negotiations and finalizing of the sale of his construction firm, visions of Melody's smiling face kept teasing his attention away from the transactions.

I wonder what she's doing right now. Maybe I should just phone her house instead of acting like a teenager with a crush, trying to go through Bobbie for information.

He sank into the upholstered chair next to the window and stared at the phone in his hand. *What if Melody gets the wrong idea? No, I'd better phone Bobbie. Maybe she'll have some news today. I have news for her, anyway.*

"Hello, Bobbie, it's Daniel. Good news: the deal is done, and I'll be home in another day or two. How is everything there?"

"That *is* good news," the gravelly voice on the other end said. "It'll be grand to have you home again. Nothin's goin' on at your house. It's all good."

Daniel swallowed his frustration and plunged in. "How is Melody?"

Was that a chuckle? "I guess she's fine, Danny-boy. Haven't seen much of her lately, though, since she's been so busy with that young man of hers."

What?

Daniel mumbled something—he wasn't sure what—and hung up. Pacing the room, he rubbed the back of his neck until it stung.

"What young man?" he muttered. "Have I totally misread Melody Jamison? Or did I blow it by being gone so long? And why did I get so flustered instead of asking Bobbie for more details? She's obviously guessed that I'm interested."

His pacing slowed and then stopped by the bedside phone. Before he could second-guess himself, Daniel plucked a scribbled card from his wallet, picked up the phone, and punched in Melody's phone number.

A husky, sleepy-sounding male voice answered. "Jamison residence."

It's true! Daniel was stunned into momentary silence.

"Hello?" the voice came again.

"Is Melody there? It's Daniel Martens."

There was a pause, and then, "Naw, I think she said she was going to that gray house down the street. May I take a message?"

That gray house? What's she doing there? I don't understand ...

"Um, no, that's okay. Thanks anyway." And he hung up.

"H–hi, Melody. Thanks for coming. I–I'm sorry to keep bothering you, but I remembered you said I should call."

The hesitancy and downcast demeanor had returned, and when Nila looked up, Melody gasped. Her right eye was swollen nearly shut, and her lip was split.

Melody moved toward Nila, but she backed up, raising a hand in supplication.

"Please don't touch me. It hurts."

Will and now Nila. Why am I so helpless to protect the ones I love?

Melody wanted to pull Nila out of the house, away from the danger she lived in. Instead, she closed her eyes for a moment and breathed a prayer. *God, help me. And help Nila. Please help me to help her.*

"How badly did Nick hurt you?" she asked gently. "Do you need a doctor?"

Nila sighed and shook her head. "It's nothing that won't heal on its own," she said. "And it was my fault, anyway."

A spark of light brightened her eyes. "I told Nick about Jesus again, that Jesus loves him and even died for him." The light disappeared. "He got so mad …"

"Oh, honey, I'm sorry." Melody fought the anger that rose like bile in her throat. *Anger won't help, I know. But God, what am I supposed to do?*

That spark returned as Nila met Melody's eyes. "If I have to choose between Nick and Jesus," she said firmly, "I choose Jesus!"

Melody dared to touch Nila's cheek. "I'm awfully glad, Nila. How can I help you?"

"Well, I was told at Haven House to plan an exit strategy, and now I'm ready. Would you be my exit strategy, Melody?" Determined hope filled the battered young face.

"Of course I will," Melody assured her. "I'll do anything you want."

"Oh, I'm glad," Nila breathed. "I put some of my stuff in this suitcase." She indicated a cloth bag Melody hadn't noticed when she came in. "Would you take it home with you? Then if I need to leave in a hurry, I'll still have some of my stuff."

"Yes, I'll do that for you, Nila. But are you sure Nick won't notice that some of your things are gone?"

"No, he only sees things like dust on the furniture or anything he didn't buy for me. He won't notice this."

Melody bit back a retort. *Deep breaths. Calm yourself, for Nila's sake.* "That's good, Nila. But if you need me, call. No matter what. Okay?"

"Okay, I guess I will."

Melody thought of something else. "What about your Bible? Do you still have it?"

Nila half-smiled. "I do. I'm reading John's part now, and I love it. I'm learning more and more about Jesus. But I have to hide it before Nick gets home."

She shivered and crossed her arms in front of her. "If he ever catches me with it, I don't know what he'll do."

Daniel had been tormenting himself with possibilities and scenarios until he was ready to tear up the documents so recently signed.

"I sold my business to spend more time getting to know that woman, and she's already moved on? Is that what I get for listening to Mother? 'Give love a chance,' she said. But did Melody give *me* a chance? Doesn't sound like it!"

He slammed his fist onto the table and appreciated the jolt of pain. "I made it on my own for twelve years. Why did I think I needed a change?"

But Melody's face swam into focus in his imagination, stubbornly staying there no matter how hard Daniel shook his head.

Finally, he sank onto the bed, his head low. "Am I destined to be alone the rest of my life? I used to thrive on solitude; now I'm sick of being lonely. God, help me. "

It seemed as though he heard a faint whisper. "Give Melody a chance to explain. Phone her."

Resistance fled as he lay there considering how little information he had about "her young man," as Bobbie called him. *Did I overreact?* He sat up and picked up the phone once more.

The husky male voice answered again. "Hello?"

Daniel took a deep breath. "Hello, it's Daniel Martens. Is Melody there yet? I'd like to speak with her."

"Um, yeah, but she's in the basement. Just a minute, please."

Daniel heard the phone being set down, and then …

"Hey, Mom, phone's for you!"

Melody opened her door with a smile. "Pastor Dave, Lydia, thanks for coming over. Please come in. I've got fresh coffee made, if you'd like some."

"Thanks, Melody," Lydia said. "I'd love a coffee." She glanced up at her husband. "How about you, dear?"

"Yes, thank you."

While Melody filled coffee mugs, Dave and Lydia settled on the couch and, holding hands, said a quick prayer.

"Guide us, Lord God, as we seek your will in this matter. Bless this house and all who enter here, we pray in the name of Jesus, amen."

Melody beamed as she handed the drinks to her guests. "That was lovely. I really appreciate your coming over on such short notice. I know you're terribly busy with the missions conference coming up."

"This is what we love to do," Dave assured her. "Lydia shared what you told her about your young neighbor's situation. Do you think she's close to leaving her abuser for good?"

"I hope so. It seems as though every time I see Nila, she's more bruised. But now she has a spark of faith, and while that gives her hope, it's also getting her in trouble. She's sharing her love of Jesus with Nick, and he can't handle it."

Melody sat down, crossed her arms and shuddered. "I'm awfully afraid for her!"

Lydia put her arm around Melody while Dave answered, "Well, we have been praying for Nila ever since you first told us about her, and we would like to help."

Lydia gave Melody a little squeeze as she said, "Yes, we would. We believe God provided that big house for a reason, and Nila just might be part of that reason."

Melody's eyes widened. "You mean …?"

"Yes," she continued. "If Nila is willing, we'd love to give her a home with us for as long as she needs it. You would be free to visit her any time, of course, and we would be thrilled to share our love of Jesus with her."

"The question is," Pastor Dave inserted, "whether Nila would consent to staying with us. After all, she doesn't know us, and with her background she may be terrified of a big homely guy like me." He grinned when Lydia murmured a protest. "Not everyone has your taste, sweetheart."

"I'll certainly suggest that option to her," Melody said. "It might be what she needs to make the final decision to leave Nick and his abuse. But are you sure you want to get that involved in such a dangerous situation? I'd hate to think I was responsible for endangering you."

"If this is God's will, and we believe it is, then whatever happens is up to him. Not you," Lydia reminded her with another gentle squeeze. "He can take care of us all."

At that point Will walked into the room. "I thought I heard voices," he said as he stuck out his hand first to Dave and then Lydia. "You must be Pastor Dave and Lydia. I've heard a lot about you. I'm Will, Melody's son."

Dave stood and clasped Will's hand with a big smile. "I'm very happy to meet you, Will. My wife and I have been praising God for your safe return to him as well as to your mother."

Will smiled wanly. "Yeah, well, it took an awful lot for me to come around." His smile disappeared. "Did my mom tell you about my friend Eli? He was a true friend, the one who finally got through to me, and he paid for my faith with his life."

"She did, and I'm sure Eli would say it was worth it, Will." The pastor waited until Will's eyes met his before continuing. "And I'm also sure you will see him again someday."

Will nodded somberly. "Yeah, I know, heaven. Eli's there for sure."

He turned to his mother. "Mom, I'm going for a walk. These stitches keep pulling, and I'm hoping a little exercise will loosen things up."

He flexed his back gingerly and then nodded to Dave and Lydia. "It was nice to meet you. Mom's been telling me about your church, and I hope I can make it there before too much longer. See you later."

When Will was gone, Melody leaned back with a sigh. "Yes, you're right, Lydia. God can take care of us all. I just wish I didn't keep forgetting that."

32

"I've sold my construction company here, Melody, and I'm coming home tomorrow. It's time for a change in my life, and I hope you'll be a part of that change. I've missed you, and I'm anxious to talk to you face to face."

Melody's voice had been filled with wonder, but some hesitancy, too. "Are you sure, Daniel?" She'd paused but then continued breathlessly. "I've missed you, too. When will you be home?"

Daniel smiled as that conversation replayed in his mind. He set the cruise control on his truck and stretched his right leg. It was just after 10 a.m., and he'd be home by mid-afternoon. Traffic was fairly light, so while Daniel drove he planned his next building project, Melody's porch.

"She agreed to that pretty quickly. Well, I've always thought that house needed a porch, and now I'll get to work on getting to know Melody better while working on her house. If things go well, I might be able to convince her that she needn't pay me. Except maybe with a kiss …"

Daniel tensed at the sudden warmth flooding his body. "Slow down, man! Let's not get ahead of ourselves. We've both got some issues to deal with. Think about the porch."

By the time he turned off Highway 16 onto the Idylwyld freeway, Daniel had the entire building project fixed in his mind. He turned right onto 33rd Street and muttered impatiently at a dawdling pedestrian crossing at the next light.

While he waited, Daniel glanced around and noticed a florist shop around the corner. "Flowers! Women like flowers."

An image popped into his mind: Angela's glowing smile as she accepted his weekly gift of roses. The expected pain didn't follow, though, and when the pedestrian finally reached the far sidewalk, Daniel pulled around and parked outside the flower shop.

Minutes later he came out carrying two wrapped bouquets. "I know Bobbie loves flowers, and I nearly forgot to get her a thank-you gift. But what if Melody doesn't want flowers from me?"

"Welcome home, Danny-boy!" Bobbie greeted him with a huge smile. "Hey, you didn't need to bring me flowers." She stepped back and grinned slyly. "They are for me, right?"

"Of course they are." Daniel tried to scowl, but his face wouldn't cooperate. Smiling like a little boy at a cookie jar, he confessed, "I got some for Melody, too."

Bobbie chuckled. "Knew it! Now, before you get busy courtin' the neighbor lady, get on in here an' tell me what all you been up to."

She tugged on his arm, leading him into the kitchen. "I made cinnamon buns just for you, and coffee's fresh. Come in, take a load off while I take care of these purty posies."

More than an hour later, Daniel nervously rang Melody's doorbell, wrapped bouquet in hand. Doubts attacked as he heard footsteps nearing the door. *Did I misjudge her feelings? Am I making a fool of myself? Maybe Bobbie's wrong. Maybe Melody is just being nice to me for Mama's sake.*

The door swung open, and Daniel had to look up slightly to meet the eyes of the young man standing there.

"Um, hello. You must be Will. Your mother said you were staying here for a while." He stuck his hand out. "I'm Daniel Martens. I live across the street. Is your mother home?"

Will took the offered hand, shook it once and let go. "Yeah, she's out back picking stuff for supper. Come on in."

Daniel stepped inside, and the two men sized each other up. Will was about three inches taller than Daniel, but their builds were similar: lean and broad-shouldered.

"Your mother told me about your accident. Are you feeling better?" Daniel passed the bouquet from one hand to the other.

Will rolled his shoulders. "Yeah, quite a bit. Got the stitches out yesterday, so now I'm able to do more stuff. I can't wait to do some real work again, but the doc says I still have to take it easy."

The back door banged as Melody carried a colander full of baby carrots and ripe tomatoes to the sink.

"Mom," Will called, "you've got company! Your neighbor is here."

"Just a minute, Bobbie," Melody said over the sound of running water. "I need to wash these vegetables and then get cleaned up. Would you like some iced tea while I change?"

She was wiping her hands on a paper towel when she walked into the living room. She saw Daniel and froze, her rosy cheeks blushing a deeper red as her eyes widened.

She's beautiful! Daniel stared. Her chin and knees were smudged with dirt, and her short pants and tank top showed off a tanned, curvy form. Her curls were hidden under a broad-brimmed hat, and her hands still showed traces of garden soil. *Wow!* Without thinking he took a step closer, only to see her throw up her hands in front of her dirt-smudged face.

"Oh no, Daniel! You've caught me at my worst." Melody backed up and darted into the hallway. "Just give me a couple minutes. Please!"

If this is your worst, I can't wait to see you at your best. The words nearly slipped out of Daniel's mouth, but he bit them back and felt his face warm.

In less than five minutes Melody emerged from the hallway, now wearing a modest sundress and no dirt. She smoothed her hair off her brow and walked up to Daniel with a shy smile. Her cheeks were still rosy. He knew he was staring, but he couldn't seem to stop.

"Welcome home, Daniel. Are those for me?" she said, looking at the wrapped bundle and then into Daniel's eyes.

Daniel thrust out the now-crumpled bouquet. "Yes. I hope you like them."

Melody cradled them on her arm like a baby as she gently removed the wrapping paper.

"Ooh, lilies and carnations!" She looked up at Daniel with shining eyes. "How did you know these are my favorites?"

"Um, I didn't. They just reminded me of you—natural and lovely."

Melody's blush deepened again, and Daniel's face mirrored hers. *Did I really say that?*

He backed toward the door. "Excuse me, I need to get home, but I would like to talk to you about the front porch. Maybe after supper?"

"Of course!" Melody's smile lit her whole face. "But would you like to stay for supper? You probably don't have much food in the house after being gone for so long."

Daniel noticed Will staring from one to the other, one eyebrow raised and his mouth a straight line.

"Thank you, but no. Bobbie made supper for me; it's waiting at home."

Daniel nodded to Will. "Nice to meet you." He looked longer at Melody. "I'll see you later," he said softly.

Will was quiet through supper, but as Melody cleared their plates away, he cleared his throat loudly until she met his eyes.

"What is it, Son?"

"Just wondering what's going on with the guy across the street. Something you want to tell me? Are you guys dating, or what?"

Melody blushed. "No, we're not dating. We're neighbors who have gotten to know each other through hard times. He's a good man, and I like him."

Will frowned. "What about Dad? Have you forgotten him already?"

Melody pursed her lips to bite back a retort. She took a deep breath, sank onto her chair, and held her hands out to her son. "Of course I haven't forgotten your father. I will always love him." She took his hands in her own and squeezed gently. "But Will, your father is gone. I can't see him smile. I can't touch him. I can't hear him laugh or watch him work."

She turned her head as tears stung her eyes. "I will always miss your father, but he's in heaven and I'm still here." She sighed and turned back to Will. "I've been lonely, Will, and I believe Daniel's friendship is a gift from God. Our relationship is new, and I don't know if anything will come of it, but I hope you'll give him—and me—a chance."

Will scowled at a spot on the table for several heartbeats. "Okay," he finally said. "I guess I can give him a chance. No one can take the place of my father for me, but I get it that you're lonely." He straightened. "But he'd better not hurt you, or he'll have to answer to me."

A week later several changes were visible at Melody's house. She'd dug up and moved the flowers from the front of the house, and the concrete step had been removed. Daniel had poured the footings for the porch, and today he and Will were setting up to pour the foundation.

Melody watched them, enjoying the banter between the two men and admiring Daniel's patience as he taught her son. A relationship was being built between the two men while they worked together on her porch.

Watching Daniel work was a pleasure, too. Melody caught herself staring at the muscles on his back as he tied rebar.

Just then a car pulled into the driveway. Pastor Dave and Lydia were smiling when they emerged from the vehicle, and Melody's face warmed as she greeted them. *I hope they didn't notice me staring at Daniel!*

"Hi, you three," Lydia called. "Your porch project is coming along nicely. I'm impressed."

"Thank you," Melody answered. "Were you at Nila's again?"

"Yes," Dave said, "and I think she's getting more comfortable with us." He grinned crookedly. "With me, that is. She took to my lovely wife right away."

"Come in and tell me about it. We'll have to use the back door," Melody said. "I have iced tea made, and I was just going to offer some to these two."

Will looked up first. "Sounds good, Mom. Bring two tall ones, please. Hi, you guys."

Daniel raised his head, dark glasses hiding his expression. "Hello, Pastor, Lydia. Iced tea sounds good to me, too. Thank you, Melody." He smiled at her, and for a moment Daniel was all she could see.

Suddenly breathless, she turned to her guests. "Follow me, please."

But before they could leave, Daniel stood, stretched his back and walked over to them. "We could use a break about now. Do you mind if Will and I join you? I'd like to hear more about the situation at the gray house."

He stood so close to Melody the hairs on her arms lifted from the electricity between them.

"I want to know how you plan to keep the trouble down there from endangering Melody and Will." He shifted his stance and raised his chin. "And you'll probably tell me to trust God," he challenged, "but that doesn't cut it for me. I need to see to believe."

∞ ∞ ∞

Melody could hear her son snoring softly in the guest room, now his room, by the time she was ready for bed. She'd been miserable ever since Daniel's challenge.

Pastor Dave didn't really help, she mused, *with his talk of God's will including trials and even death.*

"Nowhere in the Bible are we promised an easy life," the pastor had said. "Instead, we are told God will carry us through it. Sometimes we will be protected from trials, sometimes we'll be delivered from them, and sometimes we'll be carried through them to eternity with God." He'd faced Daniel directly. "His grace is sufficient. Nothing can happen to God's children without his consent. He is a good and loving father. And that's a promise we can count on."

At that point Daniel had muttered something unintelligible under his breath and said he had to get back to work. "Concrete's coming soon."

But as Will followed Daniel out the back door, Melody heard her son say, "Don't worry about it, man. God will show you what you need to see."

Melody replayed those words in her mind. She had never felt so proud of her son.

Now she sat on the edge of her bed, too restless to lie down. The air felt heavy, like just before a thunderstorm.

She slid to her knees beside the bed. "What am I supposed to do about Daniel? Was I wrong, God, about this friendship—and maybe more—being from you? Has loneliness made me vulnerable to a bad relationship? How can I love a man who doesn't trust you?"

"Love?" Her hand went to her mouth and her eyes widened. "Do I love Daniel? Oh, that makes this so much worse. Did I fail again to listen, Lord?"

But it felt as if her prayers bounced off the ceiling. Instead, dark whispers began raining down on her. "You did fail again, just like always. You failed your husband and your son, and now you've failed yourself. Failure! Failure! That's all you are. Admit it and give up."

Every mistake, every loss pounded down on Melody's head until she climbed under the covers in effort to escape. But the attacks continued. "You thought you could help Nila, but she's beyond your help. No one can help her. She's ours."

Melody felt herself sliding, slipping into another realm. "No, not again! Not now!"

She peered through the blankets and was terrified to see several grotesque beings scuttling onto the bed. She tried to scream, but four of them grabbed her by the throat, cutting off her voice—and breath. Melody struggled to loosen their grip, but their claws dug in, bringing more pain. She fought them with all her strength, even while sinking into despair.

"Help me, Jesus," she managed to whisper. The grip on her throat loosened, and she cried out, "Jesus!"

The evil creatures let go but leered at her, flexing their claws.

A soft whisper calmed Melody's panic, and she sat up and cleared her throat. The vile creatures crouched, and she said in a surprisingly steady voice, "Go! You cannot do anything to me that God does not allow. In Jesus' name, leave this house!"

She watched in awe as the horrid demons fled like so many cockroaches scurrying from the light. "Thank you, God!"

She was once again in the normal realm, and as her terror slowly subsided, it was replaced by tremors. They began in her legs and worked their way up to her arms, until every part of her was shaking.

Melody huddled under the covers and prayed urgently for Will, Daniel, Nila, and everyone she cared for until she felt the Comforter's presence covering her with peace. She relaxed, still praying, and fell asleep.

33

It was a perfect August day, sunny with high, wispy clouds and enough heat to convince Daniel and Will to go shirtless as they installed the floor of the porch.

Will's raw-looking back still made Melody wince, but today Daniel held most of her attention. She wasn't sure what to do about her attraction to her doubting neighbor, but she couldn't seem to keep her eyes away from him. She knelt to pull a few tiny weeds in the corner flower bed, positioning herself so she could admire Daniel's muscles as they flexed and bulged.

Her hands forgot to work while she gazed at him, a slight smile lighting her face under the brimmed hat. Daniel looked up, caught her staring at him, and grinned. Melody blushed and ducked her head as though searching for a nonexistent weed.

"Hey, Mom." Will's voice interrupted her reverie. "Is it lunch time yet?"

Melody checked her watch and pushed herself to her feet, brushing off her dirt-covered knees. "It is! Sorry, dear, I lost track of the time. I'll go make some sandwiches for you both."

Daniel stood and stretched, grinning as Melody's eyes skimmed him once more. "Don't make any for me," he said. "I've got some leftovers at home that need to get eaten." He picked up his discarded shirt and shrugged into it. "Looks like we're going to need a few more screws, so I'll pick some up. I'll see you in about an hour, okay?"

"Sounds good," Will answered. "See you later."

"Bye," Melody said with a smile.

She walked up her new front steps, across the porch, and into the house. "This is so nice," she said. "Will, leave the front door open when you come in so the breeze can blow through."

While Melody cleared the table, Will sprawled on the couch. Within two minutes he was sound asleep. Melody smiled when she heard her son's deep, even breathing.

Working with Daniel is just what my boy needed. He's getting exercise, learning useful skills, and regaining his strength. Lord, I can't thank you enough...

"MELODY! Help me!" Footsteps pounded up the steps and across the new porch. Melody ran out of the kitchen and caught Nila as she lurched into the living room.

"Nila, what happened?" She held the young woman away from her, taking in the split lip, scraped cheek and already-darkening eye. Her throat had angry welts, her shirt was ripped, and her legs looked as though they'd been kicked.

"H–he's going to kill me!" she gasped. "Nick came home early and caught me with my Bible. He went crazy!"

"What's going on?" Will struggled to sit up, still half asleep. "Mom?"

"Son," Melody ordered, still holding Nila, "get to the kitchen and phone 911. We need police and an ambulance. Stay on the line and in the kitchen!"

Will opened his mouth to argue, but a look from his mother sent him hurrying to obey.

Nila watched him go, her eyes widening when she saw his back.

"N–i–i–i–la!" The voice Melody dreaded roared into her house, followed by Nick himself, wild-eyed and raging.

Shaking with fear and indignation, Melody pushed Nila behind her and faced Nick. "This is my house. Get out!" she ordered through chattering teeth.

But Nick stomped even closer until Melody could see only the mania in his eyes. "Nila's mine!" he yelled into her face. "Get outta my way!"

Lord, save us!

"What's going on in here?" Will was in the kitchen doorway, phone still in hand. He took a step into the room, aggression in his stance.

"Will, stay back! I mean it!" Melody commanded, still facing Nick.

Panic swept over her as Nick laughed evilly, advancing another step. "Think you can stop me? I'll take what's mine!"

He tried to duck around Melody, but she cut him off, staying between him and the whimpering young woman.

Use my name, came the quiet whisper.

But will that work? Oh God, forgive my doubts!

She stretched herself as tall as she could, chin jutting out, and spoke to the wildness in Nick's eyes, "In the name of Jesus, get out of this house."

His eyes grew even wilder, but he backed up. Out the door, down the steps he retreated, ranting the entire time. "You can't make me! I won't go! Nila is mine!"

On the front lawn he stopped and looked around, blinked several times, and twitched. Then he looked up and saw Melody in the doorway and Nila beside her trembling from head to foot.

"Get out here!" He swore viciously. Reaching into the back of his pants, he pulled out a knife. "If you don't leave that house this minute, I'm gonna come in there and cut your friends to pieces!"

Nila's shaking hands covered her trembling lips. "I have to go, Melody, or he'll hurt you. I have to!" Melody tried to hold her back, but she pushed her away. "Let me go!"

Nila stumbled down the stairs, and Melody followed.

Will tried to grab his mother, but Melody hissed at him. "Stay back!" As Will watched, frozen in shock, his mother positioned herself between the maniac and the young woman. He tried to move, but his legs wouldn't work.

Ducking and weaving, Nick waved the knife menacingly. "All that talk about your Jesus," he sneered. "How's he gonna help you now?"

"Jesus," Nila cried, sinking to the ground. "Help us, Jesus!"

Will tried to run down the steps, but something pushed him back. He tried again. "Unh!" He was shoved gently but firmly against the doorframe. He shook his head, baffled and wary. He flexed his muscles, but he couldn't seem to move.

Nick lunged, and Melody instinctively put up her arm. She felt the force of the blade as it slid across her forearm.

"Melody!" Daniel yelled out his truck window as his tires screeched to a stop in the driveway. He yanked on the door handle, but it wouldn't budge. He tried to unfasten his seatbelt, but it held firm. Again and again he tried, but he was stuck. Horrified, he could only watch.

Melody looked at her arm. She'd felt the impact of the blade, but she couldn't see any damage.

What ... ?

Nick jabbered and danced as he continued to wave the knife. "Yeah! How's that feel, missy? Who's gonna save you now? I got the power! I'm gonna hurt you bad! And nothing can stop me!"

Trembling but standing firm, Melody felt a peculiar heat as though an oversized kerosene lamp burned in front of her. The heat was somehow soothing, and her trembling eased as the warmth permeated her body.

Nick lunged again, but this time the knife clanged against something metallic and spun out of his hand, landing behind Daniel's truck.

"Jesus!" Nila cried again, her voice now ringing with joy. "Open their eyes! Let them see!"

Nick's eyes bulged, Melody's eyes widened in wonder, and Will and Daniel stared. Between Melody—with Nila behind her—and the still-raging Nick, a tall form materialized. A towering, glowing warrior with bushy red hair wielded a massive curved sword in his right hand and held an enormous shield in his left.

Nick back up, tripped, and fell to his knees.

Daniel tried the seatbelt and door again, and this time they opened. He jumped out of the truck, pushed Nick flat, and held him there, all while staring at the angel still standing at attention in front of the women.

Will stumbled on wobbly legs across the porch and down the steps. "Eli!" he shouted, a grin nearly splitting his face. "You're alive!"

The angel turned toward Will and, grinning broadly in return, saluted as he faded from sight.

Nobody had noticed the sirens, but police and paramedics were suddenly on the scene and in control. One officer handcuffed Nick and stuffed him into the cruiser. Another headed for Melody, but Daniel ran to her and enfolded her against his chest while Will knelt beside Nila and put his good arm around her shoulders. Nila didn't flinch but leaned into his side.

"It's okay," Melody heard her son say. "You're safe now. God heard you and protected you."

Melody was shaking again and clung to Daniel. "I was so scared," she whispered into his chest, "but God was here all the time." She lifted wonder-filled eyes to his. "He sent an angel!"

Daniel tucked her head under his chin and held her even closer. "Yes, he did, sweetheart. I saw him."

Melody felt him tremble then, and she wrapped her arms around his waist.

"I thought I was going to lose you," he said into her hair. "I wanted to save you, to get between you and that monster, but God had already taken care of that."

He put one finger under her chin and lifted her face to his. "When I saw that angel, I knew God had heard my prayers, that he really does care." He swallowed hard. "The walls ... the walls around my heart are broken, Melody, just like Mama prayed."

The waiting policeman coughed. "Excuse me, you two, but I need to get your statements."

"Hey, sonny!" Bobbie came trotting across the yard. "Leave them be for a minute. I saw the whole rigamarole from my front window. I'll tell you everything!"

While Bobbie regaled the officer with a blow-by-blow account, a paramedic checked Nila's injuries and bandaged her wounds. She refused to let him lead her to the waiting ambulance.

"I'm okay. Really. But you'd better look at Melody's arm. Nick got her with his knife."

The paramedic strode over to Melody. No blood or injury was visible, but she allowed him to examine her arm anyway.

"You sure you felt the blade?" he asked. "Is it possible he just hit you?"

Melody shook her head. "It was the blade. See?" She pointed out a thin, pink line where a bruise was already forming.

The man shook his head. "I don't get it. Must have been an awfully dull knife."

"Hey! Can I get some help over here?" The younger police officer held his hand out, blood dripping from his thumb.

The paramedic and older officer hurried over to him. "What happened?" the officer demanded. "How'd you get cut?"

The young man grimaced ruefully. "Thought I'd check the knife—barely touched it to my thumb. Guess it really is sharp."

∽ ∽ ∽

By the time the police and paramedics left, it was late afternoon, and Melody's house was crowded. Jason, Faith, and baby Jessica had rushed over in response to Will's phone call, as had Pastor Dave and Lydia. Everyone seemed to be talking at once, but Melody just leaned back against Daniel's chest as they stood against the wall, his arms around her.

Every now and then she noticed Faith glancing her way from her place on the floor, questions in her gaze. Melody mouthed, "We'll talk later," and was rewarded by a satisfied wink.

Bobbie sat on the couch with Dave and Lydia, retelling in her loud voice what she'd seen.

"It was really somethin'," she said. "That big ol' warrior standin' there like he'd like nothin' better than to slice that ornery little cuss's head clean off. Never seen an angel before, but that one was downright impressive!"

"Praise the Lord!" was their stereo response.

Nila sat cross-legged in Tom's recliner, and Will hovered by her side.

Will's face still reflected the angel's glow, and awe filled his voice as he spoke into one of those sudden quiet moments. "I wonder how many people can say they were best friends with an angel of God?"

34

Sunday morning the church was packed. Daniel, Melody, Faith, Jason, little Jessica, Will, and Nila filled one pew behind Tessa, Orlando, and Carmelita. Bobbie was sitting with her friends Roger and his wife one row over.

The miraculous story had spread through the church family, and the congregation sounded like a friendly beehive. Several people came over to greet Melody and her family with smiles and words of praise. Melody squirmed in embarrassment from all the attention, but her son seemed to grow taller with every smile and handshake.

Lydia began playing the first praise song, and everyone sat down in an expectant hush. Melody sang prayerfully, tears of joy in her eyes.

"You are here, you are here,
And we're in awe of your presence.
It's by your grace that we stand, Most Holy God…"

After several songs, Pastor Dave came to the podium and boomed, "This is the day that the LORD has made!"

The response seemed even more fervent than usual. "We will *rejoice* and be *glad* in it!"

The pastor motioned to Tessa to come up. "We have a special treat this morning. Tessa has written a song and, after a bit of arm-twisting, has agreed to share it with us." He turned to Tessa, now standing beside him, and smiled broadly. "Take it away, my dear!"

Tessa replaced Pastor Dave at the podium and smiled almost shyly.

"This isn't really my song," she said. "I just wrote the chorus and put it to music. The verses came from my dear friend Melody Jamison. I call it 'Melody's Song.'" She grinned. "Hope you like it, Mel."

She looked around the crowded sanctuary and invited, "And I hope you'll all join me. It's a simple tune, and the words are on the screen."

Melody's face burned as several people turned around to look at her, but their friendly expressions eased her discomfort.

Lydia played the intro, and Tessa began to sing.

"That's the tune she was humming in the car the other day!" Melody whispered to Will.

With Daniel's arm draped over the back of the pew, Melody held her hand to her overflowing heart as her friend sang the song of her soul:

> *The enemy had bound me*
> *With chains of doubt and fear,*
> *Until your word spoke to my heart,*
> *Its message true and clear.*
> *I longed to feel the freedom*
> *That only you can give.*
> *I needed, Lord, to know you,*
> *I need your strength to live.*
>
> *And by your grace I am forgiven;*
> *Because of grace to you I now belong.*
> *You took the chains of doubt and fear away;*
> *In you I can be strong.*
> *And now by faith I am a conqueror;*
> *And by your strength the battle's being won.*
> *Your love is leading me from faith to faith.*
> *Amazing grace, I'll sing the victor's song!*
>
> *You touched my eyes, they opened,*
> *I saw the pain outside.*
> *The battle raged around me,*
> *I saw kingdoms collide.*
> *But when I fell in terror,*
> *You set me on my feet.*
> *You're teaching me to listen,*
> *To follow where you lead.*

Melody's Song

The entire congregation stood and joined Tessa for the final chorus, clapping enthusiastically in time to the music:

And by your grace we are forgiven;
Because of grace to you we now belong.
You took the chains of doubt and fear away;
In you we can be strong.
And now by faith we're more than conquerors;
And by your strength the battle's being won.
Your love is leading us from faith to faith.
Amazing grace, we'll sing the victor's song!

MELODY'S SONG
words & music by Kathleen E. Friesen

CPSIA information can be obtained at www.ICGtesting.com
Printed in the USA
LVOW082033121012
302516LV00001B/1/P